Dalriada

One man inspires Scotland
with a civil disobedience campaign.

Ron Culley

Edited by John McManus

Grosvenor House
Publishing Limited

This book is published by
Grosvenor House Publishing Ltd
Link House
140 The Broadway, Tolworth, Surrey, KT6 7HT.
www.grosvenorhousepublishing.co.uk

This book is a work of fiction. Any resemblance to
people or events, past or present, is purely coincidental.

A CIP record for this book
is available from the British Library

ISBN 978-1-83975-929-1

Previous books by Ron Culley

The New Guards/The Kaibab Resolution.
Kennedy & Boyd 2010.
I Belong To Glasgow (foreword by Sir Alex Ferguson)
The Grimsay Press, 2011
A Confusion of Mandarins Grosvenor House. 2011.
Glasgow Belongs To Me Grosvenor House
(electronic media only) 2012
The Patriot Game. Grosvenor House 2013
Shoeshine Man A one-act play. SCDA. 2014.
One Year. Grosvenor House 2015
Alba: Who Shot Willie McRae? Grosvenor House 2016
The Last Colony Grosvenor House 2017
The Never Ending Story (Editor) Downie Allison Downie 2018
Odyssey Grosvenor House 2018
The Bootlace Saga (Editor) Downie Allison Downie 2019
Rebellious Scots To Crush Grosvenor House 2020
The Odyssean Companion Downie Allison Downie 2021

Web address
www.ronculley.com

A trilogy of books dealing with Scottish independence

'Alba: Who Shot Willie McRae?'

'A brilliant book. You won't be able to stop reading'.
Donaidh Foirbeis
'A great read'. Annette Davidson.
'A controversial story brilliantly told.' John Alder.
'Fast moving, gripping and a must, must read.' Iain Allan.
'One of the best books I have read.' Graham Baker.

'The Last Colony'

'A superb piece of work.' Craig MacInnes.
'Just finished 'The Last Colony'. Recommended.'
Catherine Campbell.
*'A very important read for those interested in the independence of
Scotland'.* John Alder.
'An exciting tale of a the battle for a small country's freedom.'
Roddy Martin
'Excellent plot line, well written. A good read!' Deirdre Boyd.
*"Brilliant! When is your next book published? I'll be sure to
order it!"* Jordan Jindsay.

'Rebellious Scots To Crush.'

'Completely believable and partly based on a true story.'
J. McManus
'This is a scary premise. Brilliantly written.' Allan Thomson.
'This story requires to be told. A great read.' George Cuthbert.
*'A marvellous Scots story of political intrigue. Donald John
Morrison follows dark money to its corrupt destination -
undermining a nation.'* Grousebeater

Acknowledgements

My inspiration for writing this novel arose from a growing sense of frustration at the current stalemate in Scottish politics so my first thanks must go to those in Scotland who inspire me daily despite a regular diet of dispirited denunciations emanating from the nation's public service broadcaster. This book, in some small measure, was my way of addressing these.

As ever, my family must be thanked for their forbearance but it is to John McManus, my editor, who used his forensic eye to keep me on the straight and narrow, to whom I must tip my cap most effusively.

Thanks, all.

Chapter One

The high security Royal Naval Armament Depot at Coulport lies on the western shore of the Rosneath peninsula. The depot is also situated at the end of an unclassified, grey, Ministry of Defence road which begins near the coastal village of Garelochhead and sits, unsurprisingly, at the head of the Gare Loch just two miles from Her Majesty's Naval Base at Faslane where Britain's nuclear submarines dock and are maintained. This wide, high quality road was designed and constructed by the Ministry of Defence to provide easy access for road convoys transporting nuclear warheads.

On six or seven occasions a year, nuclear warheads are removed from underground bunkers in the Trident Area at the Explosives Handling Jetty at Coulport and taken under escort to Burghfield, just south-west of Reading in England. The route taken varies but the components of the convoy seldom does. Usually, four large articulated vehicles painted dark green carry the warheads and interspersed are several police vehicles, a bus carrying supplementary police officers, a fire tender, a breakdown lorry, a decontamination unit, a spare cab in case of need and several MOD police officers on motorcycles. Whatever route taken, the convoy always has to take smaller roads at each end of the journey before accessing their preferred motorways and 'A' roads due to the great weight of the lead-lined convoy trucks.

On a hill high above Garelochhead, high magnification binoculars followed the convoy as it travelled the five miles to a roundabout just north of the village that had to be navigated whichever subsequent route the huge lorries took.

Four warhead lorries....one, two three, four police vans, eh... seven motorcyclists...plus two at the rear and the usual ancillary vehicles. The field-glasses were adjusted to increase the magnification as the warhead convoy slowed at the roundabout. *They've, eh…seven axles…dual tyres on the rear but only single tyres on the front axel for easier handling and manoeuvrability.* The glasses were raised to view the hinterland behind the vehicles. *Perfect!…Wooded area to the rear. If I'm accurate, any bullet deals with the front tyre, ricochets off the road surface and buries itself in a tree. It'd never be found.* The convoy lumbered slowly up the road and slowed even though two motorcycle policemen had stopped traffic in all directions to provide the lorries with safe onward passage.

The binoculars were trained again on the convoy. *Only one breakdown lorry, mind you, so if two warhead carriers were taken out it would cause them a problem.* The convoy was watched until it was out of sight whereupon the binoculars were packed away and a small, folding military shovel was removed from a camouflaged army backpack.

Some three hours later, a hide had been established within a substantial yellow gorse bush in a dense wooded area. Standing immediately before it, even someone purposefully looking for signs of human activity would have been disappointed. *Add a reflective space blanket inside and neither the infra-red nor high definition cameras could detect a presence here if they sent a chopper up. The noise of their own engines down on the road will ensure that the convoy couldn't tell where or even initially how their tyres burst. They couldn't hear a distant gunshot.*

Now words were spoken audibly.
"I can do this."

* * *

The letters' editor of The National newspaper in Glasgow picked up the few letters he received by mail, most of the content of his pages arriving electronically. He spread them out on his cluttered desk next to his keyboard and read the first two, innocuous and with grammatical error, but possible entries. The next to be unfolded captured his attention immediately if only because the hand-written lettering had all been capitalised and all letters had been contrived with a sharp font. Every 'T' had been written as if the number 7, every 'O' and 'Q', indeed every curve of any letter had been squared. It read;

SIR

IT HAS LONG BEEN ESTABLISHED THAT THE DECLARATION OF ARBROATH IS ONE OF THE WORLD'S GREATEST HISTORICAL DOCUMENTS.

LET ME REMIND YOU OF A CLAUSE; 'AS LONG AS BUT A HUNDRED OF US REMAIN ALIVE, NEVER WILL WE ON ANY CONDITIONS BE BROUGHT UNDER ENGLISH RULE. IT IS IN TRUTH NOT FOR GLORY, NOR RICHES, NOR HONOURS THAT WE ARE FIGHTING, BUT FOR FREEDOM - FOR THAT ALONE, WHICH NO HONEST MAN GIVES UP BUT WITH LIFE ITSELF'.

I STATE THIS BECAUSE AS A DIRECT CONSEQUENCE OF THE OBSCENITY OF NUCLEAR WARHEADS BEING STORED ON THE CLYDE AS A PRECURSOR TO A DEVASTATING WAR, THE NOTION OF 'ONE HUNDRED OF US LEFT ALIVE' IS - AT LEAST IN THE CENTRAL BELT OF SCOTLAND - NOW AN ALL TOO TERRIBLE REALITY. THE DETONATION OF A ONE HUNDRED KILOTON BOMB WHETHER BY ACCIDENT OR DESIGN WOULD CAUSE A BLAST EIGHT TIMES MORE POWERFUL THAN THE ONE THAT DEVASTATED THE JAPANESE CITY OF HIROSHIMA AND KILLED ONE HUNDRED THOUSAND OF THEIR CITIZENS. ANYONE WITHIN FIVE KILOMETRES OF THE BLAST IN SCOTLAND WOULD DIE INSTANTLY AND COUNTLESS MORE WOULD PERISH THROUGH RADIATION SICKNESS AND BURNS. THE BLAST ZONE WOULD BECOME DEGRADED AND UNINHABITABLE FOR DECADES.

I HAVE NOW DECIDED TO TAKE DIRECT ACTION AGAINST THIS DEBASEMENT OF AN OFFENCE AGAINST A CIVILISED MORAL CODE. I AM NOW CONVINCED THAT THE BRITISH ESTABLISHMENT ARE ACTIVELY ACTING AGAINST THE PEOPLE OF SCOTLAND. THIS LETTER IS MY WARNING TO THOSE WHO WOULD SUPPORT THEM AND THE NUCLEAR ARMS INDUSTRY. I AM WELL AWARE THEY WILL NOT CEASE THEIR EFFORTS UNTIL PUBLIC OPINION REQUIRES IT. I INTEND TO BRING THIS ABOUT.

YOURS FAITHFULLY
ALBA GU BRÀTH
DALRIADA

PS. (NOT FOR PUBLICATION) I AM WELL AWARE YOU MIGHT CHOOSE TO DRAW THIS LETTER TO THE ATTENTION OF THE AUTHORITIES. HOWEVER, THERE ARE NO FINGERPRINTS ON THE LETTER, THE ENVELOPE OR THE STAMP. THE PAPER WAS FROM A REAM PURCHASED MORE THAN TWO YEARS AGO FROM A LARGE SUPERMARKET. THE CHEAP PEN ALSO. IT HAS BEEN POSTED TO YOU FROM A LOCATION THAT IS NOT COVERED BY ANY CAMERAS AND WAS NOT WITNESSED. AS YOU CAN SEE, MY HANDWRITING IS HEAVILY DISGUISED. I WORK ALONE AND NOT IN A UNIT THAT CAN BE INFILTRATED. I AM OTHERWISE A LAW- ABIDING CITIZEN.

LEST I HAVE CAUSE TO WRITE TO YOU AGAIN AND IN ORDER THAT YOU CAN ESTABLISH THAT ANY SECOND OR FURTHER LETTER IS GENUINELY FROM ME, I WILL PLACE TWO PLUS MARKS (++) AFTER MY NAME, THUS; DALRIADA++. I WILL ALSO LEAVE A CALLING CARD ON ANY OCCASION I TAKE ACTION TO ALLOW COPYCAT INCIDENTS TO BE IDENTIFIED AS SUCH.

***

The letter wasn't published but passed instead to Police Scotland where shortly it landed on the desk of Jimmy Boyd, a young Special Branch officer who asked forensic scientist, Dr. Edwin van Ossen to pass his practised eye over it.

The interview room door closed quietly as Dr. Van Ossen took a seat and opened a file on the table. He looked at the two officers before him; Boyd's sergeant, Colin Boston, insisting that he be in attendance.

"Gentlemen, I have looked at your letter in some detail and view this as a realistic threat."

Sergeant Boston looked at the facsimile of the letter before him.

"I'll need evidence, Doc. I'll have to take this up the line and if they're going to put resources behind this they'll want to be able to defend their decision."

"The writer constructs his sentences in a way that is grammatically correct. It has the feel of an educated person. No colloquialisms that might be expected of a young person so I'd say someone aged over thirty certainly. I'd say male before female but I have no evidence. It has images of masculinity but no more. The soubriquet 'Dalriada' is as you will be aware, a term to describe the Gaelic kingdom that encompassed the western seaboard of Scotland and the north-eastern corner of Ireland. At its height in the sixth and seventh centuries, it covered what is now Argyll. The writer knows his or her history and the quote used is accurate - again suggesting someone who is reasonably well-read. They appear to have insights into the kind of assessments someone like me - or you two, for example - might undertake to establish authorship and has appeared to take steps to block any likely positive outcome. As was also asserted, no prints or DNA is available."

"What about your analysis of the paper, Doctor."

"Ah, yes. I looked at that but as I say not with any real hope of unearthing anything helpful. You see, our laboratory analysis of paper takes into account its colour and opacity, the size of the sheet, its weight and thickness, its fibre content, the direction of the grain, the finish, and the watermark. Comparison in these respects with exhaustive files of domestic and foreign paper stock samples serves to identify most papers. However, if the paper is a common, low-grade type, it will yield no clues to the originator of the document except offering perhaps a broad location. In this instance, as was asserted and as could have been predicted, there is no prospect of identifying the source of purchase."

"Ink?"

"The identification of an ink is begun by determining the type to which it belongs. The three chief types in use today are gallotannic, which is the most common, chromic and aniline. Others are China ink, the coloured vegetable-dye inks, a few dark ones like those made from wolfram and vanadium, and those for special application as for mimeograph and stamp pads. Chemical differences enable the laboratory to identify these types. This ink is gallotannic. Very common."

He continued after sipping from a carton of coffee he'd brought with him.

"The pen used appears to be a ball-point pen which is more easily identified than an ordinary one as it uses an ink unique to the maker. There is a specific width of the ball point for each brand, and the surface of the ball, smooth as it may seem to the unaided eye, is really full of scratches which leave a pattern on the paper...the pen's own fingerprints, as it were. Any non-standard type of pen is the more readily identified because of its scarcity. However, the pen used is most probably a cheap Biro bought in a supermarket store somewhere - and probably over two years ago as the writer suggests."

"Handwriting?"

"The obstacles which confront a forger or a disguiser of his own writing are manifold. It is practically impossible for a writer to divorce himself from certain inherent characteristics manifested in pressure points, pen lifts, the shading of strokes, of which he is not even aware. However, our friend has circumvented this by printing letters in a contorted block form that makes identification impossible. This person knows what they're doing."

"So you can't help us?"

"Well, I suspect I *can* rather. I think you are looking for someone who has had an education, probably a male, probably older that thirty and well-read. They have their wits about them. He may come from, or now live in, Argyll. His sign-off, '*Alba gu Bràth*' and his use of a stanza from *The Declaration of Arbroath* suggests an affiliation with the Independence movement. He may or may not have a familiarity with the orthography...the conventional spelling system of a language... of Scots' Gaelic, as he accurately places a grave accent mark above the 'a' in '*Bràth*'. There are no indications of obvious mental health issues in his writing. His analysis of the nuclear threat is real and one with which many people, including myself, I might say, can identify with. He makes no reference to which tactics he...or she, I suppose...might employ but I imagine it's safe to say they may be violent."

Boston met the gaze of his partner, Jimmy Boyd.

"Yeah...I'm assuming that when he says, 'direct action' he doesn't mean pushing the button to make the Wee Green Man stop a nuclear convoy as it passes his front door."

He turned again to Van Ossen.

"So do you think this person appears to have the emotional and intellectual wherewithal to carry out violent attacks as are implied in this letter?"

"I think it's a racing certainty, Sergeant!"

Chapter Two

It was Friday and it had been a long and tiring day.

Old Archie McFarlane wearily tied one end of a waxed rope to a rusty hook on the side of his lorry, threw the tether over a cargo of pine logs and walked to the near side. Taking care to step round a muddy puddle, he tugged forcefully at the the truckers' hitch he'd created by tying a half hitch, forming a loop and tightening it, securing his load of ten sturdy pine logs.

Stepping back, he inspected his handiwork and pronounced himself satisfied before rounding the lorry once more and settling into the driver's seat. Some nicotine was called for and a carton of John Player Special Real Blue King Size was retrieved from the glove compartment. One was selected and lit. Inhaling deeply, McFarlane emitted the smoke through clenched teeth with a long hiss.

"Off to Ballindalloch," he coughed to himself under his breath, his eyes watering as a consequence of the exhaled smoke.

The B9102 from Grantown-on-Spey is a safe road. Accidents are rare but as the road leaves Lettoch it turns sharply to the left. It was here that McFarlane's knot held tight against the extra strain of the vehicle's sudden manoeuvre whereas the lorry's rusty hook surrendered instantly to the centrifugal force placed upon it. A deep pot-hole completed the *coup-de-grâce*, upsetting the load. First slowly, then with increasing rapidity, the sturdy logs began their journey to the roadside in a roaring cloud of dust and splinters. Bouncing and rolling end to end, nine of the logs were eventually rendered harmless having come to rest by the simple expedient of destroying a farmer's ancient dry-stone wall. One of the logs, however, rebounded from the tarmacadamed surface, its end rising some four feet from the road, colliding foursquare with the windscreen of a black Volkswagen Passat GTE travelling in the opposite direction, demolishing its cabin and decapitating the occupant in the passenger's seat. The driver's attempt to brake as he saw the carnage unfold was as slow as it was unnecessary, the heavy log bringing the vehicle to a halt almost immediately.

A torrent of anxious expletives spat from Archie McFarlane's lips as he limped hurriedly from his now stationary lorry to the Passat where he found the driver unconscious, an airbag having been deployed. His eyes fell upon the gory site of the headless passenger. Neurones within McFarlane's brain received these grisly sensory inputs and interacted with his medullary reflexes that controlled emesis. In a nano-second, his efferent vagus nerve relayed instructions to his pharynx, larynx, oesophagus, stomach and upper intestine resulting in the copious expulsion of the gastric contents of his gut. McFarlane spewed his load!

On his knees now, both eyes red due to blood vessels in the mucous membrane of his eye having haemorrhaged due to the violence of his vomiting, he placed a weak hand on the side of the Passat to steady himself just as the driver of a following vehicle approached on foot.

"Jesus, pal. You okay?"

McFarlane could only shake his head as the man reached for his phone and punching in nine, nine, nine, demanded every emergency service other than the coastguard.

It took but some six minutes for first the police then the ambulance to arrive from Grantown-on-Spey. One officer began coning off the area and directing new arrivals to turn round and take another route. The Sergeant attended the crash scene as the sole paramedic dealt with the yet unconscious driver.

Removing his police cap, Sergeant Angus Darroch looked inside the crashed vehicle before crouching on one knee beside McFarlane who was seated on the road, his back leaning against the rear wheel of the Passat. He placed a reassuring hand on McFarlane's shoulder.

"Can you tell me what happened, sir?"

McFarlane strained upwards still in shock. He took a moment to answer.

"The logs...the logs on my lorry, they came off at the bend."

"Yeah, I can see them. You okay, sir?"

McFarlane's eyes were tearstained. "That poor guy."

Darroch could only empathise.

"Yeah."

The younger police officer approached Darroch and signalled his attention with the upward jut of his jaw. Both officers retreated a few steps and conversed quietly.

"Just called the car in, Sarge. It's a Scottish Government car. From their car pool. That boy who's lost his heid, he could be a Cabinet Minister or something."

"Hard to tell. The face in the back is just mush. Mind you he was sitting in the front. Don't Ministers sit in the back? They do when you see them on the telly. Anyway, he'll have ID in his wallet, I'm sure."

"Aye. Right enough, sir." He changed the subject. "I've asked for back-up to handle traffic. We'll be here a while taking notes and statements."

"Good shout, Calum. You ID the dead guy and get a statement from that witness over there who called us out. I'll speak with our friend here but we'll need to get the two remaining live ones to the hospital before we take a statement and I'll need to organise a wee test to make sure there's been no alcohol involved. We'll also need those traffic cops and forensic and get the deceased to the morgue. I'll tell the boys back at the ranch to put out the news that this road will be closed until further notice. Can you handle that if the driver's still unconscious?"

"Aye. But the forensic boys from Aberdeen'll take hours to get here."

A fire engine and a low-loading recovery vehicle now appeared, their occupants showing somewhat less urgency than the uniformed responders who had first arrived on the scene.

Darroch watched them arrive.

"Aye, we'll be here for a while right enough, Calum. Better phone home and let your wife know you'll be a while. Dinner will be late tonight if you still have the stomach for it. I'll be seein' what's left of that fellah's head in my dreams."

* * *

In Edinburgh, Molly Fenwick, the First Minister's Chief of Staff reacted sharply upon taking the call that the Permanent Secretary to the Scottish Civil Service had been killed in a motor accident just outside of Grantown-on-Spey.

"But I spoke with him by phone only this morning. We're sure it is him? He's been positively identified?"

The police inspector in Grantown-on-Spey hedged his bet only slightly.

"The deceased was travelling in a black Volkswagen Passat GTE, registration K 37 JBB, a car from your government pool. The car left Inverness around three-thirty this afternoon heading for Edinburgh with him and one of your drivers, a Mister Ewan Graham who is alive and in hospital being treated for his injuries. His condition is being described as stable. He seems in no danger. Unfortunately, the passenger, whose driving license, Scottish Government buildings' access pass and bank cards show him to be a Mister Giles Merchant, is deceased and as a consequence of facial injuries cannot be identified from visual inspection alone. In the footwell of the car was a folder of e-mail and letters addressed to him...so we're pretty confident we know who he is." He hesitated. "Unfortunately, he was decapitated and what's left of his head is unidentifiable. We have a couple of officers visiting his home in Edinburgh to advise his widow and ask her to ID the body as we speak. Press have not been advised."

* * *

It was almost closing time when Angus Darroch and his police colleague, Calum Buchanan, both now in plain clothes, met in Grantown-on-Spey's small Claymore Bar on the village's High Street.

Buchanan was at the bar having just ordered a neat brandy. He acknowledged his senior officer. "Hi Sarge. Usual?"

"Aye....and it's Gus when we're out of uniform, remember." Both men were silent as the barman tended to the whisky order. "Thanks, Calum." Darroch swallowed the large malt whisky in one visit and showing the empty glass to John, the barman, invited another while signalling the addition of a large brandy as Buchanan finished his. "A big one, John." He turned to Buchanan. "Christ, the things you see in this job, eh?"

"Aye, thon poor bastard won't be having an open coffin funeral, that's for sure," responded Buchanan. "What a mess! That old driver fellah was fairly shaken up, eh?"

Darroch nodded his agreement as he lifted the glass to his lips.

"Aye. I'm prepared to bet that the Crown Office will do him for the nick of his lorry. He's got a clean driving license, no other convictions but it was *his* lorry. He owned it and it was as auld and decrepit as him. They'll fine the poor auld sod and he'll probably never drive again - or want to. But his poor loading and rusty vehicle resulted in the death of the head honcho of the Scottish Civil Service. The big cheese...the heid bummer. The powers that be'll be all over this like a rash so our procedures and paperwork better be beyond reproach."

"I'm sure they will be, boss."

John the barman finished cleaning a glass and turned to converse with the two local policemen.

"I see the toon's in the news the night!"

"Aye, we had a bit of a bump just outside Lettoch. A man died at the scene."

"Terrible, that." He lifted another glass to polish. "We were on the telly. Was the fellah local, Angus?"

"Nah. Not from these parts. Still to be identified but it wasn't one of your regulars, John."

Turning to Buchanan, Darroch gestured towards two vacant chairs at a table. The barman watched their movements.

"Don't you two be gettin' too comfortable now. It's nearly closin' time and the polis might check to make sure we're not servin' drink after hours."

Darroch smiled at the barman's quip knowing full well that a half-blind eye was taken to miscreant pub owners in the town so long as there was no accompanying raucous behaviour at closing time - which there seldom was. Grantown-on Spey was a civilised rural community where everyone knew one another, relationships were for the most part fraternal and the more vulnerable were looked after. During the day, the Claymore Bar saw its fair share of tourists but of an evening it was mostly locals using it as a community facility.

In furtherance of this ethic, Darroch lapsed into police duties.

"Tomorrow we check the paperwork then we go up to auld McFarlane's cottage. His wife has dementia, he's approaching seventy and although he's recently made a few quid from the Forestry Commission hauling these logs around, I'd bet he doesn't have a pension worth a damn and he'll be in bits. I'd like to check on him to see whether we need to involve social work or his doctor. The poor man won't be able to think straight."

"Good shout, boss.

Chapter Three

Sir Jonathan Burton, Cabinet Secretary and Head of the Civil Service in London pursed his lips as he read the message placed before him. *This rather puts the cat among the pigeons,* he thought before picking up the phone and dialling a number he used only infrequently. It was answered immediately.

"Sir Jeffery Arbuthnot's office."

"Burton here. Cabinet Office. I need to speak immediately with Sir Jeffrey."

"Of course, Sir Jonathan. I'll put you through."

Allowing only for sufficient time to elapse during which his identity was drawn to the attention of the Director General of MI5, the call was again answered almost immediately.

"Jon. Good to hear from you. Haven't seen you since we each enjoyed rather a good day at Cheltenham. You won rather more than did I as I recall."

"I was in good form then, Jeffrey. The Champagne gave me sufficient Dutch courage to ignore the advice of that pompous racing pundit who visited the box and helped everyone else lose their collective shirt."

The informalities over, Arbuthnot moved to business.

"May I take it you've called about the Scottish incident?"

"Indeed so. Whilst I will of course shortly express my condolences to family and friends, I knew you would first wish a quiet word about his replacement. The role of supporting and advising the First Minister of Scotland is so central to the smooth and efficient running of the United Kingdom, I understand full well the importance you chaps in MI5 place upon any candidates being possessed of certain additional qualities that underpins that particular post."

"Exactly that, Jon. And my immediate problem is that due to the role being so public, I can't encourage just *anyone* with those 'additional qualities' to fulfil that task. It would be observed as suspicious immediately if someone appeared as a candidate who was not firmly in the hierarchy of the civil service."

"Agreed. Let me think…let *us* think…of candidates who have come up through the ranks of the civil service who may have the potential to adopt the skill sets required by MI5 officers rather than consider MI5 officers who may have the temperament to fulfil the role of the grey civil servant."

"Exactly my thoughts, Jon. Let's talk later in the week once we've given this some further thought."

* * *

On placing the phone on its receiver, Arbuthnot lifted it once more, pressed four digits and asked his secretary to invite his deputy, Jack Strachan to join him as soon as he was free.

Half an hour passed before a light knock on his door presaged the arrival of Strachan.

"Sorry, boss. I was sitting in on a meeting with some of our friends and allies in MI6 and the CIA, each of whom are concerned about Islamic terrorists visiting our shores and those of the United States by way of Ireland."

"Productively?"

"Not really. They seem to have two types over there that they send over here, the highly educated, liberal pragmatists or the self-righteous, America-first, shaven-headed goons who look down their collective nose at all other intelligence services. Today it was the latter, I'm afraid."

The door opened and a tray carried by Miss Eldridge was brought in on which had been placed coffees for each man. Each accepted a cup graciously and sipped as the secretary took her leave.

"Well, thanks for popping up. You may have heard on the grapevine that our man in Scotland, their Cabinet Secretary, Giles Merchant was killed yesterday in what appears to have been a genuine road accident. No likelihood of foul play."

"Yeah, I knew Giles well. He and I were at Edinburgh together. His wife, Gillian will be devastated. No kids, thankfully. I'm going to make it my business to see that she's all right."

Ignoring his colleague's obvious compassion, Arbuthnot moved to address his problem."

"He'll be hard to replace. The sheer tonnage of information he supplied to us over the past three years would be literally impossible to achieve by anyone in any other post. You're a proud Scot, Jack. Any thoughts?"

"Yeah...not only did we have immediate access to all confidential briefing papers but also insights into relationships, factions round the Cabinet table, tittle-tattle, and we must remember that thanks to him placing bugs in each of their dozen or so various pool cars over time, we also overheard confidential back seats' conversations as Ministers travelled together. That legacy, at least will remain even if he has gone."

"So how do we replace him?"

"Well, it's in the hands of your friend Sir Jonathan Burton, the Head of the Civil Service here in London. There will be a number of interested parties already in Scotland but we don't have any officers of sufficient seniority to nudge them into place. The First Minister will choose from perhaps two candidates provided by Sir Jonathan. Our task is to find one who would be an obvious selection. I'd suggest two immediate filters. First, we should try to find a Scot with a Unionist perspective and secondly we should attempt to ensure that the candidate is female. Possibly someone who has earned their spurs elsewhere in the service of the crown. The second candidate should be worthy but male, boring, even misogynistic in a past life or with a flaw that could be exposed at interview."

"Sounds like a plan, Jack. I'll be speaking to Jon Burton in a couple of days, put some feelers out and see if you can rustle up some contenders."

* * *

It was lunch hour in the British Embassy in Tokyo when the phone on Catriona Burns' desk rang.

It took a moment for the quiet beep to register as she gazed mid-chew across the Chidorigafuchi Moat to the Japanese Imperial Palace, whose extensive grounds accommodated the residence of the Emperor of Japan.

She lifted the receiver.

"Miss Burns, I have John Chiswick on the line. He's from our Commercial Section asking if he can meet with you immediately. Says it's important but won't give me any detail. If you choose to accept, you have forty minutes before you meet with S suke Takeshita here to discuss next week's delegation from London."

"Isn't John Chiswick one of our Intelligence Officers?"

"I believe so."

"I'll take the meeting."

Five minutes later the diminutive figure of John Chiswick entered the room, a practised smile creasing his face.

"Ah, Miss Burns. Your secretary tells me you've another meeting in fifteen minutes."

"She's just protecting my diary," grinned Burns. "I've at least twenty."

Uninvited, Chiswick sat in a chair opposite his host, folded his hands and ensconced them somewhere near his groin in a gesture he seemed to think suggested seriousness.

"I'll come straight to the point, Miss Burns. I have been asked to convey the weight and gravity of our *confidential* conversation here today by the Prime Minister of the United Kingdom no less."

Burns didn't respond with the reverence Chiswick had anticipated. Slightly disconcerted, he continued.

"You may have read that the Permanent Secretary to the Scottish Government, reporting directly to the First Minister of Scotland...and of course the Cabinet Secretary at Number Ten... was unfortunately killed in a terrible road accident recently."

Burns nodded almost imperceptibly, still maintaining a poker face.

"Eh, well, you see, the powers that be...the Prime Minister and the Head of the Civil Service...are most anxious to fill the unfortunate vacancy and, well, your name came up in dispatches."

"Really?"

"Indeed. It would be a promotion, it would permit a return to Scotland...I gather you're from that part of our sceptred isle...our blessed plot," offered Chiswick theatrically.

"Shakespeare was referring to England not Britain and it's a misquote anyway," replied Burns stonily.

"Your knowledge of the Bard is impressive, Miss Burns."

"Where I come from, the Bard has the same surname as me."

Expecting rather more gratitude from his target, Chiswick's discomfiture showed itself.

"I thought you might be rather more excited at the prospect of promotion."

"This is my excited face."

"Please don't shoot the messenger, Miss Burns. I am to advise you that it might be in your personal and professional interest to show interest in a very important position which would be of material benefit to Her Majesty's Government. But of course if you are disinterested in advancement..."

Burns mellowed slightly.

"Mr Chiswick. Let me make a few points. First, the sun is shining here and it's warm, I have a senior position in the British Embassy; a job I love and a job I fancy I'm quite good at. I gaze from my window to the gardens of the Imperial Palace, I have begun to develop an active social life, I have a lovely apartment and have just...only just...begun to appreciate the joys of *saké*. Most importantly, I had to persuade an unconvinced husband to pack up everything he knew in London and travel to the other side of the world to allow me to advance my career. He's now happy and settled here, working in the tourism sector. I am very unsure of his reaction if I suggested another move...even to the glittering metropolis that is Edinburgh."

"Edinburgh *and London*. You'd have two masters remember."

"And I have no doubt that the fact that it is an Intelligence officer who is contacting me in regard to this opportunity means that there will be an element of the job that would involve ensuring that London was kept abreast, let's say, of the goings-on in Edinburgh. Or that I might be asked from time to time to conduct myself in a way that might not meet the complete approval of the senior Scottish politicians I'd be serving."

"It would be foolish of me to deny that you might have split loyalties from time to time, Miss Burns."

Burns consulted her watch. "I need to prepare for my next meeting. I will speak with my husband. If he gives the idea the green light, what happens next?"

"Well, if he gives it the green light, as you say, within the next two days, and you accept the opportunity, your name will be placed on a list...a *very* short list and you would become one of two recommended candidates that will be placed before the First Minister of Scotland. The post would be offered on an immediate basis and would be on an interim footing but that is merely a device to cut through bureaucracy and have the candidate installed quickly. Matters would be ratified and formalised in due course."

"And would the other candidature be a sham, Mr Chiswick?"

The practised smile returned to Chiswick's face.

"I'm sure I would never refer to anyone of my senior colleagues in the civil service in such a manner, Miss Burns."

Chapter Four

The Inverskillen Estate was comprised of over two thousand acres of incomparable beauty. Sheltered beneath the glowering and muscular Cairngorm mountain range, its soil nourished by the waters of the River Spey, its rolling hills, for the most part tree-clad, Inverskillen was home to a wide variety of flesh, fowl and fish. For over one hundred years it had been owned by the Wishart family, its most recent steward being Harold Wishart, the Laird, who had died in London only four years previously. A long time property entrepreneur, he had spent his stewardship of Inverskillen attempting to build log cabins for the tourist trade but had had his ambitions rejected by the planners. An adventure park met the same fate as did proposals for a dirt bike racing track. A large fence surrounding the entire estate was dropped due to the extravagant costs involved. Now the estate was owned and managed by Helen Wishart; Lady Wishart of Inverskillen.

Despite most early opinion supporting the notion that his wife, the plummy-accented Lady Wishart would sell up and retire to her spacious and elegant apartment in London's Chelsea, she'd defied the doubters, and within six months, had sold Inverskillen Castle and its five surrounding acres as a hotel on the edge of the estate, moved into a large four-bedroomed gatehouse with her dog, a Labrador called Rory, and joined the local branch of the Scottish Women's Institute as well as the local Green Party. Lady Wishart was passionate about the environment, and set about rewilding the estate. Buoyed by the fortune bequeathed her by her late husband's property portfolio in London, she set about developing her extensive forest in ways that maintained biodiversity and encouraged its capacity for regeneration. Freed from her deceased husband's commercial instincts and also from his mantra that a dead tree is worth more money than a live tree, she ensured ecological improvements that did not damage other ecosystems. In her endeavours she made use of the talents of one man, Lachlan 'Van' MacAskill who served as a ghillie, forester, bridge-builder and dry-stane-dyker.

MacAskill's nickname 'Van' amongst the children and elderly in the village was derived not from his given name but from his preference in living in an ambulance which he had converted into a motor home replete with bed, kitchen, toilet and shower. He lived in this custom with his dog, a Golden Retriever called Blaze. Although Lady Helen had gifted him a cottage on the estate, MacAskill preferred the ability to sleep anywhere he chose, usually close to any task he was fulfilling that day although on a few evenings each week, his matt-black converted motor home could often be seen somewhere on the edge of Grantown-on-Spey to permit a late visit to the Claymore Bar with Blaze.

Lady Wishart had one daughter, Isla, a vet who had both trained and practised in Gosforth, Newcastle. Brought up and educated locally in Grantown-on-Spey, she'd never lost either her accent or her love of her Scottish upbringing. Now home with her mother on holiday in the gatehouse she was never happier than when walking her mother's dog, Rory.

It was early morning when she and Rory walked one of the many new paths laid down upon the instruction of her mother and by the sweat of MacAskill's brow for general use by the public.

A blue sky and barely discernible breeze was masked by the dense forest until she came to a stream which opened up the vista and allowed the scenery to be viewed in all its majesty.

God, this place is beautiful, she reflected as she called Rory to her side.

"Here, boy."

She fondled his coat affectionately as the dog's ears pricked up and he trotted off along the path and round a bend, out of sight. Intrigued, she followed to see the dog seated motionless and facing what appeared to be a Golden Retriever which sat as if mirroring Rory. Both dogs seemed entirely calm and remained so until following their visual assessment, each utilised their keen sense of smell to provide vital information about their canine acquaintance's rear end. The dogs' acute olfactory senses worked overtime to identify the gender and mood of their new friend and whether it was happy, aggressive, healthy or ill. Satisfied, each dog then became distracted as Isla approached.

"Hello, you," said Isla to the Retriever. "You're a beauty."

Kneeling, she ran her hands affectionately over the necks of each dog, smiling before looking up to see where the Retriever's owner was. Seeing the path before her bereft of anyone, her gaze fell on the stream. A waterfall, perhaps shoulder-high to the pool beneath it, cascaded and burbled some thirty yards away. Beneath its shed, a man stood, groin deep in the pool, naked and facing away from her. In his thirties, she guessed and with a rippling torso. He was quite oblivious to her presence. Throwing back his head he allowed the water to spill and tumble on his face as he went about his ablutions. Isla watched for some moments before realising that she might be observed if the man turned around. She ruffled the neck of the Retriever, located its collar and looked at its name tag.

"Hi Blaze," she read. "Tell your owner he has a very nice arse!"

Standing, she again slowly dropped back into a crouch, partly concealing herself behind a gorse bush as she noticed a rifle leaning against a tree close to where his clothes had been lain.

Christ, he's a bloody poacher. That's a stalking rifle if I'm not mistaken.

"C'm'ere, Rory. Let's go report this. Quietly, now."

She led Rory into the depths of the forest and back towards the gatehouse. Blaze followed for a while then returned to the pool.

* * *

It was breakfast time as Isla returned. Her mother stood over an old and much used Aga cooker stirring a large pot of porridge.

"Ah, you're back, darling. I've made us a bowl of porridge. Enjoy your walk with Rory?"

"I did but when I was over by the old stables. There was a pool and a poacher was washing himself without so much as a care in the world. I thought we'd better phone the local police."

Lady Wishart turned and slid her spectacles to the tip of her nose and looked over the rims to her daughter.

"And this poacher...was he on his own, aged maybe late thirties? Red, unkempt hair?"

"Yes...He had a dog...He looked younger"

"Yes, he does actually. That'll be Van. His dog's called Blaze."

"It was. I met with Blaze on the trail."

"I'm sure you'll meet Van while you're up here, darling. He's an absolute godsend and I'd trust him with my life." She placed a bowl on the table and, using a large spoon, scooped two healthy offerings of porridge into it. "Here. Tuck in. It's good for you. No sugar. Salt if you must."

"Does he work for you on the estate?" asked Isla as she fetched a couple of spoons from a drawer.

"In a manner of speaking. Darling. He lives largely 'off the grid', as I believe it's called." She took a second bowl and filling it with porridge, sat down at the kitchen table opposite her daughter.

"When your dad died, I made it my business to develop the estate in a way that future generations could enjoy. Your dad was always up to some idiotic commercial adventure and, thank God, they never amounted to anything. I took the place in a different direction. One day, I was walking the estate and came across a man who was sitting, both feet in the burn with his dog, just appreciating the beauty of the trees and the water between his toes. We sat and talked. He was a quiet man. Reticent. But we got chatting and he told me he'd been in the army. The Royal Marines...actually 3 Commando Brigade Air Squadron. He retired with honour from the army in 2013 as a result of suffering from Post Traumatic Stress Disorder. He's actually a gentle soul. Badly damaged by the fighting in which he was involved. He just decided to drop out and have nothing to do ever again with the Union Jack. If you ask me he's a closet Nationalist. When I look into his blue eyes I'm sure they're Pantone 300...the same colour as the Saltire! He's a small army pension that keeps him in beer money and diesel but it's just below the level where he needs to pay much in the way of tax. He lives in an ambulance which he converted and eats anything he wants from the estate; fish, fowl, rabbits, deer. He gets eggs from the hen house and he has a couple of wee gardens near the cottage where he grows vegetables. His ambulance is magnificent. Like a wee home from home. All modern amenities other than a television. He's no time for news or current affairs. Like me, he's passionate about the environment and offered to help out on the estate. I offered to give him a job but he's refused all offers of payment. I trust him so much I gave him a blank credit card. Each month the bank sends me a run down of all expenditure on the card and each and every item is to do with work on the estate. There's not ever been an item purchased that is personal in any way. If anything costs more than five hundred pounds, he'll knock on my door and seek my permission. He's lain paths through the estate, built small bridges over burns, harvested trees and keeps the deer population under control. If he shoots a deer, my freezer is stocked - but so too are the freezers of some of the senior citizens or less well-off in the village. They just find a wee parcel on their doorstep and it might be venison or maybe a salmon or a trout fillet. The man's a saint."

"Well, it certainly sounds like the man I saw in the pool."

Smiling, Lady Wishart swallowed a spoonful of porridge. "Well built isn't he?"

"Can't say I noticed," lied Isla.

"Well, he's always working on the estate and only pops in now and again. You're only up here for two weeks so you might not cross paths. Even if you're out walking Rory, you could easily miss his van. He painted it matt black and has a dozen places on the estate where he parks it and sleeps overnight. It doesn't reflect light so it just merges with the background and can be almost invisible."

"Curious name, Van"

That's not his real name, darling. His name is Lachlan MacAskill and...'

"Lachie MacAskill! He was at school with me here in the village. He used to pull my pigtails in the playground and, as I recall, was top of the class narrowly missing out on Dux. He certainly got more Highers than me. When we were both eighteen I went to university to find a career and he joined the army to find adventure."

"Well, find it he did. But he saw enough of blood and guts to last several lifetimes and now he's happiest with animals, plants and solitude. He speaks silence fluently."

"God, he was so happy-go-lucky as a young man."

"Well, now he's my unofficial ghillie but what he doesn't know is that I've being paying a wage into an account that will be made over to him when I die or at some other earlier time as seems appropriate. He must have about seventy thousand pounds in it by now. I've also given him the old cottage over on the other side of the estate but he doesn't really use it. I've popped in on occasion and he's done it up and it sparkles inside but he prefers his van."

"Sounds like an interesting guy."

"He's a gem and d'you know, he's *always* immaculate. Collar and tie even when he's chopping wood and if you ever see him off duty, his shoes shine like he's about to go on parade. He's allowed his red hair to grow a bit but there are some parts of army life he's not forgotten."

Lady Wishart returned the spectacles to the bridge of her nose. "His only friend is Gus Darroch, our local police sergeant."

"God, I know him too. He and Lachie were great pals back in school."

"Well, Lachie and Gus drink in the Claymore Bar in the village. You should pop down one night and renew your acquaintances."

"Perhaps."

"Neither of them is married, y'know! Gus is divorced. He married dull!"

"Mother!"

"Well you are thirty-eight now and ever since you dated that horror Stanley something or other, I'm unaware of you taking an interest in continuing the family line as it were!"

"Jesus, is that all I am to you? A breeding machine? Someone who'll carry on the traditions of Inverskillen Estate?"

"Now you know full well that I don't mean that but you can't let life slip by. I suspect you're another one who'd rather spend more time with animals rather than people...just like Lachie!"

"God! You're impossible."

Placing the now empty porridge bowl in the ancient Belfast sink rather too roughly than was good for the ceramic, Isla left the kitchen and headed up to her bedroom.

Lady Helen took another mouthful of porridge.

What's a loving mother to do?

* * *

Simon Thorpe had been an Intelligence Officer in MI5 for a decade and had served his country all over mainland Europe. Recalled by his superiors to London, he now found himself in a car park above the port of Dover watching a blue Jeep and awaiting the return of its owner.

For the previous twenty minutes he had watched the arrival of the Calais/Dover Ferry as it emerged through the gloom of the evening and now took a particular interest in its disembarkation. As crowds of passengers stepped from the walkway and cars began to drive onto English roads, one gentleman of Arabian appearance, dressed nattily in a dark business suit but wearing an embroidered, tight-fitting Kufi skull cap strode towards the Jeep.

Thorpe left his vehicle and smiling broadly, approached the man.

"*As-salaam 'alykum*...Peace be upon you, my friend".

Surprised but not alarmed, the man responded automatically.

"*Va-alaikum as-salaam*...Peace be unto you too."

Thorpe offered his right hand in friendship and the man moved his briefcase from his right hand to his left to free his hand to respond. Shaking it warmly and holding it tight, Thorpe used his left hand to remove a 9mm Browning Hi-Power single-action handgun from his rear waistband. Holding it at hip-height and pointing it at his captive, he growled an instruction.

"Into your Jeep. You're driving!"

Startled, the man complied as Thorpe made his way to the passenger's seat all the while pointing the gun in the direction of the driver. He sat at an angle on the seat facing the driver ignoring both its belt and the constant bleep instructing it's deployment.

"Briefcase!"

Now more appreciative of his assailant's motives, the man affected a grim expression and handed over his attache case.

"Now drive. I'll give directions."

The Jeep progressed along Upper Road, turning left at Lighthouse Road and made its way along bumpier farm tracks to St. Margaret's Bay.

"Stop here! Keep the engine running."

Removing a file from the case, he closed it and wiped both the handle and lock with a piece of cloth used to clean spectacles. He threw the briefcase into the footwell at his feet.

"*As-salaam 'alykum!*" Smiling once again, he transferred the pistol from his left to his right hand and holding it by the barrel, he used his considerable upper body strength to strike the butt against the chin of the driver.

Dazed but not fully unconscious, it took a moment to realise that Thorpe had removed himself from the passenger's seat and had walked round to the near side. Opening the door, another two blows to the head were issued. Now concussed, the driver was helpless to stop Thorpe leaning over and releasing the handbrake. He stepped back and closed the door as slowly as the car trundled forwards until it reached the edge of one of Dover's famous chalk cliffs where gradually but inevitably it plummeted to the sea, three hundred and fifty feet below.

"*As-salaam 'alykum!*" He peered over the top of the cliff. "Obvious suicide if you ask me."

He folded the file, placed it in the rear of his waistband next to his Browning handgun and made his way back to the farm track and to the car he'd left only minutes earlier.

Chapter Five

The steps down to the basement restaurant in an alley in Tokyo's Shinjuku district were steep and the treads narrow. Catriona Burns took them carefully, holding on to a flimsy bannister. The restaurant, *Nabezo Meijidori*, was a favourite of hers and the owner Gu Zhiqiang was, as ever, pleased to see her. Speaking in English, he welcomed her.

"Mrs. Burns. It is wonderful you have chosen to eat with us again. Your wonderful husband has already arrived. Already he is drinking our wonderful Claret."

Everything was wonderful in Gu's world. He showed Catriona to the table whereupon her husband, Andy Burns stood and shook Mr. Zhiqiang's hand again before kissing his wife on the cheek and settling back into his chair.

"Mrs. Burns will share this bottle of Claret, Gu," he asserted, knowing her preference. He raised his eyebrows questioningly. "Kobe steak *sukiyaki*?"

Catriona smiled. "As ever." She turned her attention to Mr. Zhiqiang. "You make the best *sukiyaki* in Japan!"

Zhiqiang smiled bashfully. "I make it wonderful for you."

Andy Burns poured his wife a glass and toasted it with his own as she raised it.

"So what's behind this hastily contrived dinner with your husband? Problems?"

"Perhaps...although others might see it as an opportunity."

"Sounds interesting."

"I had a meeting today with an odious wee man who thinks he's God's gift. He somehow manages to strut sitting down."

"Off to a good start. Doesn't sound much like an opportunity is about to befall us."

"Well, I've kind of been offered a new job."

"Then surely that's good news."

"Its a big promotion. Permanent Secretary."

"Jesus!" Exclaimed her husband. "That's huge. You didn't expect to be in contention for a post of that seniority for another ten years."

"It'd mean another relocation."

"Ah...the downside. Where to? Some God-forsaken part of the world where no one will know how to prepare a *sukiyaki* steak and no one will understand the language?"

"Kind of....it's Edinburgh."

A silence fell on the table as both wrestled with the options.

Andy spoke first.

"Darling, we agreed years ago that you were the talent in this marriage. You have the ability to become, well, a Permanent Secretary. It's the top of the tree...the very top of the tree. I love it here in Tokyo as do you but can we really afford to pass up an opportunity like this?" He thought some more. "We decided that your career came before even starting a family. We agreed that I could find work pretty much anywhere." He thought further. "If you said 'no thanks', would that inhibit a similar offer being made in the future?"

"Given what I suspect lies behind the offer, I'd expect another imminent move - without a promotion but to the Sudan, Eritrea or some other war-torn part of the globe where *absolutely* no one will know how to prepare a sukiyaki steak and no one will understand the language."

"Why would they be so keen to see you in this post?"

"Well, you know the political situation back home. They'll be apprehensive about Scotland becoming independent to say the least and will want to count on my Scottish background but also my allegiance to the flag of the United Kingdom. They'll expect me to pass on information I glean and may even want me to carry out acts covertly that would advance their interests."

"God! My wife the spy!"

"Not sure I'm cut out for all of that."

"Then let me offer some thoughts on my part. I love working here in Tokyo. I've travelled the length and breadth of Japan on their amazing *Shinkansen* bullet trains. I adore our apartment and the people are so polite. However, I now have a smattering of Japanese, I speak French fluently, can handle a bit of German, am now experienced in an overseas travel role…what tourist or airline in Edinburgh wouldn't snap me up? We've friends there, you've a brother over there you've not seen in years, restaurants and pubs are some of the best in the world…" He ended his considerations rather lamely before picking up again. "You must make a *career* decision. Don't bother about me. We stay? I'm delighted. We leave? I'm delighted."

Catriona sipped a rather larger mouthful of red wine than she'd intended and felt for a napkin to dab the extraneous Claret from her lips.

"I've to make a decision by tomorrow. Let's sleep on it."

* * *

MacAskill's motorhome reversed into an opening in the forest he'd used on many occasions. Instructing Blaze to remain positioned on the passenger seat, he stepped from the vehicle and closed its door. Walking silently on the mossy ground before the dense tree-line forbid such growth, he moved towards a large oak tree he knew well. Circling it once to assure himself of the absence of onlookers, he placed his hand inside a large hollow in the tree and removed a piece of paper. Opening it, he read; 'Wednesday 7th. 9.30am - 9.40am. Location X.'

Committing the detail to memory, he took a lighter from his jacket pocket and set the paper alight. In seconds, as the flame consumed the paper, it was dropped to the floor of the forest whereupon he waited until the entire message was ash before grinding it into the earth.

"Wednesday 7th. 9.30am - 9.40am. Location X. I'll be there," he murmured to himself.

Returning to the old ambulance, he let himself in via its rear door and called Blaze over from the driver's cabin. He fished in his pocket and gave his dog a small treat.

"Good boy. We'll go for a walk in a wee while."

As Blaze curled up on the covers of the bed he'd constructed, MacAskill removed his rifle from a locker he'd installed on the wall of the vehicle. He cradled it on his lap and smoothed the walnut butt and recoil pad of the Remington Model 700, a bolt-action weapon to which was attached a five round internal magazine, a very high-end telescopic Leupold scope and a Harris bipod to stabilise the rifle when firing from a prone position. Some five minutes were spent inspecting the rifle and a further five checking the two attachments. A cardboard box was pulled from a compartment beneath the locker and the number of available .223 bullets were counted. Eleven. *Only need one,* figured MacAskill. *One or maybe two.*

He returned the rifle and cardboard box to their respective containers and clapped Blaze.

"Let's go for a walk, old pal."

* * *

Sergeant Angus Darroch closed the door of the office being used by the police inspector sent by Inverness to check on the various protocols associated with the road accident the day before.

Despite having had run-ins with Inspector Croft before, nothing untoward could be found. *Much to Croft's annoyance,* grinned Darroch to himself.

He turned the handle on the door behind which was a desk where sat officer Calum Buchanan typing on a keyboard. Leaning in to the room, he addressed his colleague.

"Got the green light, Calum. They couldn't find anything to shout at us about." A thought occurred. "Tell you what. I thought you handled yourself well yesterday. How about you follow things up with the local Housing Association? My calculation is that the fiscal will fine auld Archie but might easily impose a ban. If he does or if Archie decides he doesn't want to drive again, he and his wife'll be in Queer Street. They live outside the village and she has dementia. If he can't drive they have no way of getting to the shops, the doctor, the pub. Why not give the housing boys an early warning and ask whether there might be something in the way of sheltered accommodation available in the village if they decide to sell up and move out? It might be the only decent option they have. The council will make them sell the property and charge their rent against the value of their property. It's bloody shame but it might be best in the long run. I'm going to phone their doctor and the social work people and bring them up to speed. I'm sure that together we can come up with support that allows them some decency in what's left of their life together."

"Will do, boss. Fancy a pint after work?"

"Nah. I'm going to drive up to see auld Archie right now then later tonight I'm meeting Lachie MacAskill for a few pints. You know Lachie. He prefers it when it's just him and me. No offence."

"None taken, Sarge. I'll get on to housing."

* * *

The electric clock on the wall of the Claymore Bar moved its minute hand to five-past-nine indicating that the actual time was nine o'clock, John the barman always setting it five minute fast lest he required to appeal to last minute topers of the need for them to finish their drinks and move out. In his twenty-three years behind the bar he hadn't once been required to make use of this contrivance given the generally relaxed approach to public house timekeeping in the village.

Just as the hand moved, Lachie MacAskill opened the door and entered, offering a smile to John and an instruction to Blaze.

"Sit, boy." He turned his attention to the array of draught beers. "Two pints of Guinness, John. Gus'll be in in a minute."

As the pints were being given the required time to settle before being topped up, the door opened again and Gus Darroch came in. MacAskill exaggerated a look at his watch.

"You're a minute late, Sergeant Darroch. Your punctuality is slipping."

"In all my years I've never met anyone with such a fixation on punctuality as you, Lachie. It's commendable and maddening. We're in a *pub* for Christ's sake."

They each accepted their Guinness as MacAskill paid. "To you!" toasted Darroch.

"And you," replied MacAskill. "C'mon, boy."

Blaze rose and followed them to their favourite table next to the fire where he promptly laid down and began his regular pub doze.

"Not seen you for a few days, Lachie. What have you been up to?"

"Just the usual, Gus. I've hired a wee digger and I'm making a fresh path up towards the old stables. It's been good weather recently so I'm pissed at not getting out in the fresh air but it beats trying to use the digger in the mud. You?" he enquired.

"Bad accident yesterday." Darroch lapsed into the local patois he was more used to when in the company of his friend. "D'ye ken auld Archie McFarlane? He let a load of logs fall off his lorry and it took the heid aff a very senior civil servant. Poor sod would have known nothing about it. His heid was little more than mush."

"Thanks for the cheery wee story, Gus."

"You asked."

"I suppose."

The conversation continued and another round was purchased. A few more customers ventured in to the establishment while still keeping numbers well below a throng. The second of Gus and MacAskill's's pints had reached a perilously low level and consideration was being given to the purchase of a malt whisky… instead of stout…or perhaps both…when their decision-making was interrupted.

"I'm told I've now to call you 'Van'?"

Both men looked up at a slim, bedenimed woman with lustrous, dark hair that cascaded over her shoulders. Her grin was wide. Politeness and confusion fought for precedence.

"Sorry, eh?"

Both men spoke over one another trying to make sense of a beautiful stranger appearing to know at least one of them. Eventually, Gus Darroch held out his hand.

"And you are?"

"Well, *you*, if memory serves, are Angus Darroch and this other gentleman is a slightly older Lachie MacAskill who my mother tells me villagers now call 'Van'."

"The two of us are the same age," protested a still confused MacAskill.

"I know fine you're the same age. Same age as me. We were in the same class at school."

Gradually, recognition dawned on each man.

"Wee Isla...Isla Wishart?" Darroch had been first to ask.

"Only wee these days because you two are so tall." She shuffled nervously, her knuckles white as she grasped the back of the chair she'd used unconsciously as a prop. "Look, I'm only in for one drink. Can I buy you a glass before I go up the road?"

The chivalry of both men was offended.

"No you certainly can *not!*" Again Darroch was first off the mark. "We were just about to get a round in. Sit down and tell us your poison."

"I see gender equality hasn't reached the Highlands yet."

"Christ, *electricity* hasn't much reached the Highlands yet." He stood. "We're now progressing to the half and a half pint stage of the evening. You?"

"Same as you two, thanks." Darroch approached the bar and Isla smiled at MacAskill. "My mother thinks the world of you, Lachie. She told me you and Gus drank in here some evenings. I thought I'd pop in and catch up."

MacAskill surprised himself as he reached for words. Isla's sudden appearance had been as distinct and startling as a flame in darkness. Socially awkward, he chose to talk about her mother rather than her beauty.

"Your mother, Lady Wishart, is a pioneer, Isla. She's a breath of fresh air. I do a bit of work around the estate now and again, y'know."

"She told me all about you, Lachie...The two of you are ecological warriors."

"Well, I've had my fill of being a warrior."

Isla's smile faded. "Yeah, she mentioned that too."

Darroch returned. "The order's in, people. John'll bring it over soon enough. Ignoring MacAskill, he addressed Isla.

"Well, look at *you*! It must be about twenty years since we last clapped eyes on you. You left to go to uni straight after school didn't you. Where did you go and what did you study?"

MacAskill found his tongue.

"You'll need to excuse him, Isla. He's now the village's Inspector Clouseau except he's only a Sergeant. He asks embarrassing questions for a living."

"The smile returned to Isla's face. "My mother mentioned."

Three glasses of eighteen year old Glenlivet malt whisky were placed before them by John.

"Guinness'll be over in a minute."

All three lifted their glass. Isla, after pouring a drop of water in hers, was first to offer the toast.

"Slàinte mhath!"

She sipped at the malt and continued.

"After school, I left to go to Newcastle University where I did an honours in animal science then went on to do my BVMS to become a proper veterinarian surgeon. Ten years in all. I was the perpetual student but I fell in love with Newcastle and took a job as a vet. Now I'm a director of the firm. I'm only back up here for a fortnight but it's just reminded me how much I miss the place... also how much I miss my mother even though she can be an old battle-axe now and again."

"D'you like being a vet?" Darroch was asking all the questions.

"I do. I love it. What I miss is large animal practice. I tend to deal with overweight cats or dogs that have just eaten chocolate due to their owners being eejits. I'm a qualified livestock veterinarian but I couldn't tell you the last time I saw a horse, cow or sheep."

"That's a shame, right enough." Darroch was on a roll. "Tell me...is there a *Mister* Isla?"

"Err, no. I've been unlucky in love, I'm afraid. I've had three dogs over the years and they all offered me unconditional love. I've never found a man who was as reliable so I'm currently without a man *and* a dog."

The conversation continued for a further hour and two more rounds of drink until Isla called a halt to proceedings.

"I must go. Mother will be wondering where I am."

"One for the pavement?"

"No, I'm off. Perhaps I'll see you gentlemen in here again before I head south again...or maybe if you're around the estate when I'm walking Rory, Lachie." She hesitated. "Is it Lachie or 'Van'?"

MacAskill shrugged. "I suppose that in the village, weans and some of the elderly I supply with the odd trout call me 'Van' but Lachie is more me, I suppose."

Isla took her leave as each man regarded the other.

"Christ, she's a looker, eh?" volunteered Darroch.

"Aye. She's no' bad lookin' I suppose."

"And bright!"

"S'pose."

"And heiress to a fortune, eh? 'See you on the trail', she says, Lachie. You're *in*, big man."

"Fuck off, Gus. I'm quite happy with Blaze. Anyway, *you* were the one with eyes like saucers when she sat down."

"My heart kept like a salmon on the Spey, Lachie. But I'm sworn to uphold the law, not ogle young ladies in bars."

"Oh, look...there's a pig flying over the bar."

Chapter Six

Sir Jonathan Burton lifted the phone having been told that Sir Jeffery Arbuthnot, the Head of MI5 was holding for him.

"Jeffery! Good of you to call. What did you make of the file on Burns?"

"She looks perfect, old man. My chap out in Tokyo thinks she's a cold fish and has a high opinion of herself. However, I'd rather make my own mind up. She has all the right qualifications, experience, and her annual reviews are excellent. All that remains to be seen is whether she might be trusted to make sure that we continue to have an uninterrupted flow of discrete information on matters Scottish. I read other missives earlier that suggest that the natives up there are becoming more restive by the hour so we need to keep abreast of their body politic."

"Well, my secretary tells me she and her husband fly into London later this morning and you and I are due to dine with her tonight. I would have invited you to my club, Boodles but they won't allow women to cross the doorway so it'll have to be my other club, the one I use when I want to avoid politicians, the clergy, brigadiers and the aristocracy. So seven o'clock in the Groucho Club, Dean Street in Soho. No one will bother us as the place is full of ageing rock stars, comedians and actors. I suspect also that Mrs. Burns will be very jet-lagged so only a light meal, I'd suggest."

"But at first blush she appears on board with our agenda?"

"She responded in the affirmative the morning after the offer was made."

"Then I'll see you and Mrs. Burns at seven, Jon."

* * *

"The fucking machine's out of milk! How can a coffee machine advertising *caffè latte* be out of milk? Now I've got a cup of stewed espresso."

37

Jimmy Boyd wasn't happy. He thumped the side of the coffee dispenser with the heel of his hand to jolt it unsuccessfully into producing milk before surrendering and taking his carton of coffee into the small interview room.

"Coffee machine's fucked again."

Sergeant Colin Boston was wiping a large whiteboard and merely grunted an acknowledgement. Satisfied that all traces of the previous user had been cleared, he drew a large black line, north to south down the middle of the board and started to write on its west side. Still without talking, he began to form a list; 'Photographing convoys, impeding traffic, letters to newspapers, writing to politicians, setting up home in the Faslane Peace camp, placards, marches…

Boyd raised the cup to his lips and grimaced as he pondered his Sergeant's writing.

"What's this, boss?"

"These are the kinds of things we've been used to when people get their dander up about nuclear weapons. I met with the Chief Super this morning and we've been asked ever so politely to find the smart-arse who wrote that letter and make sure he doesn't do anything that annoys the self-same, bad-tempered Chief Super…who's a fuck-wit by the way…and we've to do it without spending any money."

"Didn't sound like those were the kind of things he was threatening, Sarge."

Boston stopped writing and pursed his lips in frustration.

"I *know* that Jimmy. I'm just listing them before you and I work out what he's *actually* going to do!" He moved to the right hand side of the line. "So!…"

"Canny see him accessing the Faslane Base, boss."

"Right. Let's note that…"Accessing and sabotaging the submarine base."

"Canny see it!"

"Jimmy, we're just making a list! We'll decide what's likely afterwards."

"The place is surrounded by soldiers with automatic weapons."

Boston sighed. "Jimmy, there's times whenI think I could eat a bowl of alphabet soup and shite out better answers than you... now, what else?"

"Accessing the Coulport base where they store the warheads?"

"Now you're talking." Boston wrote down the suggestion.

"Blowing up a warhead lorry?"

"So a guy who wants to stop nuclear explosions is going to explode a device under a nuclear bomb?"

"Now *you're* doing it boss. Thought we were just making a list?"

Boston returned to the whiteboard and wrote down the idea."

"Eh, poisoning the food in the Faslane canteen?"

"Jesus, Jimmy. Ideas that aren'y that far-fetched."

"Could happen, boss!"

Boston ignored the proposition but wrote; "Using a fishing boat to drop nets at the entrance of Loch Long."

"Aye, that's a good one!"

The pair continued until they had a list that filled the space available. Silence reigned as they contemplated the whiteboard.

"Not much further forward are we boss?"

"A thousand troops backed up by a thousand cops couldn't police this. He could be anywhere...do anything. The Chief Super wants it done without any expense. I'm going to have to tell him that this won't work but even then..."

"What...?"

"I wouldn't know where to start. The MOD in their wisdom have set up systems that protect the nation's nuclear weaponry." He thought again. "I mean we've not even considered that this guy isn't *already* inside one of our nuclear bases...employed there...and has access to codes, materials, technologies..." His words trailed off as he contemplated his next move.

"Our next step, young James, is to advise the MOD of this letter and ask their guidance on what supports they need from us to manage it. Then we tell the boss that we've had inter-agency discussions. If I'm any judge, the MOD will tell us that they have loads of experience in dealing with threats like this and keep us at arms' length. We stand by and wait either for something to happen, a new letter or a long period of no activity on this front."

"Sounds like a plan, Sarge."

* * *

Sir Jonathan Burton quietly disposed of the remnants of a first glass of *Saint-Emilion Premier Grand Cru Classé* as Sir Jeffrey Arbuthnot entered the Groucho Club and was shown to his table. Sitting and shaking hands with his host, he turned the bottle so the label faced him.

"I say...*Château Bélair-Monange* 2017? You clearly intend to impress Mrs. Burns, Jon."

"Not at all, Jeffrey. Completely selfish on my part. It's a delicious wine. From Libourne, north-east of Bordeaux. There's been wine grown in that vineyard since Roman times."

The sommelier poured a glass just as Catriona Burns was ushered into the presence of the two men. Both stood as she approached, offering her hand.

"Miss Burns...may we call you Catriona?" Burton emphasised the silent 'o' in her name.

"It's pronounced *Catreena*," corrected Burns. "And you may."

Some minutes were spent choosing a starting dish, dealing with Arbuthnot's memories of Tokyo, and the rather bohemian membership of the Groucho Club before Burton turned the conversation to the prospect of Burns succeeding Giles Merchant as Scotland's Permanent Secretary.

"It's an utter tragedy of course but I'm afraid in our line of work we have to be somewhat dispassionate about such things. The show must go on, as the thespians in here might have it."

Arbuthnot took over.

"Miss Burns...Catriona...at the levels at which you've been used to operating you'll have come face to face with the political and organisational nuances and subtleties that diplomats such as yourself have to confront."

Burns nodded.

"Well, I fear that at the very senior level we now wish to discuss with you, these nuances and subtleties loom rather larger and we have to be sure...*very* sure that you understand that your first loyalty is to the Crown...that is to say both myself as Director General of MI5 and Sir Jonathan here as Cabinet Secretary and Head of the Civil Service. MI5 has to sign off, as it were, *all* key appointments and this evening we find ourselves in something of a bind. We need someone appointed to this role who will have the confidence of the First Minister and who will unquestionably have the ability to occupy that post with both vigour and distinction. A cursory glance at your CV suggests that you fit the bill admirably. Normally, filling a post of this nature takes time...time we don't have. Politics in Scotland is at a feverish high and we cannot allow time to pass without a firm hand on the tiller, as it were. Our proposal is that the Civil Service appoints a candidate merely on a temporary, interim basis as a support to the Scottish Government while this process is put in place. You would be our preferred candidate and if all goes well, you would also survive the selection process, perhaps some six months down the line and become, I suppose, the permanent, Permanent Secretary."

"As you say, Sir Jeffrey, I am unused to the manoeuvres of government at the highest levels but my first thought is to ask why you don't just appoint someone with a security services background?"

"Well, for the fairly obvious reason that it would be impossible to persuade the Scottish Government to accede to a recommendation of that nature. The civil service in Scotland itself would immediately smell a rat and we'd be reading about it for months in the Daily whatever there is up there. No, it has to be someone who has had an unblemished career in the civil service. We appreciate that you might require support in, let's say, any supplementary duties, but support you would have."

"Would I be asked to undertake any tasks that were illegal?"

Arbuthnot was vehement in his denial.

"Most certainly not. But you must understand two things. First, Her Majesty's Government is firmly opposed to the proud nation of Scotland uncoupling itself from the rest of the United

Kingdom and would quickly forgive any minor deviance from normal protocols should this be necessary and secondly, we are in a fortunate legal position that allows the Security Services to authorise agent participation in crime in order to obtain or maintain access to intelligence. An agent in this context is a person....that is to say...you...who can provide intelligence on individuals or policies of interest to MI5! The legal framework is enshrined in the Security Service Act 1989. Moreover, under our 'Official Guidelines on the use of Agents who participate in Criminality', any assessment on the nature of criminality is decided not by the courts...but internally by MI5 itself. Indeed, a recent Investigatory Powers Tribunal, the body that hears complaints about our intelligence services, ruled and reconfirmed that the policy, known as 'the Third Direction', was entirely lawful and stated that MI5 officers and those in the security services simply could not function without informants who could commit crimes, often while infiltrating criminal organisations." He hesitated before continuing. "Not that for one second am I suggesting that the Scottish Government is in any way a criminal organisation but in the past we've found it necessary, as has been well publicised in the media, to have placed members of our staff in political organisations, trades unions, special purpose organisations and the like...all of which were legal entities but which may have had objectives not conducive to the well-being of the state...and in the interests of disambiguation, Catriona, *that* state is the United Kingdom."

Burns sipped at her wine.

"Well...I must say this wine is delicious. And if our evening is unsuccessful, I will remember it for this wonderful Merlot." She smiled and placed her glass back on the coaster provided. "But I must say your suggestion that I would not be asked to do anything illegal merely persuades me that I *would* be asked to participate in illicit behaviours."

Burton interjected.

"Miss Burns...Catriona...Let me be clear. This is not an open invitation to commit crimes such as violence or burglary. At best it would be in reporting conversations, perhaps passing the occasional document, possibly now and again accidentally overlooking something that might better *not* be drawn to the attention of the First Minister. That sort of stuff. All very benign."

"And if I say, 'no thank you'?"

"Then you shall return to your post in Tokyo with fond memories of an excellent *Château Bélair-Monange* although you will forget everything we discussed round this table."

"I would not be disadvantaged?"

"Miss Burns, we need willing volunteers not pressed men. That said, it may be some time before further advancement would be forthcoming. If opportunities are rejected, it may give pause for thought before others are offered."

Burns allowed a silence to hold for a moment.

"And I gather that two contenders are provided to the First Minister?"

"I shouldn't concern yourself Miss Burns. The second candidate will also be there on our behalf but will not likely commend themselves to the First Minister."

"A makeweight?"

"Precisely so, if, however, a credible one."

The starter course arrived and was enjoyed, Burns citing jet-lag, announcing that she'd forego the main course and take an early night.

"I'll be in touch tomorrow morning first thing, gentlemen. With your permission, I'll sleep on it."

She left as Burton poured the remnants of the Claret into each remaining glass.

Arbuthnot was first to offer an appraisal. "I like her."

"Trust her?"

Arbuthnot raised the glass to his lips, smiling.

"My dear Jon, in this business I've learned to trust no one. Not even the Cabinet Secretary and Head of the Civil Service."

They toasted their friendship and awaited the main course.

Chapter Seven

Isla Wishart put one arm through the sleeve of her anorak as a precursor to putting it on. Easing back the curtains in her mother's kitchen she looked up at a cloudless blue sky.

"Going to take a walk with Rory. It looks lovely out there but I've been caught before."

"You never know on Speyside," replied Lady Wishart. "Blue sky one minute, freezing hail the next. You're wise to wear something waterproof." She put a lead on Rory and handed it to her daughter. "Keep him on the leash until you get past the hen house, eh?"

"Will do."

"I think Lachie MacAskill's working up at the old cottage he uses as a base sometimes."

"Yeah," said Isla dismissively. "I bumped into him and Gus Darroch in the Claymore a couple of nights ago. We'd a good chat. Seems a nice guy."

Her mother perked up at this piece of information.

"Did you now? Kept *that* quiet."

"No matchmaking, mother. We're worlds...and miles apart."

"Wouldn't dream! Anyway, he's probably up at the old cottage."

Only half a mile into her walk, Isla removed her anorak and placed it behind her back, tying the arms together in front, creating a rear kilt, so warm was the day.

"C'mon Rory. Want to go and play with Blaze?"

The paths on the estate made for easy walking and Isla and Rory made good use of them, walking the circumference of Inverskillen before a dog's bark alerted her to the possibility of Blaze being close by. Rory scampered off in the direction of the bark and Isla rounded a further couple of bends in the trail before the old cottage came into sight. Rory had indeed found Blaze and both dogs crashed through the undergrowth and around the tall firs in playful pursuit of one another.

Isla smiled at the dogs having fun and walked onwards to the cottage. No vehicle was in evidence and stopping at the front door she could hear no engine noise, no machinery. Listening carefully now, she attempted to establish the sound of any digging or axe work. Again, only the rustle of the slight breeze and the dogs playing in the forest was evident. Diffidently she knocked the door and waited. There was no response. Curious now, she walked around the perimeter of the house, stopping to look inside the windows. The rooms she inspected were empty but, she noted, were all as tidy as would be expected were a barracks' room inspection about to be undertaken. As she returned to the front door she saw, opposite the house, what appeared to be a large kennel. A wooden bucket of water lay to one side as did a plastic container with a chute, above which was a flat pedal. Gingerly, she pressed the device with her foot and a light rumble of biscuit dog food rolled to her feet. *Perhaps Blaze has been trained to feed and water himself,* she wondered. *Where the hell is Lachie?*

* * *

MacAskill lay prone within some ferns atop a hill overlooking a roundabout close to Coulport that had to be negotiated by the warhead convoy whatever the route chosen. Wearing his camouflaged ghillie suit, he was virtually undetectable; his rifle also indistinguishable from the surrounding environment, draped in camouflage cloth. Having been in position for some thirty minutes, he had checked and rechecked the scope and the bullets and had, the night before, broken down the firearm, cleaned it and reassembled it in order to have confidence that when he pulled the trigger, his target would suffer a direct hit.

He looked at his watch and calculated that the convoy should be about to make its presence known. He lifted his field glasses and trained them on the road where it disappeared behind a clutch of fir trees. Even before the engine noise of the motorcycles used by the Special Escort Group reached the quiet glen, he saw the advance guard emerge from the firs and climb the hill towards the roundabout. Before any of the Truck Cargo Heavy Duty Carriers came into sight, the motorcyclists had taken positions at each of the roads that fed the roundabout and were in position to stop traffic had there been any in that quiet corner of Scotland.

First to pass through were the Stand Off Escorts, also known as 43 Commando Fleet Protection Group Royal Marines, who provide armed military personnel in order to counter any potential threat and and provide traffic management throughout any convoy move. Next to cross was the Escort Commander's vehicle followed by the first of the Truck Cargo Heavy Duty vehicles carrying the nuclear weapons. The Convoy's Safety Crew followed and a second of the Mammoth Majors lumbered into sight. Close behind it was the Traffic Car and a third of the warhead lorries nosed past the firs and headed slowly towards the roundabout.

MacAskill allowed the first of the Mammoths to pass unhindered as he did the Safety Vehicle. As the second warhead carrier approached the roundabout and slowed, MacAskill waited until its front tyre was in relative alignment with the forest of trees to its rear and squeezed the trigger. The .308 cartridge sped towards the near-side front tyre at a velocity of three thousand, one hundred feet per second. To MacAskill, it appeared to hit its target almost instantly. Without waiting to observe the impact of his shot, he manoeuvred the Remington to focus upon the third wagon, whose occupants were as yet unaware of the attack. Fixing the crosshairs on its front tyre and aiming again at the near side to allow the bullet to escape into the forest behind without being caught beneath the undercarriage, MacAskill fired off a second shot. As with the first, it penetrated the front tyre causing the immediate release of pressure and instant deflation. Again, because the Mammoth Major was travelling so slowly, there was no vehicular deviation but the sudden drop in elevation on the near side caused both drivers to brake and saw the armed escort in each vehicle leave the cab to inspect the damage. Initially, each escort assessed the situation as a routine, if very rare, burst tyre but when each became aware of the other puncture, a red alert saw the convoy swing into protective mode. Officers of the Special Escort Group, a specialised unit of the Ministry of Defence Police responsible for the movement of all Defence Special Nuclear material within the United Kingdom, leapt from their vehicles and took up covered positions around the vehicles or at the side of the road.

By the time the first of them had taken up position, MacAskill had collected the expended shells from his Remington, thrown a piece of cardboard with the word 'Dalriada' on it to the ground, slung his rifle over his shoulder and was one hundred yards down the mountainside, well out of sight of those in the convoy. As fit as he had been in the army, due to his unrelenting physical work coupled with regular longer distance runs around the estate, MacAskill fled downwards with ease, leaping bushes, trampling heather and striding small burns as he made his way at pace towards the hide he'd previously fashioned. Five minutes took him into the shelter of a wooded area which slowed his progress but gave him greater cover. The trees, planted twenty years earlier to take advantage of tax-breaks, had been planted in serried ranks and offered a wide ditch between each row which, other than the occasional overhanging branch, allowed more distance to be put between him and those back on the road who were as yet uncertain from which direction the attack had taken place. Now approaching the village of Garelochhead, he headed left towards the railway line that connected Glasgow with its northwestern destinations. A fence erected to stop stray cattle and unwanted trespassers on the line was vaulted by MacAskill almost without breaking his stride. He crossed over, aware of the absence of any cameras on this remote part of the rail line. One more leap took him over the fence on the other side of the line and one hundred yards later, still breathing quite evenly, he approached his hide, secreted beneath a capacious gorse bush in the shelter of a wooded area. On his belly now, he crawled within the bush scarcely noticing the sharp, sturdy thorns which caught the skin on his right cheek, bleeding him. Inside, he repositioned the reflective blanket so as to provide him with the igloo shape he sought, the green side outward, the silvered side inside rendering the interior completely dark and blocking his infrared heat signature. Using his torch, he checked his watch. Less than one minute had been employed to take care of the convoy. He'd run for thirty-five minutes and covered a distance of some five miles after having driven through the night and hiked nine miles to his earlier vantage point across rough terrain from the village of Rhu. He was tired. He pulled a small radio from his rucksack and placed both buds of an earphone in his ears to silence any ambient noise before turning the dial until he came across the frequency being used by the Special Escort Group. Listening intently to the transmissions, occasionally adjusting the dial to secure a better reception, he satisfied himself that those investigating had managed to establish that the tyres had been punctured by means of a projectile, that the bullets couldn't be found, that the direction of the ricochet marks on the road suggested a shot from where he had positioned himself and that the probable means of escape by the assailant had been by a single dirt bike as deep tracks had been found along a nearby forest track which would have permitted access onto the A814, thence to the A817 and away. *That's handy,* thought MacAskill. *They think I'm on a motorcycle.* Roadblocks were being established on all major roads surrounding Garelochhead and beyond, officers were combing the immediate environment of the attack and motorcycle officers were touring the roads and paths belonging to the Forestry Commission. As he listened, he gleaned further information that a clutch of suspects who had in the past threatened active opposition to nuclear weaponry would be visited as would residents of the Faslane Peace Camp a couple of miles down the road at the submarine base.

Turning off his torch, he set to disassembling his rifle in complete darkness as he had been taught. Cleaned and oiled, he reassembled it knowing that henceforth, any forensic examination would have to report that this weapon showed no signs of having been fired. He removed both shell casings from his pocket and using a large, sharp knife, pushed each of them deep into the soft earth beneath the yellow gorse bush under which he sheltered.

His rucksack now employed as a makeshift pillow, he turned off the radio and torch, lay back, and in minutes was asleep.

* * *

Colin Boston was leafing through the pages of that day's Scotsman newspaper when his young assistant in the 'Dalriada case', as it was now being called by the pair, knocked his door and entered without seeking further permission.

"Boss, there's been an attack on the nuclear convoy coming out of Coulport."

Boston laid the paper down immediately.

"Eh? What do we know?"

"Two shots, they think, although no one heard them. Tyres taken out on two vehicles, both carrying nuclear weapons. Both vehicles disabled. Only one recovery vehicle but they were close enough to Coulport for another to be sent out. It's still causing a blockage but they expect to be back up and running shortly. The media are all over it. We'd better be able to brief the boss quickly on this Dalriada bloke."

"Agreed. What are the MOD cops doing?"

They've set up roadblocks, checking all the wee roads and forestry tracks and have a forensic team on the way up but I have to say boss, it's pretty much what Dr. Van Ossen told us to expect from this Dalriada fellah."

Boston nodded his agreement.

"I've already sent an e-mail to the Chief Super saying that we'd been in touch with the Coulport and Faslane people and that their response was to ask us to pass them the letter but that they were trained to deal with this kind of event. I'll be advising him to wash his hands of it and allow the MOD people to handle the media. My bet is that he'll take that line rather than have to answer questions put to him by reporters. He hates press interviews and knows he's no good at them. He's too nervous in front of a camera but won't let anyone else do it in case it threatens his precious ego."

Half an hour later, having been briefed by Boston and having been ordered by the Chief Constable to answer media questions, Chief Superintendent Terrance May walked towards a circle of journalists arranged in a semi-circle bristling with microphones and cameras. Boston and Boyd walked a couple of steps behind him.

Boyd was anxious. "Think he'll be okay?"

"Probably not. He's a diddy...as much use as a fuckin' library in Larkhall! But he knows the line. I've suggested he says *nothing* about Dalriada in case it frightens the lieges, explain that the investigation is being led by the MOD police, go on to say that two vehicles were temporarily disabled but that no one was injured, there was no threat to the surrounding community and that things are now back to normal. Skoosh case!"

The BBC reporter was first to ask a question.

"Chief Superintendent, do we know who is behind this attack?"

May's attempt to look authoritative quickly faded. He cleared his throat. His nervous demeanour now all too obvious. His lips dried.

"We received a letter from someone calling themselves Dalriada and we've passed it to the MOD Police who are leading this investigation."

Boston caught Boyd's gaze and in a suppressed lips movement that would have impressed a ventriloquist, spoke quietly to his colleague.

"Told you he was a fuckin' eejit!"

Chapter Eight

Isla returned to the gatehouse with two dogs in her charge as Blaze had followed Rory and played with him all the way back.

"Mother, We have another mouth to feed. I was up at the old cottage you've given to Lachie MacAskill. He wasn't there but Blaze was and the two dogs played together. I couldn't get rid of him...nor frankly did I want to. The poor thing had been left alone with some fresh water and a device that spits out dog food. I noticed him limping so I've had a look and he has an infected paw. I'll treat it before the poor thing suffers any more."

Lady Wishart ignored the plight of Blaze.

"Oh, that's quite normal darling. Blaze spends as much time here as he does up at the cottage."

"Really?"

"Yes. When Lachie is using heavy machinery, the cabin is too small to have his dog on board and he doesn't want Blaze running around outside in case he gets injured so he either leaves him here or at the cottage and if Blaze just gets bored chasing rabbits and squirrels he comes over to play with Rory. The two of them are inseparable."

"I couldn't hear any machinery."

"Darling we have two thousand acres here. That's over three miles of forest towards Grantown and three miles up the glen. Over nine square miles. Lachie could be working anywhere."

"Well, I don't like the idea of a beautiful dog like Blaze being left to its own devices."

"Oh, I wouldn't worry. I dare say that Lachie will pop round to collect him after he's finished."

"I'm going to have a look at his paw. Where's your medical box?"

"In the kitchen, darling. Above the cutlery drawer."

Isla took a few items from the medical box and the kitchen cabinet before calling Blaze to her. The dog responded immediately and sat obediently before her.

She lifted the dog on to the kitchen table and had a closer look at each of the dog's four paws.

"I think I see the problem here, Blaze. You've a rather nasty thorn in the pad of your right front paw. It's a beauty. No wonder you were limping."

Carefully using tweezers, she caught one end of the thorn and slowly removed it. Blood started to ooze from the wound.

"Okay young Blaze, we need to clean this and dress it. Hold still now."

As if understanding every word the vet had uttered, Blaze remained seated and calm, despite the small pool of blood now gathering around her paw. Taking a pair of scissors, Isla cut away some of the fur away from the site above the wound, ignoring the mess being made of her mother's kitchen table. She filled a basin with some hot water to which she added several tablespoonfuls of salt, stirred the concoction until the salt had dissolved and taking Blaze by his midriff, heaved him upwards until both of his front legs were in the basin. For the next several minutes, she spoke to the dog who turned his head to one side as if trying to understand Isla's utterances. As Rory wandered in to see what was going on, Isla added antibacterial, anti-fungal dog shampoo she'd found below the sink and continued to soak the foot but Blaze seemed to understand that he was being treated for a sore paw and didn't attempt a breakaway. Eventually, Isla lifted Blaze from the basin and patted down the wound with paper towels before applying a bandage which travelled three inches up his leg.

"Now we need something that'll stop you chewing this or getting it wet."

A small plastic bag came to the rescue and Isla placed the pained paw inside it and taped it with electrical tape to secure the protection."

"Okay. We'll need to get you to the village vet, Blaze. I don't have the proper tools to finish this job properly. Running repairs today, I'm afraid. But that should ease the pain and allow you to hobble about with Rory. Just stay out of puddles for a while, eh?"

* * *

MacAskill had slept for two hours. As he awoke, he listened first, and hearing nothing untoward, turned on his torch. Finding his radio, he inserted his earbuds and twisted the dial again to find a frequency to overhear the conversations between members of the Special Escort Group. It took a while to hear anything clearly but eventually he was able to hear the exchanges. He listened for fifteen minutes before hearing the words he wanted to hear.

"Delta-Hotel-Niner to Alpha...the bikes are reporting no evidence of activity on the tracks around the site and our roadblocks have produced nothing."

There was white noise for some seconds before a response.

"Alpha to Delta-Hotel-Niner. Message received. Stand down all roadblocks."

Recognising that there may yet be MOD police on the hill looking for him, MacAskill twisted the dial again until he chanced upon Radio Clyde which was just about to present the lunchtime news.

"James Madison here bringing you the lunchtime news on Clyde. Our top stories today. Drama in the Scottish Highlands as lorries transporting nuclear warheads are attacked. We have a report from our correspondent, Tom Guthrie who is at the site."

Another voice was broadcast.

"At around nine o'clock this morning a convoy taking nuclear warheads from Coulport in Argyll to Burghfield in England was attacked by a person or persons unknown, although a police spokesman indicated that responsibility was being claimed by an individual known to them as 'Dalriada' who may have behind the shooting. No one was injured and repairs to the vehicles concerned allowed the convoy to continue to England without much in the way of a delay. More details later."

Guthrie took back the microphone.

"In other news, a new government order for the building of destroyers on the Clyde..."

MacAskill turned off the radio.

They've released my name? That's a surprise, but one I can use to advantage. He packed away his torch, radio and pulling down the space blanket, folded and tucked the item into a small enough parcel to shove roughly inside his backpack. Carefully, he crawled to the edge of the gorse bush checking first to ensure that no one could establish his use of the bush as a hide. Looking around the forest from his position, he used his binoculars for some minutes looking for the very hint of movement within the forest before exiting and standing erect. Movement in the trees beyond him had him crouch slowly as a deer leapt away gracefully, its white tail flashing.

Something spooked her, he decided. Lying flat again, his prone body camouflaged by his ghillie suit, he felt for his back pack and pulled out his binoculars. He heard low voices first but it took a full minute before the flash of a yellow hi-viz jacket became evident. Moments later, two MOD police officers, each carrying an automatic weapon, could be seen walking on the periphery of the tree line on the other side of the railway track. Both men conversed lightly, laughing and paying little attention to their environment. *These boys are more suited to driving a jeep sleepily around the perimeter of Faslane all right. Right out of their comfort zone today. They don't expect to find anything. They're just going through the motions.* He watched as they approached the end of the pine forest at a point where they could see down the glen. No longer able to hear the occasional word, MacAskill increased the magnification of the field glasses until he could see quite clearly the men's faces, both creased in smiles. As he reset the focus to see their full body profile, he watched them scan the glen before one of the officers gestured behind him with his thumb. As he did so, both turned and began walking up the hill in the direction from which they'd just come.

MacAskill waited until they were out of sight then gave it five more minutes. *It's unlikely but there may be a presence on this side of the track. I'll stay within the tree-line.*

Pulling on his backpack, he began the four miles hike down through the forest that would take him to the edge of the village of Rhu and his converted ambulance, sitting in a quiet but relatively hidden forestry commission track.

Again, as he approached, he sat for some minutes on his haunches in the secluded, wooded approach to the quiet cul-de-sac within which his vehicle was parked and scoured the surroundings for activity or for concealed presence. Satisfying himself that there was nothing untoward, he entered the rear of the vehicle, set his rifle in the cupboard sheath he'd built for it within the ambulance, sat in the driver's seat and turned the ignition key. He looked in the rear view mirror and caught a glimpse of his face. The scratch inflicted by the gorse bush had been quite deep and his right cheek was bloodied quite severely. If he were to be stopped on his return home it'd look suspicious. Using a paper hankie and some hand sanitiser he always carried in the glove compartment, he set to until his cheek was ruddy but no blood was in evidence. *That scratch looks quite raw, mind you,* he thought as he released the handbrake. He was going back to Inverskillen.

Mission accomplished.

* * *

Boston and Boyd stood before Chief Superintendent Pickford as he lolled back on his office chair. He had recovered his pomposity and had determined that the press conference had been a great success.

"Yes. I decided at the last moment that it would be wiser to reveal the name...or the pseudonym of the probable assailant on the basis that it may twig the memory or conscience of someone who knows an individual who goes by that nickname. After giving it some thought I felt it was more likely to help rather than hinder our investigation."

"It's the MOD's investigation, boss."

"Well, they're leading, but we're Police Scotland, Sergeant Boston and no one gainsays us on our own turf."

"As you say, sir."

"Now you two keep close tabs on this. The MOD are a fine force but they may feel they have to keep matters close at hand. We cannot countenance this. They have to share information, just as we did when we passed the the letter from Dalriada. Clear?"

"As you say, sir."

"Keep me informed of progress."

Without acknowledging their continuing presence, he opened a file and began to read, signalling the end of the conversation.

Boston recognised this message accurately and turned to leave, Boyd following suit. They walked shoulder to shoulder along the corridor outside his office, Boston clearly agitated.

"How the fuck did that stupid bastard get the job? He comes up from Cleveland where he spent his time jailing Geordie drunks, daft farmers and seaside landladies. He knows fuck all about Scots' law but still we bring these eejits in rather than promote our own people."

"Heard he had a degree in fine arts from Cambridge, boss."

"Aye, well, he must be clever as fuck then. Is that your argument?"

"Not really...but..."

Boston continued his diatribe.

"'Don't mention Dalriada', he was told but the first words out of his mouth...Honest to Christ..."

"At least he's given us free rein over the enquiries as long as we keep him up to date."

"Look, Jimmy, that fat, stupid, English bastard gets told fuck all. He gets information when he asks for it and I'll be the judge of what he gets told. I've taken a shite with more talent that that diddy."

"Borderline racist, boss, eh?"

"And how is it, Jimmy? It's all facts. *Facts*! He's fat, he's English, he's stupid and he's a bastard. He's not a bastard because he's English...he's a bastard because number one, he's an ill-mannered eejit and number two, because I *say* he's a bastard!"

"See in his office when you said, 'as you say, sir'…is that your way of telling him politely he's talking shite and you don't agree with him but in a way that you can't get reprimanded?"

"Exactly that, Jimmy. Exactly that!"

"As you say, sir!"

Chapter Nine

Catriona Burns and her husband sat in the business class section of a Boeing 767 *en route* from Heathrow to Edinburgh.

"So let me get this straight. First thing in the morning you tell the top mandarin that you're prepared to go for this post and before you put the phone down he's got you and me a seat on an afternoon flight to Edinburgh?"

"And apparently I'm meeting the First Minister tonight. They've made the case that Scotland can't function properly without an interim Permanent Secretary at this difficult time and they've already had the other candidate in to see the FM. Sir Jonathan was at great pains to point out that this process normally takes months...and it still will, but that there needs to be someone in command of the Scottish civil service during the process and it's to be one of the two of us."

Andy Burns was sceptical.

"I never realised that the business you were in was so unethical and unprincipled."

"All that and more, Andy. The civil service at its core is pretty decent, objective and supportive of its political masters but the internal politics are, I suppose as good or as bad as the internal politics of Oxford University, Marks & Spencer or Astra Zeneca. It can be pretty cut-throat although in the circumstances in which we find ourselves..."

She clasped her husband's hand as he finished her thought.

"Yeah, it appears that on this occasion, your face fits."

Catriona nodded her agreement.

"But it's still worrying why of all the people they could have chosen, they picked me."

"Raw talent, darling."

Catriona stifled a guffaw.

"Trust me there are many people in the service who are much more talented than me but I suspect they need someone senior, someone Scottish and for once, being a woman doesn't hinder."

"And your requirement to place London above Edinburgh doesn't keep you awake?"

"It does actually. I just don't know what's expected of me. I suppose most of it will be innocuous. I'm sure my weekly meetings with all of the other Permanent Secretaries won't be too difficult. Everyone knows the civil service top brass openly share information about their activities with the Cabinet Secretary. I just worry about a day, which may never come, when I'm asked to do something I'd find morally unacceptable."

"Well, don't worry about it. We'll rent a hovel in Leith and I'll take in washing."

"Then buy two pairs of marigold gloves. We both might need to!"

* * *

It was late in the afternoon when MacAskill's converted ambulance pulled in at the cottage. After spending a few minutes calling for Blaze, he figured that he'd be at Lady Helen's gatehouse and drove there.

Both dogs heard the familiar growl of the diesel engine and rushed outside to greet him. He stepped down from the cabin and hugged both dogs in a frenzy of tail-wagging, licks and cuddles.

"So you're back?"

"Isla! Good to see you."

"Blaze has been injured."

MacAskill leaned back to escape both dogs' affections and grasped Blaze's paw.

"Here, Blaze. What have you been up to?"

"He had a thorn through the pad on his right paw. I found him up at the cottage and fixed it but he'll have to go to the village vet. I don't have the necessary equipment to deal with it properly."

"Well, looks like you've done a great job but I'll fix it. No need for the vet."

"But he'll need a new dressing, might need penicillin. The wound was infected."

"I can't afford vet fees, Isla. I'm guessing you removed the thorn, bathed the wound in salt water, cleaned him up and put a bandage round his foot. The only thing I'd have done differently is not to use this wee leather thing you've put on and I wouldn't have used electrical tape. It's too flimsy. I'd have used gorilla tape it's completely waterproof and much stronger. It'd do him all day and then I'd change the dressing at night until he was better. That thing you've put on him makes him look like he's got a club foot!"

Isla was nonplussed at MacAskill's veterinary knowledge and irked by his criticism of her treatment.

"But if the infection doesn't clear up?"

"It will."

"He might need Amoxicillin or Clavulanate."

"Might not!"

Exasperated, Isla threw up her hands.

"Look I have to go down to the village in mother's Land Rover anyway. I'll speak to the vet and get some penicillin. I'll hand it in tonight to the cottage."

"It's Thursday. Tonight there's quiz hour in the Claymore. I'm seeing Gus at eight. I'll be sleeping in the van tonight."

"Then I'll hand it in to the bloody *pub* at eight. I'm not having that lovely dog go without. And if you won't use it on Blaze, use it on your cheek. What on earth have you done? That's a deep cut."

MacAskill smiled. "A scratch from a gorse bush. We'll see you at eight. Thanks for looking after Blaze." He patted both dogs again. "C'mon Blaze let's get some grub."

Isla watched as the ambulance reversed and drove off. Her mother approached from the rear.

"I was listening. Isn't he so clever? That man can turn his hand to anything."

Isla's irritation with MacAskill, coupled with the same emotion she felt towards her mother rendered her momentarily speechless. Open-mouthed, she turned, shook her head and marched off towards the mother's old Land Rover Defender whereupon she spun the steering wheel and headed off towards the vet's in Grantown-on-Spey.

* * *

Andy Burns was seated in a comfortable chair in the quiet almost deferential surroundings of the Scotch Whisky Bar of Edinburgh's Balmoral Hotel, just a few hundred yards from St. Andrew's House on the southern flank of the city's Calton Hill, where his wife was undergoing an interview. Having read two broadsheet newspapers front to back, he now mulled over whether to enjoy a fourth large malt whisky. Taking his almost empty glass and slowly walking the length of an entire wall devoted to a virtual cornucopia of excellent whiskies, he stopped every so often to take an interest in a bottle.

I've had a Lagavulin, a glass of the Macallan and a Glenmorangie...what might be a fitting accompaniment to these fine fellows? His eyes lit on a bottle of sixteen year old, Orcadian whisky, Scapa Skiren, a 2015 release from an Orkney distillery. *Aye, that'll do nicely.*

A barman finished inspecting a glass he'd just washed and polished and laid it aside.

"Sir! What can I get you?"

As he was poised to answer, Catriona came into the lounge and joined him.

"I was about to order a rather large malt. Would you care to join me?"

"Anything as long as it's large!"

He directed his wife to a table.

"We're over there."

Moments later both were seated and had sipped their whisky.

"Well? Spill the beans. Was it an ordeal or a chat among friends?"

"It was fine I suppose. Nothing to trip me up. Everyone seemed very nice and I'm advised that if successful I'll be telephoned in the first instance by the Cabinet Secretary...rather making the point that it's the British Civil Service I work for, not the Scottish Government."

Andy Burns lifted his glass once more.

"Then here's to an early telephone call."

As lunch had been skipped, it was decided that an early meal would be in order but that they would take to their hotel room, freshen up and just eat in the Balmoral.

"If this goes belly up we might be staying here only one night so I want to take full advantage," said Andy. "They've a great reputation. But if you're successful we'll want to move out as soon as possible into more normal accommodation,"

"Remember even if I'm successful, it's still only an interim appointment. If they don't think I'm cut out for this, I won't make the cut at the full interview so any accommodation will require to be temporary until the smoke clears."

Andy signed for the drinks bill and they took the lift to their room where Andy opened the minibar as Catriona undressed and stepped into the shower. Allowing a few seconds for the water to heat, she moved under the force of the water and allowed it to play directly on her face. Taking a bar of heather-scented soap, she began to produce suds which she used to cover her head and upper body. Eyes closed to avoid the sting of the abstergent, she sensed the shower door open and felt a tap on her shoulder. Placing her face under the shower-head, she rubbed the soap from her eyes and saw her husband standing outside the shower, a wide smile on his face. In one hand was a phone, in the other a towel.

"There's a woman here holding for a certain Sir Jonathan Burton. He wants to talk to you."

* * *

"Jimmy...wake up and smell the catastrophe!"

Jimmy Boyd looked up from his desk as his sergeant entered the office.

"Sir?"

"Chief Superintendent Knows-Fuck-All wants us up in his office. Apparently the press need more information about our friend Dalriada now that Big Eat The Breid has divulged his name to the media."

Together they walked upstairs to the office of Chief Superintendent May who sat as they'd left him, behind a desk pouring over some paperwork.

"Ah, Gentlemen…it appears that the Chief Constable didn't find favour with our decision to reveal the *nom de plume* of this chap, Dalriada."

Boyd sensed the bristling on Boston's neck as the Chief Superintendent continued.

"Seems now that cat's out of the bag he wants more resources put into finding out who this idiot is. I've just taken a call from our friends in the MOD Police who advise that at the site where they calculate the shooter was, a piece of cardboard, apparently torn from a packet of Kellogg's Cornflakes had the word 'Dalriada' inscribed on its blank side. The lettering was in ink and was in the same written style as was the letter we received. It appears obvious that it's our man although they've agreed to pass it to Dr. Van Ossen for his deliberations."

"Sir."

He looked up from his desk.

"So, I'll leave you two to get on with it."

Boyd reacted first.

"As you say, sir."

They exited into the corridor.

"What the fuck was that, Jimmy."

"Sir?"

"Thon, 'As you say, sir'."

"Just doing what you…"

"Aye well, that's *my* job to say that. I'm the senior officer. *I* get to be a cheeky bastard. Not you. You are Mister Dumb Insolence, got it? I am Sergeant Sarcastic. Christ you've got a lot to learn."

They walked the length of the corridor until Boston stopped, shaking his head before continuing.

"And you don't say 'as you say, sir,' when he gives an instruction. It's used when he offers an *opinion* you don't agree with. Jesus…you're not exactly the stupidest officer in this police force but by Christ, when *that* man leaves, you're het! You know of course that he'll have told the Chief that it was our idea to tell the media the name of Dalriada, don't you? He'll have dodged the bullet by throwing us under the bus."

"You're mixing your metaphors, boss but yeah, I guessed that."

"Well, when we find Dalriada I'm going to give him a new contract - to take out that fat, rude. pompous…"

"Ignorant, English bastard?" said Boyd completing the sentence.

"The same! He couldn't pour piss out of a boot if the instructions wiz printed on the heel."

Chapter Ten

"**W**ill Inverskillen United please stop talking and let's get on with this quiz?"

Gus Darroch and Lachie MacAskill gestured their acknowledgement of Benny the quizmaster's request. Darroch leaned over, pencil in hand, exaggerating his enthusiasm to a smiling MacAskill.

"Ready when you are, Bennie!"

"Off we go then. First question…Geography. What is the capital city of Nepal?"

"Kathmandu," whispered MacAskill. "Flew there from Kabul for some R&R when I was in Afghanistan."

"What is the capital city of Nepal?" repeated Bob the quizmaster, as Isla entered the Claymore.

"Kathmandu," answered Isla sitting down.

"Aye, we got that one," smiled Darroch. "It's good to see you, Isla. Hope you're good at quizzing."

"Well, so far tonight, I've a hundred percent record." She sat on the spare chair at the table, hooking her small handbag over its back. "I just popped in to have a look at Blaze's paw. I got some penicillin and Manuka honey from Donald Brodie the vet."

"I changed his dressing before I came out," protested MacAskill mildly.

"Good for you but I don't tell you how to chop down trees, build bridges over streams or shoot up downtown Kabul, do I? Your dog has an infected wound and this is causing inflammation and swelling of the surrounding tissue. Probably also pyrexia."

"What's that?"

"A high temperature."

"How d'you know?"

"Because I know how infections work, Lachie. I also brought some Manuka honey as a wound dressing. It provides osmotic debridement of the wound surface, maintains hydration of the healthy parts of the wound and to top it all, has some analgesic effects. Looking at that deep scratch on your face, you might do worse than to smear some on your cheek. It wouldn't hurt." She scanned his face for a reaction. "Do I have your permission to proceed?"

The small microphone returned to the lips of the quizmaster.

"Still geography. Where would you find an indigenous population called the Sami?"

"Glasgow," ventured Darroch with a grin.

"The northern territories of Norway, Sweden or Finland," answered Isla, her face stern.

"Okay," said MacAskill answering the earlier question.

Isla took a pair of scissors from her bag and petting Blaze, awoke him from his slumber. Skilfully she cut away MacAskill's bandage held securely by his black tape. Blaze did not resist. She observed the wound.

"'Fraid it needs some help, Lachie. You've done a really good job of cleaning the wound and protecting it but puncture wounds can force bacteria deep into the tissues and poor Blaze need a wee shot of Amoxicillin."

"Where would you find an indigenous population called the Sami?" repeated Bob.

MacAskill relented. He spoke quietly.

"Thanks, Isla. I appreciate your help."

Where's your manners, Lachie?" He spoke directly to Isla as he stood. "What can I get you? It's the least you deserve for treating this man's beautiful dog along with his ugly face."

Isla smiled. "Well, I did get a lift down from Joe the Taxi in case I was offered a glass. I'm not driving tonight."

"Then there's every chance we might win this bloody quiz for once!"

The evening continued in good humour until the quiz ended and Bennie took time to mark the returns. Following a break of some fifteen minutes, he announced that the winners by one point were the Grantown Academicals, a trio of teachers who won each and every week. Realising they had been pushed close for once, the three teachers each raised a pint in one hand while offering a good-natured two-fingered salute to the Inverskillen team. As the general merriment died down, three whiskies were brought from the bar by John the barman and set before them.

"From the Academicals. They say 'well done'."

MacAskill raised his arm in acknowledgement and lifted his glass. He offered a toast to his table.

"To healthy dogs and winning quizzes."

All three were by now quite amiably drunk and as they fell into inconsequential conversation, the television in the corner was switched on but the sound muted. On the screen, a reporter stood voicelessly outside the Royal Naval Armaments Depot at Coulport talking to camera.

"C'mon Dalriada!" A drunken shout from a merry pensioner at the far end of the pub brought laughter.

"At last someone's taking action against these horrible weapons," commented Isla.

Darroch frowned. "Aye, but you canny have someone walking around shooting at people."

"It was only the tyres of the big vehicles that were shot...not people. No one was hurt."

"Tyres today, people tomorrow. You mark my words."

"Whoever it was got clean away," said MacAskill entering the debate.

"Och, they'll get him soon. He'll be a Nationalist or someone in CND. The boys in Special Branch'll start to check their files and before you know it some names'll pop up and it'll be one of them or one of them will grass off the person who took the shot."

"Och, that's too simplistic, Gus," responded Isla. "I believe in Scottish independence *and* in unilateral nuclear disarmament but I'm not a member of either group."

"Perhaps, but you're not too handy with a rifle are you?"

"Well, *I* am and I'm not a member of any group either," interrupted MacAskill.

"Christ, Lachie. The only group you're a member of is the Inverskillen Quiz Team." He turned to Isla. "This guy is known only marginally to Her Majesty's Armed Forces Pension Scheme and to the wee guy in Her Majesty's Revenue and Customs who mainly deals with people from Her Majesty's Armed Forces Pension Scheme. He lives so far out on the edge of society he's in danger of falling off. Doesn't own a phone. I have to send up smoke signals to make arrangements for a pub visit."

"Well, I like it fine out there, Gus. You meet a better class of people in forests where there are no people."

MacAskill wanted badly to hear the commentary on the muted television but affected disinterest. He turned instead to Isla as Darroch headed for the bar.

"Thanks again for looking after Blaze, Isla. I don't know what I'd do if he was hurt. He means a lot to me."

Emboldened by alcohol, Isla found the words had left her lips before she'd taken the opportunity to measure them.

"Although not enough to worry about leaving the poor thing all alone at the cottage while you swan around somewhere else."

Taken aback, MacAskill could only mumble a response about fixing a bridge.

Biting her tongue, Isla decided she had been overly reproachful and offered some mollification.

"I'm sorry. I know how much you do for mother…and for Blaze. But I'm a vet and animals always come first in my book."

MacAskill found a measure of emboldenment.

"Auld Donald the vet on Forest Road was in here last week and was talking about retiring. Interested in filling his boots?"

Isla laughed. "You sound just like mother. She's always plaguing me to return. Her dream is for me to live on the estate, marry and give her grandchildren. If she tells me my biological clock is ticking one more time, I'll explode!"

"Not for you, then?"

"One day maybe. Right now I have a thriving vet's practice in Gosforth down in Newcastle, loads of friends and a nice lifestyle."

"Aye, but have they quiz teams that nearly win quiz competitions?"

Isla laughed and turned the tables.

"What about you? You live on a small pension, look after the estate and live in a converted ambulance."

"I love my lifestyle, Isla. I'll show you my humble abode sometime. I've put a lot of work into making it really comfortable. It has all mod cons except the TV...which I don't want. I just need the peace and quiet that comes with living on the estate but if things get too complicated for me I can stay anywhere I like because of the Tardis. If I decided, tomorrow evening I could be parked next to a beach near Stornoway or a glen near Ben Nevis."

"The Tardis?"

"Aye, like in 'Doctor Who'. I call my home the Tardis because once you get inside, it's bigger than it looks from the outside."

"I'd love to see it sometime." She paused and moved the topic on. "I suppose it's quite a different life from the one you had in the army."

MacAskill nodded.

"I've had my fill of violence. I've seen things...done things... that'll go with me to the grave. I've decided that I just want to shut myself off from society. The big estate suits me. A hundred men would feel lonesome in those woods. The only time I see people is when I meet Gus in here or chat to your mother on the estate and that's the way I like it. I trust Gus, your mother and Blaze, that's about it."

"Well, I hope in time you'll come to trust me and Rory."

MacAskill laughed. "I already trust our Rory. I forgot to mention him. He's Blaze's best friend and one of mine too."

"I have the sense that your military service may have scarred you more than that gorse bush scarred your cheek."

MacAskill didn't respond immediately, allowing his thoughts to assemble.

"These days I use a Remington rifle to shoot deer. I only kill to cull when necessary and then make use of the venison. Me or your mother usually get some of the meat and I give other cuts to some of our older residents in the village. I use small bore ordnance. Just sufficient to do the job. In Afghanistan, if I hit a man in the arm, it'd remove the entire limb from his torso. The rifles they use these days are more like canons. And why did I put my life on the line?

For what? For sleazy politicians on the make? For capitalists looking to exploit the peoples of another weaker nation? For oil? I've come to despise the absurdity of warfare. I've grown to hate the flag I once saluted and the Establishment down in London that demands it. I realised I was being aggressive towards people who were only protecting *their* wee piece of sand! I felt then and feel now, manipulated by powers I didn't and don't understand so I just resigned my commission as Captain and headed up here. I came to appreciate the old story about the sheep that was afraid of the wolf and looked to the shepherd to protect it...only to be eaten eventually by the shepherd it trusted. I decided that that represented my trust in the British establishment...so I came home."

"Back home to Strathspey..." said Isla empathically.

"...and was exceptionally fortunate to meet your mother. She's been great for me. I now lead a life of quiet contemplation with my dog. I'm out and about every day and no one bothers me. I'm doing something that benefits the planet, improves Scotland and supports the local community...and I don't charge your mother anything for..."

"Yes, she explained that to me, Lachie although she wants to provide for you. I think she's worried about you a wee bit."

"Och, I'm fine. I have food, water, shelter and the love of a good dog."

"Yes...but you live in an ambulance!"

MacAskill smiled. "You're too conventional, Isla. I'll show it to you sometime. It really is impressive if I say so myself. Everyone who's seen it thinks it's great."

"She's given you the cottage. Why don't you stay there?"

"I do...but only if I happen to be working in that part of the forest. Don't get me wrong, Isla. I'm genuinely grateful to your mother for what she's done for me. I was in a bad place when I came up here...back to the village...but now I'm a bit more like my old self. I haven't quite vanquished the demons but I can think clearly now and I'm happy doing what I'm doing and am determined to do what I can so that other young Scots don't end up in foreign wars killing strangers and dying for lying politicians and fat cats in London and Washington who will never even know the soldiers they direct once lived and had dreams."

Isla lifted the whisky that Darroch had just placed before her. "I'll drink to that!"

Chapter Eleven

Three days after the attack on the convoy, The National newspaper received another letter from Dalriada. This time, despite protestations, they chose to publish it agreeing only to remove the two pluses after his name and once more it landed on the desk of Sergeant Colin Boston.

SIR

I NOTICE YOU CHOSE NOT TO PUBLISH MY LETTER BUT PRESUME YOU INSTEAD PASSED IT ON TO THE AUTHORITIES. IT'S YOUR DECISION OF COURSE BUT YOU MUST HAVE MORE CONFIDENCE IN INCREASING YOUR SALES THAN I DO. I WISH TO DRAW MY MOTIVES TO THE ATTENTION OF THE SCOTTISH PEOPLE AND ASK YOU TO PUBLISH MY LETTER. IF YOU DO NOT I WILL MAKE USE OF OTHER NEWSPAPERS WITH FEWER MORAL PRINCIPLES.

I HOPE YOU NOW TAKE ME SERIOUSLY. I WILL BRING THE PEOPLE OF SCOTLAND WITH ME AS TOGETHER WE EVICT THE OBSCENITY OF NUCLEAR WEAPONRY FROM OUR LAND. I ALSO GIVE NOTICE THAT I REGARD THE MILITARY, POLITICAL, MEDIA AND LONDON ESTABLISHMENT AS ANATHEMA TO A PROPERLY FUNCTIONING SCOTLAND AND INTEND TO ACT TO BRING DOWN THOSE WHO WOULD USURP OUR DEMOCRACY AND PRIORITISE THE ACQUISITION OF WEALTH AND PRIVILEGE BEFORE COMMON HUMANITY.

YOURS FAITHFULLY
ALBA GU BRÀTH
DALRIADA++

"Jimmy, come over here. I think we can forget the other five copycat letters from would-be Dalriadas. Here's the one we've been waiting for. As he said in his last one, he's signed it with two pluses after his name. Copy this to the MOD people and get thon Doctor Van Ossen on the blower. Send him the original and see if he can pick up any new forensics from this second letter. The fuckin' media are going to publish this one."

* * *

Catriona Burns arrived very early taking the uniformed doorman at St. Andrews house somewhat by surprise. After an awkward exchange in which she succeeded in persuading the security guard that she was who she said she was, she was shown upstairs and introduced to her office.

"Thank you Henry," she said, reading the name on his lapel. "I imagine my pass will arrive today. Please be assured that I am who I say I am."

"Saw your photograph in an e-mail that was sent out yesterday, Miss Burns. I hope you enjoy your time in the Scottish Government. Just didn't expect you so early."

Burns sat in the chair behind her desk and surveyed her new surroundings. *Small and old fashioned...one of the downsides of inhabiting an office built in a listed, monolithic, art-deco building first inhabited back in 1939, I suppose. Somewhat removed from the minimalist, shiny steel interior of my old Tokyo office.* She rose and looked out of her window at the panoramic view of Waverley Station immediately below her, Edinburgh University, the buff-coloured south-west of Edinburgh and the Pentland Hills beyond. *Edinburgh is indisputably a beautiful city,* she thought. *I just hope I'm happy here.*

She looked at her watch and at the small pile of folders on her desk. *I've the First Minister at nine and the heads of all departments at nine thirty. Coffee with the Head of the Scottish Police Authority at eleven. An interesting morning.*

The meeting with the First Minister was most cordial and left Burns with the impression that they were going to get on very well. Promptly at nine-thirty to meet with her department heads, she entered the third floor meeting room to a light round of applause which took her slightly aback.

She smiled, slightly embarrassed.

"Why, thank you for your welcome. I'm delighted to meet you all. I've just been with the First Minister and I'm told you are an exceptionally talented group of people who have given unstintingly to Scotland over the past few years. I'm very much looking forward to working with all of you. I've read the e-mail you've all received which sets out my background but I know very little of each of you. Today and over the next few days I'll get the chance to sit with you individually and we can get to know one another a little better. But this morning I thought it might be useful if we just went round the room. You could introduce yourself, perhaps set out the main areas you're dealing with at present and the main challenges you face. Finally, in closing perhaps I could share my style of leadership. I am not by nature autocratic. I am no dictator. Rather I subscribe to the servant-leader model. I see little point in having exceptionally talented people around me and not make use of that talent so I see my job as serving *your* needs in order to assist you in achieving the goals set for us by Parliament. I'm also keen that we spread this model throughout the civil service in Scotland, so it then behoves all of us to listen, empathise and empower those colleagues who work in our departments so that they too might give of their best. This may not be second nature to some of us used to other styles of leadership but I want to support everyone in this and we can discuss it more when we meet…and when we do, please call me Catriona. We can save formalities for times when matters are more formal."

Ninety minutes were then spent listening to tales of successes and failures, savings and capital budget over-runs. Burns took copious notes. She ended the meeting by thanking everyone and saying that appointments would be made over the next few days when more detail might be gone into in respect of the issues that were raised.

"And remember, I'm keen to hear of new ideas, new approaches that might settle some of the obstacles we face. Thank you again."

She rose, stood at the door and shook everyone's hand as they left before walking back to her office. Alf Bennet, Chairman of the Police Authority of Scotland had already arrived and as instructed, had been shown into her office, had been given a seat and a coffee and was reading some paperwork he'd brought with him.

"Mr. Bennet, I'm pleased to meet you and apologise for my tardy arrival. I've been meeting the department heads and got somewhat caught up towards the end of the meeting. I see that Sheila has been looking after you."

"She 'as that, Miss Burns."

"Please call me Catriona," she replied, slightly taken aback at what she determined was the very pronounced Yorkshire accent of her guest.

"That's not an Edinburgh accent," she smiled. "Is it Yorkshire?"

"I'm a Staffordshire man, Catriona. Lichfield to be exact. It 'as to be said it's an unusual place for a man who's built a career in shipbuilding, as its the furthest place from the sea in England although some argue it's Coton in the Elms in Derbyshire but *we* 'ave a plaque in the town. They don't. And please call me Alf."

More pleasantries were exchanged and as with the department heads earlier, the Chairman was asked to set out his successes, challenges and impediments. He set to with energy, handing her the paper he'd prepared which covered recruitment, pensions shortfalls, numbers retiring, the lack of a sufficient capital transport budget and the need for investment in forensics.

Listening to his list of concerns, all of which were veiled requests for additional finance, Burns introduced an edge to the conversation.

"I've been reading some of your Board minutes, Alf. There are very seldom any items approved consensually or unanimously. Everything seems to go to a vote and is resolved by a single vote, for or against. You win some, you lose some."

Bennet raised his eyebrows at the deviation but saw an opportunity to raise another issue of concern.

"When I took chairmanship, Catriona, there were three members on Board who 'ad been there for years and 'ated my appointment. They don't have the interests of the Police Authority at heart and it colours every decision we make supposin' it's what we're going to 'ave for lunch."

"Well, that can't be healthy, Alf. Perhaps when next we meet you might offer me some views on how this might be resolved... options that is, not just a list of reasons why those who oppose you should be put to the sword."

"'Appy to do that, Catriona."

"Before we finish, the First Minister was asking about some of the news headlines. I couldn't answer as I would normally as I've been removed from Scottish politics and public life for some time. Two involved policing. There was particular concern, I think it fair to say, about the recent misbehaviour by football fans after a cup final at Hampden and by increasing support to apprehend the person who attacked a nuclear convoy."

"Cup final was handled well by police but there's this new 'abit of fans bringing flares into games. Red smoke everywhere. It makes the place look like downtown Baghdad. Only a few arrests though. Our forensic team have been assessing the evidence we've gathered in respect of this chap Dalriada. He seems to have covered all the bases and we can't find anything that would give us a clue as to where he comes from, who he is or anything else. We've been going on supposition and senior staff now think we'll probably need to wait until he strikes again and see if that gives us anything more to go on."

"The First Minister pointed out that he seems to have garnered quite a bit of support. There have been demonstrations against nuclear warfare in George Square in Glasgow and elsewhere. People are marching with banners hailing Dalriada."

"Well, you 'ave to admit that there are demonstrations about Trident missiles most months. They're not popular with most of the people of Scotland."

"Nor with the First Minister...but this attack involved firearms. No one can support opposition which may have resulted in the death of a uniformed officer."

"Quite, Catriona. I'll speak with the Chief Constable and as anything arises I'll keep you informed."

"I'm seeing him on Friday, I think. Perhaps he'll have more information then."

"P'raps."

Chapter Twelve

Prince Edward, the Earl of Wessex, is the youngest child of Queen Elizabeth II and Prince Philip, the Duke of Edinburgh. Currently only tenth in line to the throne due to the virility of his father and his elder brother, in Scotland he's known as the Earl of Forfar, a present given him by the monarch upon reaching his fifty-fifth birthday.

The regular publication of the Royal Diary issues details of official engagements undertaken by members of the royal family at locations across the UK some eight weeks in advance. By the simple expedient of reading it in the small public library in Grantown-on-Spey, Lachie MacAskill was well aware of the Prince's impending visit to the holiday home of the Royals in Scotland, Balmoral Castle.

The Royal Train pulled into Aviemore Station right on time at two-thirty-five pm. Outside, two gleaming Daimlers purred in wait. The first was to carry the Prince and his wife, Sophie, the Countess of Wessex. The second carried Edward's personal bodyguard and the Lady-in-Waiting of the Countess along with a few bags, the bulk of the luggage having been sent ahead to await their arrival. A few minutes were spent on the platform as the royal couple shook hands with local dignitaries now quite used to seeing members of the Royal Family arriving at their rail station, the closest to Balmoral.

The Craigellachie National Nature Reserve lies on the eastern slopes of the Monadhliath range of hills on the edge of the Highland town of Aviemore, overlooking its railway station. Dominated by birch woodland, it encompasses a variety of other habitats such as lochans, rocky crags and open heath. Behind one of the rocky crags, Lachie MacAskill viewed the tyres of the prince's Daimler through the crosshairs of his scope. Moving the Remington slightly, he watched the exit of the group from the station as they waved to a small but admiring crowd and waited until the four passengers had each seated themselves in the rear of the vehicles. Ahead of them, two motorcycling police officers sat ready to act as outriders. Whilst the vehicles were still stationary, MacAskill eased back on the trigger sending a bullet through the near-side front tyre of the first Daimler then took aim at the same wheel on the second car. Both tyres were punctured immediately. Calmly, he took aim at the rear wheel first of the nearest motorcyclist and shot, deflating it instantly before doing the same to the second bike. Calmly, he returned his sights to the motor vehicles and dispatched a further two shots, rendering each of their rear near-side tyres unusable. By now the bodyguard, gun in hand, had positioned himself in front of the rear side window of the royal couple urgently looking for danger as both police officers, their bikes abandoned joined him, each talking urgently to central communications. Satisfied that the four vehicles had been disabled and that the many tourists in Aviemore would be taking scores of photographs of the stricken party, MacAskill collected the spent shells, threw his Dalriada card on the ground, rose and began to jog downhill towards his vehicle, in doing so removing and stuffing his latex gloves in his jacket pocket.

It took but seven minutes of downhill running to reach his vehicle in a makeshift carpark near the main road to Aviemore. Quickly, he took the wheel but breathing out, slowly headed off along the B970 through Rothiemurchus and past Coylumbridge to the vast, wooded Glenmore Forest Park. A wide stoned path used occasionally by hillwalkers and Forestry Commission vehicles took him deep into the forest where he reversed the ambulance into an opening beneath a canopy of birch trees which rendered it invisible from the air and concealed it from the forestry trail. Again he retreated to the rear of the vehicle where he cleaned his rifle before stepping outside and burying the six shells he'd collected. *All of the bullets would have been mangled by the road and by the undercarriage of the engines. Let's see if they can identify anything beyond their actual calibre.*

MacAskill returned the rifle to its locker inside the cabinet he'd built, locked his ambulance and walked to a small burn that ran though the forest where he took the thin latex gloves from his pocket and buried them before washing his hands thoroughly to remove any powder burns that may have been deposited invisibly when he'd fired the Remington. *Any powder residue on my jacket could easily be explained by my shooting deer on the estate,* he decided. Satisfied, he stepped out onto the path and began his walk to the small hamlet of Glenmore where he intended buying something to eat from its village store.

Walking the two miles to the village, it was evident that whatever reaction had taken place had not resulted in any increased traffic or obvious police surveillance. *They'll have figured I'll have gone north to lose myself in Inverness,* he thought. *And there were some signs of trail bikes on a path near the car park so maybe they'll be off on a wild goose chase again.*

Due to the high number of tourists and walkers visiting the Cairngorm Mountain Range, the small village store in Glenmore was very used to strangers walking in to buy the necessities of life. In his waxed camouflage jacket, denims and hiking boots, MacAskill was indistinguishable from a dozen others who had purchased goods earlier that day. The shop owner, a pipe-smoking, elderly man in a grey, baggy cardigan was talking to one of the locals as MacAskill selected some rolls and fished a packet of bacon from a refrigerated cabin.

"...And apparently it was a bloodbath. A hail of bullets."

"Nah. Angus was on the phone. He says they only shot at the tyres. He took a photograph."

"So who was doing the shooting?"

"They Arabs most likely. Seems it was an attack on one of the Princes."

"Why would the Arabs want to shoot a Prince?"

"Don't know…maybe revenge for the USA shooting Osama Bin Laden."

"That's what they'd call even? The Yanks shoot the heid bummer of Al Qaeda so they try to shoot one of the Queen's weans in return?"

MacAskill decided to intervene.

"What's happened?"

The shopkeeper responded enthusiastically.

"There's been an attack on one of the Royals at the station in Aviemore. Tam here thinks it was Al-Qaeda."

"Just said maybe…"

"I've not seen any police presence," offered MacAskill.

"Well, you've maybe one polis for every hundred square miles up here," responded the shopkeeper as he held out his hand for MacAskill's purchases. "Can't see one of them SWAT Teams descending on Glenmore any minute now." He entered the items manually on his elderly cash register. "Four-forty, please."

MacAskill handed him a five pound note. "Was it on the radio?"

"Breaking news." He gave him his change. "A hail of bullets, they said."

"Anyone hurt?"

"It didn'y say but if there was a hail of bullets, *someone* must have been hurt."

The other shopper offered an opinion.

"Well, I hope they shot whatever royal waster they were aiming at right up the arse. They're all a bunch of parasites. One less mouth to feed."

"You'd better not let anyone on the other side of the mountain hear you say that!"

"Over in Royal Deeside? They're all sycophantic Tory arse-lickers over there because of the money the tourists put in their tills. These eejits fly the Butcher's Apron above their shops and don't give a fig that the local school pays more in rates than the Queen's Estate of Balmoral because of the high-paid accountants they employ to cheat the tax-man."

MacAskill lifted his goods and smiled.

"I'm wi' you, my man." He placed his purchases in his backpack and left the shop.

After walking the main road back to the small pathway that would take him in to the forest where his ambulance was hidden, he made his way into the trees and sat on a log. Checking to ensure there was no one around, he took his small radio from his back-pack and turned the dial until he came across a news channel.

Surprised the news was out on the radio before I got to the shop, he thought as he twisted the dial. *Broadcast inside the first hour? That's quick work by someone.* The white noise receded and a Scottish accent on Moray Firth Radio was breathlessly telling the people of the Highlands, Moray and Aberdeenshire of the incident.

"Authorities have confirmed that shots were fired at vehicles carrying Prince Edward and the Countess of Wessex as they left the Royal Train at Aviemore earlier today. Police and ambulances are at the scene but at this stage no casualties have been confirmed. The Prince and Countess are said to be unhurt but shocked. A spokesperson said the royal couple, who are being cared for locally before making their onward journey to Balmoral, are more concerned that the people of Aviemore were put at danger."

Aye, I'll bet! thought MacAskill.

"No one has claimed responsibility," continued the announcer. "Sergeant Angus Darroch of the local constabulary was one of the first on the scene. He spoke to our reporter Davie MacLaren.

MacAskill smiled broadly, *Christ, our Gus! a*s his friend's voice came over the airwaves.

"Six bullets were fired at two royal vehicles at approximately two-thirty-six this afternoon. There were no casualties. Each of the two royal vehicles and two police motorcycles were damaged. The royal couple have been treated for shock but are now on their way under police escort to Balmoral. There was a small crowd which had gathered to welcome the royal couple but none of them were injured. Additional police supports are presently arriving from Inverness and a search is being carried out to find those responsible."

Maclaren interrupted his statement.

"Given the time it has taken for police support to arrive from Inverness, is it not likely that the shooters will have already made their escape?"

"Local police resources have already been dispatched to secure the area. We are working to ensure the safety of the royal couple, reassure local people and to carry out an initial search."

"But this is a huge area. Surely you don't think that the few officers in Aviemore and Grantown-on-Spey can offer sufficient coverage?"

MacAskill smiled again as he discerned the irritation in his friend's voice.

"Listen, unless they came up the River Spey in a submarine, they'll have had to make use of the road network. We've more than enough officers to shut down all traffic until we see what's what."

"But if they're hiking?"

"Then they won't have got very far and our additional supports, including a helicopter that has been scrambled, will help us track them down."

The reporter turned his comments to the newsreader back at the radio station.

"So, it seems that everyone's safe, some damage to vehicles and police are checking on the use of a submarine beneath the rather shallow waters of the River Spey. Davie MacLaren, Moray Firth Radio, Aviemore."

Just before the announcer recommenced his news broadcast, the protesting voice of Gus Darroch could be heard berating the reporter..."

"C'mere, you!"

MacAskill laughed out loud, switched off the radio and put some bacon in a pan.

* * *

After listening to the police communications on the radio for half an hour, MacAskill decided that it was safe enough to venture forth from the forest and drove to the nearby workshop of Bill Anderson whose workshop was his usual destination whenever one of his chainsaws required sharpening or repair. Two of them had been in for repair for a week and were due to be collected. This was duly done and after a few minutes affable conversation about the shooting, MacAskill took to the minor roads to travel the twenty miles to Inverskillen. As he rounded a corner approaching the village of Nethy Bridge, a police vehicle straddled the road. Holding his hand out instructing him to halt was the police colleague of his friend Gus, Calum Buchanan, whom he knew.

He slowed and stopped, rolled down the window and smiled a greeting.

"Hi Calum. I've been hearing about this shooting. Al Qaeda was it?"

"Hi Lachie. Who knows? I've just been ordered to stop everything that travels along this road and make sure there are no terrorists trying to sneak away from the scene of the crime."

"I've not seen anything suspicious."

"Are you not working on the estate today?"

"Aye, but I had to pop out to old Bill Andersons'. I had two chainsaws to collect. They're in the back. C'mon and I'll show you."

Buchanan was embarrassed.

"Och, I don't need to see them, Lachie…but I wouldn'y mind a wee keek. Sergeant Darroch is always going on about how you've turned the ambulance into a real home from home."

"No problem, Calum."

As MacAskill prepared to exit the vehicle, Buchanan changed the subject.

"And how is old Bill? He was wheeched off to hospital with pneumonia a few weeks ago, I heard."

"He looked fine, Calum. We didn't talk much. I'm busy today so I just drove up, collected the chainsaws and made my way back along the road to the estate when you stopped us."

MacAskill stepped out of the driver's door and walked round to the rear of the vehicle where he opened the door, removed the two chainsaws and placed them on the ground.

"Come in, come in."

Another car arrived behind the converted ambulance and Buchanan stepped aside and waved the driver to stop before returning to the rear door and looking in.

"I'd better not spend too much time here, Lachie but wow…it looks amazing." He stepped up into its interior. "A sink, bed, chair and a desk, cupboards…"

"And a wee shower and a dry lavvy over here," said MacAskill opening a door.

"Home from home right enough, Lachie. It's a palace…Look I'd better away. Sorry to have held you up. Just drive round my car and get on your way."

"No problem, Calum. Maybe see you in the Claymore. I'm maybe meeting Gus for a pint tonight."

"Doubt that, Lachie. We'll be tied up here until top brass tells us to stand down because of this attack on the Royals."

"Aye, maybe so…"

MacAskill watched him approach the car behind him and engaging the driver before taking his seat and driving on to Inverskillen.

Chapter Thirteen

Forgoing a pint in the Claymore that night, MacAskill walked instead in darkness to a shooting club established by a farmer from Boat of Garten some five miles away. Approaching the range, he took to the wooded area surrounding it and surveilled the flat expanse of land between the breeze-blocked shooting positions and the targets some two hundred yards away. All was still, the last member having vacated the premises more than three hours previously. Stooping low and keeping within the tree-line, he made his way to the reception area. He knew that weapons were not stored at the facility but also that his intended plunder, Tannerite a brand of binary explosive target used for firearms practice, was.

Farmer Michael Forbes, who had sold a small property in Primrose Hill in London and had derived from it sufficient capital to buy a farm in Speyside, fancied himself as an entrepreneur. Reading of the new fashion in America to forsake targets on wires which had to be pulled back to the shooter to inspect their accuracy or make use of a spotter employing a high resolution scope to inspect the target rather than walk down-range, he'd been made aware of the American use of Tannerite, an explosive mixture of oxidisers and aluminium powder to create an explosion when detonated by the high-impact of a bullet. This new product curtailed more traditional methods of establishing accuracy when shooting, the feedback from rifle-owners being that it was much more satisfactory to see their target explode, producing a large vapour cloud and a loud report.

MacAskill crept closer to the side of the building and took a pair of latex gloves from his pocket before removing a small glass-cutter from a pouch in the empty rucksack he carried. A faint light fell from the window as inside, a slot machine promised illuminated winnings. Looking around once more, he rose and thumbed some malleable tack on to the window pane and cut an arc on the glass around the interior handle. Replacing the cutter in his rucksack, he tapped at the glass until it came away in one piece. He placed glass and tack in the side pouch of the rucksack and reached through to the handle. Inside, the handle had been locked but a small key had been left in place allowing MacAskill to turn it and open the window. Grimacing as the window-hinge squealed slightly upon opening, he put the dull end of a small torch in his mouth, switching it on and entering the building, again listening for a moment to discern any movements. He decided that all was well and moved quietly through the building until he came to a door which was locked by means of a warded lock, a low-security device which took MacAskill only seconds to open using a dedicated pick. The door was also guarded by a thick metal chain through a solid door handle and fastened by a combination lock. He pushed down hard on the top of the lock using his thumb making sure to exert an even force on the lock throughout the whole procedure. Maintaining this pressure, he rotated each of the dials slightly in each direction until he found the dial that was the hardest to rotate. Gradually he rotated it until he heard a resounding 'click' and felt the shackle move upwards slightly. He repeated the same process on the remaining three dials and the lock popped open. Pulling the chain through, he opened the door and entered the room. Shelving was evident on three of the walls. Boxes of ammunition of various calibre were clearly labelled and MacAskill took three packs of a box of .308 ammunition and placed them inside a large rucksack he's brought with him. *A wee bonus,* he thought. *Save me a few quid.* He continued his search until he came across boxes marked '600-mesh dark flake aluminium powder'. He placed eight of the bags in his rucksack and continued his search until he came to a shelf whose contents were marked 'Oxidiser' and contained a mixture of 85% 200-mesh ammonium nitrate and 15% ammonium perchlorate. *Perfect!* He took a torn piece of cardboard from his pocket marked 'Dalriada' and placed it carefully on the shelf next to the chemicals. A further eight boxes were removed from a shelf and placed in a now-full rucksack. He fastened the straps of the rucksack and carried it back to the still-open window where he levered it outside and exited, closing the window behind him.

* * *

It was around eleven o'clock when Isla decided that it was time for bed. She closed a book she was reading. Her mother was watching television.

"Why is Blaze still here, mother? He's been around all day. Is Lachie working with heavy machinery today?"

"Och, who knows. He's maybe just in the Claymore."

"No. He always takes Blaze with him. You know, he and Blaze are obviously fond of one another but he seems to just leave him with you at the drop of a hat."

"We have an understanding, darling. Blaze stays over anytime he wants to. I don't ask any questions. Who knows, maybe Lachie is seeing a young lady…and you'll miss your chance!"

"God, mother. You're impossible."

"You could do a lot worse."

"Mother for the last *time*. I'm not in the market for a husband and from what I can gather from Lachie, he's not looking for companionship either."

"But if he was?"

Exasperated, Isla gasped her disapproval and left the room.

Chapter Fourteen

Catriona Burns worriedly watched the wall mounted television in her office as the morning news broadcaster listed the various attacks on organs of state perpetrated by Dalriada followed by another presenter discussing the subsequent and various acts of civil disobedience being played out across the country. A Conservative spokesman condemned participants as thugs and criminals and exhorted the police to greater efforts in securing their apprehension.

"There appears to be a wave of militancy gripping Scotland at the moment. This gangster Dalriada has been able to play fast and loose with an over-tolerant society and it must stop. We are witnessing a surge in criminality as people ignore laws put in place to protect them. Stop Dalriada and we stop these copy-cat disturbances. It's difficult to believe in this day and age of high technology that the police seem stumped and have allowed this terrorist to remain at large."

The interviewer made no attempt to challenge the statement and merely handed back to the studio whereupon a light knock on Catriona's door informed her that her first appointment of the day had arrived seeing her switch off the television and attend to her guest.

Burns welcomed Scotland's Chief Constable into her office and smiled, "Good morning, Sir Andrew" as a welcome.

"I think we can dispose of formalities when we're not on a podium or in front of a committee. I'm Andy. May I call you Catriona?"

"I'd be delighted, Andy."

An affable conversation followed during which Catriona decided that she and the Chief were going to get on famously. As with the Chair of the Police Authority, Andy Shields had come prepared with two sheets of A4 on which were listed a range of talking issues which differed from those of the Authority. An invitation for her to officiate at the next graduation at Scotland's Police College at Tulliallan in Kincardineshire, reports on falling crime statistics, efforts to make progress on the Tolerance Zone allowing safe prostitution in Leith whilst at the same time being vigilant against human trafficking and the relationship that was developing between Police Scotland and British Transport Police. As these topics resolved themselves, Catriona leaned over to her desk and lifted a sheaf of newspapers.

"First of all, thanks for not just bringing me a list of desperate funding requirements, Andy. Your Authority Chairman has already bent my ear on those." She referred to the newspapers. "But all *these* talk about is the activities of this person, Dalriada. I gather from a briefing paper this morning that a note bearing his name was found at the site where shots were fired at the royal couple. And there have been an increasing number of public displays of support for his actions against the Nuclear Warheads Convoy in…" She consulted an article in the Scotsman… "Glasgow, Edinburgh, Aberdeen, Clydebank, Perth and Dundee. There have been sizeable protests outside the Faslane base at the Peace camp and now that he's been identified as the shooter in Aviemore, might we see anti-Royalist, pro-Republican displays? Within these four walls, Edward's not the most popular royal."

"No he's not but he's also entitled to get off a train in Scotland without someone taking a shot at him."

"Quite so!"

"The Ministry of Defence Police are leading investigations into the nuclear incident and MI5 seek a prominent role in the attack on Edward but we're keeping close tabs on progress. This fellow, Dalriada is a threat alright. First, because he's clearly not a member of the lunatic fringe. Our forensic people reckon he's trained, measured and very able. He's selecting targets that will play well with the gallery and is teasing us with letters which are designed to explain his motives but which are currently withstanding our attempts to glean information from them. Like I say, he's smart."

"Well, as you'd expect, the First Minister is somewhat exercised about it. It's all over TV. The government wants to see the back of nuclear bombs from Scottish waters but can hardly support someone taking action such as this chap Dalriada. So...might it be possible to keep me up to date on the twists and turns on this? I know you'll report to the Cabinet Secretary for Justice but I'd welcome a quiet note to keep me up to speed."

"That would not be a problem, Catriona. I'll see you have the same updates as the Cabinet Secretary."

* * *

In the Argyle Street offices of MI5 in Glasgow, at an address known only to the organisation and those who needed to know of its existence never mind its location, Boston and Boyd took their seats at a table around which sat officers of equal standing from MOD Police, Special Branch and a woman from MI5. Trays of lunchtime sandwiches had been arrayed on the table and had largely been consumed.

Top brass had been omitted at the behest of MI5 who wished to meet with those who had been involved operationally with Dalriada. At the end of the table, Dr. Edwin van Ossen sat reading notes he'd prepared for the meeting. Arriving late due to transport difficulties, Sergeant Angus Darroch joined the meeting in a flurry of apologies. As hosts, MI5 opened the meeting; the only woman in the room welcoming everyone.

"My identity is not important. Suffice it to say that I represent MI5 today. Government down south are increasingly frustrated at the inability of you lot up here to find and remove this person Dalriada from civilised society. We've been told to get up here to find out what's going on and to advise London on next moves."

"Good for you, hen," remarked Boston, his irascibility never far below the surface. "Best of luck."

"Officer will suffice," she replied coldly, still not introducing herself.

Inspector Jack Devine introduced himself as the MOD Escort Commander of the Warhead Convoy which had been attacked and was invited to speak.

"Let me start. Two shots were fired from a rifle positioned on a wooded ridge near Garelochhead above the roundabout which the convoy requires to navigate on its route south to Burghfield in England. The shots took out the front near-side tyres of two of the Truck Cargo Heavy Duty Carriers which stopped the convoy. Officers of the 43 Commando Fleet Protection Group Royal Marines, who provide armed military personnel to counter any potential threat, took up position to protect other vehicles and personnel and having established no immediate threat, identified gouges in the road surface suggesting the direction from which the shots were fired. By triangulating the trajectory of each groove, we were able to determine roughly the position used to fire on the convoy. At a ridge we found a cardboard card which was subsequently found to have been torn from a cereal packet and on its interior side was written in ink the single word 'Dalriada'. No one was found although the tracks of a trail bike may have suggested a speedy getaway for the shooter."

Dr. Van Ossen interjected.

"Perhaps it might be useful if I took us back a step? The two Special Branch police officers here today invited my attention to a letter sent to the editor of the Scottish newspaper, 'The National', a daily publication which supports the cause of independence here in Scotland. The letter threatened action against the UK nuclear weaponry. It was not published but our analysis determined that the person introducing himself as Dalriada had been careful to use paper, ink and a writing implement that rendered identification impossible. Equally, he managed to obscure his handwriting in such a way as to camouflage quite effectively his writing style. No fingerprints have been found. The torn cereal box card that Inspector Devine here tells us was found at the scene had handwriting and ink identical to that used in the letter. Further, a second letter was sent, again to the National although this time it was published and it widened the scope of the author's concern to include...and I'm quoting...military, political and London

Establishment figures as well as those who would usurp democracy in Scotland by the acquisition of wealth and privilege." He looked up from his notes, "He seems only to have omitted the media in his list of targets," before continuing. "Three days ago, Prince Edward and his wife, Sophie, the Countess of Wessex boarded a vehicle at Aviemore Railway Station where they had exited the Royal Train. Perhaps Sergeant Darroch could speak to that incident."

Darroch was still wiping sweat from his brow due to his dash from Queen Street Station but told the story he'd been brought down to relay.

"Again, the tyres on their vehicle and that of their support vehicle were punctured as was one tyre on each of the two motorcycles that were to be used to carry police outriders to escort the royal couple to Balmoral Castle some fifty-one miles distant. Aviemore is the closest appropriate railway station to Balmoral. A considerable number of tourists and local people were present and numerous photographs were taken many of which received prominence in newspapers and television news programmes. They were also carried on international news programmes in America and in Europe. Al Jazeera, the international Arabic news channel based in Doha, in Qatar, made the attack their main feature as did Russian Television. Forensic officers again traced the shooting position but they had to travel from Aberdeen some ninety miles away and a journey of some two hours. In consequence, while it was established that the shooter was positioned again on a ridge, high above the station in the substantial acreage of the Craigellachie National Nature Reserve, he escaped although we blocked the roads quickly and prior to the arrival of the forensic team. Again a trail bike tyre mark was found but I understand following a conversation with Dr. Van Ossen that it was a different imprint to that discovered at Garelochhead. At the scene of the shooting a further card was found. Again, Dr. Ossen confirmed by telephone that it was identical cereal box card to that found earlier and the ink and writing style was the same. No fingerprints."

The MI5 officer interrupted.

"What about the munitions used?"

Van Ossen retook the floor.

"Ah, yes. First I should mention that the two bullets fired at Garelochhead have not been found. They each ricocheted into a forest and it is highly unlikely that they will soon be unearthed. However, all were found at Aviemore. Nevertheless, I fear I have to lower expectations in respect of finding 'machining marks' on the bullets that allow these fired rounds to be traced back to a specific firearm. In reality this only works under highly controlled situations with a limited set of guns. In the real world there are just too many variables to control for. Recovered bullets are rarely pristine and the Aviemore six were all deformed, distorting the rifling marks and making any match impossible. Also, bullet diameter varies, not by much, but enough to cause the bullet to engage the rifling differently. How the bullet moves from the chamber to the rifling is also affected by variations between cartridges and causes its own markings. Finally, wear on the barrel causes marks to erode and change so after some further shots were fired from the weapon, it might easily carry markings that would not be consistent with those found. Now, Police Scotland do have a bit more luck with matching cartridge casings to specific firearms, however, in the case of each incident, the shooter took the casings with him as he left the scene of the crime. In summary we have mangled bullets and no casings. We have no ballistics evidence."

Darroch was taking notes but lifted his head as Van Ossen concluded, non-verbally inviting him to continue the presentation.

"On the evening of the attack on the royals, a Shooting Range at Boat of Garten..."

MI5 was intrigued.

"A shooting range on a boat?"

"Boat of Garten is a village in Speyside."

"You Scots have curious place names."

Boston was riled and interrupted.

"Aye, like Mincing Lane in London or maybe Fudgepack upon Humber, eh?"

He was ignored as Darroch continued.

"A shooting range only six miles from Aviemore was broken into and chemical ingredients used in the creation of small arms' explosives were stolen. Another card from Dalriada was left."

Boston wasn't finished.

"Bell-end...there's a place in England called Bell-end."

MI5 again disregarded his comment and remained on-task and curious.

"So it might have been possible - even *likely* that the shooter simply walked from the ridge to the shooting range?"

"Indeed."

"And this would have required local knowledge?"

"Not necessarily. The range advertised its wares. All it would have taken was the minimum of research on the web. A number of routes exist between the two points and it would have been easy to walk there undetected."

"Was a helicopter used?"

"It was. Almost immediately. But nothing was seen. It was daylight for the most part but cameras saw nothing."

"So firing ranges can legally sell explosives?"

Van Ossen took over.

"The explosive stolen is called Tannerite but it is supplied as components which are not themselves explosive. The ingredients taken were aluminium powder and an oxidiser mixture of ammonium nitrate and ammonium perchlorate. All legally available. Combining these components to constitute an explosive is regulated by laws on manufacturing explosives. A mixture the size of a tin of soup provides a very satisfactory loud bang and a substantial cloud of smoke. It makes it easy for a shooter on a range to determine if he or she has hit their target at a distance. However, in the quantities stolen from the range, the effect would be substantial. If the thief added further chemicals or small quantities of metal shrapnel, the effect could be very much a danger to life, either as a straightforward explosive or as a booby trap. Additionally, it would not be a particularly exotic bomb. Normally we can make strides in identifying a bomber due to their signature as we call it...the way in which the explosive has been put together. However in this instance the bomb is detonated by means of a rifle bullet and as we've seen, this shooter has unleashed a total of eight shots from distance, all of which have been aimed perfectly."

"Unless, of course he was shooting at individuals and was merely a very bad shot?"

"He is a marksman, I suspect. We have here someone with very specific goals, who seems to have no interest in harming individuals...he could easily have shot Prince Edward...he telegraphs his intentions, leaves information claiming responsibility. He is clearly measured and intelligent, claims to be working alone so infiltration or seeking informants to point in his direction are likely to fall on stoney ground. In summary we're up against someone who could strike at any time, anywhere, is resourceful and technically proficient. Our usual strategy of tracing the sale of explosives, asking our informants for information, assessing motivation, seeking confirmation of responsibility have all been taken from us as our adversary has thought through all of these and nullified them."

"So we have nothing?"

"Not quite. Dalriada signs off his letters 'Alba gu Bràth' which is Scots Gaelic for 'Scotland Forever' so it seems reasonable to suggest he may be supportive of Scottish Independence. His letters are well constructed so he has a facility that suggests a higher education. He understands munitions and is a good shot. He is capable of walking distances under stress. I'd hazard a guess that our man is a Scot aged between twenty-five and forty-five, who has undertaken tertiary education, has experienced a life in uniform...perhaps mainline or mercenary soldiering or police with training in firearms...and has a size nine shoe."

"Really?"

"Yes, at the shooting range we found a man's size nine boot-print outside the window and also inside on the floor. It's been checked and is possibly the most common and inexpensive boot available on the market, freely available from any branch of B&Q, Screwfix, Tool Station or a host of on-line DIY suppliers."

"Well, that's something."

"Not really, this chap is sufficiently creative to have merely used a boot that is say, three sizes too large for him to throw us off the scent."

"The name 'Dalriada'? Is it a Gaelic name for something?"

"It's the old name of Gaelic kingdom that encompassed the western seaboard of Scotland."

"Okay. Thank you all…"

"Hold on Mrs. MI5. We're forgetting something." Boston hadn't finished.

"Another amusing English place-name?"

"Nah! Too many to list! This guy is deliberately avoiding injury to people. It's clear to me at least that his objective is to inspire people who hold attitudes in Scotland against objects that the Scottish people already hold in contempt. There's great opposition to nuclear bombs on the Clyde, no one I've ever met likes that wee parasite Prince Edward except his mammy! There have been a rise in protests in cities all over Scotland. Many are carrying banners supporting Dalriada. He's coming across as a modern-day Rob Roy."

"A sort of Robin Hood?"

"Not at all. Rob Roy was a real person. Your Robin Hood is a fiction."

MI5 shook her head.

"Dear me. I'd forgotten how touchy you Scots were."

Darroch joined in supporting Boston.

"He's right, though. We can be fairly certain his next target will be similar to those already hit. I'd also go along with the notion that it'll likely be non-violent and popular with a certain section of the Scottish public."

'Well, I can tell you that MI5 are very concerned about anything that is popular with what you call a 'certain section of the Scottish public' as they tend to be separatists…and we tend to the view that shooting at army personnel and the royal family is usually considered a violent act. Our job…and yours…is to protect the realm, the UK realm that is, not the Scottish realm."

Boston shook his head as he replied.

"No' up here, hen! In England your cops swear an oath to the Queen but up here in civilisation our oath is to declare and affirm that we will faithfully discharge the duties of the office of constable with fairness, integrity, diligence and impartiality and that we will uphold fundamental human rights and accord equal respect to all people, according to law...according to *law*," he repeated before continuing. "Now this Dalriada fellah can't be running around shooting people and my job is to stop him doing that but not for one of your English minutes is it about protecting the British State."

"I'll make sure your comments are brought to the attention of my seniors."

"As you say, hen. I'd be grateful."

The meeting broke up as participants gathered notes and headed for the door. Darroch approached Boston and smiled, speaking to him in a low tone.

"Well said, sir!"

"Fuckin' MI5," growled Boston, still riled.

"I'm due to catch a train back north but I'm going to have a pint first. You free for a wee glass or do you have to get back to the office?"

Boston hesitated before turning to his colleague Jimmy Boyd.

"Jimmy, you get back to the office. I'm going on to another meeting to discuss Dalriada with my fellow sergeant here from Aviemore. I won't be able to be contacted if you catch my drift. I'll be in sharp first thing tomorrow."

Boyd smiled.

"As you say, sir!"

Chapter Fifteen

Deputy Head of MI5, Jack Strachan lifted his phone.

"Miranda! Thanks for calling. How did your meeting with my fellow countrymen go?"

"They're a touchy lot, boss. It wouldn't surprise me if they were all in cahoots with Dalriada."

Strachan laughed.

"Nor me. There's a lot of nationalist sentiment up there at present."

"Well, they seem capable enough. Every action they've taken seems appropriate but this fellow Dalriada has them... and us...wrapped around his finger. He seems a capable, educated guy, works alone, is a marksman, doesn't seem interested in harming people but in whipping them up into a fervour that matches his own. Forensic think he's a male Scotsman aged between twenty-five and forty-five who's been in uniform, ex-police or soldier, that sort of thing...no prints but he might have a size nine shoe. But there simply isn't any evidence we can stand on and it seems that all we can do is to wait for him to continue his efforts and hope that he makes the mistake that he hasn't up until now. It's all over the media, internationally as well, and there have been several large rallies in support of his actions."

"I see..."

"And the fact of the matter is, boss, that he's now in possession of a large quantity of explosive material which could do a fair bit of damage and we've no idea where he is, what his next target might be or when he'll strike. That said, he's in the habit of writing letters before he acts so maybe that'll give us a clue but if he doesn't..."

Strachan thought for a while before responding.

"I'm going to raise this with Sir Jefferey. Maintain a watching brief, Miranda but no operational activity. This may have to be handled creatively."

Slowly, still in thought, he replaced the phone on its receiver.

* * *

"The Steps Bar, I think, eh? D'you know Glasgow pubs, Gus?"

"I know every pub in Scotland, Colin. Haven't been in the Steps for ages. I gather it was a polis pub when the High Court was round the corner and *that* wasn't yesterday. It was always a bit spit and sawdust when I popped in."

"These days it's a bit more spit than sawdust but it's a fine wee, family-owned, no-trouble pub."

Introductions and drinks orders having being completed, small talk was next on the agenda as they sat.

"Christ, it's been years since I've been in here, Colin."

"Great wee pub. Apparently that art-deco bar is a copy of a bar on the Queen Mary."

"Decent gantry too, eh?"

"Great wee pub," repeated Boston. "Quiet...respectable!"

The conversation soon turned to Dalriada.

"I can see you're very fond of MI5," laughed Darroch.

"Och, they keep sending people up from London who don't know their arse from their elbow. But they canny fall out with us in Special Branch 'cause MI5 haven't the legal power to arrest anyone. They need us to do their dirty work but they see their job as wrapping everything up then calling us in at the last minute just to do the liftin'." He took a sip of his pint. "Also, Little Miss Crabbit was a right brammer, eh? No names, no introduction, just questions. Rude fucker!"

"Not my cup of tea, right enough. What happens now?"

"Well, she'll give me and Jimmy cover...you as well, I'd imagine. This Dalriada looks like a bit of a boy and it looks likely we're going to get the run around for a while so MI5 and the

MOD between them will take a bit of the heat off us if he's not caught quickly and my bet is that he won't be."

"I'm only a village cop, Colin. Can't see this being a career ending incident where I need to head for cover."

"Jesus, Mary, Joseph and their wee hairy-arsed donkey, you've had two of the three Dalriada incidents on your hairy-arsed doorstep."

"Aye, but he'll be a hairy-arsed Nationalist or a CND member from the Central Belt, you mark my words. A disgruntled ex-cop or army who's become a bit of a tree-hugger. All of the protests will be at nuclear bases or in the centres of population. We'll be spared that up in the Highlands. Can't see anyone blockading Balmoral Castle."

"S'pose! Mind you, like I said to thon MI5 arse in the meeting, apart from the shooting malarkey, I can see why he's so popular with many in Scotland. Nuclear warheads and Prince Edward? You couldn't find two more popular targets if you tried!"

"Aye, but it's the shooting and now the potential bombing malarkey that's keeping MI5 up at night."

Boston disagreed.

"I think you have the cart before the horse, my friend. The Establishment are far more worried about a popular uprising north of Hadrian's Wall than they are about the odd vehicle being shot at. I know MI5 and trust me…they'll come down heavy on this."

* * *

Jack Strachan knocked the door of the Director General and entered having received the nod from Arbuthnot's secretary.

"Hi boss. Thought I'd better have a chat about these Dalriada incidents. Did you get my note?"

"I did, Jack and I confess, it worried me. Have you given thought to our response?"

"I have and propose developing a select team which would operate under the Third Direction. I know that engaging in criminal acts is available to all of our operatives but I wish to spell out in advance that in the circumstances we face, any act can be undertaken that safeguards the requirements of the state. My concern is that if we merely track down and arrest this chap, he'll become a martyr to the cause. In my view, he'll have to be discredited and potentially disappeared."

"And *you* want to send out permissions..."

Strachan nodded. "Because *you* may have to sit in judgement on my decision if things go pear-shaped or become public."

Arbuthnot harrumphed his agreement. "How many intelligence officers?"

"Five. One to focus upon the nuclear side, one on the royals, one each to Special Branch and the MOD Police and one to coordinate...to lead the team and to report to me."

"And that might be?"

"Thorpe."

Arbuthnot raised his eyebrows.

"Thorpe?...Jesus! Very well! He took care of that Saudi Arabian matter quite effectively although his record shows him as something of a bloodthirsty chap. However, in for a penny, in for a pound!"

* * *

Having spent an early hour with a senior headhunter in Edinburgh in an attempt to secure a senior role within a company focussed upon tourism and foreign travel, later that morning, Andy Burns turned the wheel of his hired car and steered into RM Condor, a large Royal Marines base located near Arbroath in East Angus. Parking in an empty visitor's bay, he walked to the front door of a building that hosted a reception facility. Upon entering he found a young, lanyard-wearing Marine sitting at a desk inputing data to a computer.

"Morning, sir." Keyboard functions stopped abruptly. Full attention was given.

"Morning. I wonder if you can assist me. I'm trying to find the whereabouts of my brother-in-law. He was a member of your regiment and retired with honour in 2013 as a result of suffering from Post Traumatic Stress Disorder."

"We don't keep records like that here, sir. You might try the British Legion locally. They might help but you'd probably need to check with Navy Command Headquarters in Portsmouth down in Hampshire. I could get you their address."

"Really? I just thought that you'd have that kind of thing on tap up here. I've driven up from Edinburgh. It never occurred to me that I'd need to contact the southernmost tip of England to find local information."

"Sorry, sir."

Trying to be helpful, the Marine turned again to his keyboard.

"Hold on, sir. How recent was his discharge?"

"Eh, 2013 I was told."

"And his name and rank?"

"Captain Lachlan MacAskill. He served in Afghanistan just before retirement."

"Afghanistan?" He sat back in his seat and narrowed his eyes thoughtfully. "We've a Warrant Officer who might have been out there at that time. Look, take a seat sir and I'll make a phone call."

Ten minutes elapsed after the officer had replaced the phone on its receiver when a large uniformed man strode into the room. The soldier on reception merely nodded in the direction of Burns.

"Sir! You were asking about Captain Lachlan MacAskill?" He pronounced the forename 'Lacklan'.

"I was."

"And can I ask your relationship with the captain?"

"I'm his brother-in-law, Andrew Burns. My wife and I have just returned from some time spent overseas...in Japan, actually and we've kind of lost touch."

"When last did you see him?"

"I'm afraid it was some years ago. We've been abroad you see," repeating his explanation diffidently.

"Can I see some identification?"

Burns proffered his driving licence.

"I've nothing that explains my MacAskill connection. That's all on my wife's side."

"I served under Captain MacAskill. He was the best Marine Commando in the army. His men would follow him through the gates of hell!" He changed the focus of his questioning. "Has he ever tried to make contact with you and your wife?"

"Not to my knowledge but we have a good enough relationship. There's no obvious reason why he might not wish to meet up with his sister."

"As you said to my colleague, he left the Marines with post traumatic stress disorder. He might not want to meet up with anyone."

"Well, I suppose I could understand that. Perhaps I should just make contact with Navy Command Headquarters."

The Warrant Officer hesitated.

"Look, I've a pal who keeps in semi-regular touch with the Captain. I will tell you, he's not easy to track down but seeing as you're related…." Another pause. "Tell you what. You leave me your name and phone number and I'll get Bob Stein, that's *Sergeant* Bob Stein, to phone you if…that's if he thinks it's in the Captain's interests or would be his preference."

"I'd be very grateful to you. Thanks."

Chapter Sixteen

Having arrived back from his visit to Glasgow and having showered and changed, Gus Darroch elbowed his way past the double doors of the Claymore Bar and upon entering, hailed his friend Lachie who was seated near the fire with his dog Blaze as was usual during Quiz Hour. A pint of Belhaven Best sat unattended on the table opposite MacAskill who sipped at a full glass of dark stout.

"Good call, Lachie. Had a couple of beers at lunchtime but they merely served to whet my appetite." He took a large draught. "How you?"

"Me fine." He took a further sip. "How come you were drinking at lunchtime? Don't the polis in these parts frown on such delinquency?"

"Aye, they do but I was down in Glasgow meeting with Special Branch, the MOD and MI5 about this Dalriada stuff. It was all quite exciting for a country yokel like me."

MacAskill tensed but disguised his discomfort with a hurried mouthful of beer.

"You caught him yet?"

Darroch laughed. "Not by a long shot. This boy's good. He has MI5 in a tizzy. They've got nothing to go on and it's driving them nuts." He counted off the points on his fingers. "Male, aged between twenty-five and forty-five, probably ex-polis or army, handy with a rifle and educated." He laughed again. "Christ the description could fit you except the educated bit!"

MacAskill smiled unconvincingly. "Aye, very funny. But I'm surprised they've not picked up any clues."

"Nothing. No prints, no ballistics, nothing except a size nine footprint."

"Well, thank Christ I'm uneducated and have a size ten boot," lied MacAskill drawing his feet under the chair.

Benny the Quizmaster came to his rescue.

"Okay. Best of order. Here's the first question. What two cities represent letters in the phonetic alphabet?"

"We're off to a flyer, Lachie. Write it doon! Lima and Quebec. Right up my barra," He congratulated himself.

The quiz continued if not as productively for Inverskillen United until half way through round two when the quizmaster raised the microphone to his lips.

"A parliament is the name given to a group of which breed of bird?" He repeated the question. "A parliament is the name given to a group of which breed of bird?" MacAskill and Darroch were flummoxed until a voice behind Darroch whispered, "Owls".

"Isla!" MacAskill spotted her first.

"What's it to be tonight, Isla," asked Darroch as he stood to order her a drink.

"Whatever you two are drinking."

"We're about to start on the whisky now."

"Thanks. I'll join you."

Isla sat with the twosome and progress was made on the quiz allowing a third place finish out of nine teams. Three rounds of malt whisky had been consumed since her arrival and a fourth was rejected by Isla.

"I'm not as well rehearsed as you two when it comes to strong drink. I think I'm going to need the less convivial surroundings of the north-east of England when I return the day after tomorrow so I can recover."

"Christ! You've just arrived, girl." Darroch was exercised but became diverted as the jukebox was stirred into action when one of the still successful teachers' team thumbed a pound coin into it. The Wings' song 'Mull of Kintyre' entertained the pub.

"Great song that. Canny beat a bit of the auld bagpipes in a song. Any song is improved when you get the auld pipes on it," exclaimed Darroch.

MacAskill nodded. "Gus is a piper, Isla. He plays the war-pipes in the police pipe band." He turned his attention to Darroch, "That's why Mick Jagger insisted on some background bagpipes when the Stones recorded 'Brown Sugar'."

"Christ, I didn'y know that, Lachie."

MacAskill erupted in laughter.

"Christ, you're a top cop and you can't tell when I feed you a bare-faced lie! Some polis you!"

"I'm off-duty," he responded embarrassedly before returning to his earlier theme. "So you're off, Isla?"

"Been up here for two weeks and I've enjoyed it so much it'll be a genuine struggle to go back down. Everyone's been so lovely. It's been great staying with mother. She's getting on a bit but all of my obligations are down south. I've done a couple of locum shifts for Donald Brodie and loved every minute as it allowed me to deal with a bull with an infected ear, a cow with labour problems and even a young fawn up at Hamish Anderson's deer farm which had suspected tuberculosis. I don't get these cases in Newcastle."

"Then walk away from the Geordie cats and dogs and come back here and do some real veterinarian work!"

Isla grimaced. "Don't think I've not considered it. But go I must. My partners rely on me." She smiled. But I'll be back to see mother regularly and maybe on that trip I'll get to see Lachie's Tardis that everyone says is so amazing."

"Anytime, Isla." MacAskill entered the conversation, still quiet as he mulled over Darroch's revelations about Dalriada. He decided to scratch the itch.

"Maybe by then Gus'll have arrested Dalriada. He was just accusing me of being him when you walked in."

Darroch guffawed. "Aye, but we agreed that Dalriada was intelligent and that rules you out big time!"

Isla ignored what was clearly intended as banter by Darroch and asked, "Are you still involved, Gus?"

"Just back from a meeting down in Glasgow with MI5, the MOD and Special Branch. They're all over the place and needed the insights and assessments of a local police sergeant who knows what way's up."

"Any closer to capturing him?"

"Well, he's clearly not the greatest villain unhung. MI5 are more concerned that he'll set up a reaction in Scotland against unpopular symbols of Unionist domination. There's been protests in support of him in all the big Scottish cities and he's got them very worried…especially now that he has his hands on explosives."

MacAskill couldn't contain himself.

"Where do they expect him to strike next?"

"They haven't a clue so they're just waiting for his next letter hoping it'll give them a clue and they can stop him before someone gets hurt."

"But no one's been hurt so far," responded MacAskill.

"No, but we still don't know what we're dealing with. Could be a stable passivist who is just trying to inspire the good people of Scotland to rise against their oppressors or he could be a deranged lunatic who can't shoot straight and just missed putting a bullet through the rather thick skull of the tenth in line to the throne."

Isla took stock of Darroch as he spoke. He was still a handsome man, with a tanned, chiseled face and short, thick, wavy hair in which grey flecks had started to appear. She found her voice.

"What an exciting job you have, Gus."

"Sometimes, Isla but usually it's asking a tourist not to park in front of someone's driveway."

"Well, I know you won't agree with me but I hope this Dalriada *is* what you call a stable passivist and that you don't catch him. We could be *doing* with no nuclear bombs in Scotland and an end to the Royal Family and their privilege."

"I'm of the same opinion," echoed MacAskill, delighted at his friend's outburst.

Encouraged, Isla continued.

"In fact, I hope he turns his attention to other targets equally worthy of his attentions. There's too much inequity in Scotland and as long as no one gets hurt. I hope he strikes again. The letters' page in this morning's National supports that view."

Darroch demurred. "Well, you're right about my attitude, Isla. The man's dangerous and needs to feel the hand of the polis on his collar." He shrugged his shoulders philosophically. "Mind you, lightening doesn't strike twice and all that. If he strikes again it'll be somewhere in the Central Belt or back at Faslane. Can't see Hamish Anderson's deer farm being a target."

Isla collected a small strapped purse that passed for a handbag.

"I'm off, guys. It's been great meeting up and spending time together. I promise I'll be back soon." She bent forward and gave Darroch a kiss on the cheek before stepping round and repeating the gesture with MacAskill.

"And when I come back up, Lachie, I hope you'll invite me round to see your converted ambulance. I'll bring the wine."

MacAskill felt his face reddening.

"Ah…sure, Isla."

Both men watched silently as Isla walked towards the door and left.

"Christ, she's gorgeous, eh?" Darroch murmured. "She's obviously got the hots for you, Lachie."

"Don't be daft, man. She was just being funny. You're as single as I am now that Morag's away and re-married."

"Aye, but over the years in the polis I've learned to read people like a cheap novel. I just need to look at someone and I know instantly whether they're lying or truthful, if they've a lead pipe handy or whether they like the strong silent type. If she'd half a brain she'd make a play for a well-connected, really good-looking police sergeant with a nice house, good salary and a hefty pension but if you ask me, she's a wee soft spot for an ugly, red-haired woodsman who lives in the forest with a dog called Blaze."

"I've no time for nonsense like that,"replied MacAskill. "You ask her to bring some wine round to your place if you're that interested in her."

"We'll see," said Darroch. "In the meantime let's just agree she's a permanent member of the Inverskillen United Quiz Team whenever she's in the village. It's our only chance of beating Danny the Dominie and his two pals."

"Aye, especially with me being so unintelligent!"

"That's for sure! Another whisky?"

Chapter Seventeen

Catriona Burns sat at her desk and before attending to a weighty sheaf of papers demanding her attention, lifted the Scotsman newspaper. More protests supporting Dalriada had taken place. Images showed thick smoke emanate from red flares as protesters in Glasgow came out to demonstrate vociferously at Trident missiles being situated on the Clyde and in London news was breaking of many cars having had their tyres deflated by the wilful scattering of spikes on the roads around Parliament causing traffic jams, lengthy delays and driver anger. Cards had also been left on the road with the word 'Dalriada' on them in an attempt to mimic what newspapers had told their readers was Dalriada's *modus operandi*. At Her Majesty's Naval Base at Faslane, police had had to be called as those living in the Peace Camp opposite its gates took to the A814 and closed the road for an hour before police managed to remove them. They chanted 'Dalriada' as police officers lifted their limp frames from the road surface while television cameras captured the spirited opposition of those still not apprehended.

Her reverie was broken by her phone ringing. Her secretary announced that the Chief Constable was holding for her. She lifted her phone.

"Good morning, Andy."

"Morning, Catriona. Forgive me calling so early in the working day. I'm sure you have a lot on your plate but I suspect that you'll be meeting the First Minister at some juncture today..."

"In an hour..."

"Well I'm certain you'll be asked about Dalriada. Have you read the papers?"

"Indeed."

"It looks like we can discount the London episode as a copy-cat event. Our forensic people say the cards left signifying the involvement of Dalriada are most likely to be false. That won't provide any consolation to the poor buggers who had to wait in the pouring rain while their car was removed having had its tyres punctured. And it *does* seem to have inculcated a certain anti-Scottish attitude in the minds of many Londoners if talk-show call-ins are anything to go by."

"I'm sure."

"The Faslane and Glasgow protests were meat and drink for my officers and both events were relatively good-natured. I'm happy to talk with the FM if more info is needed but this morning, after the smoke has cleared, we're back to normal."

"And you're no closer to discovering the identity of this person?"

"MI5 are involved so they're leading but we have a team set up to pursue our own enquiries. Nothing yet, though."

"Thanks, Andy. I appreciate your call."

She hung up. *A baptism of fire right enough,* she thought.

* * *

In keeping with his arrangement with Lady Helen Wishart of Inverskillen, MacAskill steered his ambulance into a parking spot opposite the front door of her gatehouse. His task that mid-morning was to seek her agreement for the purchase of seven hundred pounds worth of rocks for a dry-stane dyke he was building at the northern end of the estate. Cheerily he knocked at the door but heard no response. The Land Rover Defender had gone. *Most likely, Isla's away into the village,* he decided. Lady Helen's Jaguar was still parked outside her house. He knocked again and pushed gently at the door as he'd been instructed to do as a consequence of Lady Helen's failing hearing.

"Helen? It's Lachie." He stepped inside. "You around?"

A second step inside allowed him access to the stairwell. Lady Helen lay prone and unconscious at the bottom.

"Helen!"

MacAskill moved swiftly to her side and took stock. Carefully he placed one hand on her forehead and two fingers under her chin, gently tilting her head backwards. As he did this, her mouth fell open slightly giving him confidence that her airway was clear. He placed his ear next to her mouth and listened, feeling her breathing on his cheek.

She's breathing okay. At this she moaned and moved her head to the right before resuming unconsciousness. *Thank, God, she seems not to have suffered any spinal injury.* Both legs were very obviously broken.

A further moan allowed MacAskill to touch her cheek and gently ask if she was okay. Slowly she came round.

"Lachie. I fell."

"Are you hurting?"

"Yes. Both legs."

"Neck okay?"

"Yes."

"How about your hip? Pelvis?"

"Just my legs. What have I done? I slipped on the stairs. Oh, Lachie it's painful…"

MacAskill held both of her hands.

"Can you feel me holding your hands?"

"Yes."

"Your head sore?"

"I hit my forehead when I slipped."

MacAskill observed a reddened and swollen abrasion on her forehead. Further inspection showed no other injury to the head.

"Looks like you've broken both legs, Helen. The good news is that it's not an open fracture so we're going to immobilise both legs and we'll get you up to hospital in Raigmore."

She slipped back into unconsciousness.

MacAskill stepped into the kitchen and opened a pantry door withdrawing a brush and a mop. Stamping forcibly on the neck of each, he took the two resulting poles to Lady Helen and went out to his ambulance where he took a length of rope from a cupboard and returned. Three small cushions from the living room settee were called into service and used to pad both legs. The poles were affixed as splints and gently but unceremoniously, MacAskill pulled at the carpet on which his casualty was lying and pulled her out to his van where he lifted her and placed her on his bed inside. Satisfied that she was stable enough for the journey, he smoothly turned his vehicle and set off to Inverness.

* * *

In a briefing room inside the MI5 building in Glasgow, Simon Thorpe waited until the door closed and spoke to the four men seated round the table.

"Okay! Listen up." He passed a piece of paper to each of them. "This e-mail gives us permission to act under the Third Direction. File it carefully in these premises before you leave them. You may well need it. It is not a document that allows anyone here to commit fucking mayhem on behalf of Her Majesty, but does permit us to engage in criminal acts in defence of the realm. Due to the significance of what we're about here, *that* may involve the regrettable dispatch of anyone who merits said dispatch. You were briefed earlier by the Deputy Director General who made the case for the apprehension of this person called Dalriada. Now, we're all operational intelligence officers but only two of us speak the Queen's English with a proper accent. Morton and Geddes speak Jockanese so they might have a head start on us three remaining civilising English people. Mr. Strachan set out our task sufficiently but my job is to make sure we're successful and to interpret his instructions. So let me be clear. I can say words that Mr. Strachan cannot. Apprehension of this terrorist is *unacceptable*. So is his public execution. He'd be treated as a fucking martyr for the separatists so nothing less than him quietly disappearing will suffice. We must engender a situation where people start to ask why Dalriada has been quiet for a while before they forget the fucker ever existed. Now, the Jock cops won't cooperate with this approach so we keep them at arm's length."

He perched himself on the end of the table.

"I have been selected to lead this team for one reason only; I'm fucking ruthless. I get the job done. I don't take prisoners and I bayonet the wounded. So, Collins. You insinuate yourself into the enquiries being made by Special Branch up here. Geddes, the same but with the MOD Police. Morton, get yourself up to the Peace Camp at Faslane and Shaw, you're coming up to the Scottish Highlands with me. Now, let me be clear. We're merciless, pitiless in this task. There's fucking revolution in the air. This fucking terrorist thinks he can have a pop at our Royal family and at the defence of our nation. Our job is to hunt the fucker down, see him off and do so without there being a ripple on the water."

He looked round the table.

"Questions?"

Morton spoke. "Looks like we'll be *needing* the insurance of this note you've given us."

"Yeah. Now, be nice as ninepence to these Jock cops up here. They haven't a clue what we're about and they think they have the upper hand because we don't have the legal power to arrest anyone. It would not be in anyone's interest for them to know that we don't give a flying fuck about arresting anyone in this case. We just need to pump them for information and elbow our way into interviewing their suspects. So we do it with a smile on our face and a Glock 19 in our waistband."

* * *

Isla turned the corner leading to the ward in which her mother had been admitted at pace, almost tripping over MacAskill as she did so.

"Lachie...I..."

"Hey, calm down, Isla. Your mum's fine. She fell down the stairs at home and she's broken both legs but they're both closed transverse fractures, the simplest kind from which to recover. She's also had a bump on her head and she's a bit woozy but that's more to do with the medication she's been given. The doc is presently setting them both and he's coming out in a moment to tell us how things have gone so take a seat and stop worrying."

"Stop worrying? Lachie, my mother isn't a young girl any more."

"She's a tough old bird, Isla. Trust me she'll..."

114

An elderly doctor appeared through the double doors. MacAskill took care of the introductions.

"Hi doc. This is Isla Wishart. She's Lady Wishart's daughter."

"Ah, then you owe this man a considerable debt of gratitude Miss Wishart. His actions have saved a very serious situation from developing. Both tibias broken, I'm afraid. Clean break, though and no appreciable blood loss. Could've been much worse, especially having regard to her age and living alone in a rural setting. I've set both legs and my colleagues are currently placing a cast on each leg. She'll be fine but she'll have to stay with us for a few days and will require support when she's discharged."

"God, I feel so guilty, doctor."

MacAskill intervened.

"Don't be daft, Isla. It was just one of those things."

The doctor agreed.

"Indeed so, Mr. MacAskill. Anyway, she'll be dancing the Gay Gordons at the next village Burns Supper. She'll just need to be a wee bit patient." He turned to MacAskill. "Nice piece of emergency first aid, sir. I was impressed."

"I've done more than my fair share of first aid, Doctor...in Afghanistan."

"Ah," said the doctor in recognition as he re-entered the operating theatre.

Isla placed her hands over her face and started to weep. She sat on a chair and MacAskill comforted her.

"Oh, Lachie. What would have happened if you hadn't chanced along?" She clutched his shoulders and continued weeping. "That's it! I'm going to phone Newcastle. I'll need to stay up here at least until she can walk unaided."

"Is that necessary, Isla? Me and Blaze can look after her in your absence."

"What kind of daughter do you take me for, Lachie MacAskill? I can't abandon my mother to a stranger."

MacAskill spoke intemperately.

"I've certainly seen more of her over the past year than anyone...including her daughter."

"I'm sorry, Lachie. That's the guilt speaking. I owe you big time and I'm so very, very grateful. I apologise. I'm just upset."

"No problem. Why don't you hang around and speak to your mother once she's settled in a ward. I'll go back and find Rory and keep both dogs until things ease. I'll look in pretty much every day in case you or your mum need anything."

Isla wiped the tears from her eyes.

"Lachie MacAskill, you truly are a wonderful person. A wonderful, wonderful person."

She hugged him tightly until MacAskill untethered himself from her grasp and bid goodbye, saying he'd look in the following day.

Chapter Eighteen

The British Broadcasting Corporation is the world's oldest national public service broadcaster. It also employs more people than any other national broadcaster world-wide. In Scotland it is headquartered in a large and unprepossessing box building on the south bank of the River Clyde.

It was six-thirty in the evening and the newsreader smiled at the camera as the theme music of the evening edition of Reporting Scotland faded. Behind her, the live, familiar backdrop of the river and its immediate environs was evident.

"Good evening. Our top stories today. In Parliament, a bill to increase the number of libraries in Scotland was presented by the government but was opposed by the Conservatives who said that the money should instead be spent on tax-cuts. Later in the programme...."

On the north bank of the Clyde, six students unrolled a large tarpaulin on which the word, 'Dalriada' had been written. Two of them tied the top corners to railings and allowed it to droop it down until it almost reached the water. Unaware of the backdrop, the newsreader continued her monologue.

Four of the students, hidden by the upper section of the tarpaulin, positioned a wheelbarrow against which they angled six powerful rockets purchased as fireworks in anticipation of successful degree outcomes and aimed them at the building across the river. One of the students stood back from the assembly and announced his satisfaction that both the trajectory and direction seemed accurate. He checked the time on his watch.

"Go, boys!"

Two kneeling students ignited the fuse on each of the rockets. Almost as one, the six rockets fired and made their way across the river at speed. Quickly, the students rose as one of them lifted the plastic barrow and threw it over the rail where it fell unceremoniously into the Clyde. Two of the rockets crashed into the wall of the embankment opposite, exploding as they did so, two hit windows behind which BBC staff were enjoying a coffee and sandwich. One exploded on the window behind the newsreader causing her obvious alarm but breaking no glass. One, however, had a direct hit near the the remote camera used by the BBC to capture the background image of a usually tranquil river. It was this rocket, upon exploding, that caused most consternation amongst the viewing public who witnessed live what appeared to be an armed attack on BBC Scotland and their living rooms. Unsure of the nature of the attack and implementing its emergency procedures, the broadcast was shut down immediately and its Test Card was shown whose central image on the card portrayed a young girl playing noughts and crosses on a blackboard with a doll called Bubbles the Clown.

Punching the air in celebration of a confrontation they had not anticipated might work quite as spectacularly as it had, the students sped off on foot across a covered footbridge behind the surrounding concert venues and disappeared into the student population of Glasgow's West End.

* * *

Andy Burns' phone rang announcing a number with which he was unfamiliar.

"Andy Burns!"

"Hello. This is Sergeant Bob Stein. I gather that you're looking for Captain Lachlan MaCaskill."

"Ah, yes. Well, to be more precise, my wife is. She's his sister. We've been working in Japan for the last while and have kind of lost touch."

"The captain likes his privacy."

"Yes, and we appreciate that but we feel sure he'd like to be reconnected."

"The captain has taken steps to make sure he's disconnected."

"But you're in touch with him?"

"Yes, sir. I'm meeting him next week. I'll pass on your contact details and well-wishes but it'll be up to him to decide whether he wants contact to be made."

"Can you at least tell me if he's safe, well and happy?"

"All three, sir. He leads a solitary existence but he has good friends around him up in Scotland and old comrades down here in England who care for him. Your brother is held in very, very high regard by those who served with him."

"So he's in Scotland?"

The line went quiet momentarily before Stein spoke again.

"I suppose it's okay for me to acknowledge that. I'll let him know of your interest. He has no phone so I leave messages for him near where he lives. I'll follow my normal routine. If he's interested, I'm sure he'll be in touch."

The line went dead.

* * *

Forbes McCalliog was eighty-four years old. In his younger days he had been a member of the Scottish National Liberation Army and had been involved in sending letter-bombs to broadcaster Robin Day and Conservative Prime Minister Margaret Thatcher. Neither had exploded and in 1993, he was arrested and at the High Court in Aberdeen, was sentenced to six years in prison for attempting to poison the water supply that served Greater Manchester. A prominent and acerbic letter-writer, always on the subject of Scottish Independence, McCalliog was visited by officers of Special Branch, informed that black powder that might appear at first pass to be gunpowder, had been found in his garden and was subsequently invited to accompany the officers to Govan Police Station where he was interviewed about any knowledge he might have about Dalriada.

For two hours, questions were asked about his activities. McCalliog was surly and unhelpful noting that there were no questions being asked about the surprising discovery of a suspicious black powder in his property, just about Dalriada.

"If it turns out to be gunpowder, you're for the high-jump, McCalliog. While forensic have a look, you're off to the cells."

Govan Police Station in 'G' Division differs from others in Scotland in that behind its high walls it has cells designed to hold Scotland's prisoners found or presumed to be terrorists or political prisoners. McCalliog was seated on a bench inside his cell and had had his belt and shoe laces removed. Half an hour after his incarceration, noises outside alerted him to another prisoner being admitted to custody.

"Fuck off, you bastards. That stuff was planted and you know it!"

A long-haired, unshaven man in his mid-thirties was thrust into the same cell as McCalliog and he too had his belt and shoelaces removed.

"Fucking bastards."

"Aye, they are that son."

"They came into my flat, searched it and found a bag of black powder I've never seen before. Now they're asking me all these questions about this guy Dalriada."

"Aye, me too."

"They're nicking me just because I had a bit of a reputation up in Aberdeen for causing trouble in the cause of Scottish Independence." He offered his hand to McCalliog who shook it. "Name's Jim Collins. I'm an academic and I publish a blog about the dominant Anglophone cultural hegemony"

"Aye, very good."

"They were pissed last week when I wrote about cultural assimilation and linguistic imperialism. I argued that Scotland's now a colony of England which I defined as economic exploitation and political control by another country, plus occupation by their settlers. I also wrote a blog arguing that we need to see more people like this guy Dalriada. Don't you agree?"

McCalliog sighed wearily.

"So, you're MI5, son?"

* * *

120

Under cover of darkness, four students, two male, two female and all studying medicine at the University of Edinburgh, forsook their studies for the evening and walked the short distance from their flats in Canongate to Queen Elizabeth House, the flagship headquarters of the Westminster Government in Scotland. A modern building situated below St. Andrew's House the administrative centre of the Scottish Government and abutting Waverley Railway Station, it houses some three thousand civil servants who answer to their political master, the Conservative Secretary of State for Scotland.

Prior to opening, a decision was made to emphasise the role of the U.K. in governing Scotland by colouring four large window panes to represent the bottom, pole-side, red, white and blue edge of the Union Flag. These windows were strategically positioned at that part of the three storey building which sits next to a road tunnel beneath the main rail line into the station.

The four students gathered together under the bridge. Ever dim, even during the day when the pale yellow lights attempted illumination, the tunnel offered some concealment. Nevertheless, aware of remote cameras once they exited their shelter into the modern cityscape of Queen Elizabeth House and its environs, the men each donned balaclavas while the women merely covered their head and shielded their face with the hoods on their garment. The two women took a parcel which was wrapped in brown paper and which had been opened deliberately at one end to expose wires. Walking briskly, one took the device which had the word 'Dalriada' written prominently on the top and placed it atop a steel litter bin some yards from the front door. The other walked directly towards the front of the building and removing a tube of super-glue from her pocket, squeezed it generously inside the keyhole on the double front doors of the building.

While this was being undertaken, the two male students had opened a tin of light brown paint chosen to match the colour of the walls of the building, poured it into a large paint tray and thoroughly saturated a fifteen-inch, long-handled, fleeced roller-pad before painting over the red elements of the flag edge, converting it at first glance from the Union Flag to Scotland's

Saltire. It took but four minutes for all tasks to be completed. Leaving the paint and roller at the site, the students re-entered the rail tunnel and walked briskly back to their accommodation slapping each other on the back and reminding each other of the need for complete secrecy lest their medical studies be compromised.

Chapter Nineteen

BC Scotland had recovered their collective nerve the following morning and led with the 'Rocket Attack' on their newsroom. Their 'Breaking News' story was of civil servants being locked out of the Queen Elizabeth House, the Saltire replacing the Union Flag on its frontage and bomb disposal experts having announced that a device left in front of the building was comprised of tins of beans and some wires. In both cases, reference was made to Dalriada about whom outraged Conservative politicians unhesitatingly called a dangerous terrorist. A police spokesman commented on the incidents saying they were satisfied that neither had been carried out at the hand of the man calling himself Dalriada but that they were serious acts of public disorder and vandalism and would be dealt with decisively.

* * *

"Another letter, boss."

Colin Boston set his coffee down and removed his spectacles from his inside jacket pocket.

"We sure it's him?"

"Looks like it. He's got the double plus after his name."

Boston took a pair of latex gloves from his desk drawer, put them on and accepted the piece of paper from Boyd. Again the letter was addressed to the editor of the National newspaper.

"The editor says he's going to publish this statement like he did the last one, boss."

"Hard to stop him! Ask him again to make sure not to use the two pluses after Dalriada's name so we can continue to identify copy-cat threats."

SIR

THIS IS MY THIRD LETTER TO YOU. AS YOU ARE AWARE, IT HAS BEEN WIDELY REPORTED THAT I AM NOW IN POSSESSION OF A LARGE QUANTITY OF EXPLOSIVES. WHETHER AND HOW I USE THEM WILL DEPEND UPON YOUR ACTIONS. IF YOU PUBLISH, MY EFFORTS WILL BE RELATIVELY BENIGN. I ENCLOSE A STATEMENT THAT I WISH YOU TO PUBLISH BUT FIRST LET ME BE CLEAR THAT I PLAYED NO PART IN ANY OF THE COPY-CAT INCIDENTS THAT HAVE TAKEN PLACE USING MY NAME. HOWEVER, I COMMEND EACH AND EVERY ONE OF THEM.

UNTIL THE PEOPLE OF SCOTLAND AWAKE TO THE FACT OF THE IMPERIALISTIC UK GOVERNMENT ACTING AGAINST THEIR INTERESTS AND PURSUING MILITARISTIC AND CAPITALIST POLICIES DESIGNED ONLY TO MAINTAIN POWER OVER THEM WHILST ENRICHING THEMSELVES, MY ACTIONS WILL CONTINUE. TO THIS END I SEEK THE INCLUSION OF THE STATEMENT BELOW IN YOUR NEXT EDITION AS FOLLOWS.

"THE BOARD OF THE BBC IN LONDON HAS BEEN FILLED WITH CONSERVATIVE PROPAGANDISTS WHO HAVE TAKEN EDITORIAL CONTROL. IT IS AN ORGAN OF THE STATE THAT NO LONGER FULFILS ITS ORIGINAL PURPOSE AND I CALL ON EVERYONE WHO IS INTERESTED IN SCOTLAND BECOMING A PROGRESSIVE, TOLERANT, PEACEFUL NATION TO STOP PAYING THEIR TELEVISION LICENCES IMMEDIATELY. ONLY BY FORCING THE BBC TO ADDRESS ITS BIAS AGAINST SCOTLAND WILL SCOTS BEGIN TO HEAR OF ALL THAT IS POSITIVE IN THE NATION AND WILL NOT HAVE TO ENDURE THE HALF-TRUTHS AND OUTRIGHT LIES IT IS BEING TOLD. I AM A PEACEFUL MAN AND MY ACTIONS ARE NOT DESIGNED TO HARM ANYONE. I URGE THOSE WHO SUPPORT MY CAMPAIGN TO FOLLOW MY EXAMPLE."

MY MESSAGE ENDS HERE.
DALRIADA++

Boston laid the paper gently on the desk before him.

"Well, I don't give a flying fuck if people don't pay their TV license. The Beeb has never been the same since they stopped showing 'The Old Grey Whistle Test'." He glanced at the text once again. "So he's going to publish the statement again?"

"Seems so, sir."

Boston thought further.

"Well, there's not much we can do to stop him. Also, if this campaign becomes a civil disobedience one rather than one where shooting and bombing takes place then that's a result. MI5 won't like it but fuck them good and proper, eh?"

"As you say, sir."

"Look, Jimmy. That disn'y work if you say it every time. You need to be more selective. And you don't say it to me. You say it to the fuds you meet in the line of work who see themselves as superior to you."

"As you say, sir."

"Fuck's sake!" he said wearily. "Get this over to forensics."

He handed him the letter and shook his head at the follies of youth.

* * *

Catriona Burns took a call from the Director General for Education, Communities and Justice in the Scottish Civil Service and was discussing the incidents of the previous evening when he asked her to hold. After a muffled conversation with a third party, he returned to his call and advised that he had just been informed of a further letter having been received at the offices of the National which had been passed to the police. He apologised once more and following another smothered dialogue, told Burns that the newspaper had decided to carry the message from Dalriada urging people not to pay their television licences.

"Shit!" The Permanent Secretary silently rebuked herself. "Sorry about my intemperance, Bob. This Dalriada thing is getting out of hand. If you'll forgive me I'd better speak with the Chief

Constable. Ministers will be in a bit of a spin over this. Thanks for your call. I'll keep you abreast of developments."

The Chief was able to inform Catriona that efforts to insinuate MI5 officers into jail cells with known nationalist and anti-nuclear activists had not proved fruitful. His officers were interviewing all of those who might be expected to have information but that it appeared that Dalriada was being accurate when he wrote in his first letter of how he was working solo.

"That makes it unbelievably difficult. We have a number of officers who have been working undercover for some years in various elements of the Nationalist and anti-nuclear movement but they've not come up with anything. These independence adherents are delighted but appear to have no knowledge of what's going on. Many crimes are wrapped up by using our powers of persuasion to have associates tell us what they know. In this instance people are either immune to our blandishments or he is a lone wolf. Either way it means that we catch him in the act, wait until he makes a mistake or he walks into my office and surrenders."

"I see."

"That last possibility isn't so far fetched. Our forensic team led by Doctor Van Ossen reckons that he may *want* to be caught... hence all of the letters...but unless and until that is true, we have a real problem tracking him down. All our officers are on alert. Our traffic boys are pulling people over and conducting legal searches in the hope of unearthing something and the MOD Police and MI5 are fully engaged. And we have to remember that it's the copy-cat incidents that are now on the front page and we have very limited capability to assess the behaviours of giddy students or enthusiastic activists in advance and interrupt their plans."

"And in the meantime, the National breaks news of the third letter telling people not to pay their TV Licence."

"Indeed."

The call ended and immediately Burns asked her secretary to place a call with the Director of BBC Scotland. It took thirty minutes but a return call was received.

"Hi, Celia, we've not met but I look forward to meeting you in person soon," said Catriona.

"Absolutely. How might I help?"

"We're not unaware of the problems you've had with the rockets being fired at your offices last night and have just been advised that this chap Dalriada is now advising his followers not to pay their TV licences in Scotland."

"God! That'd blow a hole in our finances. Things are tight enough as it is."

"Can I ask how big a hole? The First Minister will be all over this."

"Sure. Last year we raised some £340 million in revenue derived from license fees in Scotland."

"And was all of that income spent in Scotland?"

"No, only some sixty-nine percent. Between you and me, that's a real beef for us. The money is syphoned south. It's all a matter of record and we're as disappointed as the average Scottish citizen but these budget decisions are made in London. For public consumption we're one big happy family and benefit enormously from the output south of the border as Scottish viewers and listeners have access to BBC iPlayer; BBC Sounds, nine national TV channels plus regional programming, ten national radio stations, forty local radio stations as well as dedicated Nations radio services."

Burns ignored the hype. "Is it the same for Northern Ireland and Wales?"

"Not exactly. They each receive eighty-nine and ninety-two percent respectively. Again, this is all out there on the web."

"What about the percentage of license evasion in Scotland at present?"

"Well, that's another thing that gets their goat down south. Up here, there's a ten percent evasion rate while in England it's six percent. Nevertheless, if this campaign takes hold it'll cause a real tightening of belts."

"Celia, you've been a real help. Thanks."

"You must pop over to Glasgow sometime and I'll give you a tour of our Scottish headquarters. Maybe you'd even allow us to interview you."

"I don't do interviews, Celia. I leave that to Ministers but I'd be delighted to come through. I'll ask my secretary to make contact."

"Then I'll see you then. Bye."

* * *

The small grocer's shop in Grantown-on-Spey was MacAskill's usual source of foodstuffs. It was lunchtime when his converted ambulance parked outside.

"Morning, Doddie."

The owner, George Brewster looked at his watch.

"You're five minutes too late, Lachie. It's now five past twelve. We're into the afternoon," he replied affably. "I don't know where the time goes. Now, what can I get you?"

"Just some milk, four rolls and a copy of today's National."

"It's just arrived, Lachie. Take a copy from the pile over there and I'll get the other stuff."

A conversation followed which covered much of the discourse Doddie had had with other customers that morning. An elderly shopper arrived offering profuse thanks to MacAskill for his thoughtfulness in leaving three trout on her doorstep a few days previously thereby ending his chat with Doddie. He left and drove to a track near the oak tree in Inverskillen whose hollow he used to send and receive messages.

"C'mon, Blaze." He walked through pine trees until he found the oak tree. As was always his practice, he circled it and crouched to establish the absence of other people in the vicinity before searching inside the hollow for its contents. A piece of paper was removed. MacAskill read it. *Jesus, this requires some thought.*

"C'mon, Blaze. I'm going to have a read and do some thinking."

He returned to the ambulance and collected his copy of the National before reaching into the glove compartment and retrieving a half bottle of Grouse whisky. Walking quietly with his dog he reached a clearing inside the forest where a large log cut earlier by his chainsaw and left on the ground allowed him to sit.

Reaching into his pocket he removed some dried meat he kept as a treat for Blaze. He fed him from the palm of his hand and instructed him to explore while he read. As if understanding every word, Blaze left him to his task and nosed around never going much beyond the perimeter of the clearing. After a while he joined MacAskill and dozed at his feet.

Of first order was his note.

RM Condor in Arbroath contacted by a Mr. Andrew Burns. His wife (your sister?) wants to reconnect. Presently living in Balmoral hotel Edinburgh. Room 314. No knowledge of your whereabouts. Ends.

"So Catriona's back in Scotland?' he murmured to himself. *It'd be nice to see her and Andy…but not up here. I'll travel down to Edinburgh.* He opened his copy of the National and turned the pages until he came upon the piece he'd been told by a postman that morning was about Dalriada. A two-page spread condemned the use of firearms and the possibility of accidents or copy-cat incidents which used weapons but nevertheless pointed out how his actions had struck a chord in Scotland and, using their own letters' page as a gauge of public opinion, how they were endorsed by those in the Nationalist, anti-nuclear and left-wing camps while incurring the opprobrium of Unionists and Conservatives.

Looks like I'm having an impact. But where do I take this now? Let it slide or take it in a new direction? As sure as the moon moves water, they'll catch me one of these days. He looked at the dog dozing at his feet and gently ruffled his neck. *And who would look after you if I was in the pokey, eh?*

He levered himself to the ground from the log and sat beside Blaze on a carpet of pine needles, unscrewed the top of his bottle and took a swig.

I've a lot to mull over.

Chapter Twenty

The morning sun came through the half-open Venetian blinds in golden bars and welcomed Isla to another day. Yawning, she sat up in bed, tousled her hair and went downstairs to her mother's bedroom. Empty due to her mother's hospitalisation, the room looked cramped and busy with photographs, cushions and piles of books that awaited attention. *Right...a shower, then I straighten this room up, get some fresh air and go to Inverness to see mother.*

Two hours later, as she was about to embark upon her journey to Inverness, MacAskill pulled up outside and stepped down from his cabin with Blaze jumping out after him. She met him outside with a wide smile on her face,

"Well, Mr. MacAskill. To what do we owe this visit?"

"I was just going to visit Lady Helen in Inverness and wondered if you wanted me to take anything up to her."

"Actually, I was just about to leave to go there myself. She has mail...and..."

MacAskill patted Rory who had joined them.

"Well, it'd make sense for us to travel together. Will we take the Tardis? It'd give the dogs more room."

"Sure. Do you want to give me the guided tour first? You've promised me at least three times."

Grinning, MacAskill gestured towards the rear door and Isla stepped inside.

"Wow, Lachie...it's fabulous."

"Warm, too. I took the innards out but kept the electrics. Put insulation everywhere then attached a pine finishing to interior wooden battens. It's lighter in colour than heavier woods. Helps the milage. Made a bed, sink, cooking area, storage, a swing-out table and a couple of comfortable chairs...one for me and one for Blaze. I have two solar panels on the roof and every so often

I boost the battery using power from the cottage but I can cope quite easily from solar. That small fridge there uses a lot of power as it needs to be on all the time so I regulate it with a timer and it keeps things cool enough without being able to chill anything but my needs are simple so it's no hardship. A wee rug in the middle of the floor and it's home sweet home. Most nights I sleep in the Tardis but sometimes I use the cottage. To be honest, that's largely to make your mum happy. She was so insistent that I use it and I was happy to go along with it but it's the Tardis I enjoy most."

Isla opened a drawer next to the sink. It was used for cutlery.

"I knew it. Everything in here is immaculate and orderly. Even your cutlery drawer is organised. In mother's, we just chuck stuff together so we know which drawer to open for a fork but yours is orderly and uncluttered."

"Commando training. Everything in its place."

Isla looked around.

"And you're tall but there's loads of headroom." Her smile broadened. Well, I must say I'm impressed. It really is a mini-home and I can quite see why you enjoy its comfort coupled with its mobility. It's beautiful."

"Well, it saves drunk driving. I just roll up a few trees away from the Claymore and have no need of taxis." He stepped back towards the door. "Anyway, we'll be late for visiting hours. Do you want to sit up front? The dogs'll sleep in the back."

The thirty-mile journey sped past as Isla and MacAskill talked about their memories of schooldays, of Isla's veterinarian work and of the beauty of the Speyside countryside. Isla spoke of her phone call to Newcastle advising them of her requirement to stay in Inverskillen for a period of up to six weeks while her mother recovered.

"You never speak of your time in the Marines, Lachie. Was it an upsetting time?"

MacAskill drove some distance before responding.

"I loved the life, Isla. Simply *loved* it. I was lucky enough to meet and work with some top people, brave people. That I was promoted as Captain and told to lead them was an absolute privilege."

"Still in touch with them?"

"There are reunions all the time but I don't attend. I saw too much violence and death and although I absolutely love these guys, I find it easier to live in Inverskillen and worry about Blaze, Gus and your mother. These days, my biggest concern is whether I can chop a tree down so that it falls where I want it to fall, not whether my radio operator will live after having had his leg blown off." He drove on again in silence as Isla attempted to assemble her next question. After a hesitation, MacAskill continued. "There are four or five of us who meet up maybe once or twice a year. All Scots. I've another ex-colleague who lives in the Highlands. He does the odd wee thing for me and will drop off any urgent messages. I don't have a phone on purpose. When we meet, there's a rule that we don't talk about 3 Commando Brigade Air Squadron and the boys hold to their promise. It's great meeting up but I don't sleep for nights afterwards as the memories of warfare play out too vividly in my mind so it's a trade-off. I love seeing the guys but hate the aftermath as it were."

"It must have been so difficult for you, Lachie."

"These guys have made it clear that they'd do anything for me...and me, them. We were a solid unit in Afghanistan and remain so today but I make it easy for them and lead a simple life that doesn't need any supports."

"We all need help sometime, Lachie"

"Well, I've never needed anything but enjoy helping others, Isla. Usually it's the old folk in the village but today..." he slowed and indicated to turn right into the hospital... "it's your mum who needs assistance."

* * *

Lady Helen was sitting upright in bed when MacAskill and Isla entered her ward.

"Darling!" She placed her book on the bedspread."...And Lachie!"

"Look, I'll let you two have a chat and go and get us all a coffee. Here's some flowers. You're looking great Helen," MacAskill said over his shoulder as he exited the room.

"He's wonderful, isn't he? exclaimed Helen.

"I'm a fan, mother. He's everything you said he'd be."

"Oh...I can sense romance in the air!"

"Not again, mother. Neither of us are in the market for a partner."

Lady Helen grinned widely.

"When he took me to hospital he laid me down in that big bed of his in the ambulance. It was lovely. You should try it sometime!"

"*Mother*!" She changed the subject. "You have mail."

She handed over some letters which Lady Helen duly took to opening.

"Gas bill." She placed it aside and opened the second. "Your father's solicitors. I'll read that later. It's always boring." The third captured her attention and drew a gasp of astonishment. "Isla! It's a letter from Chanel Four! I'm speaking at a meeting of the Greens in Aviemore in a few weeks. They want to do a documentary on the improvements I've been making to Inverskillen and record my speech to the assembly for a piece they're doing in collaboration with *Norsk Rikskringkasting*, a Norwegian TV broadcaster on rewilding and eco-friendly developments in Scotland."

It took some time for MacAskill to return with the coffees. During that time, mother and daughter sparred verbally, initially about her ability to make the speech, then MacAskill and subsequently about the amount of care she'd need upon returning to the gatehouse.

MacAskill joined the debate. "I was talking to the doctor outside, Helen. He reckons you can go home tomorrow if you have family and community supports. If not, you'll be here for a while longer."

"I'm leaving *today*! I now have a speech to prepare!"

Really?" responded MacAskill.

"They want to film the work you've done on the estate, Lachie and they also want to record a speech I'm making to the Green Party in Aviemore. It's Chanel 4 and some unpronounceable Norwegian television company. I'm so *very* excited."

"Then you must prepare your speech from a hospital bed, Lady Helen," said the doctor as he elbowed his way into the room. "May I speak with you alone?"

"Certainly not, doctor...these two are...family." She beamed conspiratorially.

"Very well. You've been fortunate in that both fractures were clean breaks but you're not as young as once you were and we need to see your vitals improve. Both your heart and respiratory rate are a bit low for my liking. You suffered disequilibrium and fell due to you having a condition known as orthostatic hypotension. We've done blood tests to check hormone levels, blood sugar levels, and for infections. You've had an electrocardiogram to check your heart rhythm and function and an echocardiogram to check your heart health. Now, these won't stabilise by tomorrow but they will respond to treatment so I'll prescribe you some fludrocortisone but there are some lifestyle changes we'll discuss as well. In respect of your legs, in a while we'll get you back in and we'll replace your temporary casts with orthopaedic boots. They'll protect your broken bones and other muscular injuries of the lower legs and all being well, if you promise to behave yourself, I'll let you home in a wheelchair if your home accommodates one."

MacAskill interrupted. "I'm making a runway as we speak, doctor. It'll be ready by tomorrow and Lady Helen would then have the run of the ground floor of her house and could still get out to feed the hens outside."

"And would someone be home to help with toileting, cooking and sleeping."

"I'm home for the next six weeks, doctor," said Isla.

Lady Helen reacted favourably.

"Oh, darling, what great news. Now with both you and Lachie looking after me, how can I fail to recover quickly and completely? I have to be able to put on a performance when Chanel 4 come calling."

Standing just in front of MacAskill, Isla hoped that the uberstern face she used to quieten her mother was not witnessed.

Lady Helen smiled victoriously and sipped at her coffee.

* * *

Next to Glasgow Airport, at Inchinnan, an American company had located in Scotland to manufacture and sell valves and controls. Developing their company headquarters from scratch, they settled on a single story building which stretched almost the length of their land ownership resulting in a long, flat roofed building. As with all of the properties in Inchinnan Business Park, the company did not operate at night and relied upon an itinerant security presence to ensure protection against ne'er-do-wells.

Three members of the Glasgow branch of the Campaign for Nuclear Disarmament utilised the absence of a permanent security presence to advantage. Under cover of darkness, they drove their van into the car park of Integrated Solutions Ltd and stepped out.

"Right...remember...the roof has fourteen panels. The first and last two are yours boys. A nice CND logo with the initials CND beneath them. Two panels at each end. I use the middle eight to write my message. A free panel between me and you two, then the word 'Dalriada'." He looked skywards. "Every flight in and out of Glasgow must fly just to one side of this building. If we do this properly, neatly, mind...we get lots of publicity for the cause. Everyone landing or taking off will see our message."

So instructed, the three used the ladders they'd brought to access the roof. Some thirty minutes later their message to the world had been emblazoned on the roof of Integrated Solutions.

"Here's hoping the owners are sympathetic, if and when they find out about our message. This could be up for ages."

Returning all of the equipment to the van and checking to ensure that the cloth covering their number plates were still intact, the three drove away leaving no sign of their presence other than from above.

* * *

The location chosen was the quiet ambience of a deep-carpeted meeting room in the Raddison Hotel in central Glasgow. Simon Thorpe had called his team together with the representatives of the other forces of law and order who had attended the earlier convened MI5 meeting some days previously. Once again, Gus Darroch was slightly late and arrived uttering apologies to all in the room.

Thorpe had forsaken his usual be-suited apparel and was dressed in an open-necked blue shirt and denims. A lanyard round his neck held an identification card showing him to be a member of Her Majesty's Security Services. He stood and addressed the meeting once he was satisfied that all who were meant to be in attendance had arrived. All were men.

"Welcome. You don't know me but I've taken the trouble to get to know each one of you. A fine body of men." He repeated himself. "A fine body of men." He consulted some notes before laying them before him. "Together we've been tasked with bringing this mad bastard Dalriada to heel but so far we seems to be making something of an *arse* of it. Let me see if I'm up to speed on what's been uncovered so far." He looked at his sheaf of notes before raising his head. "Fuck all! That's what we've uncovered. Fuck *all*! This fucker has seen fit to open fire on vehicles going about their lawful business on the Queen's highway, he's taken a pot shot at the tenth in line to the throne and has stolen enough explosive to blow this hotel to kingdom come and he's set off a fucking epidemic of copy-cat embarrassments that now feature regularly in the morning's papers." He laid the papers before him. "Well, I'll tell you who's the fucking embarrassments...*you* fuckers. The cream of Scottish policing."

Slowly, Boston raised his right hand as if asking for permission to speak."

"Yeah?"

"Excuse me sir, but I'm only a sergeant in Special Branch here in Scotland and I don't know about anyone else, but I'm fair keechin' ma breeks at being spoken to so aggressively by a big hard man from London. I mean, I've dealt with gangland criminals, psychopaths, armed bank robbers even drunk Rangers players but never have I had to front up to some fuckin' nyaff from down south who thinks he can come up to Scotland, not introduce himself and insult everyone in the room."

"Look, my friend...I'm in charge of this operation..."

Boston half stood and pushed his chair back from the table. Theatrically, he sat back down and placed one leg, then the other on the large conference table round which everyone sat. In a separate move, he crossed them as if making himself more comfortable.

"Then you wire right in, my friend."

"Listen you,..."

Gus Darroch intervened.

"What's your name, officer?"

Thorpe stifled the urge to assault both Boston and Darroch then slowly answered through pressed lips.

"Simon Thorpe. MI5."

"Well, now we're off and running. My name's Gus Darroch. *Sergeant* Gus Darroch. From Grantown-on-Spey in the magnificent Highlands of Scotland. You have four colleagues whom I'm sure will introduce themselves as they speak, but Sergeant Boston is right. You might be the officer in charge but right now, the Scots round this table are saluting you with their middle finger. That wee introduction was deeply offensive, counterproductive and plays right into the stereotype that *we* up here, have of *you* down there, when *you* down there, come up *here*. Now it's your shout, but if I was you, I'd start again and I'd play nice."

Boston decided to be helpful.

"Aye...I mean, I'm no' an expert in cactus...but I know a prick when I see one. I'm no' a proctologist but I know an arsehole when I see one."

Thorpe, now red in the face, began to explode.

"Listen..."

One of his team, Bill Morton intervened, emphasising his Scottish accent.

"Boss!" He allowed a beat. "We're in Scotland. These guys are our hosts. Let's not be an arse."

He leaned forward, crossed his hands and spoke directly to Boston who still sat back with his feet on the table.

"My name is Bill Morton, Security Service. We are here today in fulfilment of our mission to keep the country safe. What the boss is *trying* to convey is that MI5 is anxious to secure the enthusiastic support of the Scottish forces who know far more than we do about this guy Dalriada. We've all been tasked with finding him, arresting him and seeing him put away. MI5 is keenly aware that it cannot do this without assistance...*your* assistance. In his defence, I should point out that the boss is unparalleled in his record of success. He can be, as we've seen, a little to the point, but I assure you, he delivers. He has the vocabulary of a semi-well-educated sailor, but he *delivers*!"

Boston ostentatiously removed both feet from the table and spoke to Morton.

"Where you from, pal?"

"Coatbridge via Dumfries and Galloway Constabulary." He nodded in the direction of a second member of Thorpe's team. "On my right here's Tam Geddes. From Edinburgh via Herriot Watt rugby maniacs or something or other. He can kill a man with a spoon. We're not all London gentry although this two are." He directed attention to two rather large individuals who sat on either side of Morton and Geddes.

A silence prevailed. Wearily, Van Ossen attempted to bring the conversation round to the matter in hand.

"My name is Dr. Edwin van Ossen. I'm half Dutch for what it's worth. Might it be useful to all of us if I summarise the forensic findings thus far?"

Thorpe held Boston's gaze in a manner that suggested instant extirpation. Slowly he enunciated his words and responded to Ossen.

"Please do."

Chapter Twenty-one

The letters' editor in the National was handed an unopened envelope atop a sheaf of opened letters.

"Mailroom says it looks like the envelopes and writing used by Dalriada," said the young lady who brought it to him. "Mailroom says they've been told by Special Branch to take it to them unopened."

"Aye, well mailroom can whistle. It's an offence against some Royal Mail ordinance not to read mail addressed to you, or something. Anyway, I'm going to have a wee keek inside."

In a small concession to an earlier instruction by Colin Boston, he donned a pair of latex gloves helpfully left by the sergeant and using a letter opener, slit open the envelope.

"Let's see."

He unfolded the letter.

SIR

THANK YOU FOR PUBLISHING MY LAST STATEMENT. I NOW HAVE ANOTHER I WOULD LIKE TO READ IN YOUR COLUMNS.

'SCOTLAND IS USED AS TARGET PRACTICE BY WARSHIPS AND AIRCRAFT WHICH SEND LIVE, ONE THOUSAND POUND BOMBS AGAINST TARGETS ON SCOTTISH SOIL. CAPE WRATH AND TAIN ARE ROUTINELY POUNDED BY THE UK MILITARY. LUCE BAY HAS ALSO BEEN TARGETED. NUCLEAR AND RADIOLOGICAL MATTER AS WELL AS POISONOUS AND CONVENTIONAL EXPLOSIVES HAVE BEEN AND CONTINUE TO BE DUMPED IN DOUNREAY, GRUINARD ISLAND, THE WESTERN CONTINENTAL SHELF, COULPORT, THE ROYAL ORDNANCE FACTORY AT BISHOPTON AND BEAUFORT'S DYKE.

AT DEFENCE MUNITIONS SITES IN SCOTLAND AT CROMBIE, BEITH AND GLEN DOUGLAS, MILITARY MUNITIONS IN GREAT QUANTITIES ARE STORED PRIOR TO BEING USED OR SOLD ABROAD IN WARS AGAINST THOSE WITH WHOM THE PEOPLE OF SCOTLAND HAVE NO ARGUMENT. I INTEND TO ACT AGAINST ONE OF THESE SITES IN ORDER TO DRAW THE ATTENTION OF THE SCOTTISH PEOPLE TO THE RISK OF DEATH, CONTAMINATION AND THE STERILISATION OF SCOTTISH LAND.

I CONTINUE TO THANK THOSE WHO ACT IN DEFIANCE OF THE STATE AND ASK AGAIN THAT THEY DO SO WITHOUT HARM TO ANOTHER INDIVIDUAL.'

MY MESSAGE ENDS HERE.
ALBA GU BRÀTH.
DALRIADA++

"Christ, this is a brammer! Front page stuff."

He shouted over to the editor who was busily engaged in clearing an article on a BBC calumny.

"Archie. You need to see this."

He took his mobile phone from his pocket, laid the letter flat and photographed it three times. Checking to make sure each one had worked, he folded the letter again and re-inserted it in the envelope. Inspecting each of the photographs in turn, he e-mailed them to himself as backup and searched his desktop for the card left by Boston which had his phone number.

Editor Archie Gillespie accepted the mobile phone and scrolled the image, reading Dalriada's message.

"Will I get Special Branch off our backs, Archie?"

"Aye."

He dialled from his desk and Boston answered immediately.

"Sergeant Boston!"

"Hi, it's Eddie Andrews over at the National. We've got another letter from Dalriada."

"Are you certain it's him?"

"As sure as my arse points south!"

"Is it opened?"

"Aye, we didn't realise it was him until we read the letter."

Boston sighed.

"Are you going to publish?"

"You bet your sweet bippy!"

* * *

Thorpe grinned as he read a transcript of the letter sent by Dalriada to the National. He turned to his number two, Bill Morton.

"This ups the stakes!" He handed the paper to Morton with one hand, lifting the phone receiver on his desk with the other. He tapped in numbers to the keypad and awaited connection to Jack Strachan, Deputy Director of MI5, growling at the secretary who answered he was put through before changing his tone as his superior answered.

"Thorpe here. Have you seen the latest from Dalriada?"

"Not yet."

"He's directly challenged our military. He's sent out a list of sites in Scotland we're using to train our airmen and soldiers, dump munitions or where we store explosives. He has stated that he intends to act against one of them. We need to use this boast to hunt him down and remove him."

"And we do this how?"

"We have our elite troops, there's about six hundred of them at the last count...the 22 Special Air Service Regiment, our beloved SAS, sitting on their backsides in RAF Credenhill over in Herefordshire. They are usually bored out of their tiny minds and looking for something to do. I say, why not deploy them? We have a number of sites open to this terrorist all over Scotland and can't hope to police them using conventional security measures. Most of these sites are located in the middle of nowhere and I need the SAS on the hills surrounding these facilities waiting for this separatist to make a move. When he does, they hold him and I take over."

Strachan allowed some seconds to pass before responding.

"I want to see a copy of the letter you refer to. If it is as you say, I'll clear it with the Director General but we'll need the okay from the Home Office and probably the Ministry of Defence. I know Major General Jimmy Smith personally, he's Director, Special Forces and if we get the nod, I'll brief him personally."

"That would be most helpful. I await your call."

* * *

MacAskill and Isla were returning from another visit to Raigmore Hospital where it had been decided to invite Lady Helen to stay for a further couple of days to see her vital signs stabilise.

"It's for the best, Isla. I know your mum would dearly love to be back home but 'the doctor knows best', as they say."

"Yeah. That short runway you've built at the front door will allow her to get in and out with a wheelchair or a walking frame. She'd go nuts if she couldn't get out of the house. A wee trip to collect some eggs or tend some of the flowers at the door will do her the world of good but another day or two in hospital wouldn't hurt."

The conversation continued amiably as they progressed towards Inverskillen. Suddenly, MacAskill applied the brakes and pulled the vehicle in to the side of the road.

"Shit! Wait here," he instructed gruffly as he alighted.

Isla was somewhat surprised at his abrupt exit and watched in some surprise as he vaulted a substantial fence in a single, easy leap and broke into a trot. As she watched him running across an open field, a flash of scarlet could be seen behind a copse before him. Half-way across, he stooped and collected something resembling a small droopy carpet from the grass. Moments later as MacAskill arrived at the edge of the wood, a horseman wearing fox-hunting livery emerged and engaged MacAskill in an exchange. Isla's brows furrowed as the horseman leaned forward in his saddle and attempted to strike a blow at MacAskill with his horse whip. Catching it deftly in his right hand, he pulled downwards and unseated the horseman who fell at MacAskill's feet. Swiftly, MacAskill knelt on the man's chest and in a singular movement removed his attacker's trouser belt, turned him over so he was prone, and bound the man's hands behind him with the ligature. Now kneeling on the huntsman's back, he raised the hem of his waxed jacket and took a lengthy knife from its sheath. Unthinkingly, Isla's hands flew to her mouth in horror at what she imagined was about to occur. Rather than shed blood, MacAskill placed the blade of the knife inside the man's trousers and cut downwards at the waistband before tugging and baring the huntsman's buttocks. Two paces to his right and two muscular strikes allowed him to cut two long branches from a nearby pine tree. Standing now with his boot on the shoulder blades of the downed man in order to immobilise him, he used his large knife to trim smaller branches from each limb then sharpened one end of each bough. Content that he now had the devices he wanted, he screwed one of them deep into the turf between the man's legs at his groin just above his lowered riding breeches and did the same with the second branch, this time locating it under his right armpit thereby inhibiting any movement. Finally, he lifted the bloody remains of the fox he'd collected from the field, whose body had been rent asunder by the hunter's hounds, and wiped its entrails liberally over the fox-hunters' exposed rear. As he turned and began to run back to the ambulance, he stopped, retraced his steps and reaching into his rear pocket, removed a piece of card and placed it between the man's buttocks.

Isla was incredulous as he jumped back into the driver's seat.

"Lachie! What on earth just happened there?"

MacAskill looked in his wing mirror, then over his shoulder making sure it was safe to pull out, then did so.

"The law in Scotland is that fox hunting with dogs is illegal but there's a loophole. It bans *intentional* hunting with dogs but permits the use of packs of dogs to flush out foxes as long as the *intention* is to shoot the fox before it is ripped to shreds. That man pinned to the ground in the field there is Alfred Carling. He's master of the hounds on the Glenlora Estate. He routinely ignores the law and sets his hounds upon foxes. Well, shortly the chasing hunt'll return. I could hear them howling a couple of fields away. When they get the scent they'll take an interest in that bastard's arse. I've had to watch him from afar as every time I've seen his cruelty I've been on foot. Today I wasn't."

Isla reached out and placed her hand on MacAskill's shoulder, squeezing it.

"The more I find out about you, Lachie MacAskill, the more I like you. I'm a member of the League Against Cruel Sports in the North of England and loathe fox-hunting. If I'd been in that field with you, those stakes would have been driven through his black heart!"

MacAskill smiled self-consciously. "I can't stand cruelty. Humanity seems to have more than its fair share of knuckle-dragging, heartless brutes! They start with using fireworks to blow up frogs in jars, graduate to foxes and before you know it, they're mowing down a group of villagers for having the audacity to live in an area the powers that be would like cleared of what they call insurgents or terrorists or guerrillas but are really just villagers." He struggled to contain his emotions as his smile, replaced by indignation, now turned to a glower.

"But I made a mistake. A *big* mistake!"

"What?"

He shook his head and allowed a silence as he mulled over his actions. Eventually he found his voice.

"Can't tell you...but it's a brammer!"

"What, Lachie? You're scaring me."

MacAskill answered despite telling himself not to.

"I left a calling card. It identifies me."

"Well, that's not a problem. I witnessed the whole thing. He tried to assault you and had clearly broken the law. I'd testify on a stack of bibles."

"Not that!...I'd be of interest to the authorities...for other reasons."

"You're still scaring me, Lachie! What other reasons!"

MacAskill drove on without answering Isla's question. Eventually, she attempted to prompt a response.

"Lachie!"

Further silence.

"Lachie! What other reasons?"

MacAskill partly surrendered. He held Isla's gaze as the ambulance was stopped at a halt sign on the country road preparing to turn left towards the village.

"Can't tell you.... but somewhere in Glasgow tomorrow, someone will probably be pinning my photograph to a wall."

Chapter Twenty-two

With no quiz scheduled, the juke box in the Claymore was patronised as the sole entertainment available to customers that evening. At nine o'clock, Gus Darroch entered to the sounds of Aly Bain and Phil Cunningham playing *'Charlie Hunter's Jig'* and his smile broadened as he saw his friend Lachie MacAskill seated at the fire with Blaze.

"Wasn't sure if you'd be in tonight, Lachie."

"We made no such arrangement, Sergeant Darroch. I'm just here on my tod. I decided to throw some drink at my face and have a wee think to myself about stuff I'm thinking about."

Darroch smiled.

"How much have you had to drink, Lachie? You look like a 1945 aerial view of Dresden."

"Several, eh, several...quite a lot, Gus."

"And what's brought this on, my friend."

MacAskill looked earnestly at Darroch."

"I'm an arse, Gus."

"Jesus, I've known that since Christ left Dumbarton on a sailboat."

"Aye, but, am urr..." He decided to use instead the Queen's English and corrected his use of broad Scots'. "But I *am*." He raised his voice to attract the attention of John the barman. "Haw...John! A Guinness for this off-duty polis here." Acknowledging his befuddlement to himself, he attempted to change the subject. "So... you were staying over in Glasgow last night, you were saying. Good visit?"

"Great hotel, by the way. The Raddison. The only thing that was left in my mini-bar was the fucking Toblerone. Back down to discuss this Dalriada fellah. Fuck me, the boys up from London are gung-ho to hang his bollocks from a tree."

MacAskill struggled to maintain some measure of composure.

"Have you guys no' caught him yet?"

"Naw...He's good, Lachie. He's got MI5 tied in knots and half of Scotland out on the streets proclaiming him President of the Republic of an Independent Scotland. The London boys are super-pissed." He accepted the pint of Guinness from John the barman who had begun to pour it before MacAskill had ordered it. "So, anyway...what's got you throwing drink at your face and having a wee think to yourself about stuff you're thinking about?"

"Between you and me?"

"Fuck off, Lachie. It's Gus you're talking to. Of *course* it's between you and me."

MacAskill took a long draught of his Belhaven Best and summoned up the courage to speak further.

"You know me, Gus..."

Another long swallow followed.

"Fuck's sake, Lachie."

"You know me, Gus. I like my own company...I like Inverskillen...I like the...anyway...everything's great..."

"You're having a wee think to yourself about stuff you're thinking about..and it's how you like your own company?"

"No..." A third quantity of Belhaven was quaffed followed by a long hesitation. "I was kind of thinking that maybe there's a possibility that I might like Isla Wishart."

Darroch roared with laughter. "Aye well, I think that maybe there's a possibility that Isla Wishart might like *you*."

"Really?"

"Really! It's plain to see, Lachie. It was plain to see the first time she came in here and accused you of pulling her pigtails in primary school."

"Aye...I kind of thought that as well, Gus. But I don't know..."

"Lachie! She's a lovely girl and she's clearly taken with you in my opinion."

"Aye, she's quite nice...but that's not *it*, Gus."

"Well, what's *it*, my friend?"

"I've made mistakes in life, Gus. Mistakes. When I allow emotion to supersede rationality..." More beer was consumed as Darroch waited patiently for an explanation. "Now...I am not at liberty to tell you anything about these mistakes but I'm at a crossroads, my friend. Either I settle for the possibility of maybe there being a slight chance of..."

"Jesus, Lachie! Fuckin' spit it out and I'll read it!" interrupted Darroch.

MacAskill found confidence.

"Look, I might like the lassie but I'm involved in stuff that has to remain top secret between me and the world, right?"

"Fuck's sake, Lachie. You involved with the security services?"

Seeing a way out of his dilemma, MacAskill allowed the proposition, grimacing the possibility of Darroch's assumption.

"You know I can't talk about it, eh?"

Darroch sat back in his chair.

"You are a fucking conundrum, MacAskill. A fucking mystery. An enigma. You reach exalted heights in the Commandos, get a field promotion to Captain, you're a war hero who decides they'd had enough and retires to Inverskillen, and all this time you're an undercover agent for whoever the fuck you're an undercover agent for?"

"You know I can't talk about it, eh?" MacAskill slurred.

"So your dilemma is that you don't want to advance things with Isla because you might be caught up in things that take you away for a while or put you in harm's way or..."

"Aye...somethin' like that."

"Well, your best friend's best advice is to do what makes you happy."

"Aye, but that's my problem, Gus...they both do! And now my big sister is back from Japan..."

"Catriona's back home?"

"Well, in Edinburgh with her man, Andy, a good guy... I'm going down to see them on Saturday night. So that's someone else back in my life..."

"Having friends and family around you is most important, Lachie. Let someone else fight the good fight."

"Aye, well, we'll see, Gus. We'll see."

* * *

Thorpe picked up the phone.

"Thorpe!"

"Jack Strachan. I've read the Dalriada letter and have the nod from everyone who matters. The SAS will be deployed according to the assessments made by Director, Security Forces and will be concealed around ten sites suggested in the letter. They're sending a unit of forty men from Secret Intelligence Service Operations and they sound formidable. They're formed from contingents from other elite units including the Special Boat Service, the Joint Support Group and the Special Reconnaissance Regiment and are all trained in Black Ops so I wouldn't give your man Dalriada much chance against them. And incidentally, your notion that they'd be delighted to get some kind of action hasn't gone down too well. These boys are trained to lie in a cold muddy puddle for three days just so they can pull a trigger and send someone to meet their maker but using forty of them to lie in wait for one person who is most unlikely to turn up at their location is not, I repeat, *not* as enticing as playing darts in their recreation and fitness centre."

"Tough luck! And when are they being deployed?"

"They are already on their way and we can expect them to be in position by tonight. They've selected ten potential targets. SAS men will be deployed to safeguard each target. The initial deployment is expected to last for a week but we'll review it after four days. The Minister's view is that we can't allow this fellow Dalriada to make a fool of us by announcing an attack then carrying it out successfully. Each and every one of the possible sites he mentioned in Scotland will be protected other than those at sea. They have permission to use lethal force if circumstances require it."

"That's a mistake, sir. We need to disappear this bastard. If he's shot, half the population of Scotland will turn up at his funeral to see him come down from the cross. He'll be an absolute martyr. The instruction must be to arrest and hold until I arrive. He'll disappear without trace and people will soon forget his antics."

"You may have a point. I'll make another call."

Thorpe ended the conversation and walked to the open door of his office. Putting his head out into a corridor he shouted to attract the attention of his fellow MI5 colleague, Bill Morton.

"Bill! Do you still have that old guy, McCalliog downstairs?"

A disembodied voice replied, "Aye, he's still in a cell but he's not talking."

"Okay, I'll have a go."

Thorpe returned to his office and opened a large bag containing his change of clothes, medicaments and bathroom accessories. Feeling beneath the clothes, he pulled out a brown paper parcel and unwrapped it then, pulling on latex gloves, he took the metal and plastic device he'd uncovered and walked down to the detention suite in which McCalliog was being held. He nodded to a young police officer.

"Bring McCalliog to the briefing room please."

A few minutes later, Forbes McCalliog shuffled into the room to see Thorpe sitting at the far end of a table.

"Ah, Mr. McCalliog. Come and sit by me." He patted a buff folder he had in front of him. "I've been reading all about you. You're quite something. In your younger days you must have been quite a handful for the forces of law and order." Smiling, he opened the folder and read from its contents. "The Scottish National Liberation Army...letter-bombs...attempting to poison the water supply of Greater Manchester. Quite the rebel...quite the revolutionary, eh?"

McCalliog was silent and apparently unmoved.

"But now you're eighty-four according to this file and you're past it but I'd bet my last English pound sterling that you know something about this Dalriada fellow who is making all the headlines, eh? I'm pretty sure that someone with your pedigree in Scotland's fight for its freedom knows where most of the bodies are buried." His tone turned to a more teasing aspect. "That what you're doing, Forbes, eh? Fighting for Scotland's freedom, eh?"

McCalliog remained silent.

"You been trained to say nothing, Forbes?" He moved the buff folder aside revealing the black metal and plastic device he'd brought with him.

"Now, this here may persuade you to talk to me. You see, it'll put you behind bars unless you become my friend."

He pushed it slowly in front of McCalliog.

"Now, you tell me what it says on the bottom."

Puzzled, McCalliog lifted, then turned over what he then recognised was a hard drive from a computer. Warily he inspected the device and brought it right side up before placing it back on the table.

"You've lost me."

"Well, Forbes, my old friend, let me take that back from you." He pulled the hard drive back before him. "Now, an experienced man like yourself would recognise that there are no witnesses in this room...no cameras in this room...there are no listening devices in this room because this is a room that's used to brief officers, not one in which we interrogate people who used to belong to the Scottish National Liberation Army. If you're as experienced as I know you to be, you'll also have observed that I am wearing latex gloves and have been since we sat down. Now, the only fingerprints that are presently on that hard drive are yours, and the contents of the aforementioned hard drive, I assure you, contain some of the most vicious, disgusting and frankly illegal child pornography it's ever been my misfortune to view. You're not a paedophile, are you Forbes? You don't enjoy sex with little boys do you? Because now that you own this hard drive, you're looking at spending the rest of what short time you have left on this earth in prison.

Now, we might not take this to court...deprive you of the ability to seek the oxygen of publicity in front of a judge. No, we might merely bail you but let your neighbours and the more scurrilous newspapers know unofficially that you're a fucking pederast and that those who live near you should apply for a court order keeping you from their children. And if and when the media get in touch, we just tell them that we do not comment on an ongoing investigation."

He sat back in his chair, his smile widening. "And that's it, Mr. McCalliog. You go to your grave not as a Scottish patriot and a proud grandfather but as an evil old pervert...unless of course, you tell me everything I want to know."

McCalliog's head slumped. He clasped his hands in front of him and slowly raised his head until he met the smiling gaze of his interlocutor. He was careful in his enunciation.

"Go...Fuck...Yourself!"

Chapter Twenty-three

Isla was driving to the village for a morning's stint as an unpaid but enthusiastic locum in Donald Brodie's veterinarian practice. The sunny weather that had prevailed over the previous month had changed and rain fell in a torrent like descending hyphens, spattering the road. It had begun quietly with nothing visible except tall dark clouds and a wind that increased in ferocity. A soft murmur of thunder had been but a prelude to sheet lightning. As her windscreen wipers struggled to shed the downpour, she recognised the bedraggled form of Lachie MacAskill in shorts and a tee-shirt as he ran on the opposite side of the road towards her. She slowed, stopped, lowered her driver's window, and shouted.

"Hi, Lachie. Are you running or swimming?"

MacAskill checked behind him for vehicles and jogged across to the Land Rover.

"Hi Isla, Nearly finished my morning run. Sixteen miles," he said, still breathless. "You off to the vet's?" He leaned lightly on the bonnet of the car.

Isla retreated slightly, grimacing at the force of the rain.

"Yeah. Then off to Inverness to see mother. They're saying they'll bring her home to Inverskillen in an ambulance later today...not as good as yours I'm sure," she smiled. "You going to the Claymore tonight?"

MacAskill shook his head. "No. I'm off to Edinburgh. I've a long-lost sister who's been working abroad...in Japan. Now her and her man are back in Scotland and made contact so I called them back and I'm off to meet them tonight. Must be six or seven years since we've met."

"Lachie, that'll be lovely. I'd forgotten about your sister. She was a few years older than us. You'll have a lovely evening."

"S'pect so." He stepped back from the Land Rover. "I'll get on my way. When I'm back tomorrow I'll pop round to see Lady Helen and check in case there's anything I can do to help."

"It would be lovely to see you, Lachie and mother will be delighted. She really was so very grateful to you for your prompt action when she fell."

MacAskill dismissed the warm words.

"One mile left. See you."

MacAskill checked the road again, waved farewell and recommenced his run.

Isla watched him disappear into the mist through her rear view mirror. *Lachie MacAskill is a wonderful man. A wonderful, caring, complex, tortured man...with, it has to be said once again, a simply delightful arse!*

* * *

Thorpe stepped out into the corridor connecting him with his number two, Bill Morton.

"Bill, heads up. I need you to leave immediately for Inverness."

"Sure, boss. What's up?"

"Dalriada might just have made his first mistake. He's apparently assaulted a guy called Alfred Carling, Master of the Hounds on an estate up near Inverness. The guy's in hospital with wounds to his nether-regions after being mauled by his own dogs but he's complained to police that he was set upon, tied and assaulted by someone who left a calling card sticking out of his arse. It just read, 'Dalriada'."

"Jesus! Sounds promising."

"I need verification that the card is the same as the others and we need a description of this person. This might just be the break we were looking for." He allowed a measure of realism. "Just your initial impression then get it off to forensic for confirmation. If it's a copy-cat incident we're no further forward."

"I'm on my way."

"Oh, before you go, set that old guy McCalliog free. He probably knows nothing and even if he does we'd need to disembowel him with a soup spoon before he'd give us the time of day."

He handed Morton the hard disc.

"And while you're at it would you take the prints off this, clean it and return it to my desk print-free?"

"Sure boss. What is it?"

"It's something I use from time to time to encourage people to tell me information they'd rather keep to themselves, essentially a rank bad, illegal collection of child porn I took from a dirty old bastard down in Walthamstow. Once I have someone's prints on it, they're mine!"

Morton looked at the retreating figure of Thorpe as he returned to his office, but kept his counsel to himself.

***

Boston and Boyd sat once again in front of the whiteboard in a briefing room. They were joined by Doctor Van Ossen.

"Okay," commenced Boston. "Let's see where we've got to on this Dalriada stuff." He stood and approached the whiteboard.

"Doc, tell us what we know and what we don't know."

"Well, we are still in the dark regarding the paper, pen and ink used to communicate with us. His handwriting is now well known to us but has been very effectively camouflaged."

"So, nothing there."

"Not quite. We can now clearly identify communications from him as verifiably being from him."

"Okay, so..." He wrote on the whiteboard as he spoke... "Ability to identify and ignore copy-cat communication."

"Also," he continued, "when my forensic team revisited the site from which Dalriada shot at the nuclear vehicles, they found no footprints but did find traces of *Pinus Sylvestris Beuvronensis* which is a shrub form of Scots Pine, recognised by its bluish-green needles. Interestingly, this species is very uncommon in the southern part of Argyll but is very much more prevalent in the Highland region. It grows naturally in Scotland and its altitudinal range is from sea level to just about any height on Scotland's higher mountains. While it is Scotland's national tree and is a native of the once extensive Caledonian pine forests, it finds the harsher northern conditions more to its taste as it possesses an ability to regenerate and thrive in poor soils. So...the debris left by Dalriada might suggest that he travelled to south Argyll from up north somewhere...or perhaps works in a garden centre."

Boston continued writing.

"Okay, what else?"

"We are confident that Dalriada is male, Scottish, possibly from the west, educated, a supporter of Scottish Independence, anti-the Royal Family, nuclear weaponry...and apparently now as a consequence of his latest letter, the armed forces." He consulted his notes. "He is no stranger to firearms, is resourceful and may have a size nine shoe. Finally, he has a familiarity with Scots' Gaelic."

"He might be bi-lingual, boss," added Boyd.

"Christ, that's good coming from someone who's barely lingual!"

Boston ended the list and drew a line across the board.

"However, we hear today that the firemen stationed in Faslane have gone on strike due to proposals to cut back on their numbers. This has been brewing for a while so might our man be a disenchanted fireman?" He wrote the word 'Fireman?' on the board. "We know he's handy with a rifle so..." He wrote the word 'Soldier?' on the board. "And we imagine he might have seen service in uniform...maybe as a cop...so..." He wrote the words 'Police Officer?' on the board. "Now you tell us he might work in a garden centre or, and I'm surmising here...maybe the Forestry Commission?" The words 'Garden Centre?' and 'Lumberjack?' were introduced.

"Don't know if you call them lumberjacks in Scotland, boss. Do we not just call them forestry workers?"

"We know what we mean, Jimmy. Don't split hairs. If I gave you a penny for your thoughts, I'd get change."

Van Ossen reclaimed the conch.

"It might also be worth noting that two of the incidents took place on Speyside, up in the Highlands. Marry this with the Scots

Pine discovery and perhaps we're looking for someone who hails from that region of Scotland or at least knows it well."

"Could be, Doctor." The word 'Highlander?' was added.

As Boston began writing this information on the board, the door opened and a young policeman handed a note to Jimmy Boyd who read it and, once he'd absorbed the information, exhaled loudly.

"Boss...a note from the Chief Super. There's been an incident just south of Inverness. Apparently a fox hunter was attacked and assaulted by someone who tied him up then stuck a card with the word 'Dalriada' in the crack of his arse. MI5 are heading up there as we speak. The verbal description of the writing the boss got suggests it's genuine."

Boston froze for all of a few seconds as he assimilated the information. Then he was all-action.

"Get your coat Jimmy. It can get cold up there." He turned to Van Ossen. "Thanks, Doc. Especially that bit about the Highlands. Looks like you might have hit the jackpot. We're off to Inverness."

As both men rushed from the room, Van Ossen rose wearily, lifted the ink marker used by Boston and underneath his words, 'Hates Armed Forces?' wrote, 'and Fox-hunters?'.

Chapter Twenty-four

From the breast pocket of his jacket, Boston removed the business card given him by Morton and read the mobile phone number set against his name. Urging Boyd to get a move on while he manipulated his phone, he dialled the number which triggered Morton's speakerphone.

"Morton."

"Hi Bill, it's Colin Boston here. Special Branch. I gather you people are on your way to Inverness to interview this guy who might be able to give us a description of Dalriada?"

"Hi, Colin. Yeah, I'm on my way."

"Do you not think it might be better if we travelled as a unit? Saves petrol…lets us talk tactics…shows collaboration?"

Morton smiled. "Sounds sensible. Where are you?"

"Just approaching Cumbernauld on the M80."

"Okay. I'm up ahead. I'll pull over at the Moto Service Station just off the M80 and meet you there. You alone?"

"No. Jimmy Boyd's driving."

"Too many cooks. Boyd can return to Glasgow. I'll drive us there and back. Just you and me."

"It's a deal. See you shortly."

Boyd protested. "But boss…"

"Big boys' business, son. You drop me off then get back the office to do some filing or whatever you do when you're not annoying me."

* * *

Just as Morton and Boston were speeding north along the A9, MacAskill's ambulance was making steady progress on the A9 south to Edinburgh. Afternoon summer sunshine had returned to Scotland and as he drove south, MacAskill was in pensive mood.

It'll be nice to see Catriona again. Haven't seen her since dad passed. She was always a sweetheart and she seemed to be happy in her career and in her marriage to Andy. No kids but for all I know she has a brood now although she was always a career girl. Nice to share a pint with Andy as well. He was a nice guy. He drove onwards, his thoughts becoming slightly more solemn. *God, I simply love the simplicity of my life at the minute but I've ignored family, kept my erstwhile comrades-in-arms at a distance, forsaken joys of the flesh and now look at me...menacing the power of the Union, harbouring feelings for a woman I've only recently met, on my way to reacquaint myself with a sister I've not seen in years. I've half the forces of law and order in Scotland chasing me down just at the time when I might be tempted to change the direction of my life. Are my efforts to make Scotland safer worth the candle?* His gaze fell on a small box of magnesium powder on the passenger's seat. *Well, I've one more go tonight so let's hope I'm making a difference. Perhaps only one or two more escapades, though, eh? Maybe I can retire without troubling MI5's finest and ending up dead or in the pokey.*

* * *

Unknown to each of them, Morton's car, now driving north with Boston in the passenger's seat, passed MacAskill's ambulance heading south as their vehicles made their way past McDiarmid Park, home of St. Johnston Football Club, situated beside the A9 at Perth.

Boston thumbed his finger at the football ground.

"See that? That started a revolution, by the way. Did you know that?"

Keeping his eyes on the road, Morton barely acknowledged the question.

"That, my friend, is the first all-seater football stadium in the UK. The land was donated by the local farmer, Bruce McDiarmid, who chucked in sixteen acres of his farm on condition that the club name the stadium after him. The man was a pioneer, so he was...a pioneer!"

"St. Johnston fan then?"

"Man and boy. Don't get to see them bar when they're on the telly now I'm in Glasgow. Great wee club."

He allowed some moments to pass before it was evident that Morton didn't intend reciprocating. Never completely comfortable in silence, Boston prompted further discussion.

"You a football fan then?"

"Rugby. I enjoy kicking people in the head in the name of sport."

"Jesus, you're a fucking natural for MI5."

"How so?"

"Everything's so aggressive. As an example...see that boss of yours? He's a right fuckin' nut job. Aggression on top of rudeness with a big helping of disrespect." He thought for a moment. "By the way, I didn't thank you properly for calming him down at thon meeting we had. Left to his own devices we'd all be up in court for breach of the peace right now. I can't help myself when I'm dealing with an eejit. I get all bolshy!"

"He's far from an eejit, my friend. He gets sent in to sort out all sorts of trouble world-wide and the reason he gets sent in to sort out all sorts of trouble world-wide is that he's got a one hundred per cent record...that's a one hundred per cent record...of achieving any objective set by his masters at MI5."

"So he's Mister Efficient?"

"No...he's Mister Assassin. People get hurt when they're around him. He's a dangerous man. I treat him very carefully and I'm on his fucking *team*. Trust me, you'll be on his list because you challenged him at the meeting. If he can deal with Dalriada while leaving you in a bloody heap somewhere, that'd make his fucking day. If he has his eye on you, you may as well go down and make a purchase at the rope shop, then another at the rickety stool shop and end it all because he's not one to miss an opportunity if one presents itself."

"Good to know, Bill...good to know."

They drove north, Boston doing most of the talking.

* * *

MacAskill had insisted on meeting his sister and her husband in the less salubrious surroundings of the Port O' Leith pub on Constitution Street below Leith Walk insisting that dinner in their sumptuous hotel would make him feel awkward as he only ever dressed in camouflage, denim and dowd.

"Take the mints off the pillow," Catriona had said to her husband upon hearing that her brother intended heading back north after dinner and wouldn't be staying in the put-up bed in the sitting room in their suite at the Balmoral Hotel. "Lachlan intends heading back to Grantown-on-Spey immediately we finish dinner."

At eight o'clock precisely, MacAskill walked into the pub where a table had been reserved. Shortly afterwards, his sister Catriona and her husband Andy joined him midst much hugging and smiling. Catriona gasped as her spine cracked like a book being opened for the first time, such was MacAskill's energetic welcome. Drinks were ordered along with some pub fare and the conversation flowed easily, each sibling showing astonishment at the present circumstances of the other.

"You're Scotland's top civil servant?"

"You left the military and now live in a converted ambulance?"

As it became evident that each was happy with their lot and Andy kept ordering further rounds of drinks - MacAskill confounding them by insisting on consuming only soft drinks as he had to drive later in the evening - they reminisced fondly until Catriona asked about her brother's time in Afghanistan.

MacAskill's high spirits deserted him.

"I've had my fill of warmongering. It was hard to be out there wearing a uniform I came to despise. We were being ordered to take action against what they'd refer to as insurgents. It all became so desensitised. Some of the squaddies got too caught up in it. They dehumanised the local people and saw all of them as inferior, as threats, as targets... I was lucky. I commanded a unit...a band of brothers. I loved these guys and would do anything for them... then and now. They were all mostly Jocks and several of them still stay up here in Scotland. I see them from time to time. We tried to go about our business with some measure of a moral compass but it was hard because some of the people on our side were borderline sociopaths and some of the Afghanis *were* hard-nosed killers. They were good at it. Innovative. They could dream up hundreds of ways to kill a man and I lost several soldiers who were taken out in horrible ways that even now keep me awake at night."

"It must have been awful."

"Well, I decided that I'd either eventually become as hardened to the human condition as those squaddies I detested, or I'd get out...maybe try to do something that might help compensate for all the killing and bloodshed and I was luckier than I deserved. I found an estate up in our old stomping ground in Grantown-on-Spey. You must remember the old Inverskillen Estate? Well, the owner took me under her wing. To be honest I was a broken man but she gave me a purpose, allowed me to experience peace and quiet, she gave me a cottage on the estate even though my preference is living in my ambulance. I guess it's like a safety-valve. If things ever got too much for me, I'd just sit in the front of the ambulance instead of the back and head off to my next adventure."

"Never saw you as a quitter."

MacAskill smiled.

"I'm not actually. Like I say, it's just an insurance policy. The cottage is grand. I'm still not fully back to being myself. A few weeks ago I was walking up the road to drop off a couple of trout and a wee cut of venison at an old couple's house in the village. The primary school had just come out and a wee boy behind me picked up a stick and just rattled it along a picket fence. All I heard was 'prrrrrraaaap' and the next thing I knew, I'd dived for cover and was lying prone on the pavement. Hearing what your brain tells you is an automatic weapon and protecting yourself is a nervous reaction. Never leaves you. Scared the living shit out of the wee boy, I can tell you. He was as frightened as me!"

"That's awful."

Catriona sipped at her wine and asked the question she'd been wanting to ask for some time.

"And there's no one special in your life?"

MacAskill returned her grin and offered the prepared answer he knew he'd be called on to give.

"I have a lovely dog called Blaze, I'm very fond of Lady Helen who owns Inverskillen and my best pall is Gus Darroch who's the local police sergeant."

"And is Lady Helen someone of your own age with her own teeth and trim ankles?"

MacAskill's grin widened as he forced himself to answer the supplementary question.

"She's an elderly lady whose husband died and left her the estate. I came along at the right time. Presently she's on crutches after falling down the stairs."

"Oh dear! And is she recovering well?"

"Her daughter is looking after her for a few weeks. She's a vet with a practice in Newcastle but me and Gus are trying to persuade her to take over old Donald Brodie's operation in the village. She'd be good as the village vet."

"Really...and what's her name?"

"Isla. She's nice."

"Oooh, nice enough to tempt you into a relationship? Is there a Mister Isla?"

"No, but she's way out of my league. She's a very attractive, educated professional who would have an endless queue of admirers I'm sure, whereas I'm damaged goods. A retired grunt, a woodsman who lives in an old ambulance."

Catriona held the glance of her husband.

"Andy, is it me, or has my wee brother just allowed the possibility of perhaps having feelings for a young woman?"

Now embarrassed, MacAskill took steps to change the topic back to his sister's new responsibilities.

"So what's your new job like? Hobnobbing with the great and good in Edinburgh all day?"

"I suppose so. It's genuinely fascinating. Dealing directly with the First Minister is very rewarding. Meeting captains of industry and the media moguls, such as they are in Scotland...and just dealing with anything and everything that crosses my desk. I confess I get a real buzz out of handling the various crises that happen in Scotland each and every day."

"Sounds exciting."

Warming to her subject, Catriona continued.

"Like this Dalriada person…"

MacAskill spluttered as he sipped at his glass of coke.

"He's causing chaos in Scotland right now. We have hundreds of police officers involved not only in looking for him but in marshalling the scores of copy-cat incidents and protests up and down the land that have arisen as a direct consequence of the publicity his acts of sabotage have caused. It's besieging us at the office. Every day there's another copy-cat protest, some vandalism or a march. I was informed just as I left to come here that a farmer has sprayed the entrance to the Inland Revenue's offices in East Kilbride with cow-dung. It's becoming a full scale civil disobedience emergency. He's tapped into something in Scotland that's galvanising the natives and London is most upset at the ramifications."

Recovering his composure, MacAskill empathised.

"Yeah, he must try your patience."

"Well, a forty-strong unit of the SAS have been called in. They're protecting ten of the sites he's earmarked for attack and I suspect it's only a matter of time now before he ends up jailed or dead."

"Christ," coughed MacAskill, surprised, "The SAS?"

"And MI5. And Special Branch. And Police Scotland. They're all trawling groups and organisations waiting for the clue that'll track him down before someone gets hurt."

"Aye, Gus was telling me all about it because he was first on the scene when Dalriada had a go at Prince Edward."

Catriona frowned.

"I mean apart from anything else, the cost to the public purse is astronomical."

"Surely not!" Argued MacAskill. "The cost of policing, spying on their own citizens and the army boys is a cost that'd have to be met anyway. They're all just doing what they were trained for. Surely no new money had to be found?"

"But it's the opportunity cost, Lachlan. Some of them could be down in the south-west of England helping people cope with these recent flash floods that have seen some villages washed out."

MacAskill's tone changed.

"Ach, that's what they get for living on a flood plain in houses built for profit not sustainability. One minute they're complaining about a drought, then they're complaining about floods. One minute they're telling Scots they don't have the resources to be independent, and the next they're saying that they can't cope unless they run a huge pipe from Loch Ness to West Anglia to help water their precious lawns. They have armed services all over the globe trying to pretend that Britain is still a world power. Now *they're* the astronomical costs you should be worried about! In Scotland, all that's needed are ships to protect our fishing fleet, aircraft to let us know what weather to expect and an army that prides itself in helping the United Nations maintain a peace-keeping force in world trouble spots... Just like Ireland, Norway, Sweden, Finland, Iceland...the way all the Nordic countries use their military."

Catriona replicated the same faux-surprised look towards her husband as she'd done previously.

"Wow...it looks like my wee brother is one of those Scottish Nationalist chaps we read so much about."

"I'm a member of no political party," growled MacAskill. "But I'm all for Scottish Independence. That shower down south... the ones you take your orders from...they're morally corrupt, lying, capitalist warmongers who'd sell their grannie for a tanner if they thought it might enrich them. I found the Afghanistan experience really dispiriting. If it wasn't for the opium crop, those poor Afghans would have to rely on their ability to export bloody egg-timers. It's nothing but a barren, sandy desert. A rocky, desolate country that western and Communist powers over the centuries have decided for some twisted reason they must conquer. It's been a constant foreign policy disaster, a money-pit and the graveyard of far too many men, women and weans. The sooner we're away from these bloodthirsty, militaristic eejits the better."

Andy decided to weigh in.

"I'm with Lachlan, Catriona. And to be honest, I'm with this fellow Dalriada as well. He's chosen his attacks well. Nuclear weapons, Prince Edward...and beyond him, the great unwashed have now attacked BBC Scotland and the UK Government's headquarters in Edinburgh, they've caused traffic jams in London, we've seen civil disobedience and protest marches all over Scotland...now Dalriada's attacking fox hunters..."

"Fox hunters?" MacAskill surprised himself as he almost yelped out his question.

Catriona explained.

"I was telling Andy in the taxi on the way over to Leith. We're investigating an assault on a Leader of the Hounds up near Inverness. The poor man appears to have been hospitalised after an attack by Dalriada. We're hoping he can give us a description. It'd be the first real lead we'd managed to get. The guy's damned clever but this might be his first mistake."

"Well, I hope he gets away with it," said Andy. "He's picking all the right subjects for me. And now he's targeting British arms dumps in Scotland. The man has a sixth sense of what lifts the hearts of those in Scotland who seek independence, an end to nuclear warheads, stopping conventional arms and explosives being parked or dumped on their doorstep and the ejection of a British elite which takes Scotland for granted."

Catriona, smiling, raised her arms in mock surrender.

"I give in! It looks like I have *two* Independentistas in my family. Who knew?"

* * *

Boston and Morton were admitted to the modern, pastel-painted ward in which Alfred Carling was abed. The nurse asked that they did not spend too much time with him as he required sleep. "Only a few minutes?"

Both acquiesced.

Turning his head towards his visitors as they entered, Carling pressed a button on his remote and turned off the TV news. He used his elbows to lever himself further up in his bed, grimacing in pain as he did so. Both men held their warrant cards for his inspection just sufficiently so as to inhibit much inspection but nevertheless to suggest their credentials.

"Mr. Alfred Carling?" Morton took the lead.

"It's about time! I've been horribly assaulted and was almost about to phone the Chief Constable."

Boston reacted.

"Aye sorry 'bout that. It took us a while to get up here. How's your arse?"

Morton attempted a rescue as Carling's mouth opened wordlessly at Boston's obvious impertinence.

"The nurse talked us through your injuries, Mr. Carling. It must have been a traumatic experience. Can you tell us how it happened?"

"I am Master of the Glenlora Hounds. I was conducting an entirely legal hunt when this hooligan...one of these animal welfare, anti-everything hooligans pulled me from my mount and tied me up. He then removed my riding britches and roughly smeared the entrails of a dead fox on my rear end, positioned two poles in such a way as to pin me to the ground and left me to the mercy of my own hounds."

"What did he say as he approached you?"

"From memory it was something along the lines of 'Is this fox your doing?'"

And you replied how?"

"Well, he seemed threatening so I made to hit him with my horse whip to have him stand back."

Boston intervened.

"So you struck the first blow?"

"I was quite legally engaging my right to access some of Scotland's lovely property as is set out in the Land Reform Act which gives everyone rights of access over land and inland water."

"And so, presumably was he?"

"He had an aggressive disposition."

"Did your assailant bring the fox entrails with him?"

"No. It was a fox hunted earlier in the morning." He hesitated. "Legally that is. Under Scots' Law, packs of dogs are permitted to flush out foxes as long as the intention of the hunt is to shoot the fox."

"And was this fox shot?"

"Regrettably not. Even with the best trained hounds they can sometimes become over-enthusiastic and reach the quarry before we have an opportunity to shoot."

Boston intervened once more.

"So this poor wee thing was ripped to shreds, eh?"

"As I said. It was completely legal. An unfortunate accident. I found myself removed from the hunt and was alone." Reminding himself that beyond his fox-hunting pastime he was a merchant banker more used to those around him deferring to his every whim, Carling asserted himself. "Look here, I do not appreciate your line of questioning. I was the one who was assaulted."

Morton again attempted emollience.

"Just trying to establish whether the assault was due to your fox-hunting or perhaps whether other motives were in play." He moved the conversation on. "Did the assailant speak?

"A torrent of expletives."

"Accent?"

"Local to the area."

"Can you describe him to us?"

"Tall. I'd say six feet. Muscular...wiry and muscular. Wore one of those camouflage jackets and blue denims. Unkempt red hair. A man in his thirties I'd say. Clean shaven."

"That's it?"

"Yes, I'm afraid so...actually, no...I think he had a slight scar...a wound, on his right cheek."

"Never seen him before?"

"No."

"And if we showed you photographs might you be able to identify him?"

"I'm unsure, officer. It all happened very fast and for the most part he was behind me."

Boston had decided upon entering the ward that he didn't like the man who lay in pain before him.

"Tell me, Mr. Carling. When this guy shoved his card up your arse, did you feel it was a sexual act?"

Carling spluttered his reply.

168

"Certainly not. I was not violated. For some reason the thug seems to wish apprehension and I expect you two to accommodate him."

Morton attempted to wind up the conversation.

"We'll do our best Mr. Carling. Thanks for your help. We'll leave you to get some rest. We'll have an officer come and take a formal statement from you."

Boston wasn't finished. He leaned towards the patient.

"People like you give me the creeps, Carling. And you can tell that to the Chief Constable if you want because Mr. Morton here can't hear a word I'm saying and I'd just deny it." Morton rolled his eyes. "And I read that down in England, some of the hunts actually capture and raise fox cubs so as to train their hounds by throwing these wee fox pups into their midst to train the dogs to kill. Do you do that, Carling? Do you feed wee fox puppies to your dogs so they can learn to rip them to shreds?"

"Certainly not!"

"So if officers received a complaint about your approach to animal welfare you'd be found to have a clean bill of health."

"I certainly would."

"Because I can arrange a number of visits, you know."

"I am well aware..."

Boston ignored his denials.

"I looked at the photographs of your injuries. It'll be a while before you'll be back in the saddle. That arse of yours looked painful."

"I can confirm that."

"Every cloud, eh?"

Chapter Twenty-five

Having left his sister and her husband on the pavement midst a flurry of promises to meet up again soon along with a suggestion that leaving a phone message at the Claymore Bar might be the best way to contact him other than a letter to his cottage, MacAskill headed out of a darkened Edinburgh mulling over the information she'd shared.

So they're on to me! That fox hunter is sure to give them my description. And the SAS are protecting ten bases? Well, one of them's bound to be the arsenal at Crombie. That's only four troops per base if they distribute them evenly which they won't, but they'll have to maintain a fairly tight observation close to the depot. With some luck I'll still be able to get a shot off. But they'll have night vision goggles and would see my infrared radiation signal. There'd be no hiding in the dark. He reflected further. *I'll go at first light and maintain distance. My shot had better be good but it's a big target.* He consulted a small booklet he'd earlier placed in his glove compartment and turned its pages until reaching his notes on the tidal flow of the Firth of Forth. *Actually, a dawn attack works much better. At that time, the ebb tide will ensure the tidal current is flowing seaward at its fastest rate. Much better!*

Calculating further options, MacAskill drove to Stirling and crossed the Forth in a queue of cars where it was but a river and where his journey could be made more anonymously than would have been the case had he crossed the Firth on the much closer, more modern but more public Queensferry Crossing. He drove in darkness back along the coast to the village of Torryburn, two miles from his target, turned off into a wooded area where he parked and climbing into the back of the Tardis, slept fitfully.

Defence Munitions Crombie is a military provisioning depot on the upper Firth of Forth in West Fife and is is located on the north shore of the river, south of the village of Crombie. The depot has two jetties that each jut out a a third of the way across the wide firth and which benefit from a deep water channel allowing Royal Navy warships and Royal Fleet Auxiliary replenishment vessels to moor for armament resupply. The base allows receipt, storage, maintenance, issue and distribution of conventional weapons, RAF air-launched weapons and fleet management of missiles as well as maintenance of naval mines. The Government would suffer considerable embarrassment were the site to be attacked successfully. MacAskill intended to do just that.

Waking as dawn broke, MacAskill retrieved the chemicals he'd liberated from the shooting range and took them outside the ambulance where he mixed them thoroughly in an empty plastic paint container. Satisfied, he added the small bags of magnesium powder and mixed again. *The ammonium nitrate, ammonium perchlorate and dark flake aluminium powder provides a loud bang and lots of smoke upon impact...this magnesium will ensure that there are flames as well. Should be quite an explosion if I hit it with a bullet.* Stepping back into the Tardis, he brought out a child's floating swim-ring and inflated it fully before shoving it tightly inside a string bag and tying it shut so there was some give in the net. Reaching inside the Tardis once again, he brought out a litre bottle he'd half filled earlier with petrol. Taking three polystyrene plates, he crumbled them into small pieces and fed them into the bottle. *Nearest thing to home-made Napalm once they dissolve in the petrol.* Placing the swim-ring on the ground, he lifted the round explosives' container and placed it in the middle checking that the mesh net took its weight and allowed the drum to sit comfortably within its walls. Tucking the bottle of polystyrene-infused petrol inside the net, he checked the sturdiness of the improvised explosive device and reassured, dismantled the various elements. Holding the valve of the swim-ring, he pinched it, deflating the device then placed all parts of the the assemblage carefully inside his rucksack.

It was light now as MacAskill set off for the shoreline accompanied by morning birdsong. A grey haze hovered over the firth awaiting the warmth of the sun. A tractor path led him down past some fields where sheep grazed idly. A road followed the contour of the firth towards Torryburn but this was eschewed by MacAskill who continued to the water's edge and continued his walk along the shoreline towards an old quay, long disused and built solidly of rubble which rose some six feet from the water and continued out into the firth for perhaps one hundred yards. Walking along its western length at the level of the water lapping at its base, he was completely hidden from anyone scanning the area from the munitions depot although exposed to a tug more than a mile in the distance which chugged towards his position, heading for the North Sea. MacAskill assessed its progress. *I'll be out of here before it closes on me,* he decided as he crouched down and emptied his rucksack. Once again he inflated the swim-ring and placed the already mixed explosive in its netted centre, taping the bottle of petrol to the container as he did so. Now more careful to conceal his presence, he leaned out from the edge of the jetty and nudged the swim-ring into the now fast-flowing waters of the firth which carried it away merrily downriver towards the two provisioning quays that stretched out into the Forth at Crombie. Carefully, he climbed to the top of the jetty and cautiously peered over. The swim-ring was floating in a direction that would take it directly underneath the closer jetty. *As long as it's close enough to one of the piles, all should be well,* he calculated. Still allowing only his head at eye level to protrude above his hiding place, he brought his rifle closer to his body and slowly eased it over the parapet seeking his target through its powerful scope.

Now positioned so his upper body was lying prone on the surface of the jetty, he cursed the perspective which didn't allow a precise determination of the moment it would pass directly beneath the quay. He looked up from his scope and realised that the nascent milky sunshine that was emerging cast a light shadow and that at the point where the swim-ring darkened, it would be in the perfect position. His eye returned to the scope. Two minutes passed as the explosive device closed on the jetty. To his relief, it appeared to be heading for one of the piles supporting the quay mid-way across. He readied himself and just as the yellow ring entered the gloom and darkened, he pulled the trigger. Instantly the ring erupted in an huge orange ball of flame and smoke. Aided by the creosote that had soaked into the timber pile over decades, the quay support burned brightly. Before long, the flames had reached upwards and began licking at the floor of the jetty setting it on fire too.

MacAskill watched the inflammation for some moments, shaken out of his reverie by a realisation that the tug he'd noticed earlier was now closing on the dock and he could see men on board gesturing towards him.

I'm out of here.

He placed his calling card between two rocks, collected his now-empty rucksack, took his rifle and set off at pace back along the jetty taking care to remain out of sight from those downriver at Crombie. Gaining the foreshore, he increased his speed until he was in woodland where his pace dropped to a steady uphill jog.

It was a Scots Pine that saved his life. While its primary tap root is formed early and burrows downwards in search of nourishment, the Scots Pine also has lateral roots which, in sandy or peaty soils, can remain just below the surface and in certain circumstances may protrude above the ground. It was one of these that caused MacAskill to trip just as the round fired by an SAS soldier several hundred yards away was about to bury itself between his shoulder blades. Instead it tore at his green, camouflaged jacket and carved a bloody canal along his upper left arm, throwing him to the ground in pain.

Grimacing, his instinct was to grasp his wound and in doing so, appreciated the blood loss he was experiencing. *I'll soon be incapable of movement. Must get to the Tardis. They'll have radio messages out pinpointing my location. Need to get going.*

Kneeling, he rose to his feet and continued his jog, grateful that he'd already covered most of the terrain and had only a few hundred yards to go. Shortly he arrived at the ambulance and made the strategic decision to drive rather than attend to his wound. *Not much good if I fix this just in time for them to capture me.* His left arm now blood-soaked and unable to fulfil most functions, he nevertheless manoeuvred it with his good arm so he could grasp the gear lever with his left fist, twisted the key in the ignition, painfully put the vehicle in gear before putting his foot on the accelerator and driving one-handed at speed from the copse within which he had concealed the Tardis.

The roads were still quiet and MacAskill headed north putting distance between himself and those who would harm or capture him. For fully fifteen minutes he didn't pass another vehicle on the road. As he approached the hamlet of Rumbling Bridge, he realised that blood loss was causing him to lose consciousness and pulled over. With only a cursory inspection of his wound, he pulled a wide bandage from the glove compartment and tied it loosely around his arm above the laceration before inserting a screwdriver acting as a windlass inside its girth and twisting it over and over until it tightened the ligature into a tourniquet. Taking another bandage he wrapped it around the lower aspect of the screwdriver holding it in place and fixing the compression around his arm. He reached behind him and brought forward several maps, discarding them one at a time until he found what he was looking for. Consulting it he memorised six digits.

Now unsteady on his feet and nauseous, he drove forward a few yards until he was abreast of a glazed, grey BT telephone box. Checking to ensure that no one was around, he entered the box and from memory punched in a telephone number. He thumbed in a pound coin. It was answered immediately.

"Yeah?"

"Phlegm here. In trouble. Bleeding badly. Need help. In a vehicle."

The respondent was all business.

"Map reference?"

"Coordinates November November two, two, niner, niner, zero, one, three."

"Telephone?"

"No telephone."

"Vehicle registration?"

"Romeo, niner, seven, four, Echo, Alpha, Tango. I applied a tourniquet at"...He consulted his watch... "Six oh seven. I have two hours before muscle wastage sets in."

"On my way. I'll make some calls."

MacAskill returned to the Tardis and, breathing deeply, drove on along single-track roads, his speed regulated as he strove to maintain focus. Using back roads he eventually arrived at the coordinates he'd relayed on the phone, a cairn marking the Battle of Sheriffmuir in 1715. Pulling into a small car park, he eased himself into the rear of the vehicle, lay on his bed, consulted another map, wrote down another set of six figure coordinates below the words 'Safe House' on the map which he placed on his chest. Struggling, he began to write again but managed only 'No Hosp...' before he lay back and closed his eyes.

Chapter Twenty-six

Nnews reached Thorpe within ten minutes of the explosion, his reaction being somewhat similar to that which had taken place at the pier at Crombie. On the receiving end of his fury was Bill Morton.

"What? This fucker sets the fucking quay on fire? The quay that's used to provision Her Majesty's fucking Royal fucking Navy. The quay without which we'll not be able to load ammunition onto any of our expensive warships which are required to maintain this nation in a state of readiness against the world-wide tyranny of fucking Commies and fucking Arabs? So he sets off the explosion and just fucking walks *away*! And I'm now looking at photographs taken by a passing tug boat fucking captain which will soon make their way to every fucking news desk in the fucking nation. It shows the quay ablaze and will doubtless encourage every fucking Nationalist bastard from here to fucking John O' fucking Groats to take up arms against the fucking crown." His voice rose several decibels. "He fucking *warns* us…*warns* us that he's going to pull this off…then only fucking *does* it and Her Majesty's finest can't fucking *stop* him?" His voice raised now to a pitch only dogs might hear. "I want this bastard's head on a plate! I want this bastard's balls." Shaking in rage, he lowered his tone. "I'll be in Crombie in an hour. Meet me there!"

* * *

In St Andrew's House, Catriona Burns asked herself ruefully if it had been wise to attend her desk quite so early before her media team arrived. She too had been advised of the Crombie incident and her phone was alive with print and TV journalists seeking comment. Fending them off with anodyne comment, she contacted the Chief Constable and informed him what he already knew…

that this incident was of a different order and would dominate world headlines.

"We've thrown the kitchen sink at this, Catriona. Our cops, Special Branch, MI5, the SAS...this is a blow. No question. But we must remember that it looks like he's a lone wolf. This makes it incredibly difficult to track him down. However, we have now a description of the bugger from the Master of fox-hounds and my people tell me there are a few photographs taken by a passing tug boat captain that captures Dalriada departing the scene of the crime...if it *was* him and not a copy-cat incident...so we might be closing in on him."

"The First Minister will require an urgent briefing."

"I'm already preparing it. I've also been contacted by MI5 in London who are apoplectic. They find it impossible to comprehend why we've not got this guy in chains."

"They're not the only ones!"

She ended the call as her mobile phone rang intimating that Sir Jonathan Burton, Cabinet Secretary and Head of the Civil Service in London was on the line.

* * *

Gus Darroch was at home shaving prior to dressing and attending work as news broke. The radio journalist interrupted a story about Scottish education performance to tell the story of the act of sabotage at Crombie.

Fucking hell!...He listened further. *At least it's not in my patch!* Further thought. *I'd better get down to the office. MI5 will be calling the shots now. This is international terrorism! NATO will take a view on this one!*

* * *

Isla Wishart and Andy Burns each had a similar reaction as the significance of the quay was explained to them over the radio... *Who is this guy? More power to his elbow!*

* * *

A small Ford Focus wheeled at speed into the car park hosting MacAskill's Tardis and four ex-Commandos emerged, each of whom stood over six feet tall.

"Next time we use my car, Snipe! Your shitey wee Ford couldn't hold any one of us comfortably."

Snipe ignored the jibe and was to the point.

"Let's get to the Captain. Molly, you stay at the wheel in case we need to leave quickly. Posh Boy, you take point outside the Captain's vehicle while me and the Clock check him out."

Opening the rear door, the two Commandos entered and approached an unconscious MacAskill.

"Cap!...Cap!..." Snipe gently attempted to stir him. There was no response. "Phlegm...it's Snipe."

The Clock knelt and began cutting MacAskill's jacket with a sharp knife until he revealed the wound.

"A four inch long, one inch deep avulsion. It's torn out the epidermis, dermis and subcutaneous layers and has detached tissue from the arm. From the looks of his pallor there's been massive blood loss. We're not in a sterile environment. Hospital case!"

Snipe lifted the map from MacAskill's chest and read his instructions.

"Looks like the Captain doesn't want to see the inside of a hospital ward. He's given us the co-ordinates of a safe house. Can you patch him up?"

"How long to get here?"

Snipe opened the map and quickly pinpointed the map references.

"It's a property outside Grantown-on-Spey by the looks of it. Forested area. Possibly a farm steading. I'd say maybe two and a half, three hours."

The Clock nodded his agreement.

"I'll clean and pack the wound with some hemostatic gauze, strap it up but it'll need careful attention and stitching in a sterile environment. He's suffering from hypovolemic shock and he'll need to replenish the blood loss to improve his circulation." He moved to inspect MacAskill's head.

"At first glance the arm's the only injury. Elevate his legs above the level of his head and we'll move off." He tested MacAskill's pulse. "Very low. I've got some Noradrenaline in my kit. That might stabilise things for a while and might even bring him back to consciousness. However, let's get going, but it would appear that the Captain doesn't want to deal with the authorities on this so no excessive speeding. The Captain phoned *us* instead of 999 so there must be a reason for it. It looks like he's been shot. You drive. I'll stay in the back here and pray for the patient. Give Posh Boy and Molly the map and these co-ordinates then send them on their way. Tell them to stay one mile ahead of us. We keep in touch by phone and Posh Boy's got the map so he talks us in to the safe house. If they see anything suspicious up ahead, they phone us. Try to stay off the main roads but not so much that we lose time. Let's go!"

* * *

Boston and Boyd sat together at Boyd's desk carefully inspecting five blurred images which had been taken by a hand on the tug boat as MacAskill made his escape.

Boston offered an assessment.

"These first two suggest that that quay won't be in use any time soon. Serious fire damage." He laid them aside. "So, this is our man, eh?" Silence reigned while they attempted recognition of three photographs of a man stooped and running, his face only captured in profile and at distance."

"They're blurry as fuck, boss."

"Maybe the Doc over in Forensic can sharpen them up."

"More likely MI5, boss. They've got some technology but I was told on a training course that sharpening can't correct a severely blurred image. And these look like they're severely blurred. Can't see us using them for ID purposes."

"Aye well, you'll be an expert now, eh? You've been on a *training* course." He handed Boyd the images. "MI5 already have these images. Use your considerable charm and wit to see if they'd be good enough to let us know if they can enhance them."

"Will do…and I'll maybe have a go myself, boss. I have an App on my phone that fixes a picture if I take blurry photographs of my dog."

"Jimmy, there are over a million words in the English language but I currently find it impossible to find ones that would adequately express how much I want to hit you over the head with a fuckin' chair."

* * *

Thorpe stepped from his car and walked to where his number two, Bill Morton was in conversation with a police inspector at the end of the quay. Brusquely, he interrupted the conversation.

"A word!"

Morton made his apologies and began to step aside to confer with Thorpe who started speaking intemperately as Morton was still disentangling himself from the Police officer.

"I'm fucking furious about this! Show me where the bastard set off the explosion."

Both men walked mid-way across the pier until they reached the police tape marking the scene of the explosion.

"How the fuck did he get out here without being spotted?" asked a perplexed Thorpe.

"He didn't, boss. We've interviewed the crew of the Teeling, the tug which witnessed the attack. They saw a man crouched at the end of that small pier upriver." He pointed to the rubble construction edging out into the firth which had been used by MacAskill. "They saw him take aim with a rifle at an object he floated downriver. As it reached the pile here, he shot and exploded it. There's little doubt it was the Tannerite he stole from the gun-range that was used, possibly with an accelerant to aid the flames. The army have bomb disposal boys trying to identify the explosive mix but I'd bet that was it. The SAS got a shot off but don't think they scored. They also found his calling card pinned to the rocks where he shot and followed some routes they figure he must have taken to elude them. On one hillside they found traces of blood but that could have been rabbit, deer, fox…anything. We're checking it anyway."

Thorpe struggled to find words. Eventually he settled for, "This bastard Dalriada is beginning to *really* piss me off!" He stuffed his hands into his anorak pockets and kicked frustratedly at a police cone being used to mark the crime scene and stared for some moments out into the firth before turning back to Morton, his face twisted in fury; his outrage, spittle-flecked.

"Okay...this ends now. This bastard is becoming a fucking folk hero up here. He needs to be shown up as the separatist thug that he is." He paused, his rage simmering. "Right! You keep on this. I'm going to pursue a different line of enquiry...but like I say...this ends *now*!"

* * *

The Ford Focus sped along the A9 having taken a tactical decision not to use the smaller roads via Glenn Shee due to the overly meandering route it took. As they approached the turn-off for the village of Dalwhinnie, a police roadblock was evident up ahead. Traffic was light so the two Commandos could clearly see a police officer wave on a car he'd just inspected and cleared. They were next. Posh Boy punched the speed contact button for the Clock. It was answered immediately.

"Clock, there's a police roadblock on the north-bound A9 just after the turn-off for Dalwhinnie." He consulted his map. "If you take that turn off and follow the A889, it'll take you through the village then take the B9152 all the way to Aviemore and you'll avoid it. I'll distract this guy here in case he gets curious."

So saying, he operated the Ford's light controls and started flashing the police officer up ahead who was in any event preparing to have them stop. Slowing, the Focus pulled up at the roadblock. Posh Boy rolled down his window, beckoned the officer to his side of the vehicle and spoke to him in his most affected aristocratic accent.

"Officer, there's a drunk driver heading south on the M9. The car was all over the place. It nearly collided with a minibus full of frightened children as it attempted to overtake it."

"How long ago, sir?"

"Perhaps four or five minutes. He'll still be on the A9."

The officer reached for his notebook.

"Make of car?"

Molly leaned over and joined the conversation in a broad Glaswegian accent.

"It was a black SUV. A BMW I think, officer."

Posh Boy shook his head in mock disagreement. "Thought it looked more like a Merc, myself."

He addressed the police officer. "He's not a car chap. I'd explain the difference to him but I don't have any crayons with me."

Molly affected dissent. "Try hard! Because I'm enough of a car guy to know that a Beamer's grill has perpendicular bars. The Merc has horizontal bars with the three-pointed star in the middle. And it wasn't black. It was more a dark blue colour."

"Dark blue, my backside."

Frustrated, the policeman attempted conciliation.

"Gentlemen. The longer we disagree, the less likelihood this car can be stopped from killing someone. Can we agree it's an SUV, dark colour and either a BMW or Mercedes Benz?"

Posh Boy wouldn't be mollified. "It was definitely a Mercedes, officer. My friend was too busy driving. I had a good look at the idiot driving - which was a woman, incidentally."

Molly contradicted him. "It was a bloody man behind the wheel. He had long hair, right enough."

The conversation continued for a further period until the police officer managed to list a series of possible options that might allow traffic cops nearer Perth to look out for a range of vehicles with either a male or female driver. After some cursory questions about the purpose of their trip and a perfunctory look in the rear seats, the constable waved them on completely oblivious to a converted ambulance taking the slip road to Dalwhinnie.

Chapter Twenty-seven

The Ford swept in to the dusty and rutted parking area in front of MacAskill's cottage, scattering the chickens. Some minutes later the Tardis followed suit. By the time it had arrived, Posh Boy had made light of the lock on the cottage door and had gained entry. He and Molly carried out an inspection of the premises and had declared them clear as the Clock and Snipe carried MacAskill into one of the two bedrooms and laid him, still unconscious, on the bed. The Clock took command.

"Keep his feet elevated and I'll get to work on his arm. Molly, you and Posh take out all of the blood-stained bedding and burn it somewhere it won't be found then remove any and all stains in the Captain's vehicle permanently. That'll need bleach. Lots of it. Have a look around but beg, borrow or steal what you need. There should be no trace that he'd ever had so much as a nose bleed. Burn any cloths or brushes you use. Snipe, maybe you'd keep watch outside. No interruptions. If I need you in here, be close enough to hear me shout."

"On it, Clock."

The three Commandos each turned on their heel and went about the business asked of them as the remaining Marine left his patient and boiled a kettle of water he used, once diluted with cold water, to wash his hands and arms thoroughly. Returning to the bedroom, he took a pair of surgical gloves from his pack, put them on and began to cut away at MacAskill's upper attire, removing it completely, revealing his blood-soaked arm, the bandage earlier applied now scarlet. Some minutes were spent visualising the wound and gently wiping out so the bleeding vessel in the wound could be seen. Gently, he soaked a gauze pad in a saline solution and dabbed at MacAskill's skin with it. Still blood seeped from the deep wound.

Footsteps from the porch outside alerted him.

"Clock! We have a visitor. Land Rover approaching. One occupant. Two dogs in the passenger seat."

"Be tactful. Be firm. No one gets in here."

He returned to the wound leaving Snipe to deal with the intruder. A moment later he was knocked to one side as a Golden Retriever bounded past him and began to lick the face of his patient. Clock took the interruption in his stride.

"Whoah there, big boy." He reached for Blaze's collar and drew him back. "Looks like we'll need to start the sterile conditioning all over again, eh?" He ruffled the mane of Blaze and took him out to the porch where he was confronted by a puzzled and assertive Isla who was standing with Rory at her side, her access to the cottage blocked. Snipe stood helplessly beside her more used to dealing with other warriors, not an attractive woman with dogs. Isla turned her wrath on the Clock.

"We haven't met but I'd like to know what's going on here. This man here insists I can't enter a property that effectively belongs to my mother and which presently accommodates a dear friend of mine."

"Then if he's a dear friend of yours perhaps you'd trust us to deal with a minor situation we have here. I can only ask you to believe that the four men you see here are perhaps the closest friends your friend has in the world and that he's asked for some privacy and confidentiality until matters ease."

"What on earth is going on?"

The Clock surrendered. "Look he's unwell and we're tending to him."

Isla wasn't to be dissuaded.

"Then I want to see him. I'm a medic."

The Clock's demeanour changed immediately.

"You're a medic?"

"I want to see him. We're very close and I can tell you that he'd want me to assist if he's unwell. I've already attended to a cut he has on his cheek. Whatever's wrong now?"

"What's your name?"

"I'm Isla Wishart. My family own this estate. And Lachie is very precious to us."

The Clock held her gaze, biting his lower lip as he assessed his next move.

"I'm taking a chance here, Isla. I really hope you are who you say you are." He nodded to his colleague. "Okay, Snipe."

He stepped aside and bid Isla enter. As they entered the bedroom, Isla gasped in alarm at an unconscious MacAskill, his arm now reddened again due to the Clock's ministrations being interrupted.

"My God! Lachie! What's happened?"

"As you can see, he has a four inch long, one inch deep avulsion which has detached tissue from the arm. There's been massive blood loss but I think we've just avoided exsanguination. He's been unconscious for perhaps three hours. Pretty weak pulse but it's consistent. I removed a makeshift tourniquet he'd applied within the two hour limit, cleaned and packed the wound with hemostatic gauze, and given him an injection of Noradrenaline. I was just about to clean and stitch the wound when you arrived."

Isla's confusion didn't ebb.

"Are you a doctor?"

"Eh, no. Actually I'm a clergyman...I was Chaplain to the Marine Commandos. Like Phlegm here, I've now retired. We all five of us have."

"Phlegm? This is all too confusing."

"I'll explain later." He knelt beside the pale body of MacAskill. "I'm glad you're here if you're a medic. He made it plain that he didn't want to go to hospital but to be taken here to this place. Each of the four of us served with him and owe him our lives. We're a band of brothers and would do anything for one another. He doesn't want to go to hospital with this wound?...then he doesn't go with this wound and we treat him here." He looked at his hands. "I'm no longer sterile because the dog came in but perhaps I could ask you to assist?"

"I'm a vet not a doctor but I can handle the rudiments of dealing with a wound of this nature. Yesterday it was a pig with a large wound just like this. Today it's Lachie's arm. Both the same although the pig had a noisier disposition. Let's you and I sterilise ourselves and fix this man up."

Together they cleansed and disinfected themselves and dealt with MacAskill, Isla completing the process by the careful stitching of the wound before bandaging the arm. The Clock took his pulse and detected an improvement.

"We might just have turned the corner."

Isla looked at MacAskill's still-pallid face.

"He needs fluids quickly. I have some in the practice in the village. I'll go and bring some back. Won't be long."

The Clock demurred.

"He does need fluids," he agreed. "But would you mind if I accompanied you?"

"You think I'll head straight for the nearest police station?"

"I'm sure you wouldn't but why take the chance?"

He stood and called on Snipe who came and stood at the portal.

"Hi Snipe. Myself and this young lady are going to Grantown-on-Spey. We'll be half an hour. Can you keep an eye on Phlegm and look after him if he comes to or looks like he's about to die on us...anything like that?"

"Will do, Clock."

The Marine Chaplain and Isla stepped outside where Molly and Posh Boy were still attending to the cleansing of the ambulance. Isla was first to speak as they settled themselves in her Land Rover and headed off.

"First the names? You're called the Clock?"

The Clock laughed.

"The army can be a cruel place." He stretched his arms out before him as if a cartoon sleepwalker. "If you look, you can see that I have one big hand and one little hand, hence my nickname, 'the Clock'. Born that way and both hands are perfectly functional but squaddies look for anything they can to tease you so I became 'the Clock'. Your friend indoors introduced himself upon arrival as Lachie. No problem for us Scots but the English boys couldn't pronounce the 'ch', the velar fricative. So they called him '*Lackie*' but the more he corrected him the more they pretended they were clearing their throat so eventually he was called 'Phlegm' until he was promoted to Sergeant then got a jump-step, battlefield promotion allowing to advance by two ranks to Captain and warranted a degree of respect. So, while he was known in the third person as Phlegm, he was called Captain or 'Cap' to his face."

"Well, I've known Lachie since childhood and he means everything to my mother so it's very important to her, to the estate...and to me, actually, that he recovers from this wound. How did it happen?"

"We don't know. Snipe got a phone call..."

"Snipe?"

"Again the cruelty of the squaddies. On his first posting to Afghanistan he was shot in the leg. He recovered well after an operation but it left one leg slightly shorter than the other. He walks with a pronounced limp. From behind you can see his head bobbling from one side to the other due to his uneven gait, so instantly he became known as 'the Sniper's Nightmare'... abbreviated to 'Snipe'. For the purpose of completeness, in the Captain's vehicle are 'Molly'...Quite boring actually, it's just because his surname's Malone, and 'Posh Boy', a Guardsman who's the best burglar and con-man in the army. He's Scottish but uses his posh accent so effectively, no one could imagine the levels of athletic pilferage and upper-class swindling he can undertake. In the British army, the use of surnames is too formal...a bit American, given names are too *in*formal but nicknames provide a small measure of anonymity and impudence."

"And you're a chaplain? Not a medic?"

"Well, I was called to the ministry and joined the Marines because I decided that surely God has to be present among those in the most difficult and challenging situations in the world. To be a Marine Chaplain, a posting without military rank, has been an absolute privilege. I simply loved these guys but I also decided that while I'd go out on manoeuvres with them, perhaps I could also fulfil God's work in more practical ways so I did a few courses in paramedicine so I might be of some use on the battlefield. However, just as in civilian life, I preached the word, administered the sacraments, visited the sick, buried and counselled the bereaved and cared for the anxious and lost."

Isla returned to the matter in hand.

"Very Interesting. So Snipe got a phone call?"

"Sorry, yes he took a call from the Captain who gave him co-ordinates. We rushed to his side and found him unconscious in that caravan thing."

"It's a converted ambulance. He fitted it out and lives in it when he's not here in the cottage."

"It looks amazing inside."

"So what do you think caused his injury?"

"To me it looks like he was shot. I've dealt with wounds like that before, usually accompanied by a broken bone or two. At least the Captain has escaped that complication. We'll find out what caused it once he awakens."

"Shot? Dear God! Well, Van, Phlegm, Captain, Cap or Lachie...whatever he's called today...might not awaken *at all* unless we get a saline drip into his arm so let's make haste!"

Chapter Twenty-eight

Sergeant Gus Darroch sat at his desk reading information passed to him for interest by fellow Sergeant, Colin Boston regarding the assault on the pier at Crombie. He scanned the blurred photographs of Dalriada running from the scene and narrowed his eyes the better to focus. Placing them to one side he consulted the note which summarised Forensic's assessment of the man they were seeking. He read out quietly in a mumble to himself.

"Ex-military or police, handy with firearms, size nine footprint." He turned the page. "The fox hunter reckons he's tall, with a camo jacket and denims, scar on cheek, untidy red hair, a man in his thirties and clean shaven." He lifted the photographs again and spent some moments considering them before placing them before him, rising and walking to the next door office where Constable Calum Buchanan was typing a report on a poaching complaint.

As casually as possible, he leaned round the door and tapped it to gain his attention.

"Calum, have you been in touch with old Archie McFarlane recently. I was just wondering how he and his misses were holding up?"

"They're both shaken up after that car crash, boss and he's very apprehensive about his court appearance but I've been on to the housing association and if it goes badly in terms of a big fine and/or a ban they think they can find them both accommodation in the village."

"Aye, that's good. And that poaching complaint?"

"I'm writing it up as we speak, boss. There's some evidence of a pretty big salmon haul from the Spey at Lady Wishart's estate. I'll let Lachie know and I'm sure he'll keep an eye out for them. Knowing him, he'll camp out and lie in wait in case they return."

"Aye, that's good," he repeated. "Speaking of Lachie, you mentioned you saw him the day you were checking cars outside Nethy Bridge...the day someone took a shot at Prince Edward?"

"Aye."

"You told me he was collecting a couple of chainsaws."

"Aye, he was. He had them in the back of his ambulance. He let me look in. It looked fabulous."

"Aye, it is. And you said, as I recall, that he said he'd looked in on old Bill Anderson to collect them only for a few minutes before heading back home?"

"How long had you been stopping vehicles there before he arrived?"

"About an hour maybe. Right after the shooting I was instructed to block that road."

"But you didn't see Lachie travel in the opposite direction... *towards* old Bill's workshop...you only saw him on the way back?"

"Aye...am I missing something, boss?"

"No...it's a chainsaw thing." He changed the subject. "Bring me that poaching report when you're finished would you? I'll speak to Lachie when I see him in the Claymore."

Boston returned to his office and looked again at the photographs. Again he spoke only in a murmur.

"Fuckin' eejit!"

* * *

Isla's Land Rover, with her at the wheel, screeched into the dusty track outside MacAskill's cottage. Both she and the Clock stepped from the vehicle and entered the cottage where MacAskill remained unconscious.

"Any change in the patient," asked the Clock of Snipe.

"No. Regular but weak pulse. Steady breathing. Bleeding stopped."

As he received this update, Isla was busily removing the bulb and shade from a standard lamp and positioning the tall, vertical pole next to the bed. Satisfied, she hung a clear plastic bag containing a saline solution, unrolled its intravenous line, inserted a cannula into the vein on MacAskill's right arm and allowed gravity to introduce much-needed hydration to his weakened body."

"You've done this before, Isla" said the Clock admiringly.

"More times than I care to remember. Usually dogs, but other than not having to shave Lachie's foreleg, the administration of the injectable fluid solution is precisely the same. Exactly the same 0.9 saline although this batch has a dextrose and potassium additive. Won't do him any harm and might even help. It should bring back a stronger pulse and stabilise his blood pressure."

"As long as he doesn't wake up and start barking!"

"He might make more sense if he did! I want to know how and why he was shot."

"Yeah, as do we, Isla. The four of us here who served with him each owe him our lives. In Posh Boy's case, three times over. None of us would be here talking to you if it wasn't for the estimable Captain Lachlan MacAskill Esquire, so first we save him, then we find out how the hell he came to be shot and by whom, then we make sure he's safe from it happening again, if necessary by removing the threat!"

"You mean by disabling...or shooting the person who shot him?"

"Let's hope it doesn't come to anything like that. For the moment, let's just imagine he shot himself cleaning his favourite Remington!"

Thirty minutes passed during which the Clock inspected the interior of the ambulance and pronounced himself satisfied that all traces of blood had been removed. Still, he sought more comfort.

"Molly, there's a spare single bed in the Captain's second bedroom. Remove its mattress and install it in his ambulance. Burn the one he was lying on...even though you've done a great job on it. Bury the remains. Once that's done, there's a famous country wear shop called Mortimer's in the village High Street. Can you buy another camo jacket for the Cap to replace the one we're burning?"

"On it, Clock."

"*Clock!*"

Isla called his name in such a way as to suggest urgency. Seconds later, the pastor appeared in the door frame of MacAskill's bedroom. Lachie's weakened voice hailed him in a whisper.

"Clock! Have you met Isla, the best vet in all the world?"

Clock grinned widely.

"You're awake, Lachie, you crazy bastard! Boy, have you got some explaining to do!"

"Clock! That's no way for a clergyman to speak in front of a young lady."

Isla intervened.

"Well, Lachie. *This* young lady is just as anxious to hear your story. It had better be good. We've had to treat and stitch up a deep wound in your arm. If you hadn't been found by Clock and your mates you might easily have bled to death by now."

The Clock contradicted his fellow medic.

"Well, it was Isla here who administered to your wound, Cap. I just kept you alive until we got you here to the cottage. She fixed you up properly."

MacAskill attempted to sit up but was held down gently by Isla.

"Just lie still, Lachie. You're still in poor shape. This saline drip will normalise things but just lie back and let us all shout at you."

MacAskill did as requested but inspected the bandage on his arm before relenting.

"Nice job, both!" He rested his head on the pillow. "This is embarrassing, people. I figured I might need to explain myself to the boys. I hadn't factored in being found in this condition by... by..." He struggled to describe his relationship with Isla..."the local vet!"

"I've tidied up wounds on many pigs before. You're just the first today."

The Clock's smile became businesslike.

"Captain MacAskill, sir...should we expect any visitors here at the cottage?"

"Not unless I've messed up. If you guys picked me up at the coordinates I gave you and weren't followed, we should be fine."

"How are you feeling?"

"Painful left arm, bit weary..."

Isla took over.

"Confused?"

"Not really."

"What's the name of this estate?"

"Inverskillen."

"My mother's first name?"

"Helen".

"Number plate of the Tardis?"

"Romeo, niner, seven, four, Echo, Alpha, Tango."

The Clock laughed.

"That's correct."

Isla's curiosity overtook her."

"Well, would you mind explaining that gash in your arm? To the untrained eye it looks remarkably like a bullet wound."

Years of battlefront experience, years of pastoral counselling and years of looking after squaddies in a fix allowed the Clock to intervene.

"Too soon, Isla. The poor man has just come round. Let's give him some time to collect his thoughts and allow that intravenous drip to do its stuff. We'll get all the explanations we need in short order I'm sure. In the meantime, me and the boys could do with a coffee and I'm sure you're the same. Why don't we retire to the kitchen for a bit and let the Captain recover? I'll put the kettle on."

Isla folded her arms in protest.

"I'm sitting here until I'm persuaded he's out of harm's way."

"Laudable and noble, Isla. But he needs to sleep. You're not used to your patients speaking back to you but if the Captain was in possession of all of his faculties, he'd agree he just wants to sleep for a while."

Isla moved to check this assertion with her patient and saw that his eyes were closed. Frustrated, she harrumphed.

"Very well!"

Her heels tapped out an exit on the floorboards as she surrendered to the Clock's proposition and made her way to the next room. As she left, MacAskill opened his eyes and smiled at the pastor.

He winked once and fell asleep.

* * *

Gus Darroch sat in the Claymore looking at his watch and sipping at his Guinness. His impatience getting the better of him, he emptied the pint in one smooth swallow, rose and took his empty glass to the bar.

"Another one, John."

The barman began to pour from the tap. Darroch tapped a beer mat on its edge as he waited.

"No sign of Lachie tonight then?"

John the barman shook his head.

"Lachie hasn't been in for a bit. Thought he must be off chasin' thon vet lassie."

Darroch decided to keep his friend's nascent feelings of affection to himself.

"That 'vet lassie' is Isla Wishart. Lady Wishart's daughter. She was born and bred in the village so she's got better antecedents than you, John…and Lachie's no' chasin' her. I'm not sure he'd know how to start. Right now I think he takes the view that she's a great team member on quiz nights."

"Didn'y know that, Gus. One of the teachers' team was asking who she was. I think they see your new team as a threat to their position as world quiz champions in the village."

"Aye, well, that's her!" He laid the beer mat flat on the bar and proffered a five pound note indicating that no change was necessary.

"Tips jar."

"Thank you, Police Sergeant Darroch," replied John in faux formality. "Nip round to his cottage. If he's no' in the Tardis, he'll be there I'd imagine."

"Might just do that, John."

The large flat-screen television affixed to the wall above the bar, always on but usually muted, carried images of the burned quay at Crombie.

"Here, John...turn that up would ye?"

A television news reporter dispatched from London to Fife illustrated the fact that the story was now making headlines across the United Kingdom. It took a few moments for John to find and operate the remote. The images shown reflected the damage to the wharf behind the reporter as the volume increased.

"...out of action for some time. Fortunately there is a second pier but a spokesman for Defence Munitions Crombie stated that the depot will now have to revise its schedule of military provisioning in the months ahead until the facility can be restored to its normal level of functioning."

Stock footage of a nuclear warhead convoy filled the screen followed by images of the punctured tyres of Prince Edward's vehicles and crowds in Glasgow marching in support of Dalriada. Over these pictures, the journalist listed the known impacts of the 'seditionist who is inciting rebellion against the authority of the state' before returning to a studio threesome where another presenter sat between the Member of the Scottish Parliament for Dunfermline and West Fife and the Conservative Secretary of State for Scotland. Behind them, a montage of these events had been overlaid by a library image of a man carrying a rifle and wearing a ski balaclava allowing only his eyes and mouth to be visible.

That's him nailed down as a terrorist, thought Darroch. *He might as well announce his membership of the IRA, Al Qaeda and the paramilitary wing of Hezbollah right now!*

"Secretary of State, this man Dalriada is making you look foolish is he not?"

"He is certainly a very dangerous man and whatever his political motives...and they are quite obviously linked to the separatists' agenda...he will discover, as will his sponsors, that the only way to achieve political change in this country is through the ballot box. He will be caught, tried in a court of law and will spend his remaining years in custody if he does not meet a sticky end."

"But forgive me, Minister. What possible connection can you establish between these events and your political opponents?"

"It just stands to reason, doesn't it? The Scottish Government must be cheering him on. All of his targets are British Establishment icons. The people protesting on the streets carry Saltires, not the Union Flag. Those who shout his name in approval are the same people who march under the flags of separatism."

The presenter turned to the SNP representative.

"We'll, Mr. Madden, Defence Munitions Crombie is in your constituency. *Does* this man Dalriada act on your behalf?"

"No, Joyce, he doesn't. The Secretary of State may attempt to have us associated with the acts of this man but we aren't playing politics with this matter. Our Police Scotland is actively seeking his apprehension..."

"But you would agree that his campaign hits all of the policy objectives of your party of government in Scotland?"

"It's well known that we wish to see weapons of mass destruction removed from the Clyde and it is accepted that many within our movement are of a republican mentality. Clearly, we also oppose the illegal military adventurism of the government of the United Kingdom but we would agree with the Secretary of State on one thing...the solution to these matters must be through the ballot box and so far, in Scotland, we happen to be doing rather a good job on that front."

"But not on reserved matters such as defence or nuclear weapons. The actions of Dalriada merely allow the frustrations of your membership to be addressed because you cannot influence reserved matters at Westminster."

"All the more reason for Scottish Independence, Joyce. In a modern democracy, we shouldn't have to resort to civil disobedience to right the wrongs of our society."

"Secretary of State?"

"You see, this is why the nationalists can't be trusted in government. I call this man Dalriada a terrorist and your own earlier piece to camera called him a seditionist...and that is what he is...but the nationalists call his actions 'civil disobedience'. They're soft on crime and are willing to see arms used...live rounds fired at the royal family...essential military bases set alight...our nuclear defence capability threatened...all because they want increased power in Scotland. Well, I'm here today to tell the people of Scotland that it won't work. That the might of the British Government will bring this man down. His days are numbered."

"You may well say that, Secretary of State but our sources tell us that despite advance warnings from Dalriada that he *planned* to attack your depot at Crombie, and despite the fact that you enlisted the support of the SAS in protecting that site, you still, once again, failed either to stop or catch him. You're getting nowhere fast on this are you?"

"I'm not prepared to discuss operational matters on television. I merely inform the people of Scotland and the rest of this United Kingdom that this terrorist will be caught and punished no matter how much the nationalists might hope otherwise."

The journalist smiled and turned to face the camera.

"Gentlemen, thank you. We have to leave it there."

Darroch pursed his lips and sighed.

"Thanks, John. Turn that shite off! A wee Macallan while you're at the gantry."

* * *

In Edinburgh, Catriona Burns' mobile phone rang as the interview came to a close. Once again it was Sir Jonathan Burton, Cabinet Secretary and Head of the Civil Service in London whose name appeared on the screen.

"Sir Jonathan."

"Just watched that broadcast on Dalriada. Anything further to report?"

"I've a meeting with the Chief Constable first thing tomorrow morning. I'll know more then but, no...we're no closer to finding him. The police lab is checking some blood samples we found to see if it's human. If it is, we can presume the SAS managed to get off a shot that hit him and can check for DNA but the soldier who fired said he'd seen some movement in the ferns and that the shot, whilst quite against all protocols, was more in hope than with any accuracy. The results should be with us by morning. The media has not been informed."

"Quite! Well the PM is now in something of a lather over this and is accusing everyone, you, me, the police, the Scottish Government, the SAS...everyone, of either being completely incompetent or in cahoots with this man. I'm afraid it can go on no longer and Sir Jeffery Arbuthnot has given instructions to his MI5 senior investigating officer to take such heightened action as is necessary to bring matters to a conclusion."

"As someone who is somewhat unused to the tortured argot of MI5, I'd like to know what 'heightened action' means,"

"It means, Miss Burns, that detection, tactical pursuit and containment having very obviously failed us, officers deployed in defence of the Crown in these matters can operate, shall we say, 'creatively' and with extreme prejudice to end this farce. I'll call again in the morning to learn of progress."

Chapter Twenty-nine

Thorpe had returned to his desk in Glasgow and was reviewing all information on Dalriada.

I'm missing something...I'm missing something... He shuffled through the various papers he had before him as his phone rang.

"Thorpe!"

"Arthur Glen at the lab, here, sir. I was told you wanted to be the first to hear of our findings on the blood sample that was obtained at Crombie."

"And?"

"Well, we've confirmed that the blood found at the scene not far from where the shot was fired and on a route likely have been taken by the assailant as he escaped was from a male human being, not an animal. Also, we put the results through out national database and have found no matches. Secondly, we know that redheads have a different version of a gene that prevents pigment-producing cells called melanocytes responding to a hormone that instructs them to make dark pigment. The DNA sample from this sample carries the mutated genes so the odds are around ninety-six percent that your man is red-haired. Typically in the western world, about two percent of the population has red hair, but in Scotland the figure is much higher at around thirteen per cent or thereabouts. There is also a ninety-seven percent chance that this person's eyes are either blue or light grey. Further research could show the percentage likelihood of this man having illnesses like diabetes, Huntington's neurological disorder and the like but I suspect that these details won't trouble you at the minute."

"They don't. But it tells us that the SAS shot hit its mark, eh?"

"Not really. It must be remembered that while DNA collected from a crime scene can either link a suspect to the evidence or eliminate a suspect, similar to the use of fingerprints, DNA testing cannot tell us *when* the suspect was at the crime scene or for how long. The blood could have come from an accidental cut hand of a local man walking his dog, it could have been left the night before, it may have lain for a couple of days…"

"It might as well have been coloured tartan. It was fucking Dalriada all right and we've shot the bastard. So you confirm that there are no matches in the database but that he is very likely to be red-haired and blue eyed?"

"Correct. I'll send this over in written form."

"I'm obliged!"

He sat for some minutes thinking before taking his pen and listing the known factors that identified his quarry, underlining some. He lifted the phone and called Morton.

"Thorpe here. We've got the DNA results. It's him alright and we shot him. Check every hospital from John O'Groats to fucking Lands End. If we shot him and he's the lone wolf we think he is, he'll need medical attention. Find out where. Also I want an update on all the informants we have out there. Even if this bastard *is* a lone wolf, *someone* must know something. Break a few bones if you have to but get me some fucking information I can use to nick this Jock terrorist!"

He placed the phone on its harness and thought further

A needle in a fucking haystack. If he's not at death's door, I need him to break cover…I need the bastard to make a mistake.

He sat back in his chair and placed his feet on the desk before removing his pistol from its drawer and inspecting it while he thought.

Extreme prejudice…extreme prejudice!

* * *

The Clock had decided to trust Isla to visit her home to see to her mother and to return with foodstuffs for those at the cottage. She returned with not one but two dogs and entered the cottage smiling her way past Snipe who remained on guard at the front door.

"Right, I have enough soup to feed an army and sufficient rolls and sausages for the army it opposes." She began to unpack a large bag. "How's our patient?"

The Clock smiled. "Why don't you ask him yourself?"

Isla left her foodstuffs and made her way to the bedroom, following the dogs which were fussing over MacAskill as he sat up in bed.

"Hi Isla," he grinned as he ruffled and patted both dogs with his right arm, his left remaining limp.

"Well, someone looks on the mend."

"Thanks to you and Clock. You guys probably saved my life."

"Probably to no purpose as I propose to murder you here in front of your ex-soldier pals if you don't explain how the quiet, self-effacing woodsman who cares for my mother ends up shot and bleeding."

MacAskill's smile widened. "Who says I was shot?"

"That was a bullet wound. It dug a deep channel across your upper arm and fortunately for you, missed your humerus bone and even more fortunately, your brachial artery. Had it been severed, it would have resulted in unconsciousness in as little as thirty seconds and death in as little as two minutes. You don't know how close you came to dying." Tears welled up in her eyes as she sought a response. "Lachie?"

MacAskill remained silent for a moment before replying.

"Isla...Clock...I don't want to lie to anyone...especially you two. But I'm not sure that explaining how I came by my injury would help things." He quietened again for a moment, uncomfortable at the tears that rolled silently down Isla's cheeks. "Look...what can I tell you?"...He pondered further. "Listen... I'm *not* up to no good...but I just *might* be up to some minor mischief! The authorities may be mildly interested in my apprehension but I am at peace with my actions. There's nothing you should worry about. Once my arm heals I'll be back good as new and working on the estate."

Slowly, Isla raised her hand to her mouth. Her head began shaking in denial as she stepped back slightly from the bed.

"My God...you're...you're that man...the one police are looking for...you're Dalriada!"

MacAskill grimaced and allowed a silence before he answered.

"Look...I can't lie to either of you...but I'm not about to say something that might cause us problems in the future should the authorities ask questions of any of us. So let me repeat...I'm at peace with my actions. I am working to bring about a peaceful, socially just, independent Scotland. I wish harm to no one but I also believe in actions that bring people on to the streets to fight for these same objectives...and from what I gather from reports on this fellah Dalriada, there appears to have been a positive reaction in many quarters to his actions. But if you ask me directly if I'm Dalriada, I respectfully choose not to answer."

There was a period of silence before the Clock responded.

"I understand, Captain." He turned to Isla. "You mentioned something about rolls and sausages?"

Isla's gaze was fixed on MacAskill. A silence was broken only by the ticking of a vintage mantelpiece clock in his bedroom until, wordlessly, she took herself from the room and made for the kitchen.

The Clock watched her go. "We have your back, Captain. I'll speak with Isla." He stood. "Can you face a roll and sausage? Coffee?"

MacAskill's eyes still focussed upon the doorframe through which Isla had exited."

"Speak with her, Clock. I'm on the side of the angels."

As the Clock left the room, MacAskill spoke after him in a stage whisper.

"Clock!...Two sugars!"

* * *

Isla had busied herself frying sausages and had thrown some bacon into the pan for good measure. Her communication with the ex-Commandos had been monosyllabic, her focus solely upon the bright copper utensils and their contents atop the small Aga cooker in MacAskill's equally *bijou* kitchen as she wrestled with her earlier conversation with him.

The Clock stood in the doorway handing out plates and mugs as they became available. Requests for 'any more?' allowed Isla further time to herself as she complied. Only after a third round of rolls had been distributed did the Clock interrupt Isla's reverie.

"He's a good man, you know. If I were to tell you the tales of his heroism and kindnesses, we'd be here 'till midnight. Four of us answered his call for help instantly and without thought. Every one of us owes him and there's not a man in the regiment that wouldn't do the same. He's a legend who decided that he'd seen enough bloodshed and sought the quiet life up here where he was raised as a boy." Isla continued to move pots around. "You'll know him as a shy woodsman but he's a warrior who's hung up his gun. Whatever he's been up to...whether he's Dalriada or not...he'll only have been acting in the interests of peace and maybe Scottish Independence...he was strong on that in the regiment." Isla began to cut and peel vegetables she'd brought to make a pot of soup, saying nothing. The Clock continued. "I only know what this Dalriada guy has been up to, same as the rest of Scotland...by watching it on telly. He's caused a bit of trouble when he halted a nuclear convoy, embarrassed a junior member of the Royal Family, chastised a fox-hunter and stopped arms being loaded onto ships that would carry those weapons to poorer parts of the world to kill those deemed disposable by the British Establishment. In doing this, he hasn't hurt anyone or caused violence other than the fox-hunter, and he'd struck the first blow according to you."

Isla continued her silence, allowing the Clock to continue.

"Your attitude clearly matters to him. He asked me to speak with you as you left the bedroom. Are you two close?"

Isla stiffened as the question prompted an unexpected reaction.

"I don't *know* what we are! I just thought of him as a wonderful guy who looked after my mother and now I find you calling him a warrior who's causing chaos all across Scotland. There are people in the streets chanting his name, there are students firing rockets at the BBC, others tearing down the Union Flag...I don't know what to think."

"Do his causes offend you?"

"On the contrary! I've been cheering on Dalriada along with everyone else in the pub. It just never occurred to me that he'd be sitting next to me as I did!"

"Well, let's remember that he hasn't confessed to being Dalriada."

"As good *as*! His non-confession was obviously a device to allow you and me to deal with the inevitable police questioning." She cut some more vegetables then turned to face the Clock directly. "If I'm honest, I'm worried about what'll happen to him. There's a nation-wide man-hunt. Police and soldiers are looking under every hedgerow for him and he's lying next door with a bullet-wound that could have killed him had it been an eight of an inch to the left."

The Clock smiled as he gestured towards the two dogs.

"That pair look like they could do with a walk. The men have been fed and the soup can wait half an hour. Would you walk with me?"

Isla looked wordlessly at the open door to MacAskill's bedroom. The Clock empathised.

"He's just had two rolls and sausage and coffee with two sugars. I suspect he'll cope without us for thirty minutes."

Isla dried her hands on a dishtowel.

"S'pose."

Initially the twosome focussed upon Blaze and Rory as they cavorted together on a path round a small lochan close to MacAskill's front door. After a few moments Isla opened the conversation.

"I can't keep calling you Clock like your army pals. Have you a proper name?"

Clock laughed. "Yeah, I do. I'm just a simple priest. A Jesuit actually. The Reverend Michael McSween. You have the choice of Reverend Father Michael or simply Mike. I *much* prefer Mike."

"Are Jesuits allowed to participate in the military?"

"Many faiths permit their soldiers to be supported. Jesuits place considerable emphasis upon flexibility which allows us to become involved in a great variety of ministries and missionary endeavours in all parts of the world. It's been a good fit for me. In some ways, the Jesuits are the Commandos of the Roman Catholic faith. Our present Pope, Pope Francis is a Jesuit...he's the first Jesuit to be elected Pope mind you. We're not always the most popular order. I've a small clerical responsibility in a rural parish in Renfrewshire although I have other responsibilities that needn't trouble us today. While I've retired from front-line service with the Marines, I still make the time to offer such assistance as I can to those who have retired and live in Scotland. I do quite a lot of fund-raising for fallen comrades and those who have been wounded either physically or mentally. The army top brass and the charities I plague for resources don't know whether the Reverend Michael McSween wants to lift their heart or their wallet."

"And your assistance includes rescuing and patching up shot Commando Captains who have the British Establishment in turmoil?"

"Precisely so...an individual whom I love and respect beyond all others outside of the church had urgent need of my medical and practical services and I responded without a second thought knowing that had the call been made in the other direction, the Captain would have moved heaven and earth to assist me...and to assist me without regard to whether I deserved it or not." He allowed a silence as Isla considered his words. "You're a vet, Isla. You care for your flock, *literally* care for your flock. You don't offer a lesser service to one sheep because it's troublesome. I have a vet down in my parish who operates regularly on the dumbest bulldog ever to grace a living room sofa. He routinely eats his owner's slippers and requires an operation on its stomach to remedy matters. Sam, my vet friend, doesn't give up on the dog because the poor thing can't see the causal relationship between a tasty slipper and a sore stomach...he just operates and tries to save the dog."

"I'll bet he also encourages the owners to stop wearing slippers."

"I'm sure he does...but his love for animals is unconditional, as is mine for Captain Lachlan MacAskill." They walked on.

"I also happen to believe that the Captain's analysis of the political situation in the United Kingdom in general, and in Scotland in particular, is spot on." He stopped and turned to Isla. "If one of your animals started to horde food it couldn't eat and stopped other hungry animals eating anything, you'd intervene and redistribute the food or at least write a doctoral paper about something previously unknown in the animal world...but in *our* society if someone amasses more great wealth than they need and denies it to others, they put him in the House of Lords. I spent countless nights round a campfire with Lachie as he explained his view of the basic unfairness of the system of government as it affected the people it was supposed to serve. Sometimes we had some Eton and Cambridge-educated officer join us to bestow the wisdom of the ruling classes on the squaddies. On every occasion, without being disrespectful, Lachie tore their arguments to shreds. The Marines in the regiment loved him. Not only was he ferocious in looking after them, not only did he know the names of their wives, their kids, their dogs, even...but he could fence verbally with superior officers and win hands down. Many of those wives and kids I mentioned wouldn't have a husband or a father if he hadn't put his life on the line to save them. So...if I'm asked why I care for the man, it's because I owe him personally, because I love and admire him and because I actually agree his analysis of Scottish politics. If he's now come to the conclusion that he needs to ratchet up the action needed to bring about the change he sees as necessary, I'll stand shoulder to shoulder with him...that is, of course if he actually *is* Dalriada."

Isla turned from her companion, attempting to hide her tears. As he'd done with Marines and parishioners on countless occasions before, The Reverend Michael McSween gathered her in his arms and hugged her until she had recovered some composure.

"Mike...I'm so worried about him. We're just getting to know one another but even without everything you've just told me, I knew he was a very special man. Seeing him helping my mother...d'you know, all the work he does on the estate, all the help he gives, not just to mother but to villagers who need a bit of assistance...he does it all for no pay. He refuses every offer of finance my mother makes. He lives on his small army pension and what he takes from the land in terms of plants, fish, flesh and fowl. He lives in his silly converted ambulance so that if he finds things too stressful, he'll just get into the driver's seat and head off somewhere else."

"And you wouldn't want that to happen, would you, Isla?"

Isla shook her head.

"No, I wouldn't, Mike."

"Then let's you and I make sure it doesn't."

Chapter Thirty

Three days passed during which Dalriada's attack on Crombie Pier slipped gradually from the headlines although the item remained high on the agenda for discussion between Catriona Burns and Chief Constable Andy Shields at their weekly meeting in St. Andrew's House. Ever convivial, Sir Andrew drew attention to progress in identifying the individual who attacked Crombie and empathised with the SAS soldiers who had allowed him to escape.

"We have his DNA now along with increasing definitions of his image although they are too blurry to be of much use and would certainly not be of any merit in a court of law."

"You're certain it was his blood you found?"

"No. But there's a decent chance it's his. That said, we have found no hospital or medical establishment which admitted anyone with a wound where we couldn't establish the *bona fides* of the patient so perhaps it was a very light wound or else he's lying dead somewhere."

"The First Minister's under pressure to announce a capture."

"Yes...as is the Prime Minister, but the London decision to send in the SAS who then watched him escape despite having received prior warning of his intentions, leaves Westminster vulnerable to accusations of incompetency. That said, if he *is* a lone wolf, and he appears to be so, it makes his apprehension extremely difficult. We need him to make a mistake and he hasn't done so yet. Because he doesn't appear to be part of a group or movement, all of our usual lines of enquiry...all of our informants...are rendered null and void. The groups you'd expect are cheering him on but no one seems to know anything about him. Our forensic people have been in touch with the University of the West of Scotland which has a Criminology Department. MI5 had people attend a meeting there and we sent one of our sergeants who's noted for his irascibility just to annoy them. London spooks do tend to have a supercilious attitude when they venture north. Anyway, the group included behavioural scientists, social scientists, forensic scientists and criminal investigators, all professionals involved in the practice of criminal profiling."

"What's that?"

"It refers to any means of inferring the traits of individuals responsible for committing criminal acts. Generally, profiling methods tend to focus upon diagnostic evaluations, criminal investigative analysis and to a some extent, investigative psychology. Their findings suggest that Dalriada is an ex-police officer with firearms training or possibly a retired soldier. They reckon he's male, educated, Scottish, fit, mid-thirties, street-wise and probably lives in a rural area of Scotland, either the West of Scotland or the Highlands. There was disagreement over his psychological profiling. Some thought he was a stable extrovert whereas others figured he was a stable introvert. They agree he's stable...we're not dealing with a crazy person...although we now suspect that he's a red-head."

"And he'll strike again?"

"We think so...and it might be our best chance of catching him. The trail's pretty cold."

"So I'll tell the First Minister you'll have him in handcuffs by tomorrow?"

Sir Andrew smiled broadly.

"I only wish you could."

* * *

Thorpe sat at his desk re-reading the profiling paper on Dalriada for the umpteenth time. *Needle in a haystack...a fucking minuscule needle in a giant fucking haystack of needles. I need to get out of here and make things happen.* Frustrated, he stood and walked to the office of Bill Morton who was on the phone to a hospital.

"You're quite certain?" Morton wrote some notes on a piece of paper. "Well, thanks for your help. We'll follow up these names." He placed the phone on the receiver and spoke to his superior. "Hi, boss. We're still checking hospital admissions in case he's turned up after a few days wait. We're collecting names and will follow them all up to check alibis."

"Extend the search to hospitals in the north of England. Check the morgues too, here and down south. Just in case those arseholes in the SAS managed accidentally to kill the bastard."

"We've already done due diligence on the morgues, boss. There's no one dead who fits the bill. We'll keep looking though, just in case he's died a slow death."

"Keep your shoulder to the wheel. The shrinks reckon he's living in a rural setting somewhere in the west or north of Scotland. We'll need to focus on both but first I'm going north. I'm going up to see that sergeant who comes down to the meetings. The fox hunter assault seemed opportunistic which makes me think he has his base up there. Where is that Sergeant Darroch based?"

"He's in Grantown-on-Spey. A small village just past Aviemore."

"Next to where the attempted assassination of a member of the royal family took place and near where the explosives were stolen?"

"The very same."

"Exactly... I may be incommunicado for a while. If I get a scent, I will almost certainly take executive action. You'll hear about it after the fact...if, indeed, anyone hears about it at all."

* * *

The afternoon glare required that Darroch pulled down the sun-shield on his windscreen as he sat in a police Land Rover which he'd reversed into a small tree-lined bay overlooking the River Spey, a location he'd used many times on a dark night in order to maintain watch on a stretch of the river used not infrequently by poachers. Half an hour had passed and he'd not moved an inch. His face impassive, he turned over in his mind the facts as were known about Dalriada and came to an assessment.

I must be wrong…I must be wrong. He's my best pal, but everything I know about this Dalriada fits his description. If I confront him and I'm right, what's my next move? Jail him? If I'm wrong, how much does it bruise our friendship? He lifted a Manila folder that contained paperwork relating to Dalriada, reading its contents without assimilating a single word. Eventually he focussed upon the blurred photographs of Dalriada making his escape from Crombie. He shook his head. *That's fucking Lachie. No one on this planet could identify the individual from this photograph but as sure as haggis is a health food, that is Lachlan MacAskill…I'm almost certain!* His gaze turned again to the quiet waters of the Spey. *Me and Lachie used to fish these waters as weans.* He smiled. *'Poached' them would be a better word. Now I'm a cop tasked with stopping others doing what I used to do with Lachie.* His gaze rose to the muscular mountain range of the Cairngorms which framed the river before him. *We learned to ski together up there. We climbed these hills in the snow when experienced mountaineers told us not to. We go back a long, long way and I'm now a cop who is pretty persuaded that he's the man who is causing mayhem in the body politic and who should be arrested on sight.*

His reverie was interrupted by an old man beginning to wade out into the Spey wearing waterproof overalls and carrying a fly-fishing rod. Resignedly, Darroch placed his police hat on his head and stepped from his vehicle and cupping his hand to his mouth, shouted.

"Willie….Willie Primrose….Willie!"

His third attempt caught the attention of the fisherman who turned from the burbling waters of the Spey to establish who had called his name.

Darroch stood atop a high bank of the river, his hand still cupped to magnify his voice.

"Willie…Have you bought a permit since I spoke to you last week?"

Willie Primrose grimaced a hard of hearing look which attempted also to convey innocence.

"Willie…don't make me come down there and lift you. If you have no licence…" He reached for words that might convey his frustration… "Just bugger off back hame! Away back hame to Jean and don't let me catch you poaching during daylight hours. You're just taking the piss and not making my job any easier."

Resignedly, old Willie Primrose turned and slowly shuffled his way through the shallow waters to the northern bank of the river as Darroch mildly castigated himself.

So there we go. Instead of jailing someone for an offence, I bend the law to make it fit the culture and circumstance of the Highlands of Scotland…but auld Willie's not wanted by the Crown, not sought the length and breadth of the land…so how do I deal with Lachie?

Chapter Thirty-one

MacAskill placed his right hand on the shoulder of the large axe and gingerly grasped the throat of the handle with his left as he'd done thousands of times before.

His four ex-Marines stood around him a few steps back.

"You're sure this isn't too soon, Captain?' asked the Clock.

"Feels okay so far."

Using his right arm, he lifted the weight of the axe above his right shoulder and sent the blade crashing down upon a log, which splintered.

"See? My left arm is just to guide and offer balance to the blow. It's all in the right arm. Even with no muscle there to speak of, I can still wield an axe and get some work done about the place."

"Well, we'll see what Isla makes of that suggestion, eh, Cap? I'm not so sure it's a good idea."

Right on cue, Isla's Land Rover turned into the area at the front of the cottage and she and Rory stepped from the vehicle, the dog making straight for MacAskill's kneeling position and a cuddle.

"So what's going on here, then?"

MacAskill freed himself from Rory.

"I'm just testing if I have any semblance of power in my left arm. Made a decent job of using the axe on that log."

"Bit soon, Lachie. Your upper arm is still swollen and you might burst your stitches if you're not careful. The bullet missed your triceps but took a lump out of your deltoid muscle. I know you'll say you'll ignore the pain but it won't help your recovery if you damage further what your body's trying to repair."

MacAskill changed the subject.

"How's your mum?"

213

"She's as pig-headed as you. Wants to run before she can walk…but she's getting around…wondering why she hasn't see you in a week."

"What d'you tell her?"

"That you had summer 'flu and that I was now attending to two patients. She's made you soup. It's in the Land Rover. How do you feel today?"

"Okay. Didn't sleep well and I'm still a wee bit tired but I'm eating properly and taking money off these four at cards of an evening so all's well."

"Well, your body will replace the lost blood volume within a couple of days but it'll take maybe four weeks for your body to completely replace the red blood cells. Still, if you're eating well and taking these iron supplements I gave you, you're in a good place."

"Can I run? Exercise?"

"Only if you go with Mike…I mean the Clock. And run only a short distance and run slowly and…"

"Och, I may as well sit in the parlour and read a book. Can I not work up a sweat?"

His question went unanswered as Darroch's police vehicle swept into the yard and braked in a cloud of dust. The four Commandos aligned themselves in front of MaCaskill who smiled reassuringly and placed the axe carefully on a pile of logs.

"It's okay boys, he's a pal of mine."

Darroch stepped from his car, leaving his police hat inside. He hailed his friend.

"Lachie!"

"Hi, Gus."

Still partly obscured by his fellow soldiers, he put his left hand in the pocket of his jeans, anchoring his wounded arm, and stepped forward, offering his right hand in friendship.

"Here, Gus. Let me introduce you to my friends. They all served with me in the Commandos. This here's Mike. The big chap is Stewart, there's Molly, real name Robert and finally Duncan. You know Isla, Blaze and Rory."

Darroch shook the priest's hand and merely waved a greeting to the others, acknowledging only Isla in a monotone that only just passed for friendly.

"Hi, Isla."

MacAskill continued.

"We've been having a wee reunion. Because I'm not on the phone, they just descended on me unannounced and we've had a few days of strong drink and weak hands at cards. Sorry I've not been in touch."

Darroch's face remained impassive.

"I was hoping for a wee chat."

"Well, I was thinking of taking the boys down to the Claymore tonight if you were thinking of popping in for a few glasses."

Darroch shook his head.

"Nah, I need a chat now if that's okay."

Isla intervened.

"These guys were just going off for a run, Gus and I was going to make coffee. You two have a blether in the living room and I'll get the kettle on, eh? I've some home-made soup as well."

Still not smiling, Darroch nodded his agreement and followed Isla into the cottage while MacAskill spoke quietly to his friends.

Seating himself in a small armchair, Darroch rehearsed his opening lines as MacAskill took the matching chair.

"Good to see you, Gus."

"Aye." Darroch laced his fingers and leaned forward. "Mind you told me that there were bagpipes on that Rolling Stones record?"

MacAskill grinned. "Aye, 'Brown Sugar'?"

"Well, I know you were taking the piss but for a moment, I believed you. I believed you, no matter that it was preposterous, because I *always* believe you. We've never lied to one another. You've been my best pal since primary school. We've looked after one another through thick and thin…"

"Christ, Gus, you're awful serious today. Everything alright?"

"No…not really. I'm up to my ears in this Dalriada stuff and wondered if you could help me."

"If I can, Gus."

"MI5, Special Branch, the SAS, every bastard in a uniform north of Carlisle is looking for Dalriada. They've come up with a profile for him. Scottish, smart, fit, ex-cop or soldier, mid-thirties, possibly a Highlander...probably red-headed." He took a folded piece of paper from his uniform pocket as he spoke. "Think of anyone this describes?"

MacAskill's smile hadn't left his face.

"Thought we'd agreed in the pub that I fitted the description except the 'smart' bit?"

"You aced all your exams at school and could have walked into any university. But you wanted excitement and rose from a squaddie to Captain in the Marine Commandos, a decorated war-hero. A sharpshooter. By any measure you're no fool." He unfolded the paper. "Lachie, you fit every aspect of the profile."

Instinctively, MacAskill found himself running the tip of his tongue over his dry lips as he marshalled a response. However, Darroch continued.

"You've got to admit, Lachie. It's all a bit too close for comfort." He shook his head remorsefully. "Earlier when I was getting warm, you allowed me to think you might be working for the authorities on an undercover basis. I didn't think to challenge it because you're the closest human being to me I've ever known. But now..."

Isla appeared in the doorframe with an inverted biscuit-tin lid on which she'd placed two cups of coffee along with sugar and milk.

"Lachie, you lead a life of lunatic frugality. Buying a wee tray wouldn't kill you." She laid the lid down on a small table and began to place a cup beside each man. She stood erect. "Tell him, Lachie. Tell Gus or I will."

MacAskill looked at her askance.

"Eh?"

Isla allowed a deep sigh and sat on a hardback chair that served as a dining chair whenever MacAskill had cause to eat from his table, which was seldom.

"I suppose we had to tell you sometime, Gus. Lachie and I are involved...we're lovers. Whenever he's not been with you in the Claymore, he's been holed up here with me. We look after mother together, we walk the dogs together and when we're not doing that we're...well, we do what lovers do. Now, I've been back here in Inverskillen during the entire period that this chap Dalriada has been tormenting you and we've pretty much been joined at the hip. Now, there must be scores of men who fit the profile you've just described and while I'd love to think that my boyfriend here was Dalriada because I happen to support every action he's taken, it's not been Lachie. I can assure you. In fact, I find it laughable. Actually, when that pier was set on fire in the Firth of Forth, Lachie's ex-Commando pals were here with us in the cottage."

Darroch and MacAskill looked at one another. Each face a mask of confusion, if for different reasons.

Darroch spoke first.

"You two?"

MacAskill summoned up a facial gesture that he intended should convey bashful acknowledgement as Darroch handed the blurred photograph of MacAskill to him.

"Tell me that's not *you*."

Isla crossed the small room and seated herself on the arm of MacAskill's armchair, inspecting the photograph along with its subject. She demurred.

"And who's this meant to be, Gus? Are you saying it's Lachlan MacAskill?" She took the paper and held it closer. God, this could be *you*, Gus. Is your implication that this is a photograph of Dalriada and you think this coloured blur is Lachie?"

"That's what I'm asking."

Isla was defiant.

"Then you're barking up the wrong tree, Gus. This could be absolutely anyone."

Darroch nodded and leant down to the side of the fireplace where a pair of MacAskill's training shoes were sitting. He picked one up and looked at its sole.

"Size nine. You told me you were size ten, Lachie. Dalriada is size nine."

"Different shoes, different sizes, Gus."

"And when you visited old Bill Anderson's workshop to get your chainsaws repaired, you met Constable Calum Buchanan manning a roadblock outside Nethy Bridge on your way back home. He had been there for an hour and although you said you'd just popped into Bill's for a moment, he didn't see you on the way there. There was a roadblock because someone had just taken a shot at Prince Edward."

MacAskill was silent for a moment.

"Jesus, Gus. You're *serious* about all of this."

Darroch stood.

"And maybe it's just as well for you that I am, Lachie." He walked to the doorway and turned.

"Listen. I'm still your best friend. Always will be. But MI5 now have a DNA sample of this person's blood. That'll point the finger at him sure as fate if he is ever apprehended. It places him at the scene of the Crombie attack. They have his shoe size and type from a print at the Boat of Garten shooting range when Tannerite was stolen. They have this photograph." He hesitated. "Now, I'm delighted to hear of you two being a couple. I really am. And it provides you with an alibi. A flimsy alibi but an alibi nevertheless. But if MI5 get their hooks into it, it might unravel."

He walked towards the outer door as Isla and MacAskill each rose and followed him out. Upon reaching his car Darroch offered a parting comment.

"I know that half of Scotland is cheering this Dalriada person on. Many have taken to the streets but given our chat, let's just say that I've decided that my suspicions here today are unfounded but hear this...I hope that this Dalriada person screws the fuckin' bobbin before someone else who is more sceptical than me takes a closer interest. The way I see it, this guy is ahead of the game at the minute. He just might get away with everything that he's done so far but if he gets lifted for so much as droppin' fuckin' litter and somehow ends up having to provide a DNA sample, then the fuckin' balloon goes up, eh?"

He opened his car door and seated himself.

"See you at the pub quiz. But before you arrive, work out whether you were here at the cottage with your Commando pals as Isla says or in Edinburgh with your sister when that pier was attacked as you told me in the Claymore. And look after that left arm you're protecting. It looks sore!"

Slowly, he engaged the clutch, turned the car and headed back to the village. Neither of the twosome spoke until the car's engine could no longer be heard. MacAskill broke the silence.

"Thanks for that Isla...but that just might have been the daftest thing you've ever done."

"And why is that?"

"If I really *am* Dalriada and the authorities arrest me, that alibi wouldn't stand scrutiny and you'd be charged with being an accessory after the fact."

Isla looked at MacAskill squarely.

"And what if I thought it worth the risk to keep you out of prison?"

"Well, I'd be humbled, but you'd still be daft!"

Isla folded her arms and looked disconsolately at her shoes, awkwardly attempting to decide whether to discuss their relationship or her friend's predicament. *Business before pleasure,* she decided.

"Okay. Look! Gus is no fool. He's obviously conflicted and he's clearly giving his best pal a break along with some good advice. So, a couple of things. I'm going back to the gatehouse. I know for a fact that my dad had size ten shoes and that mum has never been able to throw out any of his clothes or belongings. He'll have a pair of walking boots. I'll get them for you and you get rid of those boots you're wearing...just *in case* they match the footprints found at Boat of Garten," she said with a chuckle.

"Might not be a bad idea."

"And when Mike and the lads return, you tell them what happened. I think Mike's a really sharp guy and he might have some ideas about how to make this all go away. They all need to be told anyway given their involvement in bringing you back here. You might want to discuss your Edinburgh visit with them so there's consistency." She unfolded her arms and smiled wanly. "I'll be back in an hour."

She turned and headed towards her Land Rover but stopped as MacAskill hailed her.

"Isla...I just wanted to say...well, thanks for what you did back there. I actually found some of what you said, eh...nice."

Isla nodded slightly and continued walking. He shouted after her once more.

"Thank your mother for the soup. I'm feeling better already."

Isla raised her hand in acknowledgement without looking back. MacAskill stood and watched her drive away while pondering his situation.

So everyone's looking for me are they?...Bet they don't know that the woman who's heading up the posse is my big sister.

Chapter Thirty-two

Thorpe took his Browning pistol from the leather holster under his left arm and placed it in the glovebox of his Volvo. Levering himself from his seat, he locked the car using a button on his ignition key and strode through the front door of the small police office in Grantown-on-Spey. Constable Calum Buchanan was standing at the front desk writing in a ledger. There was a smile in his voice as he spoke.

"Morning, Sir. Can I help you?"

Thorpe displayed his MI5 identification and asked for Darroch by name.

"He's up at old Mr. and Mrs. McFarlane's house, sir...an old couple that's had a tough time recently. He'll be back shortly if you want to take a seat.

"I'm not good at waiting, son. Can you get him on the blower and get him down here?"

"Is it urgent, sir?"

"A matter of the highest state security, son. Life and death."

Buchanan looked at him evenly, anticipating his boss's preference, in doing so remembering the disparaging comments he'd made about his MI5 meeting with Thorpe in Glasgow.

"You wouldn't be the MI5 chap who's hunting this Dalriada fellah, eh?"

"All the way from London," he growled.

Buchanan pursed his lips.

"I went to London once. On an art trip. Stayed on the coach." He nodded in the direction of a blue upholstered bench seat. "Anyway, like I said, if you'd take a seat..."

"Son, if brains were gunpowder, you wouldn't have enough to blow your fucking ears off!"

221

"Aye, some people tell me that. Anyway, sir, if you'd sheath that sharp London wit for a moment and take a seat, Sergeant Darroch will be back in a jiffy."

Thorpe leaned across the desk and contemplated punching the young constable but thought better of it. His temper subsided.

"I'll be outside having a smoke."

"Certainly, sir. And try not to litter. There's a waste bin attached to a lamppost on the pavement for cigarette butts."

Thorpe's irritability, never far from eruption, simmered as he reconsidered his decision not to leap over the desk and assault the young man. As he made a fist, the door opened and Darroch stepped into the office.

"Well, look who it is. We're honoured!" He clapped the angered Thorpe on his shoulder as he passed him. "Social visit is it Mr. Thorpe?"

Thorpe sighed deeply and tried to compose himself.

"I don't do social."

"Are we talking Dalriada?"

Thorpe nodded and was shown into a small office used occasionally by Darroch but was more often where pies and beans were heated by microwave and consumed by those on duty. After some small talk, Thorpe cut to the chase.

"I don't intend to head back south without the scalp of that bastard Dalriada, and those exceptionally clever geeks back at the ranch figure he's based up here in your neck of the woods. So I'm here to ask who you have on your suspects list and what you're doing about it."

"Well, of course it's given the highest priority but yesterday we had a big Hielan' coo break loose from a field just outside the Bridge of Brown and it needed recapturing. Big traffic jam. Must have been six...maybe seven cars involved. Chaos! Both directions too! Then of course we heard tell of poachers over by the Old Military Road at Speybridge. Too good an opportunity to miss but they'd buggered off by the time we got there. Busy, busy."

Angered, Thorpe's temper rose again.

"Look...Since I've arrived, I've had nothing but cheek from your young cop out there and I won't be patronised by the likes of you. You fucking Jocks up here don't seem to give a fuck that there's a terrorist walking about shooting at people."

"What on earth makes you think he's up here somewhere?"

"Because two of the incidents were on your local turf and the third...also only a few miles away...was *opportunistic*, it wasn't planned. It tells me that although he could be hid out at John O' Groats, there's a decent chance he's around here somewhere and you idiots don't seem in the slightest perturbed about that."

"I'll grant you that perturbation isn't common up here. I'll grant you that, alright. We've a well-ordered, well-behaved community up here. Decent folk. A couple of scallywags, but nothing too troublesome. We know everyone and everyone knows us. If there was a gunman running amok, we'd know who it was and where to find him. I've looked at the profile you chaps have produced, made one or two enquiries and I've satisfied myself that there's no one up here I can think of who fits the bill. Maybe you'd be better off looking into your John O' Groats idea."

Thorpe drummed his fingers on the desk, one of the many tells that signified his impatience.

"I've driven all the way up to Brigadoon here to catch this bastard and I won't be returning south without his head on a stake. My people in London will be contacting your boss in Inverness and telling them in the strongest terms that you're not cooperating with our enquiries."

He stood as if to leave. Darroch leaned back in his chair and reached for the rear of an electric kettle which he switched on.

"Just you wire right in, Mr Thorpe. You have every right. I expect they'll ask for examples of our non-cooperation here in Grantown-on-Spey and when you can't give them any, they'll just lift the phone and ask me to be a wee bit more diplomatic. Then you'll come back and maybe find me just about the same, diplomatically speaking, and I'll still be telling you that I don't have a list of potential terrorists that may or may not have been involved in shooting up the royal family. But don't you go away thinking that I'll be getting a rocket up my arse due to your complaining." He took a mug from a desk drawer and inspected it for cleanliness. "No, that isn't going to be happening any time soon Mr. Thorpe."

Thorpe bristled as he placed his hand on the door-handle.

"I'm armed and fucking dangerous, Darroch...armed and fucking dangerous. I'll be around here 'till I nail this fucker. Just don't get in my way. You might get hurt!"

He left, ignoring the cheery wave from Constable Buchanan at reception.

Darroch took some milk from a small fridge and sniffed it to establish its freshness, determining that it was good for tempering perhaps one more coffee.

I think you might just be as armed and dangerous as you say, Mr. Thorpe. I'll need to put my thinking cap on...and be careful!

* * *

Catriona Burns arrived in the conference room where sat her senior officers, chatting amiably amongst themselves as they awaited her presence. She smiled a welcome as she settled in her chair and opened a buff-coloured file which she consulted for a moment before speaking.

"Morning everyone. Sorry about the short notice but as you can imagine, the FM is anxious about the number of protest marches taking place all over Scotland on Saturday, especially the large one here in Edinburgh. I've just come from a meeting with the Chief Constable and he has his force on full alert. We're not expecting much in the way of violence but we also have some information that there will be attendance by those opposed to the antics of this Dalriada chap, and that may have the potential to produce a flash point. The Chief has people on the ground who, let's say, have *associated* themselves with both groups and who will provide up to date information on any potential trouble spots."

A casual hand was raised only slightly from the officer responsible for transport. Catriona nodded her permission to contribute.

"This campaign of Dalriada seems to have welded together those who support Scottish Independence, those in CND who oppose nuclear weapons, the anti-monarchists, the far-left, the Greens, civil rights people and even the animal rights activists. There are local marches in support of Dalriada scheduled for Oban, Aberdeen, Stirling, Perth, Galashiels and Dumfries on Saturday. It's clear that there's been considerable coordination here and, frankly, it's been helpful as it reduces the numbers attending the big Glasgow and Edinburgh events. That notwithstanding, the pressure on the road network and rail services will be immense. There are no plans to increase train services so I'd encourage the Chief Constable to ensure a presence at rail hubs as not everyone who wants to get on a train will be able to do so. Football matches in Glasgow, Edinburgh and Perth will also compound matters. Road networks may be jammed."

"Sir Andrew tells me he's already spoken with the Transport Police and they're as ready as they can be although, as you imply, it's going to be a gargantuan task to deal with the transport problems this throws up."

Another hand.

"Any closer to apprehending Dalriada?"

"I'm afraid not. As you'd imagine, there are a number of leads being followed up but being honest, we're not much further forward."

A third hand.

"Our PR team tell us that BBC Scotland and STV, in fact all of the broadcasters, propose to downplay coverage of the marches unless they're forced to televise some incident that occurs."

"That's helpful but social media will ensure that it's widely covered. We can only hope that it all goes off uneventfully."

PR continued.

"We've also turned our minds to how we deal with the potential apprehension of Dalriada and the prospect of him being hauled in front of a court. There could be significant challenges maintaining order not to mention the problem of finding a neutral jury. He's managed to split the nation with many viewing him as a

Scottish hero and others as an outlaw. Selecting fifteen people who are open and measured in their views of him might be difficult."

"A bridge to be crossed at another time, Johanna. We have to catch the blighter first!"

* * *

With Molly Malone in the lead, the four ex-Commandos completed their run and returned to the cottage, sprinting the last few hundred yards. Wreathed in sweat, they each fell on the grass, exhausted by their efforts, their tops darkened considerably by copious perspiration.

MacAskill walked from the cottage and threw each of them a towel before sitting on the grass beside them.

"Boy, am I out of condition," gasped the Clock.

"You've done well for an old man who only gets exercise chasing altar boys round the confession box," countered Snipe.

"That's when the real exercise starts," chipped in Posh Boy. "When he catches them!"

Father Mike McSween merely lay back and smiled at the banter, shaking his head in disapproval as MacAskill called them to order.

"Guys, listen up!" He allowed a distraction as Blaze sat beside him looking for some attention. "Now, it seems obvious that I'm being fingered as this Dalriada bloke. All four of you have taken an oath of allegiance and have sworn that you will be faithful and bear true allegiance to Her Madge, her heirs and successors, according to law, so help you God. One of you is a priest which maybe suggests that he takes *that* oath…and the broad requirement not to bear false witness given it's one of the Ten Commandments, a tad more seriously. Now, were I to 'fess up to being Dalriada, it'd put you in a position of having to have me taken into custody, or lying about it should you ever be asked to spill the beans. In the case of Clock here, it'd mean he'd have to spend all day praying for my mortal soul or join me in Hell when his time's up."

The group looked uneasily at one another. Finally Posh Boy spoke up.

"Well, the way I look at it, Captain, is that we're no longer Marine Commandos. We're all *retired* Marine Commandos, *ex*-Marine Commandos, so the oath has been retired as well. I happen to be a big fan of the Queen if not so much of her heirs and successors, but my allegiance, for what it's worth, is to my brothers-in-arms. To you in particular. I answered the call as I did to offer whatever assistance I could to a comrade who needed my help. That still stands. I can't speak for the others."

Almost as one voice, Snipe and Molly agreed. MacAskill turned to Mike McSween.

"Where does the Reverend Michael McSween stand on this?"

"Well, unlike these three, while I'm no longer a Marine Commando, I haven't retired from the church. Telling the truth is important to me as it is for the church. If I were to be aware of you as a wanted fugitive, then my duty as a citizen might be to see you drawn to the attention of the authorities. However, in my business of faith, I am constantly faced with dilemma. I was pastor to you chaps when you were engaged in dealing death. Not very Christian. I not infrequently kept your drunken misdeeds from your commanding officers...even from Captain Lachie MacAskill here...*that's* bearing false witness. Not very Christian. I even remember helping Captain MacAskill steal a pool table from the Royal Engineers so we had some distractions at camp and remember also chastising myself that I so easily broke the seventh Commandment in doing so." He smiled. "*Certainly* not very Christian, so I'm far from perfect. None of us are. I take the view that the confessional need not take place only in the Confession Box and so, if Captain Lachlan MacAskill wishes to confess, I would hear his unburdening and keep it confidential."

"Even though he's a renowned atheist, Clock?" asked Snipe.

"I was pastor to one hundred and twenty men out in Afghanistan. I'd say perhaps twenty were believers and of *them*, maybe only a dozen were Roman Catholics so I'm pretty used to hearing confessions from men who don't have the same faith as me, particularly in moments of great stress. I'm at peace with this."

He turned to MacAskill.

"So, anything you'd like to share Captain? It appears you have our confidence."

Chapter Thirty-three

Thorpe stepped from his car and entered the portals of the Old Bridge Inn just outside Aviemore where Tam the barman was gingerly placing some additional fuel on a log-burning stove already ablaze.

He stood as Thorpe waited at the bar, wiped his hands on his denims and smiled a welcome.

"Good morning, sir. What can I get you?"

Thorpe was inquisitive. "Log fire on a sunny day?"

"Customers like the atmosphere it creates and it's seldom warm enough up here to melt an ice-lolly. Anyway?"

"A Macallan whisky with lots of water."

"You'll be ruining a great whisky, sir. The Macallan has a reputation as one of our finest whiskies. Distilled in Craigellachie just up the road. At best maybe a wee splash of water but more than that, well...up here that'd get you hung!"

"Thought the customer always knew best?" responded Thorpe sourly.

"Indeed they do sir." He removed the glass from beneath the Macallan optic. "I'll let you pour your own water."

Thorpe filled the small glass almost to the brim with water and took in his surroundings.

"Nice pub!" He sipped at his drink as he paid. "Wonder if you can help me...I'm a journalist with the Sunday Times and I'm writing a piece about Post Traumatic Stress Syndrome and what life is like for ex-soldiers and well, uniformed people who've retired from their service and are now living a rural life. I figured that the best place to ask around might be the local pub. Any of your regulars fit that description?"

The barman gave this some thought.

"Well, there are two I can think of. Both their seventies. If you chat with them make sure to set aside a couple of days and ensure that you have deep pockets as they'll talk the hind legs off you about them being warriors if you buy them a glass."

"I was thinking more of people in their thirties, maybe forties."

Further thought was given.

"Not really. Just old Bob and Neilly."

Thorpe nodded and took a long quaff of his whisky. He hesitated, then produced the photograph of MacAskill taken at Crombie from his pocket.

"Know this man?"

Tam placed his spectacles atop his nose and contemplated the image.

"My God, it could be anyone. Bit too grainy to allow recognition, I'd say."

"Yeah...not a great shot." He retrieved the photograph and placed it inside his jacket pocket. "Tell me, what pubs in Aviemore are used by the locals as opposed to tourists?"

"Och, the locals round here'll drink anywhere. I'd say the Winking Owl and the Balavoulin are your best bets."

Thorpe finished his drink and placed the glass back on the bar.

"I'm obliged."

Watching him as he left the inn and entered his vehicle, Tam the barman took note of his number plate and wrote it on the palm of his left hand. Stepping back, he picked up a phone used mostly by topers to call a taxi and dialled the number of the Aviemore police station. It was answered by Constable Calum Buchanan. Before Buchanan could complete his practiced introduction, Tam was talking over him excitedly.

"Calum...Calum. It's Tam here from the Old Bridge...quick... is Gus in the office?"

"He's out at the minute, Tam. Something up?"

"Aye, there was a guy in here a minute ago. Said he was a journalist from the Sunday Times doing an article about old soldiers or something. Thing is...he showed me a photograph of someone...couldn't make it out...but when he put it back in his pocket I was sure I could see a gun in a holster under his arm. Now I might be wrong but..."

"This guy, Tam...about six feet? English accent? Carnaptious?"

"Aye, that'd be him. I took a note of his number plate."

"Read it out to me, Tam. That might be helpful. In the meantime, I wouldn't worry. He's known to us and he's no danger to you or your customers. What kind of car was he driving?"

"Black Volvo. Registration EU19 XEJ."

"You're a pal, Tam. I'll let Sergeant Darroch know and I'll maybe pop in for a pint after work...but don't worry. This guy's harmless."

"He wanted to know other pubs to visit. I told him the Owl and Balavoulin."

Buchanan thanked him, finished the call and contacted Darroch by radio asking him to return to the office when convenient.

* * *

It was dusk as MacAskill assembled his four friends in his small living room and bid them sit. Low-wattage lightbulbs did little to illuminate the room although the log fire offered some assistance.

"Guys, I've given this a lot of thought and have decided that this fellah Dalriada should hang up his boots. I've decided to come clean and own up to my activities. This gets you off the hook as the police would have no further interest in you. Scotland is now in a bit of an uproar which is what I had intended should happen. Now, I propose to draw a line in the sand...but not until I complete two final acts tomorrow evening. I mention this only because of my wounded arm." He patted his upper arm still swathed in bandages beneath his shirt. "I might need assistance to achieve my objectives. Half of Scotland appear to be taking to the streets in support of Dalriada and against those injustices I've attempted to highlight by my actions. The day after they get home, I hope to have something broadcast that'll put it all into context but first, I intend to remove seven padlocked gates which Lord Hanbury has newly erected in what has been, since time immemorial, a public right-of-way in the Glenburn Estate just south of Moy, near Inverness. I propose to throw them in Loch Moy. You may have read in the papers that in order to protect his ability to bring well-heeled toffs up to Scotland to shoot grouse, he wants no locals, no hill-walkers, no environmentalists on his land. He's breaking the Scottish Land Reform Act which gives access rights to almost all land and inland water in Scotland provided people respect others' privacy, safety and Scotland's environment and he's no slouch at using his deep pockets to pursue legal actions that maintain his position. Poisoning raptors, setting baited ground-traps for any creature that might prey on a grouse, keeping hill-walkers off his land, was certainly not what was intended by the Act. Lord Hanbury has made a lot of newspaper headlines but tomorrow evening, under cover of darkness, I propose to rid the right-of-way of his impediments and allow people to exercise their rights once again. Following that, I propose to visit the BBC Highland headquarters in Inverness and take advantage of their empty studio to record a message for the people of Scotland. I accept that this will identify me and will see me apprehended by the authorities but I will have achieved my objective. You all served with me under fire and appreciate the importance I place on achieving any mission in which I am engaged."

"Sure this is wise, Captain? asked Snipe." He took the remnant of some roll-up tobacco from the tip of his tongue and continued. "Can't speak for the others but I'll be with you tomorrow night and I certainly won't be saying anything to anyone about you or Dalriada no matter how much the cops or anyone asks me to. Seems to me we could maybe carry out both tasks and still have you remain incognito."

"It's maybe about time I outed myself, Snipe."

Molly Malone intervened.

"We can discuss that later, Captain. I can see how together we could easily remove those gates you describe but how on earth will you be able to make use of all the technical equipment necessary to broadcast your announcement?"

MacAskill smiled. "If my plan works...with the help of you guys...I won't need to. I've checked out the BBC Studios in

Inverness. They're mainly used for radio broadcasting and some televised content for BBC Alba TV. They're only on-air for about seven hours a day and shut up shop after their last broadcast at eleven. From midnight onwards, there's only one doorman playing solitaire on his computer at the front desk. If I can see him entertained at the front door, I'll have ample time to make my way up to the studio where I just turn the lights on and speak into one of your modern mobile phones with a video camera. I'd use the studio used by BBC News and it'd be indistinguishable from the real thing when I put it out on social media."

"Aye, Cap, but you'd be identified immediately and you'd be off to the pokey in jig time...maybe for quite a while," responded Posh Boy.

"The trial would be entertaining, though."

The Clock demurred.

"Not if they held it in-camera, Lachie. Not if they brought a charge under a terrorism act and allowed a judge-led decision in chambers rather than a jury trial."

MacAskill paused in thought.

"Hadn't considered that, Mike." He shook his head dismissively. "I'll think on it, but first we agreed that we'd have a beer in my local tonight, eh? Quiz Hour at the Claymore awaits... and tomorrow evening, once darkness falls and all these marches in my support have ended, can you assist in my last two acts as Dalriada?"

A smiling murmur of agreement prefaced the noise of chairs being moved as the men stood and readied themselves for departure.

MacAskill placed his right hand lightly on Mike McSween's shoulder and spoke quietly.

"Listen, Clock...how about you and the guys walk down to the village. It's only twenty minutes. I'll drive over to Lady Helen's. I want to explain my thinking to her and to Isla. They deserve to know what I've been up to and how I propose to accept my fate."

"You sure, Captain?"

"Yeah. I'll join you immediately afterwards…Isla too, if she's in the mood." He smiled, hoping it looked reassuring. "I'll see you all in the Claymore. Mine's a pint of Guinness."

* * *

Gus Darroch perched on the end of his desk and quizzed his junior colleague.

"So Thorpe's taken to visiting our pubs with a gun under his oxter and he's frightening the horses?"

"Seems to be. I've asked around. He's been in all of the pubs in Aviemore. I telephoned Manus Maxwell over in the Country Inn in the Boat of Garten. He's been there and seems to be making his way through all of the villages in Strathspey. If I'm right, he'll be in Nethy Bridge soon. I've asked Willie McDonald in the Nethy Bridge Hotel to phone me if he shows up there."

"So he'll be in Grantown-on-Spey by tonight at this rate, eh? I was going along tonight for the pub quiz with Lachie so I'd better get home, get changed and make sure there's no trouble if Thorpe turns up with his shooter. It's one thing him speaking to people during the day…quite another at night when everyone's pissed! Anyway, we don't want these London boys getting lost or getting into difficulties."

As he fastened his top shirt button in readiness to leave the office, a phone rang and was answered by Constable Buchanan who listened momentarily and waved Darroch over, the phone still to his ear. He covered the mouthpiece with his hand as he spoke.

"It's that police sergeant from Glasgow. Special Branch. Colin Boston."

Darroch nodded acceptance and took the receiver from Buchanan.

"Hi Colin. Caught Dalriada yet?"

"I'm hamstrung with a halfwit for an assistant and a diddy for a boss. I'd be lucky to see him lifted if he walked in with a big sign round his neck saying 'I am Dalriada'."

Darroch laughed as Boston continued.

"Listen, I was talking to that number two in the MI5 team, Bill Morton and he was telling me that his boss, thon arsehole Thorpe was making his way up to your patch. Thought you should know."

"Aye, he's already been in to see me and pass the time of day. He's now apparently walking about the place causing trouble, asking questions and upsetting people."

"Got room for another polis causing trouble, Gus? There's hee-haw happening down here."

Darroch agreed instantly. "It would be great to see you, Colin. I've a big house with four bedrooms and there's just me at the minute. I can put you up and we'll go look for trouble together. It'd be nice to see you."

"I might have to bring stupid-lookin' with me. Just for shits and giggles."

"The two of you would be very welcome. Just call me when you get here."

"I'm leaving now, Gus. Just need to get wee Jimmy Boyd out of kindergarten and fill the tank."

Chapter Thirty-four

The Claymore was busier than usual, partly given MacAskill's increased team numbers. Good natured banter flowed as the teachers' team shouted their denunciation of his use of 'four obvious professors' as a ploy for his team to win the quiz for the first time. MacAskill's rebuttal that not one of them had as much as an 'O' Grade to their name drew smiling shouts of derision from his new team members; Snipe claiming proficiency in woodwork and metalwork as evidence of academic excellence. Just before the Benny the quizmaster commenced proceedings, Isla entered to further shouts of scoffing and booing as the Inverskillen team now numbered six. Initially perturbed at the welcome, Isla took comfort in the ready smiles of all around her and took a seat next to Mike McSween.

Benny raised the microphone to his lips.

"Remember to write the name of your team at the top of the answer sheet. I failed my 'O' Grade Telepathy so I need to know which team I'm scoring…"

Some who'd forgotten took a few moments to comply, some teams arguing briefly over the name of their team.

"Okay…let's start…How many years must a Scottish whisky mature to be considered whisky?…That's, how many years must a Scottish whisky mature to be considered whisky?"

"In this pub, aboot hauf an hour, Benny", shouted one of the locals to much laughter. The bar's ambient noise level dropped as whispered conversations took place within teams, MacAskill's group quietly discussing whether it was three years or ten, finally resolved by Posh Boy, who was known as a whisky *aficionado*. Three years was settled on as an answer. Just as the hubbub ebbed, the door opened and Thorpe walked in, slowly taking a sense of the atmosphere as he approached the bar. Caught up in the quiz, few took notice of the tall stranger.

"Just a glass of water, barman."

John the barman busied himself preparing the drink as Thorpe scanned the room.

"Busy tonight, eh?"

"Quiz nights are always a bit busier."

"Local crowd then?"

"Aye. They're pretty much all regulars."

Thorpe took his crumpled photograph from his pocket.

"Recognise this man?"

John's spectacles hung on a lanyard round his neck. He placed them atop his nose and peered at the photograph, slowly shaking his head.

"Bit blurry. Could be anybody."

"Remind you of anyone round here?"

"Could be half the village."

Thorpe retrieved the photograph and continued to scan the bar, stopping as he noticed MacAskill's unkempt red hair. Placing some coins on the bar he collected his drink and walked over to the Commandos.

MacAskill's head was bowed as he consulted his teammates over a question about Sir Walter Scott.

"Don't I know you?"

MacAskill raised his head and considered his interrogator.

"Don't think so." He shook his head as he replied.

"I think I know you from somewhere. Did you not wear a uniform...maybe still do?"

"Don't think we've met, my friend."

Thorpe's voice took on an edge and he leaned forward in a threatening posture.

"Answer my question!"

As MacAskill leaned back in his chair affecting nonchalance, the four large ex-marines stood as one man and glared silently at Thorpe who, realising his tone had caused offence, attempted retrieval of the situation.

"No offence, mate. Just thought I knew you from somewhere."

As the confrontation became noticeable to other quizzers, a silence fell on the room just as the door swung open and revealed

Gus Darroch. One glance told him a confrontation was brewing between Thorpe and MacAskill's friends. Four paces took him to the side of Thorpe.

"Ah, Mr. Thorpe. I see you're acquainting yourself with one of our quiz teams. I'm usually a member but they'll have to come last without me tonight. I was just going to have a drink at the bar. Care to join me?"

Thorpe held MacAskill's gaze for moments before allowing himself to be led to the bar by Darroch.

"Looks like you're upsetting the natives. When I've a uniform on it's my job to see that no one does that. Tonight I'm off-duty but I still have the same attitude."

"That guy...he's got red hair. Same build as the guy in the photograph."

"Well, if you got the same report as I did today you'll maybe have noticed that the forensic boys added a footnote to the effect that thirteen percent of Scots have red hair. There's about five million Scots. That makes it about six hundred and fifty thousand of our people who are gingers...and that's not counting Highland coos."

"Know him?"

"Aye, I know him. He's a gamekeeper and general handyman on the Inverskillen Estate just outside the village. Name's Lachlan MacAskill. And to add to your sense of coincidence, he was a Captain in 3 Commando. Field promotions and decorations as long as your arm. He's a quiet man. Lives alone. Very popular in the village."

"Fits the profile perfectly."

"Sorry to piss on your chips but as you'd imagine, he's been checked out. He has watertight alibis and witnesses who'd testify to his being where he said he was on those occasions when Dalriada was active." He called on the barman who was busily washing glasses. "John, can I have a pint of lager and get this man a big Glenmorangie. We can't have you drinking water. We have a saying up here. You should never have water without whisky. Nor should you ever have whisky without water."

"I'm driving."

"So are half this room."

Thorpe swallowed the remnants of his glass and placed it on the bar.

"You fucking Jocks think everything's a laugh and a lark, don't you? He's the nearest thing we have to a suspect. I expect to be having a few words with him when he's not surrounded by his army."

Darroch took on a new tone.

"Well, you'd better bring your 'A' game, Thorpe. You couldn't beat him with five aces. He's quiet and inoffensive like I say, but he's able. He's also non-violent. I happen to know that he has renounced all violence as a consequence of his overseas experiences with the Commandos. He wouldn't harm a fly."

"We'll see about that."

Turning on his heel, Thorpe walked from the Claymore, fixing MacAskill with a glare as he did so. Oblivious to his departure, MacAskill was deep in conversation with Isla but four pair of eyes followed the MI5 man as he stepped out onto the pavement.

Darroch stood at the bar alone sipping at his pint. After a few minutes he was joined by MacAskill.

"Who's your friend, Gus?"

"Name's Thorpe. A name synonymous with eejit. He's MI5 and he suspects you of being Dalriada."

"Does he now?"

"Aye, he does. And although he's an eejit, he's also a very nasty piece of work. I told him you had alibis but he reckons you fit the profile perfectly."

MacAskill captured the attention of the barman. "A Macallan, John. Big one...and a Glenfiddich chaser for Gus." He turned his back to the bar, leaned against it and spoke quietly to his friend. "This'll all be over in a couple of days, Gus."

"Christ...now you're worrying me, Lachie. These people play for keeps. I've checked this guy out. He works alone and has a reputation for not taking prisoners. He's armed. You always had the ability to talk me into a burning car but there won't be much I can do to help if he throws the British State at you."

"I need two more days. If you could keep him off my back until then it'd be appreciated, Gus. I'll explain everything then. Promise!"

The Inverskillen Quiz Team had largely forsaken the quiz and had missed the last three questions. At the edge of the group, Mike McSween and Isla were deep in conversation.

"I don't know whether to feel pride that the man I've been cheering on is my friend...or whether to feel sad at the prospect of him being hurt or ending up in prison...I've become very fond of him and was beginning to imagine that maybe he was becoming fond of me too, Mike."

"Och, you need have no doubts on that matter, Isla. It's as clear as day that he has feelings towards you. He's just a big feartie. Brave as a lion on the battlefield. 'Wee, cowrin', tim'rous beastie' in affairs of the heart."

"I think the Burns' line is, 'Wee, *sleekit*, cowrin, tim'rous beastie'."

"Well, if half of what's been going on is down to him, I'd have to concede sleekit," smiled McSween.

"Indeed." She reached across the table and squeezed his arm. "Mike, you're a very special person...I feel I can talk to you. It's just...well..."

"Yes?"

"I don't want to lose him..."

McSween placed his hand over Isla's and pressed it reassuringly.

"Nor do I. And I have the semblance of an idea. Perhaps I could walk you home and we could discuss it. Might your mother still be up at this hour?"

"Oh, certainly. She's a late bedder. But how might she assist?"

"I'll explain as we walk. Let's go."

"Let's get Blaze. Lachie asked if we could look after him over the weekend."

Darroch's mobile phone rang.

"Gus Darroch."

"Hi, Gus. It's Colin Boston. We're just approaching Aviemore."

"Jesus, Colin. You must have broken the world speed record to get up the A9 so fast."

'Aye. If I hadn't been a cop I could've been a great get-away driver! I'll have paperwork to fill out when I get back wi' all these speed cameras."

"Aye, so." He glanced at MacAskill. "Look, I'm in Grantown-on-Spey. My house is on the edge of the village. Number one, Braemoray Avenue just as you enter the village from where you are. I'll get a lift from Joe the Taxi here and should be back before you get there. Is your young constable with you?"

"Aye. Brought him just to feed me mints and keep me awake while I broke every speed limit known to man."

"See you shortly, Colin. I've all the beds made up. There's a bottle of Glenmorangie I want to show you both."

A laugh on the other end of the phone signalled the end of the conversation. Darroch turned to MacAskill as he pocketed the phone.

"That's Special Branch, Lachie. One sergeant and a constable. They're up from Glasgow and they're joining the fray. They're staying with me for a few days." He looked around to ensure he wasn't being overheard. "Look, Lachie, I'm your best friend and always will be. But I'm a cop and my job is to bring this Dalriada fellah to heel."

"He won't exist after Sunday, Gus…"

"Look, it's obvious they're circling you. MI5 and now Special Branch. You take care and I'll do what I can to stay their hand. I won't perjure myself so there are questions I won't ask because don't want the answers to them. Okay? I can only do so much."

"Thanks, Gus. I'll explain everything shortly."

"Take care, Lachie. Stay out of trouble and don't do anything I wouldn't do."

"Can't promise, Gus…but I'll be careful and I *do* promise this'll all end soon."

Chapter Thirty-five

MacAskill knelt before the ancient log-burning stove in his living room and fed the nascent flames some small sticks as a precursor to heavier logs he had beside him.

"Make yourselves comfortable, boys. Snipe, you're nearest, maybe you'd bring that bottle of Grouse through. There's glasses in the kitchen as well. We could maybe have ourselves a wee nightcap before turning in. You have the cottage to yourselves. I'll sleep in the Tardis tonight."

The three marines did as requested.

"Where's the Clock?" asked Posh Boy.

"He's walking Isla and Blaze back to her home. He'll be with us shortly," responded MacAskill, still tending the fire.

The whiskies poured and all four seated round what was now a blazing fire, MacAskill toasted them.

"*Slàinte mhath*, boys. Thanks for everything."

"Our pleasure, Cap," replied Snipe. "You've fairly got Scotland riled up. Anything we can do to help...although I'm not daft about the idea of you revealing yourself openly. Why not continue to evade the forces of law and order just like you've done from the beginning?"

"Well, they're closing in on me. That fellah in the pub tonight was MI5 and there's another two boys from Special Branch in the village. Now, I'm not crazy about leaving all this behind me... spending my time in a cell rather than the great outdoors but I have to face up to the fact that the British State is closing in. I don't want anyone to get hurt and maybe if my trial was public, I could make a statement explaining my actions and showing the injustices under which Scotland labours due to British exploitation."

"And what about Isla? asked Molly. "That lassie seems pretty soft on you."

"Aye, I've given that a lot of thought...a lot of thought. Her mother matters to me too. Lady Helen needs support as does this estate but still...I can't wish away my situation. There are now going to be dozens of marches on Saturday. Scores of thousands of people will take to the streets in towns and cities all over Scotland to denounce the very inequities I've been railing about. So, I've kind of made my point. Scottish Independence is the one way we can guarantee the removal of those obscene weapons of mass destruction from our soil and the introduction of a more legitimate social structure in Scotland. As I said earlier, I propose to make a public announcement using the good offices of the BBC in Inverness so that when these foot-soldiers get home and rest up, they can hear me speak on social media the following morning in quite a dramatic way...and in the run-up to that, I can do a bit of damage tomorrow night to Lord Hanbury's determination to keep the *lumpenproletariat* from interfering with his moneyed toffs and grouse shooters."

"What in God's name is the *lumpenproletariat*, Cap?" asked Molly.

"The rabble, the great unwashed, the riff-raff", Molly... "*You* actually!" he grinned.

Outside the living room window, Thorpe stood in the shadows listening carefully. Footsteps approaching saw him take cover behind the hen house as Mike McSween closed on the cottage, a light from his torch guiding the way. He wiped his boots roughly on a rusty metal doormat and entered the cottage. A rise in the decibel count inside as he did so allowed Thorpe to take undetected to the path just used by McSween and return to his parked Volvo concealed within a copse of fir trees on the B9102.

* * *

Darroch had just put his jacket on a hanger when a car drew up outside his house. Anticipating the arrival of Boston and Boyd, he looked through the curtains to check his assumption, switched on his outside lights and opened the door, exchanging waves of welcome with his guests. After some handshaking, Darroch showed them each their room and invited them through to a comfortable living room where a selection of Scottish pipe music played quietly in the background. Three whiskies were poured.

"So you travelled at the double, but safely?"

"Aye," replied Boston. Driving at night makes me sleepy so Eat-The-Breid here kept me awake by feeding me mints all the way up but his dull as ditchwater patter is so boring I'm glad you live in a bungalow in case I need to throw myself out your window through losing the will to live if his chat doesn't improve."

"Bit harsh, boss!"

Darroch smiled.

"Don't fret, Jimmy. I used to have a sergeant like yours when I was wet behind the ears. Big North Uist teuchter called Hector George McLeod. Made me a tougher person. We ended up great mates. He taught me a lot."

"It's been an experience right enough…mind you the boss has seen and done it all."

"Always wanted to be a cop?"

Boston interjected.

"He ran away to join the circus but he took a lift in the clown car and the doors fell off outside Pitt Street. The polis was the next best thing."

"There's more clowns in the polis than Billy Smart's circus, boss."

Darroch laughed.

"Anyway…your health, Colin! To you, Jimmy."

Boston raised his glass.

"*Slàinte mhath,*" replied Darroch.

"*Slàinte,* toasted Boyd in response to both."

"So you want to join the fun and games up here looking for Dalriada?" asked Darroch of Boston.

"Och, we know he could be anywhere but when we heard that thon MI5 arsehole was up here we figured he might know something we don't and it gave us an excuse to get out of Glasgow and get some fresh air."

"He's been going round the pubs in villages all along the Spey valley here showing everyone that photograph of Dalriada that resembles just about every male that's not a midget or sixty pounds overweight, and hopes to have him identified. Before you guys arrived tonight he nearly lifted a guy in the local pub just because he had red hair."

Boston took another sip of his whisky.

"I had a drink last night with Bill Morton, Thorpe's number two. By all accounts your man's a bit of a bastard. Morton reckons he's been used by the security services all over the place when they need a bit of tidying up done. He always works alone. It was pretty clear there's no love lost between Thorpe and Morton but it was also evident that Thorpe's held in very high regard because of his ability to bring about resolutions to awkward problems that might otherwise embarrass the government."

"Can't say I've taken to him myself."

"Don't think he's up here to find Dalriada and read him his rights, Gus...and he won't want him pleading 'not guilty' in court with all the publicity that'd bring. As a cop, I find myself more worried about the likelihood of *him* offending the law of Scotland than this guy Dalriada."

Darroch nodded his agreement. "Aye, people in the pub are cheering Dalriada on. He's looked on as a bit of a hero."

Boston agreed. "He can obviously shoot straight. He could have shot the drivers of those vehicles in the nuclear convoy, he could have put a bullet between the eyes of thon wee daft prince, killed the fox hunter, used that explosive to take lives...but he didn't."

A silence ensued as the threesome absorbed Boston's words. It was broken by Boyd.

"Then maybe *we* need to get a hold of Dalriada before Thorpe does..."

Boston smiled.

"Son, we'll maybe make a polis of you yet!"

Darroch looked pensively into his glass of whisky and weighed Boyd's proposition.

* * *

Thorpe inspected his mini bar, emptied the contents of a miniature bottle of Grouse whisky into a glass tumbler he'd taken from the bathroom and filled it to the top with tap water. Before drawing the curtains, he looked out of the window of the Cairngorm Hotel opposite Aviemore's railway station where only days before, shots had been fired at the entourage supporting Prince Edward. A train bound for Glasgow slowly pulled out. He watched until it had gone, closed the curtains and sat on the single chair provided for the room. Long moments preceded his first lengthy draught of whisky before he decided on his next action.

Reaching into his case, he withdrew a pair of disposable gloves and put them on. Next, he took the hotel pen and scribbled on the back of an envelope to ensure that the ink was flowing before taking a sheet of the hotel's notepaper. Carefully, he folded the top of the page so that the hotel's logo and address were isolated then carefully creased the fold before tearing the top strip from the rest of the sheet, leaving only a white sheet of paper. Throwing the strip in the bin, he devoted his attention to the blank page. Before writing, he withdrew a green folder from his case, opened it, and inspected a copy of the notes sent by Dalriada to the National Newspaper. Copying the capitalised lettering used by Dalriada, he ensured that all letters were hand-written with a sharp font, that all 'T's were written as if the number 7, and that every 'O' and 'Q', indeed every curve of any letter had been squared...just as had been done by his quarry.

Reading the note back, he smiled at his handiwork.

SIR

THIS IS MY LAST LETTER TO YOU AND ITS PURPOSE IS TO OFFER AN APOLOGY TO ALL SCOTS WHO WERE DELUDED ENOUGH TO BELIEVE THERE WAS SUBSTANCE TO MY EARLIER ACTIONS. I BELIEVE I SUFFER FROM A SEVERE BIPOLAR DISORDER AND TOOK THESE ACTIONS DURING A TIME OF MY LIFE WHEN I WAS HYPOMANIC. I NOW REALISE THE ERROR OF MY WAYS AND WISH THINGS COULD RETURN TO NORMAL IN SCOTLAND.

AS MY MOOD CHANGES I HAVE COME TO THE VIEW THAT I HAVE UNLEASHED MISERY ON THE PEOPLE OF SCOTLAND AND THAT THE ONLY WAY TO ACCEPT RESPONSIBILITY FOR MY ACTIONS IS TO END MY LIFE. IF YOU ARE READING THIS, MY SUICIDE WILL HAVE BEEN ACCOMPLISHED SUCCESSFULLY. WHAT I'VE DONE HAS BEEN VERY WRONG.

YOURS FAITHFULLY
DALRIADA

He read it a second time. *Pretty good,* he decided. *My prime goal is to kill Dalriada and to make sure that his body is never found. Failing that, he has to commit suicide and be found with this note on him. One way or another...he perishes.*

A third read prompted him to place two plus marks after the name 'Dalriada' in order to authenticate the letter as coming from the man himself.

Reaching again into his case, he withdrew an A5 sized plastic evidence bag into which he placed the folded letter. Carefully, he tightly closed the clear, resealable Ziplock plastic pouch and placed it in his inside pocket. Finally, he removed his thin latex gloves and placed them in the bin. He took another long mouthful of whisky, removed the Glock 19 from his shoulder holster and inspected it.

Tonight, I heard a confession from Dalriada's own lips... Tomorrow...one way or another...he dies!

Chapter Thirty-six

Catriona Burns unzipped her anorak front and ordered a whisky from the bar in the dank and musty interior of the stone-built Bannerman's pub in Edinburgh's Cowgate. Although it was just after opening time, the pub was busy, a great many of the customers wearing Saltires and paraphernalia indicating their support for CND, Scottish Independence or animal rights. Many appeared dressed for hill-walking. Anoraks were *de rigueur*, it seemed. All seemed in good spirits.

Catriona sat at the edge of a group, so dressed, fussing over a large hound that had been attired in tartan livery and which proclaimed support of Dalriada.

"Would you pass me that water for my whisky, please?" asked Catriona.

"Sure," answered an elderly woman who handed her the small glass she'd used herself for the same purpose only moments before.

"That's a lovely dog. Hope it's not too warm in its beautiful outfit."

"Made it masel'," replied the woman. "If it rains, it keeps her dry."

"And it shows support for Dalriada, too!" responded Catriona empathically.

"Aye, it does that," smiled the pensioner."

Catriona took a beat and launched into her mission that day.

"I was going to go on the march myself today," she lied... "But I'm still unsure about Dalriada's use of violence."

The woman reacted as if slapped.

"Violence? The man's just stickin' up for Scotland. The Poll Tax was violence. Nuclear bombs on our doorstep is violence. Austerity is violence. I mean, d'ye think people don't suffer just as much when decisions are made in England but cause hurt up here?

Politicians moan about it but now we've got someone who puts his money where his mouth is. Dalriada is a national hero and everyone in this pub supports him."

"I can see that. I absolutely sense the passion right across Scotland. People are fed up and want action on these issues but is firing a rifle at people the right way to go about it?"

"No one's been hurt. Even that wee nyaff of a Prince."

"I suppose so..."

"Look at me...I'm nearly seventy year old and here I am out on the streets of Edinburgh wi' ma big dug on a Saturday morning when I should be in the hoose doin' the inside of ma windaes. Me an a' them like me are fed up tae the back teeth about all of they things Dalriada's gaun oan aboot."

"I must admit that I did expect a younger contingent to be on today's marches."

"Ah'm young! Was Nelson Mandela a teenager? Was Gandhi a wean? James Maxton?" She took her whisky in her hand and offered it in a toast. "Here's tae you, hen. You're young wi' yer hale life afore ye. Dae ye really want Scotland to disappear in a cloud of smoke if there an accident on the Clyde? Are you happy that that bunch of scroungers live in luxury in palaces when auld grannies like me have tae go tae food banks? Why wid ye celebrate our young men and women killing *other* young men and women in foreign fields over disputes that have got hee-haw tae dae wi' us here in Scotland?" She took a long sip of her whisky. "Maybe your life is different, hen. Maybe you're happy wi' the way things are but I can tell ye, see everyone in this pub...see everyone on these marches all across Scotland the day...*they're* no' havin' it anymore. Ah willn'y see too many more years on this earth but ma grandweans will...an' *that's* why the insides o' ma windaes are manky the day!"

Catriona touched the lip of the woman's glass with her own.

"I don't think I've heard such a passionate political speech... and I've heard a few."

"Then join us on the march, hen."

"I must go, I'm afraid...but I wish you well."

Finishing her whisky, Catriona exited the bar and walked the half mile to the Whistle Binkies pub in the Grassmarket where she went through the same exchange with a group of animal rights activists before stopping for a coffee in the Filmhouse Café Bar on Lothian Road.

Sitting this time on the edge of a giggling group of older teenagers she wondered about the wisdom of engaging them in conversation before asking the young girl nearest her if they were going on the march down the Royal Mile.

"Once the rest of our pals arrive we're all on the march."

"Sorry to be inquisitive, but what is it about the march that you're protesting?"

"We all want Scottish Independence."

"Forgive me asking, but do I detect an accent from the Home Counties?"

"You do. Weybridge. I'm a student up here but I propose to stay once I qualify."

"What are you studying?"

"Medicine. Up here you still have a Scottish NHS. It hasn't been sold off and I don't believe the Scottish people would ever stand for that. You've more nurses per head of population, more hospital beds per head of population, more doctors per head of population, you're serious about merging health and social care and I want to be part of that...so do my friends. Everyone at this table will be a doctor one day and half of us come from England... apart from Wendy, she's from Cardiff but she wants to stay up here as well."

"So, Scottish independence then?"

"Yes, but also all of the other issues that Dalriada has brought to the surface. I support animal rights, want rid of the royal family once the queen dies, want rid of nuclear weapons, and want an end to foreign adventurism. Britain is no longer a world power and has long been relegated to the second division. Leaving Europe was the final straw that brought me to Edinburgh to study and to this march to protest."

Catriona continued chatting for a while longer, finished her coffee and left, walking the short distance to the Caledonian Hotel where her husband, Andy was looking lovingly at a large and expensive Campbeltown 1973 malt. He was awakened from his reverie as Catriona placed her hand on his shoulder prior to sitting beside him at the bar. He leaned over and kissed her tenderly on the cheek.

"Hi, darling. How was your adventure on the Dalriada march?"

"I'll have what you're having, thank you, Mister Inconsiderate."

Andy caught the attention of the barman and signalled another large malt before turning his attention again to his wife.

"So, Mrs. Top Civil Servant, how was your voyage of discovery?"

"Hardly scientific, but depressing and inspiring in equal measure."

"How so?"

"When last did an estimated two hundred thousand people take to the streets of Scotland in support of anything other than free whisky and haggis?"

"You knew that before you left this morning."

"Yes. But I had no real idea of the strength of feeling that lay behind their commitment." She hesitated. "Look, I know there is another perspective out there...people who genuinely see benefits in the Union, people who believe we're safer with a nuclear deterrent, people who are Royalist to the core..."

"Yeah?"

"I think the mood's changing. I think that the people who held these views belong now in the era of Harold MacMillan and Harold Wilson...the 'Harold' era. The people, young and old, that I spoke to...well..."

"Well?"

"I honestly couldn't disagree with any of them."

* * *

The sun had reddened the sky and had dipped below the tree-line when McSween emerged from the firs and hailed MacAskill who was continuing his attempts to chop wood using one good arm and one guide arm.

"Thought we were going to have to leave without you, Mike," he smiled.

"Just having a word or two with Lady Helen and Isla before the off."

"You're seeing more of Isla than me. Should I be worried? I've heard all about you parish priests."

"Yeah…mother and daughter…the communion wine helped!"

They both embraced, each grinning. MacAskill nodded towards the Tardis.

"We're about to set off. Everything we need is on board. I just need your assurance that you have your posh phone that will record my deathless prose when I take to the airwaves."

McSween took his mobile phone from his pocket.

"Charged it specially. We're good to go."

MacAskill invited his friends around him. All five were wearing battle fatigues and could have passed for a military unit.

"Guys…I want you to know how much this means to me. All day, the radio has brought news of scores of marches in towns and cities all across Scotland. People have taken to the streets in great number. They support the efforts I've made in drawing attention to inequality, warmongering, spending on inhuman and unusable nuclear warheads rather than on poverty and education…and animal rights. I've made it clear that my mission is accomplished… almost. Tonight with your help, we'll make a wee dent in the arrogant belief held by Lord Hanbury that he and he alone will decide who walks on what he thinks of as his land but which is land that belongs to the people of Scotland. When we take care of that, we head for Inverness where we've discussed our plan to enter the BBC Highland headquarters and record a message…a final message that will end the reign of Dalriada. It might well see the back of me for a wee while but I'm counting on you to visit me with a cake with a file in it."

"Permission to speak openly, sir," asked Snipe standing to attention.

"Speak your mind, Private McKechnie."

"Sir. Me and the boys have been talking and have formed the view that you are a fuckin' eejit!"

"Reasonable assessment, Private McKechnie. Have you established a rational argument behind your assertion?"

"Me and the boys see no reason why you should end up in the pokey, sir. Me and the boys think what you have done is admirable but that you should not end up in the pokey, sir. If the law got a hold of you, you'd be entitled to a full jury trial by firing squad."

MacAskill smiled.

"Gentlemen. I love you all...I really do... and I have no great desire to end up in the pokey as you would have it but facts are facts. The forces of law and order are circling. I have almost achieved my objective. One more shove and I'm over the line. Forensic science may soon aid those forces of law and order and I will be brought to justice. No amount of alibis, no number of testimonies of honourable service will dissuade the Establishment from hanging me from the nearest lamppost. But the service I will render humanity, never mind Scotland, is far, far more important than anything they can do to me."

"Permission to speak openly, sir," asked Posh Boy.

MacAskill nodded.

"Most of us think that Private McKechnie is an idiot, sir. But we do agree that it would be better if you avoided the clutches of the forces of darkness. We are collectively of the view that dealing with the several gates you'd like removed tonight is straightforward but that the proposal to make a *visual* statement from the BBC HQ in Inverness is an avoidable folly." He looked around for support. "In that regard, sir, we are of a similar view to that of Private McKechnie, that you are a fucking idiot."

Mike McSween intervened.

"With your permission, sir." He stood atop a large log, allowing him to loom large over the group.

"We have all served under Captain Lachlan MacAskill...our 'Phlegm'. We have all cause to thank him for his judgement, his support and his sacrifice in caring for all of us here and for all of those those who served under his command. Not once...not once ...under fire or under the influence, did I hear any disputation regarding the wise instructions of our leader...not once did I experience a superior officer countermanding his decisions." He smiled. "We have been privileged. Can any of us here tonight claim with any substance that they would be alive tonight if it wasn't for the leadership of our Captain? But now, for the first time, we see fit to question his decisions?" He stepped down from the log. "Gentlemen...I share the love our Captain has for each of you...but I am prepared to accept his judgement. I encourage all of us to act as we would have done had his instructions been made as we lay on the sands of foreign lands. Tonight we are asked to act on his commands. I know, without asking, that we will not let him down." He lifted a small backpack and shouldered it. "Snipe, Posh Boy, Molly...we have gates to remove. Let's get on our way."

There was a unified movement as the group moved silently towards the vehicles. MacAskill, placed his arm around McSween.

"Mike, you're up there with Churchill when it comes to making speeches."

"I was aiming for Wallace at Bannockburn, but as long as it raises the hackles!"

Chapter Thirty-seven

The Tardis and Snipe's small Ford bumped their way down the sandy, unadopted road to the main B9102 road towards Grantown-on-Spey, their progress eased by Posh Boy and Mike McSween travelling in the converted ambulance leaving more room for Molly and Snipe in the smaller vehicle.

As they accelerated along the main road, a Volvo eased its way from a lay-by and followed them at a distance. Every so often, a car was allowed to overtake and supplant the Volvo as the car nearest to Snipe's Ford in order to permit the notion that he was not being shadowed. After half an hour, the Tardis indicated a right turn and began to navigate its way along a Forestry Commission track into pines. The Ford followed.

Thorpe chewed his lower lip as he considered following but decided that he'd be spotted almost immediately and turning off his headlights, reversed his car some distance before parking it across a farmer's gate, fifty yards behind the turn-off.

No one will use this access gate in the dark, he decided as he began to jog after the two vehicles now lost in the darkness ahead.

Although fit, Thorpe wasn't in the kind of condition that allowed MacAskill and his four men to run at pace for an hour before tiring. Still, despite a stumbling run along a darkened path, Thorpe managed to reach the parked vehicles, a short distance into the glen. Breathing deeply, he rested for a moment before straining his eyes and listening to ensure that no one had been left behind to safeguard them. Satisfied, he moved slowly as he heard voices up ahead of the men's vehicles.

Standing over the first of seven gates, MacAskill took his heavy bolt-cutters and snapped the padlocked chain that prohibited entry. A metallic rattle ensued as it was withdrawn from the gate before muscular Posh Boy and Molly lifted it from its hinges. Quietly, MacAskill pointed to his right.

"Loch Moy is about three hundred yards downhill. Submerge it. I'd rather it wasn't found easily. Once it's under, join up with me along the path."

Adjusting their grip, the two marines lifted the heavy gate as if it were made of balsa wood and made off into the blackness of the trees.

"Next one up ahead," whispered MacAskill.

The three remaining men moved forward as one. Standing behind a large pine tree, Thorpe decided that further efforts to follow would be folly and that the odds were that once they'd completed their task, a return to their vehicles and further progress to Inverness was inevitable. He'd await their return and would assess opportunities to deal with Dalriada in Inverness.

He stood silently behind a large fir tree until he could hear no more movement in the forest then sought out a fallen tree between the vehicles and the main road on which he sat in order that he could see the men as they returned from their mission. A cigarette suggested itself and was lit and inhaled deeply as he waited.

* * *

"Jimmy...would you give me and Sergeant Boston here a moment?"

Boyd rose without demur and stepped outside Darroch's living room, and to ensure he was following the request with complete compliance, placed himself outside the front door where he sucked deeply on an electronic device that simulates tobacco smoking. Darroch gestured to Boston that he should sit. Both men faced one another.

"Colin...you're a good sort. I can tell. How long have you been in the force?"

"Near on thirty years, Gus. Man and boy."

"You're nearly at retirement then."

"Canny wait."

"I've a bit to go...see...the point is..."

256

"Spit it out, Gus."

"You and me, we've been round the block once or twice, eh! We know what way's up."

"Gus, that's no' spittin' it out...that's worryin' me that you've something to tell me and you think I won't approve."

Darroch grimaced his acknowledgement.

"I can't afford to make a mistake here, Colin. I need to trust a cop I've only shared a few beers and a bottle of good whisky with. For all I know, you could be a rules man...someone sent by a sleekit HQ to mess around with us unsophisticated Heilan' polis."

"I'm no jobsworth, Gus. I'm a practical man and a pain in the arse to my superiors. I've seen my best years. It used to be that I could wrap up a case at the drop of a hat but these days I often can't find the hat. I'm no glory hunter...just a crabbit old man looking forward to retirement."

Darroch hesitated once more before sharing his thoughts.

"Look, Colin...suppose I suspected a good man of being Dalriada? The cop in me says I should just arrest him and allow justice to take its course. But last night in the Claymore, I could see in the eyes of Thorpe that he believes he has found his man...a man who is relied on by the old folk of the village. Whether he's right or wrong, my worry is that he'll take steps to remove him from this earth and use the breadth of MI5's rules of engagement to nullify him by killing him. He looks like someone who'd accept collateral casualties without losing any sleep. As you said earlier, there's no way he'll want him testifying in court with all the attendant publicity that'd bring. So I have two problems. First, I must find him and try to protect him from Thorpe and secondly..."

"Aye?"

"Secondly, if we come to the view that he has to be lifted, I want it to be done by you. I don't have it in me to lift a good man and I don't want MI5 involved. They can't arrest him anyway but I need to feel he'll get a decent shake of the stick...and I reckon that you're the very man who could see to that."

"I'm comfortable with that, Gus...so what's his name and where do we find him?"

"His name's Lachie MacAskill. *Captain* Lachie MacAskill. Marine Commando, retired. Now a woodsman. He lives in a converted ambulance called the Tardis and he could be anywhere in the Inverskillen Estate. He also has a cottage on the estate, we'll try there first as he's a few pals up from the Marines just now... and if they're still up, he'll have used the cottage as a base. We'll use my car."

"Well, with the measures you pour, you'd better let my young constable drive. He's only had the one whisky. Let's go."

* * *

Each gate took longer to dispose of than the previous one as the right-of-way deviated upwards from the shoreline of the loch, necessitating lengthier periods there and back. As the men reached the top of the glen, only one more gate remained to be dealt with. As with those previously attended to, MacAskill cut the padlocked chain with ease and withdrew it before inserting his 'Dalriada' calling card at a weld at the top of the gatepost. Snipe and Posh Boy lifted the gate and set off downwards towards the loch.

'We convene at the vehicles once you're finished," instructed MacAskill as the three remaining men began their walk downhill. It took twenty-five minutes to approach their meeting place, Snipe and Posh Boy having joined them some ten minutes into the downward journey. As they closed on the vehicles, MacAskill suddenly stopped, stooped and using a tactical hand signal used countless times on manoeuvres, held his right arm out, fist clenched at head level. His left arm waved them to the floor. Instantly, the men froze and squatted, awaiting further instructions. McSween was closest.

"I smell it too, Captain," he whispered.

"Cigarette smoke. Out here in the middle of nowhere at one o'clock in the morning," he breathed quietly. "It could be a poacher or a courting couple but we'd better make sure." Still crouched, he pivoted on his toes and wordlessly drew a circle in the air with his hand. Silently, the men formed a knot around him.

"We can smell cigarette smoke. Someone's out here. Molly, you take the right flank. Out to the main road through the trees then return and report. Posh, you take the left. Do not engage unless provoked. Snipe, you and Clock guard the perimeter of these vehicles. I'll make my way along the track to the road. Complete silence. Be invisible. Back here in ten."

Noiselessly, each man went about his task, stepping carefully where it was possible to see the ground beneath the dark canopy of fir. Ten minutes later as instructed, the five men reconvened. Molly was first to report 'no evidence of hostiles', as he put it. MacAskill reported similarly but as Posh Boy re-emerged through the trees he had news of a different nature.

"We have an individual seated on a log in a clearing smoking a cigarette roughly half way between the vehicles and the road. It was very dark but he seemed to me to be the man who spoke with us in the Claymore Bar last night. No evidence of weaponry. He hadn't a clue I was yards from him. I could take him out easily."

A barely perceptible shake of the head signalled MacAskill's disagreement.

"We can't be sure he's alone or in communication with others." He thought further. "I had no sense that there was anyone on the hill when we were opening up the right-of-way. If it *is* MI5, they'll be interested in other matters. I was told that this guy works alone and that he's dangerous. I was also told he'll be armed. Our job is to stop him, disarm him and immobilise him so we can deal with our next mission unimpaired." Further thought. "Okay, we test whether he's alone. We walk normally to the vehicles and drive back to the road. I'd expect him to have parked somewhere close...probably to the rear of the track opening if he followed us. When we get to the road, the Clock and I turn right towards Inverness, Snipe, you take Posh Boy and Molly and head left. If he knows I live in the Tardis, he'll follow me. If you find after a mile that no one's following you, Snipe, turn and chase me. When I see your headlights, I'll slow and stop. You block off his retreat. Posh Boy and Molly, you disarm him, Mike checks his ID, Snipe takes the air out of his rear tyre. I'll keep my distance." He stood and the others followed suit. "Any questions?"

There were none. Normal conversations followed as they made the last thirty yards to the vehicles.

Each man sat as directed and MacAskill took his time turning the Tardis. Snipe did similarly with his Ford and both drove to the road end where they separated.

Thorpe had made his way quickly back to his vehicle and had concealed himself by ducking below the level of the dashboard. Somewhat taken aback at one of the vehicle's lights illuminated his Volvo in passing, Thorpe turned in his seat and peered at his wing mirror, establishing that the vehicle that had passed him, heading away from Inverness, was the Ford. As MacAskill had anticipated, he decided to follow the Tardis and did so initially without headlights, keeping a distance behind him. A full moon allowed him to track the ambulance without further use of his lights and he travelled in this way for some time before becoming aware of headlights behind him. Ambivalent now, he was in two minds over his decision to drive without lights. The car behind him was sure to flash him as it became evident he was driving at night without lights. He decided to drive on side lights and made that adjustment just as he turned a corner to see MacAskill's vehicle stopped at a narrow bridge and a large man in army fatigues walking towards him. Braking, he realised that the other following vehicle had closed and was now immediately behind him. With no means of manoeuvring, he stopped, took his Glock 19 from his shoulder holster, concealing it beneath the steering wheel and with a practised movement, disengaged its three safety mechanisms, readying it for firing. He opened the driver's window as Mike McSween approached.

"Evening, sir. You were driving without lights."

Snipe emerged from the car behind and knelt at the nearside rear wheel. Posh Boy and Molly approached and took up position at each of the rear doors of the Volvo.

Nonplussed at the turn of events, Thorpe remained open-mouthed as McSween continued with an accomplished confidence.

"I'm afraid I'll need to see some identification, sir."

Gathering himself somewhat, Thorpe reverted to type.

"Who the fuck are *you*?"

"First things first, sir. Your identification please."

With a move that was almost perfectly synchronised, Posh Boy and Molly opened the rear doors and slipped into the rear seat of the car.

Molly spoke. "Do not make any sudden moves, sir. We have you at disadvantage. Please slowly pass your weapon to my colleague. If you do as instructed you will not be harmed. If you do not follow our instructions I will simply shoot you in the back of your head."

"Who the fuck *are* you," Thorpe repeated.

"Final chance, sir," replied Molly.

Thorpe made a calculation. Three large men now surrounded him and one claimed the ability to shoot him. He took the Glock by the barrel and held it above his left shoulder. Molly took the weapon and stepped from the car.

McSween opened the driver's door.

"If you'd be good enough to step out of the car, sir. I'd like to see ID and I want to check that you have no other weapons."

Thorpe's internal rage, never far below the surface, exploded as he got out of the car.

"I'm an officer of MI fucking 5 and I'm going to make it my business to see each one of you fuckers hung from the nearest lamppost for this."

McSween continued his requests evenly.

"Wallet?"

Angrily, Thorpe took his wallet from his trouser pocket and opened it to show a photographic ID describing him as 'MI5 Securities Head 3c, Simon Thorpe'.

McSween considered the likeness and satisfied, returned the wallet which Thorpe took angrily. "Thank you sir, please face the car and spread your legs."

Molly appeared from the rear of the car holding Thorpe's Glock 19 which he waved at him, encouraging compliance.

Seething now, Thorpe permitted a check. McSween removed a small knife from a sheath strapped to his right calf.

As he did so, Snipe appeared at his side.

"Done!"

McSween smiled at a furious Thorpe.

"Thank you for your cooperation sir. We won't trouble you further."

The four marines turned on their heel and each returned to the vehicle they'd left only moments before.

As the Ford overtook the stationary Volvo and joined the ambulance *en route* to Inverness, Thorpe hurried to the boot of his car where he rummaged among some loose blankets and emerged with a compact Beretta 9000 pistol which he readied for firing. Pointing it in the direction of the disappearing vehicles, he fired just as the tail-lights of the Ford vanished round a bend. Enraged he fired a further three shots aimlessly into the darkness.

Returning to close the boot of his car he noticed his nearside tyre deflated.

"Fuuuuck," he screamed, several times bringing the butt of the pistol down hard on the boot, causing a wound to his the palm of his hand where the gun tore at his skin.

Chapter Thirty-eight

Darroch returned to the police car used by Boston and Boyd to report that there was no one at home in MacAskill's darkened cottage.

"He could be anywhere on the estate but the fact that none of his army colleagues are here suggests that either they've all gone home or that they're all off together on some escapade." He thought only for a moment. "There's nothing for it. I'll have to wake Lady Helen and Isla. They might know something."

He invited Boyd to drive on along a dusty earthen track which became metalled as they approached the gatehouse. The property was in darkness as they approached and they were welcomed by the barking of two dogs unused to visitors during their sleep time. A light shone from an upstairs window as Isla drew back her curtains and peered through the window at her visitors. Recognising Darroch, she slipped on a dressing gown and went downstairs where Lady Helen was shuffling through a doorway, assisted by a walking frame.

"Mother, it's Gus Darroch. Away you back to bed and I'll see what he wants."

"My house, my rules. I welcome all guests who trouble to visit."

Sighing, Isla opened the door and bid Darroch enter.

"Sorry to trouble you at this hour, Isla but it's essential I know where Lachie is."

"How on earth would I know, Gus?"

Darroch became intemperate.

"No games, Isla. Last time we spoke you told me you two were lovers and spent all your time together…"

Lady Helen let out a yelp as Isla cast her eyes to the floor anticipating her mother's reaction. She didn't disappoint.

"Darling. I'm delighted. How wonderful! You and Lachie!"

Darroch ignored her outburst.

"His life might be in danger. I have two officers in the car outside and we need to find him before someone else does. Now, where is he?"

Isla and Lady Helen exchanged glances.

"He's in danger?" asked Isla, seeking confirmation.

"Mortal! And we need to get to him soon. It might already be too late."

A further nervous, non-verbal communication took place between mother and daughter before Lady Helen spoke.

"He's a good man, Gus. You know that. If you harm a hair on his head, I'll have your guts for garters." She paused, still uncertain before making up her mind. "Now...he and his four army friends have currently gone for a midnight walk. When that's completed they propose to move on to BBC offices in Inverness where Lachie proposes to make a speech using their facilities." She looked at her watch. "They'll have finished their walk by now."

"So BBC HQ in Inverness?"

"I suspect so...but remember Gus...you're dealing with a potential son-in-law of mine so *no mistakes!*" She held up a finger in admonition as Isla cast her eyes to the floor once more in embarrassment.

Darroch turned and returned hurriedly to the car without a word of farewell.

Lady Helen spoke more to herself than to her daughter.

"I *do* hope we've done the right thing."

"I'm getting dressed," announced Isla. "I'll warn Lachie about Gus."

"Indeed you won't, darling. I can't have you driving like a maniac in the wee small hours. It's too dangerous."

"I'm going, mother. Make yourself a cup of tea. I'll phone if there's any news."

She rushed upstairs, taking the steps two at a time. As she disappeared into her bedroom, Lady Helen remembered her earlier outburst and spoke again quietly, almost to herself.

"And congratulations once again on Lachie. He's a good man!"

* * *

Old Sam Hendry finished the evening paper and licking his right thumb, peeled back the pages until he reached that day's crossword, the simple one; the cryptic crossword always confusing him. Before starting, he checked the multi-screen control panel in front of him. Black and white images of the front door, reception where he sat, and the lifts on ground, first and second floors showed no activity and he returned to his crossword. On an hourly basis, he'd dutifully take his ungainly bulk and limp up the stairs to each floor. Night lights on the stairwells did not necessitate the use of a torch thereby allowing him to carry his small radio for company, as he did.

Set back one street from the River Ness, BBC headquarters in Inverness is a Grade 'B' listed, two-storey Georgian townhouse built in 1830 which had been extensively refurbished to provide additional office space, a news room and an ALBA TV studio. During the day, it was a busy news and entertainment hub but after midnight as the last person left, it was completely empty other than its security guard.

During his seven year tenure, Sam had only had to deal with five or six incidents and his usual experience was sitting at the front desk finding things to do to entertain himself. He liked country and western music as a background to his evening shift and quizzes, crosswords, solitaire and reading crime novels occupied him until five o'clock when the cleaners arrived, shortly followed by those preparing to deal with the news that had occurred overnight.

On the street to the side of Culduthel Road where the now darkened BBC was situated, MacAskill parked the ambulance and watched as Snipe pulled in behind him. All five men congregated at MacAskill's driver's door.

"Okay, boys. We've discussed this. Snipe, you stay with the vehicles. Molly and Posh, you have your berets?' Both men nodded as they pulled their old Marine Commando berets from their pockets, placed them on their heads and tugged them down above the right ear, putting the finishing touches to their military fatigues. "Good... you look convincing. Posh, we need your best accent tonight!"

"Absolutely, old chap," enunciated Posh Boy in his best, cut-glass English accent.

"We'll need twenty minutes if all goes according to plan."

"Roger that, Cap."

Posh Boy and Molly moved off and walked downhill to the front entrance of the BBC. Nimbly, McSween and MacAskill leapt over the side wall of the building, emerging through bushes into a small car park. Three levels of light scaffolding had commenced in view of necessary repairs to the roof. Crouching, they ran beneath the first level of scaffold and, deciding the way was clear, scuttled to a rear window where MacAskill produced the glass-cutter he'd used to enter the shooting range at Boat of Garten. As with there, he thumbed some malleable tack on to the window pane and cut an arc on the glass around the interior handle, removing the glass. Because the window had been double glazed, he repeated his manoeuvre then opened the window using the handle. Pulling the opening so it lay horizontally, he and McSween entered the premises and each of them switched on their torch. MacAskill retraced his steps and placed a 'Dalriada' card on the windowsill before turning and shining his torch round the room. Whilst he was so engaged, McSween casually retrieved MacAskill's calling card and put it in his pocket.

Silently, MacAskill nodded towards the office door which led to the corridor outside. Quietly he opened it an inch and put his ear to the crack. Thirty seconds or so later, a doorbell could be heard followed by the scraping of chair legs on the floor as Sam rose slowly to answer the visitor. As the night watchman's voice was heard over the intercom, MacAskill opened the door and, checking that the guard was indeed occupied now by Posh Boy and Molly, gave the signal to McSween to move. Quickly they moved to the stairwell and stepped quietly but swiftly up the stairs to the first floor.

Downstairs, Molly was explaining their visit.

"I'm driver for General Sir Archibald Mortimer, sir. He has an interview scheduled for oh seven hundred hours."

Behind him stood the imposing figure of Posh Boy, ramrod straight, arms behind his back. All that was missing was his swagger stick. Sam looked at his watch.

"But it's only five past two in the morning."

"We've travelled up from Catterick Garrison near Richmond, sir. Made better progress than expected. The General is to be interviewed about the new proposals to locate our new Logistics Corps here in Inverness."

Sam was flustered.

"But I wasn't told about this. I'm not allowed to let anyone in....under any circumstances."

Posh Boy took a step forward and spoke into the microphone set next to the door.

"You have a military look about you, sir. Spent time in the forces?"

Still muddled, Sam answered tentatively.

"Black Watch...Army Catering Corps, sir," he replied. "*Demi Chef de Partie*...a Lance Corporal."

"Excellent, man. The army marches on its stomach!"

"Long time ago, sir," muttered Sam, inherently accepting the officer's seniority. "Look, I'm very sorry, but I'm not allowed to permit anyone to enter this building."

"BBC's being somewhat circumspect, eh?"

"I suppose so," agreed Sam diffidently, not knowing the meaning of circumspect. "It's not the BBC. We're contractors. My boss is in Glasgow. I'd better make a phone call."

"Take your time, soldier," smiled Posh Boy. "No rush."

Sam returned to his desk where the monitors continued to show no activity, MacAskill and McSween having already pushed open the heavy door into the soundproof studio that housed the Alba newsroom.

MacAskill switched on the lights in the windowless studio, pulled some sheets of A4 from inside his fatigues and unrolled them.

"Okay. I've got my notes. It's only a short commentary. I figure maybe four minutes." He dimmed some lights and increased the illumination on the news desk from which he'd be speaking. "I'll have a seat behind the desk. You tell me if it looks okay."

He moved behind the BBC desk and held his notes below a small raised edge so located to allow the newsreader to see his or her transcripts whilst concealing them from the camera.

"Looks great, Lachie. You look like Kirsty Wark...more war-like than Wark-like, mind you. Just speak up. We're not using their microphones, remember."

"Okay," smiled MacAskill. "Just tell me when your phone is ready to record my deathless prose."

McSween took up position to one side of a large mobile camera and nodded his satisfaction to MacAskill.

"Anytime you're ready, Lachie. Just speak into the BBC camera as if you really *were* on the air."

MacAskill cleared his throat.

"My name is Lachlan MacAskill and for the past few weeks I've become better known as 'Dalriada'. I'm speaking to you from the BBC headquarters in Inverness where I've entered their studios without their permission in order to record a message to Scotsmen and Scotswomen everywhere who've shared my passions and concerns over many years and have now found the confidence to express them through direct action...through civil disobedience. I have been much cheered by the efforts fellow Scots have gone to to protest the obscene presence of weapons of mass destruction only a few miles from Glasgow. And to those who protest our cause on the streets of London? Well done! Take them on in their penalty box...while we defend ours."

Equally, those who have taken to the streets up here in opposition to animal cruelty have my undying respect. Our good friends, the Windsors must by now understand that while they might be lauded in certain parts of the Home Counties, in certain quarters of the Commonwealth and indeed by some up here in Scotland, the vast *majority* of us see them as an anachronism and hold the view that their time has come. Scotland must hold a referendum on whether we'd like the class system they perpetuate to continue or whether we'd like to live in a country based upon merit and equality rather than who your father was...a country where your contribution is based upon *what* you know rather than on *who* you know. The House of Lords has no place in a modern democracy."

"I was a soldier. I fought overseas and I have seen for myself the idiocy of sending young men to die on a hill for a cause about which they're ignorant, pitting them against other young men, also sent to the slaughter in support of the convictions and enterprises of older men who stay safe and make profits from their blood loss. Scotland has arsenals in many of its rural nooks and crannies all dedicated to offering aid to those engaged in war. We have no need of these and Scots have no interest in the sands of Iraq or on the rocky outcrops of Afghanistan. We should be a peaceful nation, offering assistance to other peacekeeping forces and protecting our borders. We have no need for aircraft carriers, destroyers, warplanes or nuclear submarines. Ireland, Norway, Iceland, Sweden, Finland, have none of these. And it's no accident that whether we look at the health of democracy, the lack of corruption, trust between citizens, safety, peace, social cohesion, gender equality, equal distribution of incomes, or many other global comparisons, you find the Nordic countries in the global top spots. If England wants to continue to see itself as a major world power...a deluded notion, I must say...then include us *out*! But beware their sleekitness. There's a real truth to that old saying that 'the sun never set on the British Empire'. It was largely because God couldn't trust the English in the dark. Never forget that! So, don't allow the war machine in Whitehall to fool you any more."

"Tonight, I removed a series of seven gates put in position and padlocked by Lord Hanbury on his Glenburn Estate south of Inverness to frustrate the legal public access rights of every Scot.

The gates were put there to stop ordinary Scots from enjoying their own environment in the beautiful hills and glens of their own country. They were put there to allow Lord Hanbury and his wealthy friends to shoot grouse with impunity without having to trouble themselves with witnesses to their avarice and selfishness. The way is now open for walkers to once again tread the paths as once did generations of Scots before them and I hope that many will take the opportunity to show Lord Hanbury that his wasteful use of land in Scotland will be resisted.

In finishing, I'd like to remind us of the words of French philosopher and political activist, Simone de Beauvoir, who said, 'The oppressor would not be so strong if he had no accomplices among the oppressed', and in testimony to that, would like to thank the Director General of the BBC and his Scottish acolytes for their hospitality in allowing me to broadcast from their studios where normally viewers and listeners are permitted to see and hear only news fit for a colony. It'll be the first time that the true voice of Scotland has been broadcast from their buildings. Time and again, people have had to listen to the half-truths, embroidered falsehoods and downright lies pushed by their correspondents, all designed to maintain the colony of Scotland as the passive recipients of whatever Olde England decides they should pass our way while at the same time robbing our country blind, just as they did to India, Pakistan, the fledgling United States, and every African country they raped and plundered. The BBC that operates in Scotland today is a colonial, British State enterprise, aimed at toppling the elected government of Scotland. Even most of our political parties and all of our newspapers are owned by foreigners from outside our country whose interests are not our interests and the BBC uses them to provide a daily diet of virulent anti-Scotland bias to their news content. Well, I am here tonight to tell them all that their time is up. Scotland will not accept this anymore. Most Scots hold the BBC in deep contempt and view the legal requirement to fund them only to see their licence fee go to London to pay for the propaganda designed to have Scotland remain a vassal state as extortion and completely absurd. Today, I am calling for all Scots to withhold their licence fee as a wake-up call to London that we will not be treated this way. Enough is enough!"

"I have been made aware that the lawful powers of the United Kingdom have had enough of me and that they may even be circling this building as I sit here tonight. I wish no harm to any human being. My actions have all been designed to draw attention to iniquity and to encourage others to take up the cause, not to occasion injury, either to man or beast. The response over the weekend demonstrated to my satisfaction that I have been successful and my grateful thanks goes to every one of the more than two hundred thousand people who demonstrated in the towns and cities all over Scotland. These marchers have come increasingly to understand that within the present United Kingdom arrangement, Scotland remains an occupied country and this is reflected in the fact that Scotland's social institutions are run predominantly by a Unionist establishment elite whose allegiance is not, and never can be, primarily to Scotland. This leaves Scotland and the Scottish people subject to continued colonisation, exploitation and oppression."

"I have identified myself tonight in order to bring my leading part in this effort of civil disobedience to a conclusion but I look forward to others taking up the role I have played while I continue to act in a supporting role once the authorities have finished with me. I know my strengths. Any jackass can kick a barn down but it takes a good carpenter to build one. I leave that task to others."

"*Alba gu Bràth.*"

McSween pressed a button and lowered his phone.

"I take it back. That was powerful. You *would* give Kirsty Wark a run for her money."

Chapter Thirty-nine

Jimmy Boyd was being encouraged by his sergeant to drive ever more quickly, even as Darroch sat in the passenger's seat, hands against the dashboard in the brace position. Two miles behind them, a Land Rover driven by Isla powered its way up the A9 towards Inverness, gaining on them.

"Even with a big drink in me, I'd be a better driver than you, sonny-boy."

"If you say so, sir."

They drove on, closing on the Highland capital.

* * *

Having made his phone call and having been advised it would be acceptable to permit the two soldiers to make themselves comfortable in the reception area inside the BBC studios, Sam made his way slowly round the reception desk to advise his visitors of the decision.

"Sorry 'bout that, people but rules is rules. I've to admit you to reception and offer you coffee."

"That would be excellent," responded Posh Boy stepping inside as the door was opened. As they settled, Sam began to boil a kettle in a cupboard behind his desk, now revelling in the unexpected company and the re-telling of tales of derring do in the military kitchens of his youth. Still unsure if more time was required to permit MacAskill and McSween to complete their task, the two Marines encouraged chat about Sam's military career in kitchens the world over, allowing a charming and interested Posh Boy to seat himself on the edge of the reception desk, in so doing masking the security monitors.

Unseen by any of the three men, MacAskill and McSween returned behind them to the exit office and to the open window where MacAskill noticed that the Dalriada card he'd left had disappeared.

"Must have blown away," he muttered as he replaced it with another piece of cardboard with his name inscribed, this time leaving it on a nearby desk. As he turned to open the window, McSween pocketed the card as he'd done the first.

McSween exited the window first and, placing his right foot on the ledge, dropped the short distance to the ground. MacAskill was in the process of following suit when a gun butt struck McSween's head, knocking him to the ground unconscious.

Instantly, MacAskill recognised the form of his MI5 nemesis, Simon Thorpe who swiftly manoeuvred the Beretta, pointing it now directly at him.

"Down!" instructed Thorpe.

"I'm unarmed," said MacAskill. "Both of us are."

"Down," repeated Thorpe. "I don't give a rat's arse if you're carrying an AK47 or if you're a fucking Amish preacher. I'd shoot you without hesitation. I kill for a living and it wouldn't upset me one bit. In fact, I'd fucking enjoy it after that fucking nonsense on the road earlier."

MacAskill considered his options and sitting on the sill, dropped the short distance to the ground, facing Thorpe who took a step back to distance himself from any prospect of attack.

"Name?"

"Johnnie Scobie."

"Scobie?"

Quietly at first, MacAskill began singing lines from the the refrain of Scottish music hall song, 'We're No Awa' Tae Bide Awa'...

"Says he tae me, 'Could ye go a hauf?...Says I, man that's ma hobby'."

Infuriated, Thorpe stepped forward and caught MacAskill full on the forehead with his Beretta, cutting him.

"You're fucking Dalriada and we both know it. So we're going a short run in my car, Mr. Dalriada. Any funny business, I'll just shoot you dead. I promise you, your absence from the face of this earth won't be missed." He signalled with his Beretta that

MacAskill should move to his right towards the car park and followed him. Reaching the corner of the building, MacAskill back-heeled his captor violently on his shin and pirouetting, brought his right elbow into sharp contact with Thorpe's cheekbone. As Thorpe stumbled, MacAskill turned the corner and ran along the planks of wood serving as a walkway on the scaffolding. Nimbly, he climbed a ladder taking him to the next, incomplete level. Placing one foot on the second rung, Thorpe grasped MacAskill's left foot with his gun hand until forced to release it due to being kicked by MacAskill's right boot, the Beretta dropping to the ground. Realising that he'd nowhere to go but down, MacAskill readied himself for a leap into the darkness of the surrounding bushes when Thorpe climbed upwards, grasped his jacket and wrestled him to the makeshift floor. Aggressively, he moved behind and yanked MacAskill towards him, wrapping his arm around his neck. Pulling him upwards, he adjusted his forearm so that it was around MacAskill's neck and placed his other hand behind his head. Bending his elbow he flexed his arm and applied pressure to the side of MacAskill's neck. Trained in martial arts, MacAskill knew full well that the carotid choke hold would shortly block blood to his brain and render him unconscious. Two moves resolved the problem. With his right hand, he straightened his thumb and drove it over his shoulder into Thorpe's right eye occasioning screams of pain from his adversary. Secondly, he threw his legs forward and sat down urgently, bringing Thorpe to the floor, easing his grip. Still in his partial embrace, however, MacAskill placed both feet against the wall and heaved. The entire structure, still incomplete and not well anchored, teetered some distance from the wall before settling again. As it did so, MacAskill heaved once more. This time the scaffolding swayed, held its balance as if deciding whether to return to the wall or collapse, before slowly deciding to allow gravity to take the entire steel frame to the bushes below.

Now freed from the choke hold, but unaware that Thorpe had lost his Beretta, MacAskill took to his heels, crawled through the bushes and leapt the wall to where the vehicles were parked. Lying next to the driver's door of the Tardis, Snipe lay unconscious, a head-wound streaming blood. Quickly placing his index and middle fingers on his neck at the side of his windpipe, he felt a strong pulse. With no time to offer further assistance, he ran across the road and made his way at pace along a dark lane festooned by variously coloured wheelie bins. Behind him, cursing at the darkness, ran Thorpe. With a disabled left arm and blood oozing from his head wound, MacAskill decided that evasion offered better chances of survival than engaging in combat with an armed man so he ran. At the end of the lane, a road followed the contour of the River Ness and close by, the Infirmary Bridge; a suspension bridge of wire rope and trusses which spanned the river and offered a public footbridge to those seeking to cross it.

MacAskill tripped on the first step and sprawled on the narrow walkway allowing Thorpe to close on him. As he rose he realised that the wound on his left arm had re-opened and that the bleeding from the cut above his eye had begun to impair his vision. Unsteadily he rose to his feet, now only yards in front of Thorpe who shortly made up ground and hauled him to the floor of the footbridge, again seeking to put him in a choke hold. This time, MacAskill had anticipated the move and had placed his wounded left arm at his neck, inhibiting the move and, clutching Thorpe's neck with his good hand, pulled him over his shoulders leaving him on the seat of his pants before him. Grasping his collar, he dragged him back a few feet and kneed him forcefully on the back of his head but to no avail. Breathing heavily and bleeding from the assault on his right eye, Thorpe rose and faced MacAskill who drove the heel of his right hand into Thorpe's face, stunning him. With a roar, Thorpe bent forward and ran at MacAskill as if attempting a rugby tackle. Deftly, MacAskill rolled backwards on to his shoulders and using Thorpe's momentum, placed his right foot under his belly and pushed upwards with as much force as he could muster.

The Infirmary Bridge is designed for foot traffic. The elegant 'B' listed crossing, built in 1882, has a a low-height railing to provide pedestrian containment. Unfortunately for Thorpe, it signally failed to contain his person and clipping his head on a cast iron strut, his frame escaped the parapet and he fell several feet into the murky depths of the River Ness. Equally disadvantageous for Thorpe was his earlier youthful insistence that he had no desire to learn to swim. This incapacity and the blow to his head as he fell saw him plunge to the cold waters below and fail to surface.

Rising unsteadily to his feet, MacAskill looked over the latticed parapet at the blackness of the muscular River Ness. Still weak from his efforts, his left wrist bloodied from the blow to his upper arm, he began to move towards the entrance to the bridge as a prelude to gaining access to the grassy slope down to the river. As he reached the bank, McSween appeared, his face bloodied.

"I saw a man overboard. Who was it?"

"That MI5 guy." They both limped painfully to the water's edge. "He hasn't surfaced," muttered MacAskill.

Although only six miles long, the River Ness has one of the highest average discharge rates in the United Kingdom as it opens into the Beauly Firth, thence to the North Sea. While at the Infirmary Bridge close to the eastern bank the water forms white gashes where it boils over boulders, the main body of water is deep, powerful and cold.

"Let's walk the bank to see if he surfaces," suggested MacAskill.

"Don't think he'll be coming up any time soon, Lachie. We'd be better off tending to Snipe. He has a head wound. I dragged him into the Tardis and he's conscious now but I'd like to check him over. You look like you need some attention, too."

MacAskill allowed himself to be dragged away from the scene and retraced his steps along the quiet lane behind the houses that fronted the river. As they approached the illuminated street ahead, McSween placed his arm across his friend and bid him stop. Blue flashing lights bounced their presence off trees and houses around them. Cautiously, they peered round the corner to see three fire engines parked below their two vehicles. A number of firemen were also in evidence although there was no hint of urgency or drama.

"The scaffolding," whispered MacAskill. "The guy inside must have called them."

One of the fire engines began to pull out, the Crew Manager having decided its response was unnecessary. Staying on the other side of the road from the appliances and not attracting any attention, both men made their way back to the vehicles where, inside the Tardis, their three colleagues were in conversation. Posh Boy was applying a bandage to Snipe's forehead.

"Everyone okay? asked MacAskill.

"Aye, we're fine, Cap. I was surprised from behind and knocked unconscious. Didn't see who did it."

"We're good, Cap," said Molly speaking for himself and General Sir Archibald Mortimer who was till tending to Snipe's wound.

"Then let's get out of here. Posh, you and Molly seem in best shape. You both drive."

Both men moved instantly to take the wheel of each of the two vehicles and unhurriedly manoeuvred them out and round the two remaining fire engines before heading for Inverskillen.

As they waited to turn into Haugh Road, MacAskill shouted, "Pull over, Posh!" Two cars travelling fast past their road-end headed speedily towards the BBC buildings. The occupants of the first vehicle couldn't be identified but the second was clearly driven by Isla in her mother's Land Rover. Quickly, if painfully, MacAskill opened the door and stepped out.

"Wait here, Posh."

He took a few paces behind the Tardis and, opening the Ford's passenger door, asked him to follow the Land Rover.

It was only a short distance to the flashing blue lights where both vehicles had stopped. He recognised Gus who was now engaged in conversation along with two other men and a fireman. Leaving the Ford, he instructed Molly to follow the Land Rover and walked briskly to Isla's passenger door which he opened, entering it.

"God! Lachie! You frightened me half to death...wha..?... You're bleeding...!"

"Afterwards! Gently take a left, Molly will follow us. Take a further two first lefts and it'll bring you up behind the Tardis.

We then take a more circuitous route out of Inverness. I'll answer questions on the way. We've three casualties."

"Then why don't we head to the vet's. Me and Mike can look you over."

"Mike's one of the casualties. No one's too serious but your good work on my arm has been wasted, I'm afraid. The stitches have burst."

Both vehicles came up behind the Ford. MacAskill leaned from the window and asked Molly to follow on. The convoy drove slowly down towards the river and along Ness Bank towards the city centre. Ahead, the fire engine earlier dismissed had pulled in beside the river, lights still flashing and had disgorged its crew who were standing in a huddle with two other men. A figure lay on the ground. Two firemen were kneeling.

"Pull over, Isla."

Stepping out, MacAskill moved behind the Land Rover to the Tardis.

"This requires your talents, Posh. That group up ahead surrounds what looks like a body. Can you amble past without engaging and see if you can pick up any info. When you return, head for old Donald Brodie's vet practice in the village. We'll drive on." He advised Molly of directions and returned to Isla, guiding her towards the A9 and back to the village.

Chapter Forty

Posh Boy had reconnoitred the scene, had established only that the body being tended to was now a corpse and that there was some significant measure of consternation present. He returned to the Tardis and turned towards Grantown-on-Spey only moments before Darroch, Boyd and Boston arrived at speed, braked and left their vehicle in the middle of the road, its hazard lights flashing.

* * *

Darroch flashed his warrant card as he approached the firemen.

"Police Scotland. What do we have here?"

One of the two fishermen present interjected.

"A fuckin' scandal, that's what. And you fuckers won't cover this up. Not this time. First chance I have I'm phoning the newspapers!"

As two firemen continued to attempt resuscitation, another fire officer explained.

"These two chaps were fishing the Ness and they dragged this body from its waters." He nodded at his two kneeling colleagues. "This pair are trying to revive him but he's well gone. It would appear to be suicide."

"Aye, it was me that found his note!" The second of the two fishermen made his presence known.

"Note? Can I see it, please?" asked Darroch.

"Jimmy?" The Crew Manager invited his colleague to pass the note. "I suspect this'll put the cat amongst the pigeons."

Darroch opened the Ziplock plastic pouch and removed the single sheet of paper. Instantly he recognised the style of writing and read the suicide note Thorpe had planned for MacAskill. He handed it to Boston.

"Well, we've all fucked up some evidence now. I don't have any latex gloves with me and there will be firemen's prints all over this. May as well make a meal of it!"

"Jesus Christ!" Boston read the page as Boyd looked over his shoulder."

"There's more," grimaced the fireman, handing him Thorpe's wallet.

"Well, fuck me gently," intoned Darroch as he inspected it. "Colin...look at this!"

"Aye," growled the first fisherman. "He's only MI5 and he's only admitting he was Dalriada!"

The second man chipped in.

"And there's five firemen and two fisherman here who'll testify in court that MI5 employed Dalriada. You canny cover this up. This is a scandal. You'll be able to read about it in the papers tomorrow."

Darroch knelt and inspected the body.

"Aye, it's Thorpe all right. Dead as Partick Thistle's cup chances." He stood. "Okay, everyone. This is now a crime scene. We'll need statements, but right now I need everyone to leave the body as it is and stand back. The local boys will tape this area off." He turned to Boston. "Well, Colin. This looks like it's fallen right in your lap, my friend. It has Special Branch written all over it."

"Kinda does, eh?"

* * *

Isla opened the door of the vet's practice and bid people enter. She sat everyone in the small waiting room and hurried to a store room from which she reappeared carrying a box of various items. Despite his bloodied head, McSween was tending to the medical needs of Snipe.

"Okay, what have we got here? asked Isla of him.

"Snipe needs a head wound stitched. No concussion apparent. Lachie has a deep cut on his forehead and he says his arm's needing attention. I've a cut on my head as well. Hope you've enough surgical thread."

"Who's worst?"

"That would be Lachie, Isla."

Isla grinned. "Okay soldier-boy. Over here with you."

Half an hour later everyone had been tended to.

"I'd suggest we all get some shut-eye," suggested Isla. "I know *I'm* going home to bed."

"Good idea, Isla. Your poor mother will be having kittens." MacAskill stood and clasped his hands in front of him, bowing slightly. "Lady and gentlemen. I owe you all…big time. I needed a bit of help tonight and you all came through. Now…for the moment at any rate, let's keep our evening's activities to ourselves, eh? I dare say it'll all come out in the wash once my speech is broadcast but what's complicating matters is the apparent death tonight of that MI5 guy. We can't yet be sure it was him who was pulled from the Ness but it looks likely. We don't know how much of a fuss this'll cause but I'd imagine it'll be substantial. I intend to face that alone. So let's all get back up the road, have some kip and we'll see what tomorrow brings."

* * *

Darroch, Boston and Boyd had remained at the scene for an hour until the local officers had arrived and taken statements. At Darroch's suggestion they agreed to accompany him to Thorpe's hotel in Aviemore before turning in. Waking the receptionist from her reverie, they were accompanied up to his room where they asked her to remain outside.

"MI5 certainly know how to look after their officers, eh? Either that or Thorpe enjoyed staying in small rooms with views of concrete walls," opined Darroch. Clothes remained unhung in a soft suitcase, no toiletries were evident in the bathroom and as a consequence of the 'Do Not Disturb' notice on his door, the bed had remained unmade, but unused. Thorpe had obviously slept on top of the bed, presumably clothed, thought Darroch, rather than *in* the bed.

"Look at this!" invited Boyd as he proffered a waste paper bin containing three empty miniature bottles of whisky along with a strip of paper. "It looks like he's torn off the top of the hotel paper. My bet is that the forensic boys'll match this to that suicide note we read at the river."

Boston looked in the bin and met Boyd's gaze.

"Son, you'll be Chief Constable in a fortnight if you keep this up!"

Darroch checked the bin.

"You're right, Jimmy. And I'll bet they'll match this hotel pen here to the ink used." He sat on the sole chair and attempted a summary. "So what do we know...probably...? We know that Thorpe is dead, that he was pulled from the River Ness, that inside his pocket was a suicide note which can be traced back... probably...to this room here in Aviemore and that he admitted to being Dalriada. Now...he clearly *wasn't* Dalriada and there will be unimpeachable witnesses who will testify to his presence elsewhere during periods when Dalriada was doing his business. But there are five firemen and two fishermen who will nevertheless testify to his suicide and to his admission. That's going to give the conspiracists a lot of house room to make mischief. It'll also make any court action against the *real* Dalriada much more difficult as any defence would make mincemeat of the prosecution. What say you?" he asked Boston.

Boston sat on the edge of the bed and peered again into the litter bin.

"I have colleagues who would disappear this evidence, Gus. I might need the help of an incorruptible cop who won't be silenced."

"Aye, well...I *am* that soldier boy!"

"You're right about Thorpe. He was an arse, a psychopath and a bully but he wasn't Dalriada. He clearly intended to plant the note on the real Dalriada in order to take some of the potency out of his appeal to the masses. That said, you're right. If we ever caught the *real* Dalriada, I'm not sure it'd be possible to persuade fifteen objective men and women of good public spirit that there wasn't something a bit iffy about his prosecution. A decent QC would see this booted into touch before it even appeared in court."

"I'll get our forensic boys over here from Aberdeen as quickly as possible. I'll also submit a report up the line and see that it has a wide readership. You have to follow your own protocols but it's difficult to see how anyone can silence two separate police reports, witness statements from two fishermen and a group of firemen, especially if they carry out their threat to speak to the press."

"It's been done before, Gus," replied Boston.

"Well, I intend to ensure that it doesn't happen this time, Colin."

Deciding to call in at his office before heading for bed, Darroch dragged his two Special Branch colleagues out of the car.

"One more stop before retiring, boys."

A lone constable manned the desk.

"Oh, morning, sir. Got your messages about the incident on the River Ness last night." He stepped back towards a grey suspension file trolley and removed a paper. He consulted it to ensure it was the one he sought and handed it to Darroch.

"They found a pistol in the middle of the collapsed scaffolding, sir. It had been fired recently. Four bullets missing from the chamber. A Beretta, apparently. They've dusted it for prints and they're off for analysis."

"Thanks, Alex." He turned to Boston and Boyd. "Any money says it's Thorpe's.

Darroch thought quickly.

"Okay! Look, I'll drop you two off at my place and you get some shut-eye. I have one visit to make before I turn in but it needn't involve you guys."

"Mischief, Gus?"

"Not at all. Just a wee domestic errand I have to take care of."

Darroch handed the keys to Boston and, upon arrival at his house, changed cars and set off for Inverskillen Estate.

If four shots were fired, I want to make sure that one or more of them didn't end up in Lachie's head, he thought. *Let's hope I'm not breathalysed!*

It took but a few minutes anxious driving for him to screech to a halt outside the cottage. The Tardis was parked next to the hen house. Anxiously Darroch thumped on the door, trying to peer through the window into its depths and occasioning the illumination of the cottage as the four Marine Commandos were wakened.

"Lachie! It's Gus."

A curtain was pulled back and the sleepy face of MacAskill appeared at the window. Moments later, he opened the door, and stepped outside.

"Christ what happened to you?" asked Darroch, seeing the stitched wound on his forehead.

"Horseplay with the guys. They play rough."

"But you're okay?"

"Sure. Why wouldn't I be?"

Darroch seemed relieved.

"It's a long story but that MI5 man who confronted you in the Claymore has been found dead in Inverness. Looks like suicide. But it looks like he had a pistol and four bullets had been fired from its chamber. I was worried that one of them might have been reserved for you."

MacAskill yawned.

"Don't know why you'd think that, Gus. Only met the man once. We didn't seem to take to one another but I can't see him shooting me over that. Me and the boys went on a midnight march just like old times...came back...went to sleep."

Darroch nodded his understanding.

"It's late. You get back to your bed. If you've half an hour tomorrow, I'll bring you up to speed on what's been happening."

"We're all going to see Lady Helen's speech that she's making for the documentary tomorrow evening and then heading for wee Benny's final Claymore Quiz for a glass or two. The boys are all away home the day after tomorrow. Maybe we'll meet up in the Community Centre in High Street?"

"Sounds like a plan. Lachie. I'm just relieved to see you're all right. I was worried."

He turned to make his way back to the car only to find four large Marine Commandos standing silently behind him, arms folded, listening intently. Two of them also sported stitches on their foreheads. Darroch looked at them and shook his head.

"Jesus Christ, remind me never to go on a midnight walk with you guys."

He brushed past them, got into his car and drove off in a cloud of dust.

Chapter Forty-one

Catriona Burns accepted the call from Sir Jonathan Burton, Cabinet Secretary and Head of the Civil Service in London. His curt tone was materially different from the one she'd encountered in the Groucho Club when offered her current appointment.

"This has not gone well, has it, Ms. Burns?"

Surprised, Catriona took a moment to gather her thoughts.

"Do you refer to the Dalriada situation?"

"Indeed I do. It's been a complete disaster. You were sent up to Scotland specifically to ensure that matters of this nature were handled sensitively but successfully."

"And I believe we were well on our way to doing that, Sir Jonathan. Our forensic people had determined his age, sex, background, hair colour, eye colour, shoe size and approximate location. We were closing in on him, but London sent up an MI5 man who thought he was Wyatt Earp and compounded the felony by dispatching an elite force of SAS troops who, although alerted to his target, managed to allow him to set fire to one of the key military provisioning sites in the UK. Then, to put the icing on the cake, your MI5 officer writes a suicide note confessing to being Dalriada and jumps off a bridge into the River Ness. Were these actions predicated upon instructions given him by his London masters or was he freelancing? Either way, it seems to me that actions taken in Scotland were rational, proportionate and were producing results. London-based decisions seemed unorthodox, high-risk, clumsy and ultimately unsuccessful. In addition, it has probably rendered any successful prosecution under Scots' Law very unlikely and has been a veritable *gift* to the very people and organisations you so desperately seek to diminish in Scotland. A propaganda *coup* beyond their wildest dreams!"

There was a long silence on the other end of the phone as Catriona fumed at her end.

"Thank you for your considered response, Ms. Burns. I understand the points you make but feel that perhaps you mistake your current role as one championing the Scottish people and their institutions rather than addressing those which matter somewhat more to London in general and to Westminster in particular." He made a decision. "As we discussed, in some months the post you occupy will be re-advertised. Of course you may apply for it but I would not, in all conscience, encourage any optimism. I suspect we shall thank you for your efforts in Scotland but seek other opportunities to harness your undoubted skills elsewhere. Goodbye, Ms. Burns."

Catriona stared at the phone for some moments before replacing it in its holder. She rose and looked from her window at a bustling Edinburgh, still trying to make sense of her conversation with the Cabinet Secretary. Her phone rang for some moments before it registered with her. She lifted it.

"Your husband, Ms. Burns."

"Yes...put him through please." A click presaged the call being transferred. "Hi Andy."

"I have news."

"So, it appears, do I. You go first."

"I've just heard back from those headhunters. Initially they were interested in using my talents in the tourism sector but after some pretty non-specific interviews, I've been offered a job managing a distillery!"

"What?"

"Actually it's a *group* of distilleries that wants to boost their export market in the far east and particularly in Japan. Big salary and based in Edinburgh!"

Still shaken by her previous conversation and close to tears, Catriona only managed to issue a tepid response.

"Well done, darling. Do you need an assistant?"

* * *

MacAskill sat behind the four Marines in the back row of the hollow steel-framed chairs with green canvas backs set out in serried ranks to accommodate what was evidently going to be a full house. Grantown-on-Spey wasn't used to one of their own being the subject of a television documentary, and allied to Lady Helen's popularity, not only curious locals but the entire domestic Green movement and Scottish Women's Institute had turned out in force. Isla stood at the side of the raised stage, her mother having earlier been hoisted up on her wheelchair, the facility not yet being possessed of disabled access to the podium.

"Nervous, mother?"

"I have my speech. They seem nice people, the Norwegians. They've been interviewing me all day on the estate so I'm comfortable with them. I'll be fine, darling."

"I'm just going to sit at the back with Lachie and his friends if you're okay."

"You young people get on with it. Don't bother about me."

As Isla and Lady Helen were concluding their conversation, Mike McSween moved from his seat at the end of the row and sat beside MacAskill.

"Change of roles, Lachie...I'm afraid I've something to confess to you!"

"Priest confesses to wanted criminal. I've heard it all now."

"Actually, that's what I wanted to mention...I'm not at all sure you're a wanted criminal."

"Really? And how do you work that one out?"

"Well, if an MI5 operative had been found dead and if your card had been found in the BBC studios, don't you think someone might have paid you a visit given his suspicions and the fact that he'd shared these with the local police sergeant?"

"They could be surrounding this community centre as we speak."

"I lifted your calling card last night...both of them, actually."

"Eh?"

"Sorry, Lachie. I acted against your orders as a captain but took the actions I did as a friend." He stooped slightly in his seat to bring himself closer to MacAskill and lowered his tone.

"I spoke with Lady Helen and Isla after your speech to us at the cottage. We agreed that you announcing your identity as Dalriada made no sense so we decided that I would not, repeat would *not* film your speech from the BBC. Instead, I recorded an audio account. Isla and Lady Helen transcribed it during the day today and Helen has incorporated it in her speech tonight so it'll get even wider...and possibly more authoritative coverage."

MacAskill stroked his chin thoughtfully before speaking in a harsher tone than was usual for him.

"I've been walking around all day just waiting on someone telling me I was under arrest. I put on hold any thoughts I had about...about...well, any thoughts I had about the future. Why didn't you tell me earlier?"

"In case you overturned the democratically-arrived-at decision of me, Isla and Lady Helen to save you from the gallows." He stood as Isla arrived and surrendered his seat to her. He knelt and continued in a stage whisper. "We couldn't have imagined that the MI5 guy would commit suicide and take his suspicions to the grave."

"Well, to be honest..."

"I arrived just in time to see him vault from the bridge in a suicidal leap. I'm a priest and can't tell a lie."

"Aye, but..."

He stood as Gus Darroch entered the hall and walked towards the group at the back. McSween issued a whispered growl into MacAskill's ear.

"Don't bugger this up!"

Isla moved along one and allowed Darroch the end seat as McSween moved back into the row in front.

"Evening, all."

"God, you even say 'hello' like Dixon of Dock Green."

"I'm off duty, Lachie. Just a pleasantry." He looked past MacAskill. "Looking forward to hearing your mother speak, Isla?"

"I'm nervous for her."

"She'll be grand." He allowed a beat. "So your pals are off home tomorrow!"

MacAskill nodded. He affectionately squeezed the broad shoulders of Posh Boy who sat directly in front of him. "Posh Boy here, Stewart Murray, talks like he's just out of Cambridge. Sure, he spent a few years in the Guards where he perfected his cut-glass accent but he's from Bonnybridge near Falkirk and he's going back to manage the mountain guide and tour company he owns and runs from Glasgow. The Sniper's Nightmare, our Snipe, AKA Duncan McKechnie, goes back to Strathclyde University where he's studying to become a PE teacher. Molly there, Robert Malone runs a horticultural company in Glasgow where he looks after posh people's gardens and cuts down their dangerous trees. And of course, the Reverend Michael McSween goes back to his parish in Renfrewshire."

"That guy's a priest?"

"He was as much a Marine Commando as any of us but he was our Royal Army Chaplain who doubled as a paramedic. A great man...a great man!"

"I'm impressed. Sounds like a good bunch."

"Yeah. I'll miss them when they go home."

"So will I," offered Isla. I've come to know them a bit. They're pretty extraordinary people."

Darroch changed the subject.

Here, that was a terrible carry on last night in Inverness, eh?"

"Heard something on the radio. Some guy drowned in the Ness?"

"Aye. Suicide apparently. Turns out he was an MI5 officer... the one who dug you up in the Claymore because you had red hair...and he had a confession in his pocket that he was Dalriada."

"Really?"

"Aye. He *wasn't* Dalriada, actually but that's beside the point. It kind of puts the forces of law and order behind the eight-ball. He was a smart-arse MI5 man who we *think* intended to plant the confession on the real Dalriada once he'd offed him. Although God alone knows how he thought he'd find him. But there are now a number of witnesses first, that the dead man was MI5 and secondly that he had a pretty persuasive note in his pocket saying he was Dalriada. It's going to make any further investigation difficult…especially if the guy who *was* actually Dalriada *screwed the fuckin' nut* and…excuse the language, Isla… didn't go on any more of his adventures. Right now, there are really no clues as to his identity, not even much in the way of circumstantial evidence. If the guy who's been doing all these things just, how can I put it… *screwed the fuckin' nut*…excuse the language again, Isla…he'd probably be able to write off the entire story until he was in his dotage and could tell his grandchildren."

MacAskill looked straight ahead saying nothing as Darroch continued.

"I mean that's just my twopence worth. For all I know, the real Dalriada could want to shoot out the tyres of a warplane landing at Lossiemouth or something but if he didn't…and *screwed the fuckin' nut*, he'd probably escape detection." He shrugged his shoulders. "But here, why am I telling you two this?" he asked rhetorically. "You're here to hear your mother make a speech to the nations of the United Kingdom and Norway."

MacAskill looked at him evenly.

"The United Kingdom is a state, not a country. *Scotland* is a country!"

Isla squeezed his pained left arm to gain his attention.

"Lachie, *screw the fucking nut*, would you?"

The room darkened and a light shone on the stage illuminating Lady Helen. Darroch wasn't yet finished.

"Oh, Isla, before your mother starts, Lachie was telling me how fond he was of you and how he'd love to take you out to dinner at the first possible opportunity." He smiled broadly, stood and moved to the side where he leaned against a pillar, folded his arms and prepared to listen to the evening's speaker.

Applause greeted Lady Helen as she sat in her wheelchair, smiling, her notes in her hand.

She allowed the acclamation to end before starting to speak.

"Ladies and gentlemen. As you may know, the wonderful people at Channel Four and *Norsk Rikskringkasting*, our favourite Norwegian TV broadcaster, have an abiding interest in rewilding and have been interviewing me all day about the efforts that Lachie MacAskill and I have been making on Inverskillen Estate. They're here tonight to capture my words and I want to make some serious proposals about how Scotland might do more to protect and preserve its magnificent Highlands. But first, if I may, I want to make what I view as a public interest announcement and I trust that our broadcasting friends understand it's significance and incorporate it in any eventual production."

"All of us in Scotland over the last wee while have been riveted by the actions of someone called Dalriada who has set out to challenge a number of issues that trouble a great many people in Scotland." A few cheers emanated from the audience. "Now, it is rumoured that last night in Inverness an MI5 man was pulled from the River Ness and had upon him a note to the effect that he was Dalriada. He was *not* Dalriada. There is compelling evidence that he was an MI5 operative determined upon a scheme to use a false flag to discredit Dalriada. I know this as today I received a statement from the *real* Dalriada who still walks among us and who appears to know of my passions and of my speech tonight. With your permission I'd like to present this to you now." She took her spectacles from the lanyard round her neck and began reading her notes.

"I have been much cheered by the efforts fellow Scots have gone to to protest the obscene presence of weapons of mass destruction only a few miles from Glasgow. Equally, those who have taken to the streets in opposition to animal cruelty have my undying respect. Our good friends, the Windsors must by now understand that while they might be lauded in certain parts of the Home Counties, in certain quarters of the Commonwealth and indeed by some up here in Scotland, the vast *majority* of us see them as an anachronism and hold the view that their time has come. Scotland must hold a referendum on whether we'd like the class system they perpetuate to continue or whether we'd like to live in a country based upon merit and equality rather than who your father was...a country where your contribution is based upon *what* you know rather than on *who* you know. The House of Lords has no place in a modern democracy."

She continued in this vein having carefully filleted any remark that might identify Dalriada, and gave added lustre to his comments about land use, animal cruelty, public rights of way and the environment.

Finishing the statement, she removed her spectacles.

"Now, I've destroyed the original notes I received from Dalriada, but to enable the forces of law and order to establish to their own satisfaction that my comments are authentic, I conclude by advising that he signed it off with his own name, stated *Alba gu Bràth* at its conclusion and had two plus marks after his name. He advises me that *that* information is sufficient to alert the authorities to the provenance of his notes. He concludes his message by telling his followers that he will meet them on protest marches in the future but that he will pull back from further actions of the nature that have brought him to such notoriety in Scotland and further afield. He leaves the field of civil disobedience and active protest to the hundreds of thousands who have already shown their willingness to oppose these various iniquities he's highlighted. Dalriada has been able to throw some sand in the gears of the British establishment but only the people of Scotland acting in concert can advance these ideals and bring about the change we need if the nation is to prosper in a peaceful, environmental, safe and socially just way."

She smiled at an audience which gazed at her somewhat open-mouthed.

"And for those involved in setting the forces of MI5 against the issues that trouble the people of Scotland and who sought to use underhand means to traduce a Scottish hero, I say…beware the law of unintended consequences! Now, let me say a few words about Inverskillen."

Asbjørn Larsen, the Norwegian producer, turned to his counterpart in Channel Four and spoke quietly into his ear.

"Beware the law of unintended consequences." He pursed his lips. "I believe we might have the title of our documentary."

* * *

Lady Helen took pride of place at the Inverskillen Quiz Team Table where all five retired Marine Commandos and Isla sat. Next to them, Team Plod consisting of Darroch, Boyd and Boston sat in jovial conversation. Attempts to get the quiz underway were thwarted by the number of people who wished to pass on their congratulations to Lady Helen and by the increased number of teams due to many of the attendees at her speech ending their evening in the Claymore.

"So what are you saying, Gus? That me and Jimmy here should head off back to Glasgow?"

"What I'm sayin'," said Darroch, slurring his words, "is that there is not one scintilla of evidence that this Dalriada fellah is associated in any way with this part of the world and while it's been great hostin' you two, if you want to stay longer, you'd be very welcome but it'd be because you enjoy the social life up here and want a few days R&R in my place in Grantown-on-Spey. Not because you think you're getting closer to nailin' Dalriada."

"But you, yourself thought it was maybe that guy MacAskill over there."

"Nah...I was just sharing what Thorpe thought and that was just based on his idea that it had to be someone with red hair. You could try to see if that'd stand up in court but ah hae ma' doubts!"

Boyd interjected. "Thing is, boss, Thorpe had years of experience in MI5. Maybe we should pay attention to his hunch."

Boston's dislike of Thorpe influenced his attitude to Boyd's comment.

"See, the trouble wi' you, Jimmy is that you need to learn to judge people's character properly or you're goin' to wake up in a flat in Maryhill missin' a kidney." Mellow now as a consequence of his alcohol consumption, he changed gear. "Here...Chief Constable elect...I'm going to start on the whisky. Mine's a wee Glenfiddich."

"As you say, sir." Boyd gestured to Darroch. "Another Guinness?"

Isla waited until her mother was talking with Mike McSween before slipping her arm through MacAskill's.

"So, you're fond of me?"

"Wha...?"

"Gus says you told him you're fond of me and wanted to take me to dinner."

"Och, well, Gus says more than his prayers."

Isla smiled. "So, I'm an ugly hag, eh?"

MacAskill began to protest, eliciting a giggle from Isla.

"It's just that I've been on the phone all day to Newcastle and I've come come to an agreement with Donald Brodie up here and my partners in Gosforth that I'll sell up down south and take over his vet practice in the village. I'm quite excited and was hoping to celebrate my new life here in Grantown-on-Spey."

"God...that's wonderful news, Isla...and you're no ugly hag... in fact you're... you're completely presentable!"

She laughed. "*Completely presentable*! That's the best you can come up with, Lachlan MacAskill?"

"Words aren't my strong point, Isla. Fact is...I'd love...simply *love* to take you to dinner."

"Then I'm going to presume you're fond of me as well!" She adjusted her position so she was looking him in the eye. "So, are you fond of me as well?"

MacAskill blanched as he reached for the words.

"Very fond."

She reached over and tugged at her mother's sleeve. "Mother... *mother*...Lachie's taking me to dinner and he's very fond of me! Very fond."

Lady Helen placed her glass on the table and beamed at her daughter.

"*Knew* it...I just *knew* it, darling! A match made in heaven!" She reached over and hugged Isla, winking at a somewhat nonplussed MacAskill over her shoulder.

Benny the quizmaster at last managed to have the microphone work, inviting best of order as the quiz began.

"First round is a topical news round. First Question. There's been a lot in the papers recently about this guy Dalriada.

First question...he always signs off his letters using the Scots Gaelic saying, *Alba gu Bràth*. What does *Alba gu Bràth* mean in English?"

Before he managed to repeat the question as was his custom, the Inverskillen table, surrendering the point, raised their glasses and shouted joyously as one for the entire pub to hear, *"SCOTLAND FOR EVER!"*

www.ingramcontent.com/pod-product-compliance
Ingram Content Group UK Ltd.
Pitfield, Milton Keynes, MK11 3LW, UK
UKHW032313070225
4507UKWH00001B/70